# ENIGMA
# BLACK

## SARA FURLONG-BURR

# ACKNOWLEDGMENTS

I firmly believe that writing a novel is a team effort, and I'm grateful to have a wonderful team of people by my side to help me through the process. First, I'd like to thank my husband and daughters for putting up with my late nights and time spent glued to my laptop. Without your unconditional love and support to keep me sane, I wouldn't have been able to get through the process.

To my beta readers and proofreader, who spend hours of their own time to make sure my novels are up to par, I thank you. Your time, attention to detail, and friendship mean more to me than I can adequately express.
To my readers, your overwhelming support on Amazon, Facebook, Goodreads, and Twitter has been more than I could have ever hoped it would be. Thank you for purchasing my novels, taking the time to read them, and reviewing them.

# PROLOGUE

*Where you used to be, there is a hole in the world, which I find myself constantly walking around in the daytime, and falling in at night. I miss you like hell.*

~Edna St. Vincent Millay

CLOTHED IN SHADOWS, neatly tucked away atop a stone ledge, I wait for him. In the months since I'd been whisked away from my former life, waiting was all I seemed to do. Waiting for the day I could return to that life; waiting for the day I would die in triumphant vindication for the sacrifices I had made; waiting for the day I would finally obtain the vengeance I so dearly sought.

Vengeance. A simple word for such a complex action. How I'd dreamt of nothing but it for the last ten years. It consumed me, forcing me to drink it in until I'd become intoxicated with its essence. It'd been the single pervasive thought haunting my existence, continuously running through my mind in a sadistic loop. Unable to sober up, I'd stumbled through the last decade of my life plagued with the inability to think of anything else but my last memories of them and the day of carnage that took them away from me. Vengeance was almost within my grasp. Soon, I would have the power to attain it. However, such power– I'd learned–does not come without a price; and this particular price had been paid with my life.

The autumn air whipped through my hair caressing what little skin still remained exposed to the elements. Before becoming the property of The Cause autumn had been my favorite time of year. The smell of the chilled air was invigorating and the leaves on the trees aflame with crimsons and golds were positively mesmerizing. It always amazed me how something could be so beautiful as it lay dying. Perhaps, the same could be said about me now. I was an empty shell left abandoned on the beach unable to facilitate life. Even if I had wanted to feel alive again, it just simply wasn't allowed of me. The colder and more desensitized I was, the more liable to kill without blinking an eye I would be.

My former home had fallen into despair these last ten years. Strewn throughout the once prosperous metropolis were dilapidated buildings and empty store fronts creating a virtual ghost town where life once reigned supreme. Most of these dwellings had been abandoned by those who chose to leave the confines of the city in favor of secluded locations where the presence of the New Order was not yet evident. Little did they know, however, these locations no longer existed but were merely destinations of mythological proportions.

I spent many a night lost in my thoughts, and it was often during these times of contemplation atop my precipice that I would get what I was waiting for. For me, seeing Chase Matthews was the only remaining bright spot I had left in this world. He kept my heart beating, unwittingly providing me with reassurance that I wasn't quite dead yet. Through his dimly lit window I watched him.

I knew that I shouldn't be here, but his aura was like a magnet pulling me toward its glow. His grip on me was strong making my visits to this ledge so frequent that I was beginning to ponder whether a permanent imprint of my rear would become forever indented in the cement. My former life with him had been nothing short of perfect. In his arms, I'd regained the feeling of safety and security that was ripped from me in my youth. His blue eyes looking into mine always had a way of making me feel weak, a feat of which nothing else had successfully been able to accomplish. I'd been strong in my former life without even having been manufactured to be as I was now.

A tear streamed down my cheek, burning my skin on its descent. Yet another sign of the weakness I was forbidden to display back at my new home; but this ledge was not my home and I couldn't help it anymore. A glimmer of the Celaine Stevens I used to be still existed under the mask I was made to wear. That was something they would never be able to take away from me. I'd given them my life, my body and my mind but my soul was all mine and would remain so until my dying day.

Chase was every bit the awkward brand of perfection I remembered him as being. Often, I would find myself unable to break my gaze away from him for I never knew when or if I'd ever get the chance to gaze upon him again. Closing my eyes, I envisioned our former life together and, for a moment, I could almost feel his lips on mine again–a feeling I hadn't been able to experience in what seemed like an eternity.

He rummaged through his dresser drawer, pulling out a pair of neatly folded shorts and methodically laying them out on his bed. I could tell by the way he stumbled around his room that this particular night had been a trying one for him. Fumbling with the buttons on his shirt, he proceeded to undress, causing a familiar burning sensation to spread across my cheeks. A part of me felt as though I should avert my eyes as the sight of my former lover half-naked would do little to help my present situation, but I couldn't help it. Instead, I scanned every inch of his toned physique, affectionately remembering the nights when I would lay next to him with his broad shoulders encasing me.

Moonlight shone down upon my ledge as a passing cloud gave way. And, in that instant, he looked up in my direction as if suspecting my presence. He would never see me. I was trained to stay in the shadows; to be the perfect assassin. The light in his room flickered out, bathing it in darkness. They would be expecting my return soon. With a sigh, I stood up, bracing myself for my descent from the ledge and, with one effortless leap, flung myself off it, letting the wind tear through my body. It was time to get back home to my prison; to my destiny; to my own personal hell.

# BOOK ONE

# MY FORMER LIFE

# 1

# THE INCIDENT AT THE FLAMINGO RESORT

HE WEARILY PACED the casino floor wanting nothing more than to join his sleeping family back in their room. Unfortunately, as a chronic sufferer of insomnia he knew that any effort at attempting sleep would be fruitless and his restlessness would only disrupt his wife and son from their slumber. Instead, he forced himself to meander through the aisles of slot machines in an effort to build up enough fatigue to hopefully knock him out.

How he hated those machines. On top of the shrill, deafening noises emanating from them, he found himself having to shield his eyes away from the flashing lights the ones at this particular casino seemed to favor. Further adding insult to injury, the dreadful apparatuses were specially constructed to tie in with the ultra-annoying beach theme of the Flamingo Resort and Casino. When he and his son had first arrived at the resort earlier that day, he couldn't resist whispering a quip involving a flamingo throwing up after an acid trip under his breath. This jab had naturally changed his son's expression from one of horror to one of sheer amusement. His wife–needless to say–had not been amused.

Despite its attempts at depicting a cutesy family vibe, it was still a casino with the same droll neon signs marketing poker, blackjack, and craps all while using the potential of various monetary jackpots to lure the masses in hook, line and sinker. Like fish with torn mouths, its prey always took the bait, only to continue coming back for punishment time and time again.

Atlantic City had been his wife's idea. Had it been up to him, he never would have set foot in the place. But, for her, it was the perfect culmination of her love of the ocean and machines that flashed and clanged–or so he suspected–that lured her here. Certainly, none of what this eyesore had to offer held any interest to him. If he had his way, they would have vacationed somewhere sunny, warm and somewhat educational such as the Alamo or the Mayan ruins. Unfortunately though, as she so often did, his wife had won the argument, meaning that he and their teenage son were once again forced to endure yet another one-sided vacation.

After a half-hour of strolling aimlessly on the casino floor, he decided he'd rather not endure a migraine on top of his persistent insomnia, choosing, instead, to catch some air on the boardwalk–though, within seconds of his stepping outside, it became immediately apparent that the casino may be the lesser of the two evils. The frigid December wind caught him off guard, assaulting him with everything it had. Ignoring the stabbing cold, he walked across the deck where he noticed a solitary figure looming in the darkness. The sharp contrasts of the man's face were revealed to a small extent by the flame of the cigarette between his lips. As he drew nearer, he could hear the man mumbling while struggling to keep it in place.

"It's enough to freeze your cojones off out here," the stranger spoke. "If it weren't for this damn addiction, I'd be curled up in bed snuggled up nice and warm next to the saucy redhead I picked up earlier."

He smirked at the man's vulgarity. Unsure of what to say but not really wanting to keep the conversation flowing, he offered up a quick retort, "What are you waiting for then? Put that thing out and get back up there."

The strange man chuckled, flicking away ash from the end of the cigarette. Preferring to be alone, he left the stranger on the deck and walked down the stairs that lead out to the boardwalk. Each of the weathered, wooden steps creaked under the weight of his descending footsteps until his feet hit the ground. Pausing under a light post, he put his hands in his pockets for warmth, gazing upon the ocean from the shoreline to the point where it became one with the night sky on the horizon. Another blast of wind cut through his skin, and he found himself laughing at the irony of the moment. In that instant, his surroundings matched the mood that had hung over him like a dark cloud for the last several years.

He loved his wife dearly but was confused as to whether this love was coming from his heart or from the feeling of indebtedness he harbored for her having supported him during a prolonged battle with prostate cancer. He'd been diagnosed shortly after the birth of their son and the disease had struck him unmercifully, wreaking havoc upon his body until there was virtually nothing left of it. It was only after several grueling rounds of chemotherapy and an extensive amount of recovery time that the cancer went into remission. In its wake, however, he'd been rendered a frail shell of a man with the treatments not only having robbed him of his dignity but also stripping him of his manhood as well. His inability to produce any more biological children with his young wife had robbed her of her dream of having a big family. And since they had neither the resources nor the interest in adoption, it'd all rested upon his shoulders, leaving him feeling as though he'd somehow failed her.

Be that as it may, despite his illness and her disappointment with the path her life had taken, her devotion to him never wavered. So it was, on a day fourteen years ago, an unspoken promise was made by him to give his wife the world in exchange for the life he was unable to deliver to her. Years later, this well-intentioned promise felt more like a life sentence and he was beginning to see his debt to her as having been paid in full with inflated interest. In his mind, their son, Ian, was the only thing keeping him tied to her anymore.

He stood in placid contemplation, staring into the black hole unfolding before him while the wind swept around him, chilling his body to the bone; the lone figure on the illuminated boardwalk. Exhausted, he removed his hand from his pocket and looked at his watch. It was nearly three o'clock in the morning. Figuring he should return to thaw out and attempt to rejoin his family, he walked back toward the steps to the deck of the casino.

A shudder overcame him as the casino came back into view, but oddly it wasn't due to the cold. It was his body's response to the mere sight of the garish pink flamingos whose animatronics made them dance around the entryway. *Why did I let her talk me into this?* he thought.

Further frustrated, he opened the entryway door where he found himself simultaneously greeted by a rush of heat and a synthetic palm tree leaf slapping him in the face.

Somewhat deserted, the gaming floor stood unusually quiet. But even in the tranquility of the moment, a sense of impending doom overcame him. Invading his thoughts with each step, the threatening feeling followed him onto the gaming floor, persisting throughout his journey across the casino toward the guest rooms. On the news, he'd heard about a string of attacks that had been taking place across the country. These attacks, in the form of bombings, appeared to be occurring at random and without any clear purpose other than for pure shock value and the sick, homicidal amusement of their perpetrator. Such attacks had even prompted him to foolishly suggest to his wife that they postpone their vacation until the world returned to normal again, but she wouldn't hear of it. She'd accused him of backing out on her, causing him to concede defeat.

With a sigh and a shake of his head, he turned around to appease his unrelenting uneasiness by doing a quick sweep of the gaming floor and the remaining people on it. Not surprisingly, nothing seemed to be out of the ordinary in either respect. *Oh great, I must be losing my mind along with my sleep*, he thought. Satisfied with his survey of the room, he hypothesized that his sleep deprivation was causing pure paranoia to take over his thoughts.

"Get a grip," he mumbled under his breath, turning back around to walk down the hallway.

Then it came. A violent, earsplitting commotion erupted from behind him, throwing him to the floor. In stunned confusion, he looked up from the pink and green palm tree-etched carpeting in time to see, to his horror, a wall of fire overtaking everything and everyone in its path moving steadily towards him. In macabre slow motion, the casino's plastic ambiances melted in the scorching heat as did its organic patronages, going up like dry kindling in a tidal wave of flame. Screams escaping the mouths of the few in the path of the devastation were forever quieted by the fire's wrath. Any time for him to take evasive action had long since expired, and he knew that any effort to do so now would be nothing short of suicide.

Resigned, he put his fate in the hands of another and remained face down on the floor, shielding his head with his arms as the flames consumed him.

# 2
## THE BEGINNING OF THE END OF MY LIFE

LIKE MOST SEVENTEEN-YEAR-OLDS, I'd been oblivious to what was going on in the world around me and the inevitable ramifications the recent string of attacks would have on my life. All I knew back then was that I was happy in my own little world–as dull as it may have been.

On an overcast day in December nearly a decade ago, I sat in chemistry class, running my fingers along the grooves of the table while staring blankly at the world outside my window. The first snow was going to fall soon, or so they said. *Hooray*. Why my parents had chosen Maryland to live and not some tropical haven, I would never understand.

Next to me, my lab partner was studiously taking down notes like he always did. Derek was your average run-of-the-mill science geek. Feverishly documenting every bit of Mr. French's more-rambling-than-informative-lecture, he completely ignored the fact that his glasses were sliding ever so precariously down his nose. Though, despite his nerd-like tendencies, he was still a pretty good-looking kid with thick, dark hair and piercing eyes the color of kiwis. What was evident to me, however, was the way his face had a tendency to turn various shades of crimson every time I even so much as glanced in his direction. From the beginning, I'd made it clear to him that I wasn't allowed to date. Okay, so that was a lie. A lie made all the more interesting by confiding in him that my father was an avid gun collector with a split personality.

Although my aversion to dating seemed to be somewhat of a relief to my parents, I suspected they were nonetheless starting to wonder about their teenage daughter's lack of interest in even broaching the subject with them. In fact, I was fairly certain that my mother was chomping at the bit for me to bring a date home to give her an excuse to take me shopping for prom dresses, makeup and all that other frilly, girly crap. Alas, it wasn't meant to be for I had ulterior motives with my selection of Derek as my lab partner.

Derek was a science phenom; so, when it came down to choosing lab partners, let's just say it was a no-brainer for me. And it never ceased to amaze me that, regardless of his academic intelligence, all it ever took for me to win him over was a simple bat of an eyelash and a lip-gloss infused grin. It'd been one of only a handful of times I'd used my feminine wiles to my advantage. It wasn't as though I were incapable of passing the class based on own merits. Quite the contrary, I selected him because of my capabilities. He was a genius and I was of slightly above-average intelligence, which translated into me not having to do too much to ace the class. Some would call it laziness; I called it efficiency.

I'd always been an honor student without even trying. I considered it nature's way of making up for everything I wasn't graced with: artistic skills, athleticism, and the uncanny ability to walk into a room without tripping over my own two feet. Classes were just an unnecessary formality for me.

"Ms. Stevens," Mr. French called my name while leaning dangerously too far over the overhead projector near the front of the classroom.

His stomach was almost as pompous as his ego. When he leaned over the projector it brushed against the ink on the transparency, smudging the glass and leaving yet another stain on his two-sizes-too-small polyester shirt. He'd just completed his lecture and was scanning the jungle for unassuming prey to devour with humiliation. Today, I was his target. *Oh crap.*

"Ms. Stevens, what is reverse osmosis?"

I looked at Derek, giving him a big smile as I turned to face Mr. French. "Reverse osmosis is a method of producing pure water by forcing saline or impure water through a semi permeable membrane across which salts or impurities cannot pass."

Out of the corner of my eye, I saw Derek giving me the thumbs-up from underneath our table. Mr. French wore a clear look of disappointment, signaling that I'd again robbed him of the opportunity to reprimand me for not having paid attention in class.

"Very good, Ms. Stevens."

"Thank you," I replied in a tone peppered with a hint of smart ass.

"I think you just stole the wind from his sails," Derek whispered to me in amusement.

"Nah, he has enough hot hair left to move the Titanic," I replied.

Derek did his best to stifle his laughter but not before he received a warning glance from Mr. French. It was apparent that I was becoming somewhat of a bad influence on the future valedictorian. Pleased with myself, I smiled at Derek and resumed my descent into la-la land, staring out the window at a lone snowflake falling from the sky.

"I have this theory," my friend Lucy announced from her aptly named "co-pilot" instead of "shotgun" position in my Taurus as we were pulling out of the school's parking lot.

I'd basically been Lucy's chauffeur since obtaining my license a little over a year ago. Her parents didn't much care for teenage drivers and weren't about to add to the problem by allowing their daughter to join in their ranks. But, for some reason, they had trusted me as I–in their words–had 'radiated maturity beyond my years'. I supposed it was a compliment seeing as how whatever exactly it was they thought I radiated was apparently enough of a reassurance for them to leave their daughter's life in my hands.

"Oh, really? What pray tell is this said theory?" I asked.

"Quite simply, the world is ending."

Lucy's proclamation nearly caused me to miss a stop sign, forcing me to brake rather abruptly, clearly annoying the person in the car behind me.

"Okay," I said. "You have my attention. I would love to know where you came up with this theory."

"Just look at all the chaos and destruction going on right now with these bombings taking place. I mean…what else could it possibly be? There must be some reason for this kind of erratic human behavior. All the attacks that have been going on, and they only seem to be getting worse. Someone or something has to be sparking them."

"What? Because psychopaths don't exist? Come on, Lucy. There are a lot of evil, psychotic people in this world. The only difference between now and, say, fifty years ago is the fact that people now have better access to more tools of destruction. Take the Internet, for example. There are websites devoted to the sort of chaos that has been going on lately. Plus, there's way more media coverage than there used to be. We just hear more about everything that goes on now, so maybe it's just that it seems like there is really more happening than there truly is."

Lucy was my best friend even though she'd always been the overtly analytical, paranoid, conspiracy theory type of girl. These traits tended to wear thin on most everyone else who knew her, but I'd become accustomed to–if not somewhat amused by–them through the years. Whenever she suffered so much as a cough, she'd find herself on the Internet researching it, developing speculations as to its origin. Instead of the usual viral causes, she'd more often than not come to the conclusion that some freak pathogen had been released into the air. Over the years, I discovered that if I could reason with her by providing cold hard facts, or well-spoken bullshit, she was quickly brought back down to reality.

"I suppose you're right," she agreed.

"As always."

"So what are you planning on doing over Christmas Break?" A puzzled look must have overspread my face as Lucy shot back, "You completely forgot that today was the last day of school before break, didn't you?"

"So sue me for not owning a calendar. Besides, I finished all of my gift buying weeks ago. I guess I just felt like I could forget about the whole Christmas thing."

"You're one strange creature, Celaine."

"One person's strange is another person's unique. Now get out of my car."

Lucy laughed, rolling her eyes at me as she opened the passenger side door of my car now parked in her driveway.

"I'll give you a call this weekend."

"Thanks for the warning."

She shook her head, closed the car door and proceeded up her driveway. It was nice having a friend who understood me. I'd made several acquaintances and quasi-friends over the school years, but none of them seemed to appreciate my dry humor like Lucy Pierce did.

Methodically, I backed out of the Pierce's driveway, avoiding the various ceramic pots and ornamental statues planted at the end of it. A minor infraction last summer on my part had forced us to make a mad dash into town to replace a couple of potted geraniums that had somehow ended up underneath my tires. Narrowly avoiding another disaster, I backed out into the road and drove the two blocks from Lucy's house to my parents' split-level complete with white picket fence. My folks took the whole American dream thing to the extreme.

By late afternoon, the wind had picked up, howling in sheer protest. It all but took my breath away as I opened my car door. I absolutely hated this time of year, and that's probably why I always allowed myself to forget about it so easily. The true meaning of Christmas, as far as I was concerned, had been lost years ago in the age of advertising and keeping up with the Joneses. Now, it seemed as though the holiday was becoming more of a time for parents to buy their children's affections after a year of neglect masked by the use of television as a babysitter and having a "headache" when their children asked them to play catch in the backyard.

Much to my relief, I was the first one home. I threw my keys into the wooden bowl next to the front door that served as a catch-all for all of our miscellaneous junk. There were days when I treasured solitude, a fact of which my mother and little brother never could quite seem to grasp.

My mother, Carol, had yet to catch on to the fact that I was none too interested in the daily gossip around town. Nor did I care to partake in standard "girl talk" with her. Small talk for me consisted of a lively discussion of a novel or a stimulating debate about some hot topic issue. When I tried to institute such talk with Carol, it was like hitting a brick wall, prompting me to give in to her while patiently sitting and listening to her stories of how the dignitaries in town lived their lives. I knew everything about Mayor Anderson's extramarital exploits and Sheila from down the block's five hundred dollar pumps. I'd made half-hearted attempts at smiling at all of Carol's stories when she regaled me with them and was always amazed that she still couldn't understand why dances didn't thrill me; why being a cheerleader never really appealed to me; or why I had no interest in befriending those daughters of the social elite in our town. The answer was quite simple: I would not allow Carol to live her life vicariously through me.

Don't get me wrong, I'd been dealt a decent hand in life. Carol and George, my father, always ensured that my brother, Jake, and I had everything we needed. George was head of the pediatric unit at Hope Memorial Hospital. Carol was a journalist for the local newspaper with her main expertise–surprise, surprise–being human interest stories. Landing that job had been like receiving manna from heaven for her as there was no one more interested in how others lived their lives than Carol.

George was the only thing standing between me and the loony bin. My father was a little more low-key than my mother, preferring to stay at home instead of attending social gatherings. Carol and George were complete opposites who fit together perfectly like pieces of a jigsaw puzzle.

Jake and I were the quintessential brother and sister team. We pretended to despise each other, often refusing to be in the same room for more than what was absolutely necessary. However, if one of us were in trouble, the other would walk on hot coals to kick the ass of whoever warranted it. After all, if anyone was going to do bodily harm to my brother, it would be me.

Yes, we lived the perfect, all-American, white picket fence kind of life until one late December day everything turned upside down.

After grabbing an apple from our fruit bowl, I plopped down on my bed, wrapped myself up in my down comforter and turned on the television. While flipping through the channels, a news bulletin appeared on the screen, grabbing my attention. This particular bulletin detailed yet another bombing. This time the bomber had struck an Atlantic City casino. That would make twice this week and four times within the last month that an attack had occurred. Thankfully, this time the casualties were minimal since the casino was struck in the wee hours of the morning.

I turned the channel only to find yet another news organization replaying the same story. A perky, blonde anchor woman who appeared to have had numerous cosmetic procedures to the point where being surprised was the only expression she could muster recounted the attack:

"A blast killed three people and critically injured five more at the Flamingo Resort and Casino in Atlantic City shortly after three o'clock this morning. The explosion took out the lobby of the casino, damaging much of the gaming floor. Fortunately, due to the timing of this travesty, there were minimal people on the floor at the time. The cause of this incident remains under investigation, but many believe it to be linked to similar incidences that occurred in Philadelphia, Dover and Baltimore within the last month…"

I turned off the television and lay on my bed staring at the ceiling. What if Lucy was right? There had to be a reason for all of this. This couldn't just be random, could it? After arriving at the conclusion that I was becoming just as paranoid as she was, I put all thoughts of Armageddon to rest and closed my eyes.

"Celaine, dinner's ready," Carol called.

"Huh?" Groggy, I sat up and looked at the clock on my desk. Apparently, I'd fallen asleep. Who would've thought that staring at the ceiling wasn't stimulating enough to keep a person conscious?

"Celaine."

"I'll be right down," I said. It was time for another rousing Stevens' dinner. I stood up, slowly making my way downstairs. Not surprisingly, they'd already started eating without me. When it came to food, my family meant business.

"So nice of you to join us," my father said sarcastically.

I dished up a plate of lasagna for myself. Besides grilled cheese and spaghetti, lasagna was just about the only other thing Carol knew how to make, ensuring that we ate those three meals quite frequently. Suffice it to say, she was no Betty Crocker.

"I was talking to Claire today at work," Carol began. "Apparently, her and Bob are considering building a bomb shelter in their backyard what with all the mayhem that has been happening around here.

"Is that a fact?" my dad replied with slight bemusement.

"Yeah, they're really freaked out. Bob says that if there's another bombing he's selling the house and moving out of the city altogether."

"Bob has always been one to overreact."

"You think?"

"Yeah. Why?"

"Well, these attacks…they seem to be occurring more frequently…in more populated areas. I mean, what if they start bombing highways –or schools."

"Carol."

I stole a glance over at Jake, relieved to see him building a garlic bread town in his lasagna, completely oblivious to what was being discussed.

"Carol," my dad began, exasperated, "more than likely these attacks are being carried out by copycats. The problem lies with the media…they sensationalize this crap to the point where those psychopaths tune in to see it. They think they'll get their names in the history books if they set out to best what has already been done. It's their attempt to instill further panic. By building a bomb shelter or uprooting our lives we'd be doing nothing but fanning the flames they've created."

George hadn't been himself lately. His unflappable demeanor had changed overnight. We'd all noticed that he seemed slightly more anxious lately, but couldn't quite pinpoint the reason behind it. Our best guess was that it was due to more stress being put on him at work. He was well-respected by his colleagues and peers. Some even speculated that he would be in the running for the chief of staff position when the current chief retired later next year. Whatever it was, George wasn't talking about it and repeated enquiries from Carol were doing nothing to lighten his mood.

"Well, I suppose you're right," Carol said, deflated, "But still, these incidences are a little disconcerting."

My fork scraped the bottom of my plate creating a bloodcurdling shriek that brought me back down to reality. Something about my parents' discussion surrounding the attacks hadn't set well with me.

"Thanks for dinner, Mom," I said as I stood up.

"You're welcome, sweetie," she replied. "Oh, Celaine."

"Yeah?"

"We're going to the mall tomorrow to pick up some last minute gifts. Do you want to come with us?"

"Darn skippy." I was happy to hear the conversation returning to an iota of normalcy. My father chuckled.

"She's one strange child," I heard my mom mutter.

"You got that right," Jake said.

"Jake, what the heck is that?" my father asked.

"I'm building a replica of Washington, D.C. See, here's the White House, the Lincoln Memorial, the Washington Monument..."

"For Pete's sake, Jake, eat your dinner," George grumbled. I could tell George wished he'd just stayed at the hospital tonight instead of coming home.

"And you think *I'm* weird," I called out as I headed back upstairs.

"It's not being weird, it's channeling my creativity," Jake called after me.

"I've heard that President Brooks thinks the attacks are becoming more organized," Carol said, returning to the topic of my and George's disdain. "He believes we may be dealing with a domestic terrorist organization bent on staging some sort of a coup. They're talking about institutionalizing a nationwide curfew because of it."

I stopped in my tracks halfway up the stairs as I strained to listen.

"That will never happen," George countered. "It would be like spitting on the Constitution. The people simply wouldn't allow it."

# 3

## THE LAKES

MY FATHER, MOTHER and brother were murdered on a snowy December afternoon just days before Christmas. In hindsight, I know a part of me died with them.

Carol, George, Jake and I made our way into the mall packed with the usual traffic the Christmas season generated. This time of year, the city turned into a claustrophobic's worst nightmare. Sure, an aura of glee and merriment flitted through the air. It was, after all, just mere days before the big event. Permeating the atmosphere was the aroma of evergreens, sugar cookies, and cinnamon, acting like effervescent buffers to keep the usual smell of exhaust fumes at bay. Those sights and smells are what I firmly believed prevented a person from going insane as they spent an eternity in line buying something that was probably only going to get returned anyway. *Merry freaking Christmas.*

The Lakes was a plethora of retail paradise where all fads were exploited to the max, ensuring that every last penny was squeezed out of the pocketbooks of the unassuming. Fads weren't my thing. I marched to the beat of my own drummer, much to the dismay of George and Carol. But what I lacked for in compliance with the usual social norms, I made up for with my academic achievements and overall uneventful teenage years, thus earning my parents' trust. So, when Jake decided that my hair looked better with Smoothie in it, they didn't protest to my sudden need to break away.

"It's not fair," Jake said. "She always gets to go out on her own."

"Well, Jake," my father chimed in. "Perhaps your mother and I could trust you, too, if we weren't so sure something would be lit on fire in our absence."

"That was *one* time," Jake protested.

"Tell that to Ms. Jacobson's cat," Carol added.

It'd taken a full year for ole' Smokey's coat to grow back after Jake's infamous experimentation with bottle rockets, and still the cat just wasn't the same. Poor Smokey now walked with his head tilted and the smell of singed hair never fully left him. In a sick, twisted way, I had to laugh at the irony of this occurring to a cat named Smokey. In the aftermath, Jake had learned that, like elephants, cats, too, never forgot being wronged. Since the incident, every time Smokey would see Jake outside, he'd crouch low to the ground with a maniacal stare etched across his feline face, plotting his revenge.

"Meet us at the third floor parking ramp at five-thirty," George said.

"No problem, Geo...Dad." My parents were very liberal when it came to us using their first names, but my dad still managed to wince every time his name escaped my lips, forcing me to keep my "Georges" and "Carols" to a minimum.

I thanked my parents for the moment of freedom, making sure to stick my tongue out at Jake as I bounded away. It was a juvenile move, but I knew that it nonetheless managed to get under his skin and, well, wasn't that my job?

I'd always felt such a profound sense of freedom after breaking loose from my parents. So much so that, without someone being there to tell me what to do and when to do it, I usually ended up just wandering around aimlessly. There was nothing I needed to do, nor was there anything in particular I really wanted to look for, which didn't help matters. After scouring through a few stores, I decided on one pedaling memorabilia from the 80's. I didn't know what it was about the 80's that drew me in and theorized that I was subconsciously channeling my parents' long-forgotten youth, when they were just a young couple in love with no children to blow up random animals.

From the moment I entered the store, I was in all my neon, bangle bracelet, big-haired, legging-wearing glory, and it was apparent that the store's employees took their jobs very seriously. With stirrup pants and oversized off the shoulder sweaters they looked like something straight out of a Tiffany video. While canvassing my surroundings, I rummaged through hair ties, abnormally large t-shirts, and striped leg warmers. I then meandered through the store, killing time more than I was actually browsing. After finding a sales bin, I managed to do a bit of digging and located a pair of neon pink hoop earrings to make my time in the store worth it. The electric yellow leggings stuck to the earrings I selected were still a bit of a stretch for me, but I figured I'd graduate to them eventually.

Upon purchasing the earrings, I walked back out into the mall where I found my way through a maze of oversized candy canes, swam through a sea of impatient children, and maneuvered through the crowds until finally locating a restroom. As far as public restrooms go, The Lakes wasn't half bad. It still wasn't clean enough to meet my standards, but if it were an emergency I would suck it up and hover. When I entered the restroom, Christmas carols were blaring over the speakers. It would have been a welcoming sound, deviating from the utter chaos of the mall, if not for the fact that I'd been forced to listen to *Jingle Bells* for the last two months. I was beginning to loathe the Holiday Season and all its ho-ho-hokey glory. After setting my purse down on the sink, I removed the earrings from the neon green plastic bag and fastened them to my earlobes to inspect them in the mirror.

"Not too shabby, Celaine, not too shabby," I said to myself, much to the amusement of those within earshot.

I decided to pin my hair back to let my new earrings take center stage. Just as I brought my arm up into view, however, I happened to take a glance at my watch and was struck by the time. 5:45! There goes my freedom for the next couple of months. Without hesitation, I bolted out of the bathroom sprinting, not too gracefully, through the crowds of people, eliciting gasps, expletives and overall general irritation in my wake. I wasn't an athlete by any stretch of the imagination, but I could run when I had to. My hope was that my parents had lost track of time, meaning that I would remain the dependable, punctual daughter they thought me to be. No such luck.

Jake stood beaming as he watched me approaching. This was no doubt his vindication for my earlier sisterly gesture.

"There you are," my mother proclaimed. "Really, Celaine, we've been worried sick."

"I'm sorry, Mom, I just lost track of time and, well, there was a long line to get into the bathroom and..."

"To what? Check out your new earrings? Young lady, I'm not as gullible as you make me out to be. If there's one gene of mine that I know for sure I passed on to you, it's an aversion to public restrooms."

*Damn.* "I'm sorry, Mom. It won't happen again."

"Let's get going," George said. "It's starting to snow pretty hard out there."

Dejected, I followed my family out of the mall to the parking ramp with Jake snickering beside me the entire time. The weather had taken a turn for the worse; that much was evident even in the cement sanctity of the parking ramp. Snow flurries whipped through rows of automobiles, ricocheting off their plastic bodies and inevitably embedding themselves in my flesh. I shuddered, trying not to think about the fact that I'd neglected to wear any other means of protection from the elements other than my hooded sweatshirt.

After taking a couple of wrong turns and attempting to break into a vehicle that happened to be the identical twin to ours, we made it back to our car.

"Celaine, could you give me a hand with this, please?" Carol asked me.

"Sure thing."

I grabbed the packages out of my mother's hands and located room for them in the corner of the trunk.

"Bag lady," Jake sneered.

"Is that the best you got, little man?" I asked.

"Enough," George quipped.

George started the car as I strapped myself in with my iPod to prepare for the hour journey back home in our winter wonderland. With my mind at ease, I began sensing that something wasn't quite right. Something was missing; something whose identity presented itself just as we were about to pull out of the third floor parking ramp.

"Do you have any gum by chance?" Carol asked me, leaning back from the front seat.

"Yeah, let me get my p..."

26

"Your what?"

"My...uh...purse."

"Okay. So, where is it?"

"Do you really want to know the answer to that question?"

"Oh, Celaine," George said, aggravated.

"It's in the restroom, isn't it?" Carol asked.

"I do vaguely remember setting it down there."

In the rear view mirror, I could see the vein in George's neck beginning to bulge, his face turning a bright shade of red.

"How could you be so careless?" Carol asked, digging in some more.

At this point, Jake was giggling like a school girl. Christmas had come early for him.

"I will drive you to the entrance of the third floor, and we'll wait for you there," George said. "No side trips, young lady. You will go straight to that bathroom and come back to the car. Do you hear me?"

"Dad, I made a simple mistake. No need to brand me with a scarlet letter just yet."

George parked just outside the doorway to the third floor mall entrance, motioning for me to get out with a big sigh. I shut the door and gave him an apologetic smile through the glass before I turned around to reenter the mall.

Had I had any inclination that this would be the last time I'd ever see them, I would have stolen another glance in their direction. I would have done anything I could muster to save them, to capture the very essence of their faces, to engrave them in my mind forever. Of course, I couldn't have known that that final imperfect moment was going to be the last time I'd ever see them.

With speed that would make even an Olympian proud, I ran through the mall. The crowds had thinned out somewhat, but not enough to make my journey to the restroom a walk in the park. Around me, the usual monotony of screaming children, of people stopped haphazardly in paths made for travel, and of others gathered around in idle chatter about their holiday plans conspired against me. As the minutes ticked away, I could visualize the vein on George's neck bulging out further and further until it finally burst in a bloody mess. The thought of this made me shudder, prompting me to decide that the only way to get around my problem was to go through it.

"Excuse me, pardon me, coming through; girl on the move here." I pushed my way through the mobs of holiday revelers. Crowds were just one more reason to hate the holidays – as if I needed another one.

It's funny how, when you're in a hurry, time seems to stand still, making a simple trip to the restroom seem like a hike across the Yukon. Of course, knowing that George was growing closer to having a coronary by the second didn't help matters. After what felt like half a century, the restroom came into view. In my elated rush to finally get there, I neglected to look where I was going, and it was only after I crashed to the floor that I saw the felled candy cane that had mysteriously managed to jump out in front of me. Attempting to compose myself as I stood up in pain, I muttered some words that most certainly would have eradicated my name from the fat, jolly man's "Good List."

The fall managed to pop a cork of negativity in my mind, forcing me to realize that, even on an average day, the odds that my purse was still exactly where I'd forgotten it were pretty slim. Nonetheless, I knew if I were to come back empty-handed I would hear about it from George and Carol for at least the rest of the year, and Jake for a good six months. I let out a sigh, preparing to meet my fate as I limped into the ladies room discovering, to my amazement, that the fates were smiling upon me. My purse was there in all its denim glory on the sink where I'd forgotten it. Whether or not my wallet was still in it was probably a whole different story, however. For now, the mere presence of the purse itself would be enough to appease George and Carol. I'd have plenty of time to worry about what was or wasn't still in it later. With a relived smile, I snatched it by its faded, denim straps and made a bee line out of the restroom.

My knee was throbbing from having been bashed against the linoleum floor. Great, I was probably the only person to have ever suffered a battle wound from a hard day of shopping. I hobbled along until I came to a bench that just so happened to be located next to the same candy cane of doom that had attempted to foil me. In pain, I rolled up my pant leg to inspect the damage. Already I could tell that my pasty skin was beginning to bruise around the point of impact, and it was noticeably beginning to swell. Disgusted with my lack of coordination, I pulled my jeans back down and headed back in the direction of the third floor parking ramp.

It's amazing how life can change in just a mere matter of seconds. One moment you're walking through a mall browsing for Christmas presents for your loved ones; and the next, everything goes black. Exactly two things happened before my world was quite literally ripped out from underneath me: First, there were a series of pops resembling those of an automatic firearm; then a flash of light appeared so bright I swore the sun had crashed into the earth.

Amidst those thunderous blasts and that flash of light, life as I knew it came crashing to an end.

# 4

# THE LEDGE

I'D NEVER BEEN through an earthquake before, nor had I ever heard of one of this magnitude occurring on the East Coast. Therefore, in hindsight, an earthquake seemed like an odd conclusion for me to have rendered as I felt the Earth shake beneath my feet and beheld the sky falling in around me.

In response to the chaos unfolding around me, I attempted to steady myself against a railing separating the third floor from a sixty foot drop. Discernible screams of fear and shocked surprise erupted, breaking through the commotion. Intermingled with those screams were gruesome cries of anguish whose presence was silenced by the sound of concrete striking the floor. Smoke invaded The Lakes, blending in with the hurricanes of dust generated with each explosion–three in all–creating the perfect storm. In the aftermath of the final explosion, the railing that served as my sanctuary began to buckle.

The steel squealed in defeat as the piece supporting my body suddenly swung out over the center of the mall, bringing me with it. In shock, I looked down at the floor below my dangling feet, noticing that the majestic thirty foot fountain, the crowning glory of The Lakes, now stood in nothing more than piles of broken concrete.

My heart raced inside my chest as my body hung over the chasm. Tears welled inside my eyes from the fog of smoke encasing me, impairing my vision. A sudden tremor shook throughout the mall causing the third floor to shift once more, and the portion of the railing I clung to with every ounce of my being creaked as it began to break away from its foundation. Determined, I tightened my grasp on the metal bars, knowing that if I didn't act fast I, too, would be in pieces like the concrete beneath me.

I slid my body upwards to the third floor. Inch by inch, I hoisted myself along the railing in a near vertical climb up the side of what had once been the floor beneath me.

"Keep going, Celaine, you aren't going to die here – not like this," I repeatedly told myself.

Halfway to relative safety, further disaster struck. Droplets of water rained down from the mall's sprinkling system, dripping down the sides of the metal railing, rendering it a virtual slip-and-slide in my hands. Any grasp I'd had on it was suddenly compromised, forcing me to slide back down. If I couldn't find a way to battle my way back, I would be in dire trouble.

Before that day, I hadn't realized just how amazing the sheer human will to live was. At the point when I should have lost my grip, my adrenaline kicked in. With this new burst of energy came an overpowering determination that only intensified as I forced my body back up the railing. Before I knew it, I'd surpassed the point where I'd slid down. Water continued pouring in steadily from both the sprinkling system and the remnants of the mall's ceiling, soaking me to the bone. The bitterly cold December air from the outside began creeping its way inside, sending my damp body into shock.

"Inch by inch," I repeated to myself. I could feel the veritable mountain I was climbing beginning to tremble again, making me aware of the fact that I didn't have much longer before the final avalanche struck. It was a culmination of every horror movie I could think of, except I kept telling myself that the lifeless figures scattered on the floor below me were nothing more than mannequins. That illusion was shattered when I saw the blood.

The railing shuddered again, forcing my body to swing precariously back and forth. I looked back up the metal pole and gasped in shock upon realizing that less than an inch of steel was left binding it to the rest of the railing. In desperation, I made one last heave, propelling myself away from the pole and, to my relief, my hands managed to grasp the jagged edge of the third floor foundation. With all the remaining energy I could muster, I pulled my body safely to the floor just as the railing broke loose, crashing to the rubble below.

On the debris-covered floor, I lay sobbing. Dust and smoke created such an impenetrable haze that, if not for the mini fires spouting from the perforated gas lines, I wouldn't have been able to see at all. In pain, I managed to stand up and assess myself. There were a few minor cuts on my arms, but they were otherwise unscathed. That wouldn't be true elsewhere. When I inspected the burning pain in my thigh, I noticed blood flowing down my leg from an extensive cut leading from the upper thigh halfway to my knee. My jeans had been torn all the way down on one leg, exposing my skin.

With my thoughts beginning to clear, I remembered the whole reason why I was even still in the war-torn mall. I let out an audible gasp, the tears welling in my eyes. *Oh God, no,* I thought, remembering that George, Carol and Jake were waiting for me outside. In pain, I ambled towards the department store that separated me from the parking ramp. It was in this direction that the explosions had come from.

Above me, a piercing snap erupted. I looked up in the direction of the sound, finding myself forced to dive out of the way of a falling skylight. It crashed to the floor, sending shards of glass flying in my direction. Dazed, I picked myself up from the floor. Broken glass had cut into my hands, but neither that nor the pain mattered to me at the moment. The entrance to the department store was just yards away, and I was going to make it or die trying. I scaled the mountain of debris comprising the remnants of the department store entrance. Survivors who'd been in the store at the time of the blasts were scrambling to get out, looking at me as though I were suicidal for wanting in.

"You're heading to the worst of it," a woman, covered in dust from head to toe, shouted at me.

I ignored her, continuing my climb into the department store. To say that this was the worst of it had been an understatement. War zones probably didn't look much different than the sight that was before me.

Clouds of smoke infiltrated my lungs, bringing a bout of incessant coughing so unrelenting that my ribs began to ache. In my attempts to counteract the assault, I crouched down to crawl in the more breathable air on the floor, my hand touching something that felt familiar. A scream escaped my lips as I realized that I was holding a hand that was no longer connected to a body. Sickened, I threw the hand off to the side and continued my crawl toward the ramp. My stomach turned, and I knew that I had to keep my eyes trained forward if I was going to make it without passing out.

*Almost there*, I thought. The door to the parking ramp was close to being within my grasp; a virtual blinding beam of light shone through it. A beacon in the blinding fog. At that moment, I found it funny how I hadn't noticed there being a light at that door before. The department store had always seemed so dark in the direction of the ramp. Even more amazing still was that the entryway appeared to be intact. With my target in sight, I took a deep breath using my remaining strength to spring to my feet, running the rest of the way to the door.

The automatic door was more manual than automatic. I banged on it with my fists, attempting to do the job the explosion had been unable to accomplish. When that failed, I braced a leg on one side of the frame and, with my aching arms, attempted to pry the door open like a human crowbar. No luck. After a couple more minutes of kicking, smacking and invariably flipping the door off, I realized that what I was doing was not going to work. Undeterred, I scanned the rubble for an idea. A piece of scaffolding stuck out like a sore thumb within the concrete. With a plan forming in my head, I lunged towards it, praying it would be suitable enough to pry the door open. But just as I bent down to grab it, I felt one hand on my shoulder and another one around my waist attempting to pull me back.

"What in the hell do you think you're doing?" A man whirled me around to face him. His eyes were wild, his hair gray from soot. He appeared to be a security guard or an officer of some sort. It was too hard to tell based on what was left of his tattered uniform. "There's nothing left. Do you hear me? The ramp is gone. You're going to get yourself killed trying to go out there."

Even though I heard the words he spoke, they made no sense to me. What did he mean when he said the ramp was gone? It had been there just twenty minutes ago. Deciding that the good officer must be crazy, I broke away from him and proceeded onward in my quest to pry the door open, grabbing the piece of scaffolding from its concrete tomb.

"No," he yelled at me again, moving to restrain me.

I'd had enough. As much as I didn't want to do it, I felt like I had no other option but to disable the officer, as reasoning with him was clearly not going to work. I raised my arm and swung at him, striking him in the chest. The force of my elbow to his rib cage caused him to release his grip on me enough to where I was able to break away. Once free, I whirled around swiftly, kicking him in the legs as hard as I could in the hope that it would incapacitate him long enough for me to pry the door open.

I fetched the metal bar from the rubble and jammed it between the seal and the frame of the doorway, pushing it with all my strength. At first, it put up an admirable fight, but after several solid jabs it finally conceded defeat, squeaking open. Smoke–thicker and black in color– poured into the store from the outside, sending me into another coughing fit. Undaunted, I gave the bar a few more solid pushes until enough room opened up for me to squeeze my entire body through the door. Through the clouds of smoke, I took off down the crumpled concrete. In the suffocating fog, snowflakes stabbed my face like tiny daggers, grinding salt in my wounds.

My eyes worked to focus in the direction I'd left my parents' vehicle. I walked down the pavement, looking for the familiar sight of the garage, realizing that I should have been there by now. The smoky haze slowly became less and less dense the further out I walked until a wayward gust of wind blew past me, punching a hole into the unknown. What it revealed was a scene I hadn't expected.

Instead of the familiar ramp, I found myself standing on the edge of a ledge with the rest of the city spread out before me. Sirens surrounded me. I shielded my ears with my bloodied hands. A strange sound approaching from above drew my attention to the helicopter that was circling the mall. The hurricane-force wind it generated pushed my broken body in all directions. Did I take a wrong turn? Was I *that* disoriented?

No, I wasn't. This was where I'd left my parents and Jacob. They had been right here waiting for me. A thought occurred to me then; a thought that rendered my delicate stomach as fragile as an egg shell. Numbness overtook me as I staggered to the edge of the cliff, peering over it to see what I had feared and somehow already knew would be there.

"No! God, no," an involuntary scream escaped my lips.

Atop the ledge overlooking their fate, I dropped to my knees and sobbed. In anguish, I repeatedly punched the pavement, only stopping after my hand hung limp from my wrist. The physical pain from breaking my hand, however, was not something I remember feeling. My body was already too numb from the emotional shock. Over the edge of the newly-formed cliff, my family's fate had been revealed to me. Strewn in a mass of broken pavement were pieces of steel in every shape, size and color. Attached to these pieces of steel were tires, antennas, and license plates. My father, mother and brother were somewhere down there at the bottom of that ledge. The parking ramp had been the epicenter of the blasts. On the pavement I laid, immobile and unfeeling. I was wet, cold, broken, and I didn't care about anything anymore.

From what I was later told by both my doctors and from watching reports on the news, I remained on the ledge for about an hour before firefighters were able to remove me from my sepulcher. My motionless body was on the national news, serving as the perfect illustration for the devastation that had transpired that day.

One of the firefighters who rescued me from the ledge carried me to an ambulance where EMTs stripped the soggy clothing from my body. I must have been shaking pretty badly as they wasted no time enveloping me in blankets. After I was secured, the ambulance raced to what I assumed would be Hope Memorial Hospital.

"Poor thing," a pretty, young EMT said while attaching various tubes to my body.

I heard the other EMT, a man who'd obviously been the more seasoned veteran of the two—with salt and pepper hair and a stare devoid of all emotion—speak as he radioed ahead to the hospital. "Teenage female with probable hypothermia, smoke inhalation and a possible broken right hand...possible bilateral rib fractures and multiple contusions. Estimated time of arrival is eight minutes."

The woman EMT, whose last name was "Topper"—or so I gathered from the badge dangling around her neck—caressed my cheeks. She then began humming a familiar tune I recognized from my youth, and the volumes of lullabies my mother used to sing to me at night. This instant memory of my mother sent a new wave of pain coursing through my body, forcing a small tear from the corner of my eye.

"She looks catatonic," she said. A worried tone flowed from her voice.

"They'll do an MRI at Hope Memorial," the elder EMT replied, unfazed. "She's probably just in shock. There's no telling what she's witnessed today." Topper winced, continuing to stroke my cheek.

The last thing I remember that day was the ambulance pulling up in front of Hope Memorial; the hospital that'd become like a second home to me through the years. My stretcher was unloaded to a throng of trauma-hungry physicians. It was a sight that would have made George proud. A handful of residents gathered around me, some of whom I recognized through my frequent meanderings in the halls, and rushed me through the doors of the Emergency Room.

"Oh, my gosh. Is that Dr. Stevens' daughter?" one of the doctors asked.

"All pretty girls look the same to you, Scott," another retorted.

It was then that my memory cut off.

The rain and sleet came splattering down against the umbrella I clutched in my good hand; one lone umbrella in the sea of black umbrellas gathered together in a tight circle. In the middle of the circle stood three oak coffins, each covered with a bouquet of roses, my mother's favorite flower. Next to me, Lucy was nearly as devastated as I was.

Everything went by in one big blur that day. I'm not sure whether I could recite a single word of Reverend Logan's eulogy or any of the heart wrenching memorials given by my father's colleagues. In fact, I'm pretty sure that I couldn't even remember the names of most of the people who attended the funeral. I couldn't describe the faces of the individuals who embraced me while passing along their condolences. All I could focus on were the three oak caskets sitting side by side being pelted by balls of sleet.

Why had I been spared? What made me so special? These were the questions I yearned to have answered, but of which I knew answers did not exist. My father had done so much in the advancement of pediatric medicine and had so much more yet to offer. Why him and not me? None of this made sense; none of this was fair. I watched as the caskets were lowered into their final resting places while the crowd dispersed to their vehicles. With Lucy still at my side, I continued watching them until they were no longer visible–half tempted to ask for a hole to be dug for me, too.

"Celaine," a soothing voice behind me said, "are you ready?"

I turned to see my Aunt Tasha looking at me sheepishly. "Yeah," I replied.

"Okay. Wait here and I'll pull the car around."

Carol's sister, Aunt Tasha, must have drawn the short straw, and it was she who would be my guardian for the next year. This meant a move halfway across the country, but I really didn't care. Nothing existed for me here anymore. Lucy was devastated, but I reminded her that the year would go by fast and we always had the Internet. That had seemed to appease her for the time being.

"You're like a sister to me, you know," Lucy murmured almost incoherently through her tears.

"Don't...don't get all emotional on me right now, Luce." I broke my gaze away from the coffins and turned to face Lucy, wrapping my arms around her. And as much as I tried to fight it, I just wasn't strong enough to keep the tears away.

"Now look who's getting emotional."

I gave Lucy a small smile, releasing her from my grip. "You'll always be my sister, too." With the sleeve of my overcoat, I wiped the tears from my eyes. "I'll be back, Luce. I promise."

"You'd better be." She looked over my shoulder just as my aunt pulled the car off to the side of the path behind us.

"Well, I guess this is goodbye, then?" she sighed.

"Only for now."

After giving me one last quick hug, Lucy, too, wiped a tear from her eye, and with a forced smile, waved to me before leaving to walk to her parents' car. Aunt Tasha must have sensed that I wanted one final moment alone with my family. For not being good with such "delicate situations", she was handling me like a professional. I stared at each individual resting place, the places that would eternally hold my father, mother and brother.

# 6
## The Aftermath

THROUGH THE WINDOWS of the vehicle, I could see their faces staring at me–pleading for me to free them. I had exactly ten seconds to save them....nine...eight. The department store door jammed, forcing me to scan the rubble for the familiar metal pole. Success. I grabbed the pole from the severed hand's grasp, releasing each finger from its death grip around it. Time was running out...seven...six...five. Giving up on prying the door open, I threw my body against it, shattering it into a thousand pieces. The clock ticked away...four...three...two...I took off running towards them. I was going to make it this time. Finally, I was going to be able to save them.

But just as the scenario always seemed to unfold, when the final second faded away a dark figure appeared before me. My body became rooted to the ground in response to the apparition's menacing countenance as though his very presence froze every thread of my being. Even though I couldn't make out the specific features of this dark entity, his identity was no secret to me, and I knew what was coming next. The Man in Black threw his arms up into the air, summoning an enormous explosion, throwing me back into the store. In the glare of the explosion they were gone.

I shot up in bed, a cold sweat trickling down my face. Ten years had gone by, and still the vivid nightmares of that horrible day continued to plague me unrelentingly. My hand wiped the sweat from my forehead as I allowed my eyes to adjust to the darkness. In my chest, my heart was beating uncontrollably, making breathing difficult. Unable to quell my panic attack, I guided my fingers over the contents on top of my nightstand, stopping when they hit the hard plastic cover of my cell phone. It was three o'clock in the morning, but I knew he wouldn't mind. He never minded. In the two years I'd known him, I'd only seen him upset a handful of times, all of which were work-related.

He picked up on the fourth ring. "Hey, you," he answered groggily, further intensifying my guilt.

"How did you know it was me?"

"My other girlfriend already called me hours ago." I could almost see the smirk forming on his face.

"Very funny," I retorted.

"Did you have another nightmare?"

"Yeah, that makes four in a week." Tears began forming in the corners of my eyes. A single one emerged to run down my cheek. "Will this ever stop? Haven't I been tortured enough already?" My quivering voice was bordering on a sob.

"Shh…shh… it's going to be all right, Celaine. I'm here for you. In time, the nightmares will fade away, leaving you and I to our life together and…"

"Stay with me tomorrow night," I interrupted, more of a plea than a request.

"Hmmm… getting to hold an incredibly beautiful woman for a whole night… I don't know. I'm really going to have to think about that. I mean, I do have a pretty busy schedule and all, but I'll see if I can rearrange some appointments and pencil you in."

"Other than me, you're the only person capable of mustering sarcasm this early in the morning." My sobbing subsided. A half-smile returned to my face.

"That's why we're perfect for each other. We're the soul mates of smart ass."

"I love you."

"I love you, too. Now get some sleep. You've got a busy day ahead of you tomorrow. Loans to decline, lives to shatter, you know, fun stuff."

"Thank you. I'm not sure what I would do without you."

"Well, fortunately that's something you'll never have to worry about. See you tomorrow, beautiful."

I hung up the phone, letting my legs stretch over the side of the bed. It'd be at least another hour before I would be able to fall back asleep again. My fingers found the switch to the lamp on my nightstand and switched it on as I stood up from the bed. Tired, I walked down the hallway of my apartment to my cold, uninviting bathroom. Its tile floor was like sheer ice underneath my feet, causing me to shudder. I reached for the plastic cup on the basin, turned on the faucet, and filled it with water. Not only did the nightmares affect me emotionally, but they also took a toll on me physically. My throat was dry and the same knee I'd smacked on the floor in the minutes preceding the explosion throbbed in eerie phantom-like pain. Some nights I swore that glass was still embedded underneath my skin; some nights it felt as though I'd lived through the devastation all over again.

I opened the drawer of my bedroom nightstand, taking out the worn photo album. My photo album had been one of a few possessions I salvaged from my parents' home before moving to Iowa with Aunt Tasha. Its cloth cover was somewhat faded from years of wear and the pages were beginning to yellow. My fingers turned each page with care, stopping when I found what I had been looking for: the last family photograph ever taken of us.

There I was in all my awkward teenaged glory, smack dab in the middle. We were all wearing our identical photograph attire: matching blue sweaters and khaki pants. It'd been Carol's idea, of course. How I missed Carol. She was naturally gorgeous in this particular photograph with her hair, the color of toffee, pinned back. George looked so regal, so professional, and so proud. Then there was Jake. I often wondered what he would look like now as a young man. Would he be in medical school following in George's footsteps? Married with children of his own? Anger overtook the sorrow as my feelings over the injustice of it all came flooding back.

"There will be a day," I spoke to them as though they could hear me. "I promise you. One way or another, there will be a day of retribution."

I tucked the loose photograph back into the photo album and turned off the light. While lying back down in bed, my thoughts drifted to the aftermath of the explosion. My Aunt Tasha had done everything she could think of to make my life as normal as possible and, considering the circumstances, she'd done a wonderful job. Of course, she was nothing like the hawk Carol had been. Under Tasha's supervision, I'd been allotted way more freedom than any teenager should possess. At times, she'd seemed more interested in playing the role of the big sister to me rather than acting as my maternal role model but, when push came to shove, she managed to step up to the plate, ensuring that my grades were always up to par and that I kept relatively out of trouble. Not that there was a whole heck of a lot of trouble I could have gotten into. After all, there really wasn't much to do in Iowa outside of porta-potty tipping.

Much to Tasha's chagrin, after graduation I decided to come back home to Maryland. Some would argue that I was a sadist with a glutton for punishment. Regardless, I still felt at home here. On top of that, a part of me needed the closure in seeing the Memorial site that was erected two years after the explosion at The Lakes. In a strange way, seeing the Memorial had given me a sense of peace. It was something tangible. Of course, Lucy had been beyond thrilled with my decision to move back. We'd ended up attending college together; she studying psychology and I, finance.

However, my decision to move home inadvertently became the best decision of my life the day I met Chase Matthews. Shortly after my father's death, Hope Memorial Hospital created a scholarship in honor of him specifically for those young medical students interested in studying pediatrics. Catching wind of my return, the hospital contacted me requesting that I present the scholarship to that year's winner. At first, I was a little hesitant. I wasn't sure how I would react to all the stares and inevitable awkward conversations, but I knew that my father would have wanted me to do it.

Every presentation ceremony started out with a memorial to my father. Dr. Taylor, the pediatric surgeon who'd served as a resident under George, gave the speech every year. From my vantage point on the stage, I could see the admiration in the doctor's eyes as he spoke about my father. I'd sat on the stage scanning the audience, looking for any familiar faces. That's when I saw him. He was boyishly cute with shimmering, sky blue eyes and the smirk of a hardcore smart ass. He was resident Chase Matthews. A fan of my father's work with the pediatric unit, he was as close to perfection as I had seen, and he was staring at me.

A rush of heat poured into my cheeks, alerting me to the fact that I'd probably turned twelve shades of red. As much as I tried to, I couldn't divert my attention from him. I was so entranced that, when it came to be my turn at the podium, my name had to be called twice to snap me out of it. Two years later, I was still under that same trance.

With memories of my initial encounter with Chase Matthews flashing through my head, I managed to fall peacefully back to sleep.

The sun beamed into my fourth floor apartment, creating a makeshift heating pad on my back. It was yet another fabulous workday morning. Another day of fun and finance awaited me at the First American Bank & Trust. In this age, I felt fortunate to have a job. Unfortunately though, like many careers, it had just grown too mundane for me.

It was a perfect summer day and, if not for the presence of armed soldiers on every block, it would have also seemed like a normal summer day. Their presence was an omnipresent reminder that things were still far from normal here. We were still living in the nightmare of unwavering paranoia with every person, parked car and building being a potential target for lethal destruction. Pure anxiety had reduced a once bustling, crowded city street to just a few brave souls using it to commute warily back and forth to work.

The attack on The Lakes created a fork in the road for more than just those whose lives it'd directly impacted. A Pandora's Box had been opened in its wake, unleashing a chain of events overseen by the Brooks' Administration. Military enforcement of Brooks' new order swept through the nation, generating a false sense of security. The fall of democracy had been met with praise by Congress and the highest approval ratings of any President in history. President Brooks was keeping us safe; President Brooks cared about society. Bullshit. At least, that was my opinion.

After the revocation of the Twenty-Second Amendment allowing Brooks at least one more term in office, suspicion rose amongst us more cynical members of society. The more vocal members of this opposition–radicals they were called–were said to be launching a rebellion against President Brooks as they considered him just as dangerous as The Man in Black. The Man in Black or any other responsible party still hadn't been apprehended and, although conditions had become markedly calmer over the last couple of years, there were still random attacks occurring.

The decline in instability was due, in part, to the appearance of an inexplicable duo who'd mysteriously appeared on the scene in the last couple of years. Many thought them to be subhuman, robotically engineered by the Department of Defense to counteract The Man in Black; a means to putting an end to the insanity. Robots or not, something was different about them. Their abilities were not of this world. Normal humans simply couldn't make the graceful yet deadly movements that they could. Normal humans couldn't leap into the air at the staggering heights nor possess the speed they do. Normal humans couldn't take on The Man in Black. They were our nation's very own "superheroes", sent to destroy The Man in Black and make our world safe again.

In some ways, I loathed the necessity for their existence, but mostly I longed to have the abilities they mastered. To be able to deliver the fatal blow and watch the life leave the eyes of the person responsible for the attack on The Lakes just as they must have watched my family die would be the best form of justice.

I was a block away from the bank when I heard a commotion coming from the corner of the block behind me. The newspaper had just hit the newsstands and, from the sounds of it, it appeared as though there had been another attack. Curious, I did an about-face, heading back in the direction of the commotion.

"Can you believe it?" a red-headed, freckled woman cried out. "It's terrible, just terrible."

Another woman chimed in, "It just proves this madness will never end."

I stood up on my tiptoes to peer over the crowd in order to catch a glimpse of the headline:

### Hero killed after confrontation with The Man in Black

A wave of nauseated shock ran over me. How could this be? These super humans… they were mortal? I guess I shouldn't have been too surprised. The duo had to have been at least partly human, and there wasn't exactly anything man-made out there that wasn't entirely indestructible. Nonetheless, it was shocking to me, and I had grown almost immune to shocking over the last ten years. In disbelief, I headed back down the sidewalk.

The mayhem didn't recede when I entered the usually quiet, mundane atmosphere of the bank. Everyone was abuzz with the news of our hero's demise.

"How could this have happened?" Travis, one of the other loan officers and a constant thorn in my side with his by-the-book attitude, enquired.

Veronica, a teller and my closest friend outside of Lucy, piped in, "Geez, Travis, nothing is impossible, nor is there anything that's indestructible. Besides, this would be a great career opportunity for you now that there's an opening."

"Oh, really, how do you figure?"

"With that hard head and that thick hide of yours, it would be almost impossible for a bullet to wound you." A snicker erupted through the crowd. Travis was not exactly a favorite amongst our usually tight-knit group.

"Hi, Celaine," Veronica greeted me with her all-too-cheery-for-this-time-in-the-morning voice.

"Hey," I replied. "I see we're starting in early on Travis this morning."

Travis let out a disgusted groan as he headed back to his office. Veronica was one of the first people I met when I moved back to Maryland. At first, it seemed as though we had nothing in common, but after learning that we shared nearly the same unfortunate story, we instantly bonded. Both of us had had family members killed in an attack by The Man in Black, and we found ourselves leaning on each other in hard times like an emotional crutch.

Veronica flipped back her long raven hair, the envy of every woman at the bank, and followed me into my office. "So, do you have any big plans tonight?" she asked.

"Actually, yeah, Chase is coming over tonight, and we plan on going out to dinner. Last night was another bad one, and I think he feels sorry for me," I replied with a stifled laugh.

Veronica looked at me with concern growing in her eyes. "You had another nightmare? Celaine, this is really getting ridiculous…maybe you should get some help."

"Are you implying that I'm not quite right in the head?"

"No, of course not. That was something I already knew." She shot me a smirk as she adjusted some paperwork on my desk. "That ship sailed a long time ago."

"Thanks."

"What I mean is that maybe there's something more behind your dreams. You know, like… like psychological or something. Maybe you need to work your inner demons out with a licensed professional. Doesn't one of your friends work in that field?"

"Lucy, yeah. Believe me, she's given me more than my fair share of free counseling throughout the years. Actually, I'm pretty sure she uses me as an exemplar for the mentally ill when she's in session with her patients."

Veronica laughed. "I just worry about you, Celaine."

"I really appreciate it, Veronica, but Chase takes great care of me."

"I'm sure the boy wonder does," she said with a wink. "I just don't know how, for the life of me, you can be around that human encyclopedia all day. He would give my brain a knowledge overload."

"What can I say? I like 'em nerdy."

"That you do." With that, she leapt from her perch atop my desk, nearly spilling my coffee in my lap in the process. She then proceeded to her booth in the front of the building, offering up another jab in Travis' direction for good measure. A quick retort of 'Bite me' rang from his office to which she replied, "Is that all you got? I'm sorely disappointed, *Weiner*."

"It's pronounced *Wine-ner*."

"That's not how it's spelled, *Weiner*."

Besides the obvious monetary gain, there were definite advantages to coming to work.

# 7

# THE SHADOWS

"YOU LOOK AMAZING," Chase said, admiring me from across the small, entirely-too-cramped, wooden table.

I could feel my face turning redder than the merlot I was sipping. No matter how much time passed, I still felt the butterflies in my stomach whenever I was around him. He was like kryptonite to me; my one weakness. It was a profound feeling that was riddled with contradiction being both frightening and exhilarating at the same time, but I basked in it with the knowledge that some of the best things in life made absolutely no sense.

We were at our favorite hole-in-the-wall pub just a block from my apartment. Chase and I were not much for appearances, preferring the rugged, manly atmosphere that our pub offered. We'd spent many a date night here without it ever having grown old, even as the atmosphere around us grew more unsavory. It was unusually quiet tonight with only one other couple seated a few feet away from our table, and a couple of men playing pool in the corner. I liked the quiet, but this was a tad unusual, even for this place.

Chase took a sip of his water, swishing it in his mouth as he rolled the glass around in his hand. "Tap water, vintage 2009," he announced discerningly.

I couldn't stop myself from bursting into laughter, revealing the dreaded snort that came whenever I was thoroughly amused by something. The other couple near our table looked up in surprised amusement, causing my face to flush in response.

"Adorable," he proclaimed, happy with himself.

"I bet you won't think that in twenty years," I said.

"Twenty years? I was going to trade you in for a new model after ten."

"Ha, ha."

"Celaine, I love you with every fiber of my being. Until my dying day, my heart will be yours. Unless, of course, you become sick of me."

"Chase Matthews, the day I get sick of you is the day that pigs sprout wings and take to the sky."

"You know that isn't entirely impossible…" He began breaking into what I affectionately referred to as his "nerd lingo," which usually involved talk of DNA, chromosomes, surgical procedures and pretty much anything else related to the human body and how it worked.

"I'm sorry," he stopped. "I think I'm boring you."

"No, not at all," I lied.

"Really? Your eyes were starting to glaze over."

"I just like it when you go all nerdy on me."

"Thanks. I think."

Chase glanced up at the television on the wall to check the final score of the baseball game taped earlier that afternoon. Since the curfew, many professional games were taped as opposed to being aired live, allowing the public an opportunity to attend the games. The taped games were then broadcasted at their normal times for the rest of the country to view within the safety of their homes. This not only abided by the curfew laws but also served as a deterrent for The Man in Black. The shock value of an attack on a taped game was significantly less catastrophic than if the attack were to take place during a live broadcast.

I looked up at the screen just in time to see a recap of the day's news scrolling across the bottom of it. "What do you think of the death of one of our supposed superheroes?" I asked.

"It's weird," he replied. "I can't say that it surprises me, but it surprises me."

"I know what you mean."

"There's nothing out there impervious to everything. Whatever this psychopath is, he can and he will be stopped. It's only a matter of time. What makes me wonder is what will take his place...if something hasn't already."

"What do you mean?"

"Doesn't this all seem a little odd to you, Celaine? We voted to basically give up some of the basic principles of democracy by being fed the explanation that it was for our own safety. How does that even happen? Do you think the public would have been so quick to give up any freedom, no matter how small, if The Man in Black didn't exist...if there were nothing to fear? Do you think that President Brooks would be serving in his third term now? There's just something fishy about this whole thing. Yet the people approve of this madness. They think just because the attacks have decreased by a couple of percentage points over the last few years that what he's doing is working and we're going to win this battle when, if you ask me, we've already lost."

"I think that's one hundred percent plausible but not probable," I said in a tired, half-hearted attempt at sounding half as eloquent as him.

He smiled his crooked smile. "Well, Ms. Stevens, I do believe we need to start heading back, as Big Brother will sick the Feds on us if we break curfew."

"Hey, you have a hospital badge," I said with a sly, I'm-trying-to-live-on-the-edge smile. "You know the curfew doesn't technically apply to you."

"That may be true when I'm actually on duty, but right now I'm just a humble civilian. Nice try, though."

"Can you blame me for trying to live dangerously for once?"

"Yeah, you're a real rebel." He rolled his eyes at me from across the table.

I took Chase's hand as we walked out of the pub back onto the street towards my apartment. It was a spectacular night, perfect for a solitary romantic walk under the stars, and I couldn't help but think that it was too bad we couldn't be on the streets past ten o'clock. One thing I've never been able to get used to is walking through a city completely devoid of people at a time when logic says it should be teaming with activity. Perhaps there was some truth to Chase's theory. In moments like this, it made perfect sense.

Despite the absolute perfection of our moment together, however, I couldn't shake the feeling that something didn't feel quite right. Upon turning down the alleyway leading to my apartment building, it seemed like someone watching us, calculating our every move. My body tensed, my stomach shifted from euphoric butterflies to a sudden sickness as though something terrible were about to happen. In a flash, I whirled around to face the dark, empty street stalking our footsteps.

"What are you doing?" Chase asked with uneasiness in his voice.

"I don't know what it is, but I have this strange feeling that someone is watching us."

"Oh, man, I knew this would happen someday. The fresh air has made you delusional," he said. "That's it; I'm never letting you out of the house again."

"You may want to check your faucet; your sarcasm's leaking," I said in annoyance. "I'm serious, Chase. I feel someone watching us. We're not alone. I mean…we are alone, but we're not…it's just…oh…you know what I mean."

Chase placed his hand on my shoulder. "Celaine, there's no one there. If there were, we would've noticed it. There are only so many places a person can hide on this empty street." He was right, although I would never have admitted it. Behind us stood nothing more than a dark, deserted alleyway; ahead of us, more of the same. After realizing that I wasn't going to let it go, he opted for a compromise. "Okay, if someone had been following us they obviously aren't now, but if they still are, I hope whoever it is enjoys the show." Scooping me up into his arms, he pressed his lips to mine in a passionate embrace; one that I wished would last for an eternity, but instead ended entirely too soon. "Well, we had to make it worth their while, right?" he said, still holding me close to him.

"Uh-huh," was all I could reply. Great, not only was I paranoid, now I could hardly walk.

In the shadows, at the exact location—down to the coordinate—where they told him he would find her, he waited for her. Impatient, he lit a cigarette and checked his watch. It was nearly curfew, which meant that she should soon be within his sight. The hunter would have his prey.

Amused, he slumped down the side of the wall, wondering whether she would come with him willingly or if she would need to be dealt with. He hated dealing with people; it left such a mess.

Moments later, she emerged from the pub. As instructed, he cautiously took a step out from his place of hiding to engage her, quickly backtracking at the sight of someone else with her. *Oh, great, a boyfriend,* he thought. *They didn't say anything about there being a boyfriend.*

With no other option but to remain hidden, he watched his new target. She was beautiful, he observed. Tall, dark-haired, with a nice figure–from what he could see of it. Nothing about her screamed "killer", making him wonder whether they'd completely lost their minds in their selection of her. When they had first informed him that she would be a "she", he envisioned a woman with more girth and slightly more muscle. After all, she was the first woman they'd ever chosen.

His target turned down an alleyway with her boyfriend in tow. He couldn't allow himself to lose sight of her. At all costs, he had to stick with her until his job was done; no matter what the outcome may be. With the cigarette still aflame between his lips, he leapt onto a fire escape, scaling the side of the building lining the alleyway. Along the edge of the roof he walked until he saw her further down the darkened street. Her boyfriend was clutching onto her in a passionate embrace almost as if it were the last time they would see each other. Who knows, depending on how his mission turned out, perhaps it would be.

Love. It was the dirtiest four letter word of them all. The dreadful emotion rendered a person weak and vulnerable, which was unacceptable to him. It was a hypocritical state of being. Not only did it instill immense pleasure, but it also served as a catalyst for excruciating pain and suffering. It was unexplainable, and he didn't like the unexplained. Besides, nothing lasts forever, so why pursue an impossibility?

He removed his cell phone from his pocket, deciding to approach her tomorrow. The boyfriend was too big a risk for him to take tonight.

"Blake," the response to his call rang into his ear.

"I've located Stevens and will make contact tomorrow," he said. Without waiting for a response, he shoved the cell phone back into the depths of his pocket, stomping the cigarette out on the roof. He wondered how long she would last.

The stars glittered above us from our haven on the rooftop of my apartment building. We weren't supposed to be there, but we didn't care. With the expert lock-picking skills I'd acquired during my teenage years of forgetting my house key paired with a bookend from my apartment, we were able to both prop and open the fire escape door. It was our spot. A regular retreat used by us as a means of escape from the monotony of daily life.

The one positive aspect arising out of the mass exodus of the city had been revealed to us during the first clear night we visited our rooftop sanctuary. The barren city allotted for an uncompromised view of the night sky. There were no city lights remaining to compete with the natural luminescence of nature. It was in its uninhibited, natural state.

I held Chase tightly with my head on his chest just over his heart, running my hands through his hair. Most couples had a song to define their relationship; we had a star. And it was shining proudly over us as if realizing its significance. Our star was the last star comprising the handle of the Big Dipper and was chosen because it was one of the few stars I knew I'd always be able to find. Chase tried explaining the constellations to me once but his lecture had been drowned out by my snoring. "So, do you still feel like someone is watching you?" he asked.

I sat up to meet his eyes. "Yeah, but somehow it doesn't seem as foreboding."

"I guess I need to try a little harder then," he chuckled. "It's getting late, we should probably go inside."

"Party pooper."

"Don't blame me; blame our employers."

"What? Are you telling me you can't do your job on only a couple of hours of sleep?"

"It's not me I'm worried about, it's my patients. Would you want to see your surgeon yawning only a couple of minutes before he was scheduled to cut into your body?"

"Point noted."

The flame from the candles bounced around my bedroom walls,

creating a ballet of light that illuminated Chase's bare torso. As we lay in my bed, I ran my fingers along the lines on his abdomen. He worked out obsessively when he wasn't at the hospital, and it really paid off for him. My head rested on his broad shoulders while his hands caressed my back. It was a moment bathed in perfection. It was a moment I wished could last forever.

*"Have I told you lately that I love you,"* my futile attempt at singing brought a smile to his face.

"Ripping off Rod Stewart, are we now? Bravo."

"Rod who? I thought it was an original."

He laughed, moving his fingers up my back, tracing my spine until he reached my head, where he proceeded to stroke my hair.

"When are we going to move in together?" he asked curiously.

"My guess is that you're enjoying this just as much as I am."

"Immensely."

Even though we'd been together for two years, the whole idea of the big "C"–commitment for those brave enough to use the word–scared the hell out me. It wasn't as if I imagined my life without Chase, because I didn't. I was just afraid of the unknown. I'd never been married, nor had I ever lived with anyone I'd been in a relationship with, so the whole prospect was rather frightening.

"I don't know. I was always taught that people should be married before they live together," I asserted in an attempt to grab hold of the topic and steer it over a cliff.

"So... you want to get married?"

"No... no... Oh, my God, no... I mean... You mean, right now?"

He laughed. "Not this very second, but thanks for the confidence booster."

"Chase, you know how I feel."

"I know. You're afraid of commitment, and I think that's the most intriguing thing in the world because I've never met another woman who seemed to have that problem." He rolled over to face me, cupping my cheek with his hand. "I also know that the majority of that issue stems from the loss of your family. Trust me Celaine, come hell or high water, I'm not going anywhere. I'm afraid you're stuck with me."

"Promise?"

"I promise."

I leaned in to kiss him as he ran his finger tips from my neck down to my back, creating an electric tingling sensation through my body as he pulled me closer.

"Do you want me to stop?" he asked.

"Never."

"Promise?"

"I promise."

I opened my eyes. It was morning, and it was raining. Terrific.

"*You are my sunshine, my only sunshine. You make me happy when skies are gray. You'll never know, dear, how much I love you, please don't take my sunshine away.*" Chase kissed my cheek. "Good morning, beautiful," he greeted me.

"So, it's all right for you to rip off songs but not me? That's really unfair."

"Hey, when you're as suave as I am, you can make anything sound good."

"What time is it?"

"It's about time for the both of us to get up and get ready for work." I groaned.

"My sentiment exactly."

"Well, it was good while it lasted," I said.

"Yes. Yes, it was." At that moment, the alarm on my nightstand went off. Chase leaned over me to turn it off.

"What? No snooze button?" I teased.

"I have to pull a double shift and will be on-call after my shift for the rest of the week, so I'll pretty much be M.I.A. for the next few days." I gave him the best pathetic looking face I could. "Don't look at me like that," he said, turning his gaze to the ceiling, staring off into space.

"What is it?"

His gaze remained fixated on the ceiling as though he were in some sort of intense concentration. After a moment, he spoke. "How about you and I have dinner at Angelo's on Saturday?"

"Angelo's? What's the occasion?"

"No occasion. I just figured we could use a change of pace from our normal routine."

"It's a nice thought, Chase. It really is. Isn't it pretty expensive there? After two years, I think we're well beyond having to impress each other. I don't want you to spend that kind of money on…"

He put his index finger to my lips. "Don't worry about the money. I have some extra funds lying around just itching to take my beautiful girlfriend out."

"Well, when you put it that way."

"Angelo's on Saturday, then?"

"Consider my arm twisted."

# 8

# THE PROPOSITION

IT WAS POURING outside as I unfolded my umbrella, venturing out from the sanctity of the awning in front of my apartment building. Rain ranked right up there next to Christmas in my book of dislikes. Water splashed up from the sidewalk, saturating the inside of my heels while I trudged down the street, cursing myself for not having invested in a pair of galoshes. *Nothing like having cold, wet feet to start your day out right,* I thought, annoyed.

Shortly into my walk, I began experiencing the same sensation I felt the night before. There were eyes on me. I knew it. Although it seemed like a weird thing to think as there were several other people walking along the same drenched pavement. Still, I couldn't shake the feeling. It was more overpowering than it had been the night before. Unable to take the persistent paranoia, I spun around in an attempt to catch the culprit, nearly knocking over an annoyed brunette in the process. She flashed me a dirty look and scowled at my feeble apology.

*Show yourself, you bastard,* I thought. Of course, no one was there to reveal themself. Everyone on the street seemed focused on reaching his or her own destination; they were concerned with their own lives, not mine. No one seemed suspicious; no one stood out. Worried that I was becoming certifiable, I turned back around and walked down the sidewalk a little faster. But the foreboding feeling continued to surround me.

When I was safe inside my office, I unfolded my sopping wet umbrella hanging it on the hook behind my door. Either I was partially wet or the air was cranked unusually high today as my body shivered from the cold. *No, I thought, it's not the temperature, it's that icy stare you felt following you in here.* I shuddered at the thought.

I took out the black cardigan I kept in my desk drawer, slipping it on to warm up. Chase loved the fact that I chilled easily, as it made me cling to him like a human heating pad. He always got this cheesy grin on his face whenever I would wrap my arms around him trembling because the temperature had dropped a degree or two. At that moment, thinking of Chase and the night we'd spent together just a few short hours ago managed to pacify my uneasiness, making me feel flushed in the process.

"Someone had a good night last night," Veronica stood in my doorway, looking every bit the supermodel she always did, impeccably dressed with her dark hair framing her porcelain face. If it wasn't for the fact that she swore like a sailor a person may actually believe that they were in the presence of an angel. "So, tell me about it. I want all the dirty details."

"There's not much to tell," I said. "We went to the pub, then back to my apartment, and… we had a great night."

"Wow. That's boring," she said, arching her eyebrow. "I'm disappointed in you, Celaine. The look you had pasted on your face when I walked through the door screamed pure, blissful ecstasy. I could have sworn you'd just gotten in after a passionate night of hot, steamy…." An elderly man walked into the bank, whirling around to face us upon overhearing Veronica's candor. He stared at her in disbelief, his jaw hanging slightly ajar. "Welcome, Sir." Veronica didn't miss a beat. "Is there anything I can do to assist you with your banking needs today?"

"No, Ma'am. Just going up there to the tellers." The elderly gentlemen gestured to the teller booths at the far end of the bank. A red tint spread across his face as he hurried toward the back of the building. Vulgar or not, she drove men of all ages absolutely insane.

"Veronica, you do realize that you're a teller, right?" I asked.

"Details, details. Anyway, you're banned from speaking to me until you come up with something good," she said as she turned to leave my office.

"Wait, Veronica," I called.

"Banned, I say."

"No. Seriously."

She feigned frustration at my request as she turned back around. "You do realize that *I'm* a teller, right?" she stated, pointing to herself.

"No fair using my lines against me. Seriously, have you ever felt like someone was watching you?" I was desperate to extinguish my paranoia.

"All the time. I just wheel around and kick them where the sun doesn't shine. That usually solves the problem."

"What if you wheeled around and no one was there?"

"You mean, like a ghost or something? Celaine, didn't I tell you not to take those pills with alcohol... geez... kids these days."

"Damn. That would explain the slurred speech and the soiling of myself. Really, Veronica."

"Seriously? Well, if you want my opinion, I would say you're probably being a little over imaginative as logic should tell you that, if there is no one there, there can't possibly be anyone watching you."

"That's kind of what I thought."

"Quit sweating it. If it happens again, call me up and I'll take you to the place with the lovely padded rooms and the stylish white jackets." She winked at me.

"Thanks, Veronica... I think."

"Anytime." Veronica walked back to the front of the bank, launching her daily assault at Travis on her way.

*Ding. Ding. Ding.* The tone sounded, startling me, causing the file I'd picked up from the corner of my desk to fall out my hands. In the middle of the lobby, a monitor methodically lowered down from the ceiling, turning on in its descent. Around the same time as the institution of the curfew it'd become mandatory for all public facilities to install these monitors. They were to be used, presumably, in the event of an attack or for evacuation notifications. In my opinion, President Brooks just wanted to have the undivided attention of his flock hanging on his every word. Simultaneously, everyone stood up to leave their respected posts in order to gather around the monitor. Seconds later, President Brooks came into view.

"My fellow Americans," he began.

"How original," I muttered. Veronica shot me an amused look.

"A horrible tragedy has befallen our country with the sudden death of one member of a rogue vigilante duo. For the past few years, this duo has heroically charged themselves with the task of seeking and destroying what has become a very real threat to our country: The Man in Black. Unfortunately, it was during one such encounter recently that one of our country's own superheroes met their fate…"

I rolled my eyes and headed back to my office.

"Celaine, aren't you going to watch this?" Travis asked, shocked with my insubordination.

"Nope, I've had enough hot air for one day. I'm beginning to break a sweat."

Veronica giggled. President Brooks continued, "Our resolve remains strong, and our fight to make our country safe again will continue. We as The People will take down The Man in Black and right the injustice that has been brought upon us…"

I closed my office door.

The rain let up during the lunch hour, allowing the sun to peek out from behind the clouds. I decided to go out for lunch to take in the fresh, moist air–the one good thing about the rain. Before leaving, I took my cardigan off and made my way outside. My morning talk with Veronica had helped to set my mind at ease, for now. Everything she'd said made perfect sense. It's funny how logic could bring you down to earth when your head was in the clouds.

Adjacent to the bank sat a small diner with a lived-in feel. The atmosphere wasn't great, but the food more than made up for that. It was a grease lover's haven of saturated fat, and I both loved and loathed its proximity to me. Thankfully, the line wasn't very long today, allowing me to walk directly up to the counter to order my usual turkey sandwich with soggy french fries. Then, with tray in hand, I walked over to a booth in the corner of the diner and sat down.

As I sat down to eat, I took my phone out of my purse, revealing a missed call from Carrie, Chase's mother. Shortly after we'd begun dating, I adopted Chase's family as my own. They'd reminded me so much of what I'd lost. Through them, I almost felt as though I'd reclaimed a part of what I'd lost at The Lakes. Chase's sister, MaKayla, had the same mischievous nature about her as I remembered Jake having. She and I had hit it off right away. Like Chase, I couldn't picture my life without any of them.

After only a couple of bites of my sandwich, my comfort level was beginning to dissipate again, giving way to an eerily familiar feeling. It was stronger than ever now. With Veronica's advice replaying in my head, I tried ignoring it, but it was just too strong for me to disregard this time. Without lifting my head, I looked up from my table to scan the diner for its source. There were people all over as the place was starting to fill to almost near capacity now that the rest of the lunch crowd was filtering in. Across tables filled with business men in suits, my eyes searched. Like me, most of them were on their lunch hours and probably didn't have the time to put into stalking at the moment.

Intermingled with the business-types were a couple of lone families who'd bravely ventured out of their homes, testing their fates for a slice of one of the diner's famed pizzas. I scanned around some more… nothing… nothing… then… bingo. He was sitting alone in a booth on the other side of the diner. His very stare pierced my face like a blade. I could feel my skin getting hot as though his eyes were emitting heat. The man wore black. Black slacks and a black button down shirt. His hair, slicked back, was also dark in color; his eyes were a deep chocolate, even deeper than my own. I guesstimated his age to be somewhere around thirty, perhaps thirty-five. As creepy as his staring was to me, I had to admit that he was ruggedly handsome. Yet his look reflected one who was troubled, too. The staring was blatantly obvious. He didn't try to hide it and, even though I wasn't looking directly at him, I could tell he knew that I was on to him. Should I look up and acknowledge him? Should I just leave? I wouldn't get the chance to explore the answers to these questions as, at that moment, he was walking to my booth.

"May I have a seat?" he asked more politely than I would have expected.

"Actually, I was just leaving," I replied, standing up. "It's all yours." The look on his face turned to one of shock. Obviously, he'd never had a woman be anything but complicit to his requests before.

"Wait, I'd like to speak with you."

"I'm sorry. I'm in a relationship." I grabbed my tray from the table.

"I didn't come over to ask you out on a date. Actually, I wanted to speak with you about a business proposition."

"I'm sorry. I'm not for sale, either." I was beginning to get annoyed and was close to breaking out the mace that was tucked away in my purse for just such encounters as this. He laughed. I'd apparently made his day.

"No, not *that* kind of business proposition," he chuckled.

"Fine, I'll humor you if you answer one simple question for me." I set my tray back down on the table, trying to sound threatening but, from the looks of this guy, he didn't threaten easily.

"My name is Blake Cohen."

"That's not what my question was going to be." We were both sitting down, staring at each other from across the table.

"All right then, what is this mysterious question?" His smugness was quite upsetting.

"Why have you been following me?" The smile vanished from his face, revealing that I'd taken him off guard. I clutched my purse tighter, prepared to use it as a blunt object if necessary.

"So, you knew that I was following you?" he asked. "Maybe they haven't made a mistake after all. Your instincts are quite impressive." He paused for a moment before speaking again. "The answer to your question is contained within my purpose for being here with you right now."

"I'm listening."

"Have you ever had a feeling of utter helplessness? A feeling like you should be able to do something, but you know that you aren't physically able to do it, nor do you have the means with which to carry it out?" My thoughts returned to the day of the explosion, to my family and to the knowledge that I could do nothing to save them. He studied my expression thoughtfully and continued. "What if there was something you could do? What if you could be given the tools to defeat The Man in Black? What if you had the power to ensure that no one else suffered the same loss as you have?"

Tears clouded my vision, but I couldn't tell if they were tears of anger or of agony. "That's impossible." My mouth made the words, but my ears didn't hear them.

"But it's not. I was sent here by my superiors to find you. They've been observing you and believe that you hold the potential to do just that.

If you come with me, they can provide you with the means along with the abilities you will need to fight and defeat The Man in Black and... replace my partner."

My eyes shot to his face. "Wait... your... your... partner? But that means that you... that you... wait... what?"

"I'm going to have to ask you to keep your voice down. Our conversation isn't something that should be broadcasted. Put two and two together, Celaine, and you will get four." The smug smile returned to his face.

"How do you know my name?"

"Out of this entire conversation, that's what concerns you the most?"

"Okay, so you're a superhero whose mission it is to seek and destroy The Man in Black, and you're asking me if I want to replace your partner who was recently killed."

"No, I'm a government agent, not a superhero. Trust me, there's nothing super about this life."

"Okay. So how do I know, with any degree of certainty, that you're not just some psychotic nutcase who's going to lure me away with some wild story, throw me in the back of his trunk, and hold me hostage in his basement while ordering me to 'rub the lotion on its skin'?"

"You don't."

"That's comforting."

"Funny, I didn't take you to be one for dry humor. I have a feeling you and I could get along just fine."

"Am I just supposed to agree to this and then you whisk me away? I need details, I mean, if I were to agree to this, I would need to give my work notice... my friends, my..."

"I can appreciate your need for the clarification of all the details, but you need to understand that I would only be sticking my neck out even further on the chopping block than I already am now if I were to divulge such information to you. Besides, if you choose to accept this position, you will not be permitted contact with anything or anybody related to your former life."

"What? You're telling me that I have to cut off all contact with my friends, my job, and my life? How do you expect anyone to agree to that?"

"Well, obviously, there were at least two of us who felt such a sacrifice was warranted for the sake of the greater good."

"I'm not saying it's not admirable. I'm saying it's not something I can very well agree to right at this moment."

"I'm not asking you to accept anything this second. This offer is extended for another seventy-two hours."

"So basically, I have but a mere three days to make the decision to end my life as I know it so that I can move on to a new one cloaked in uncertainty?"

"Basically, but let me ask you this, Celaine... If it were ten years ago, would you be so hesitant?"

In my mind, the scene of the decimated parking ramp and the images of the crushed SUV containing life as I knew it unfolded. "How did you know about that?" I asked in a whisper.

"Again, that surprises you? This is really getting quite old. Look, just think about your feelings that day and the feelings each time you wake up in a cold sweat night after night because the nightmares just won't end. I'm sure you made a promise to your family, just as I did to my loved ones."

"You lost someone, too?"

"Why else do you think I'm sitting here today? This isn't a life for the faint of heart. It's lonely, tiring, aggravating and every other negative adjective you can possibly think of, but I'm doing it for them. In my mind, that makes it worth it. I'm sure that in the last several years you've accumulated other people in your life worth protecting as well as the ones you've lost."

I glanced up at the clock on the wall. My lunch was supposed to have ended ten minutes ago. "I... I need time, and I have to get back to work. Do you have a card or a number or something?"

He laughed. "Do you think my line of work would allow me to carry contact information of any kind? Seventy-two hours. Meet me on the roof of your apartment building. You can give me your answer then. In the meantime, make no mention of our encounter to anyone."

I nodded, standing up to make a hasty retreat.

"It was nice meeting you, Ms. Stevens," he called out to me as I opened the door.

I nodded again as I stepped out of the diner and onto the sidewalk.

Blake Cohen pulled out his cell phone. "Contact has been established," he reported.

"What's your impression?"

"I think she's going for it."

"Good. Are you clear on what to do if she doesn't?"

"Is there no other way?"

"Blake, you're not backing out on your mission, are you?"

"This one seems different from the others. I don't think she'll talk."

"That's not a decision for you to make. She already knows too much. If she chooses not to join us, she must be dealt with. Is this clear, Blake?"

"Crystal."

Blake ended the call and stared out the window at the front of the diner. It had been a long time since he'd been able to appreciate the gift of a nice day. He sighed, stood up and walked out of the building. This was the part of his job he hated the most.

The sky could have crashed to the Earth where I sat. The planet could have split in two and I wouldn't have noticed any different. I was in a haze, drifting through the rest of my day after the weight of the world had been placed upon my shoulders. It was a burden that was verging on becoming too heavy to bear. In meetings, I tried to remain focused and professional, but I knew my clients could tell that my mind couldn't have been further from their loan applications and refinancing enquiries. My mind was on my life, not theirs.

If I didn't accept the offer Blake presented to me, would I regret it? I finally had what I'd been dreaming of for the last ten years within my grasp. Finally, I was getting the opportunity to back up every promise I'd made to my family in every speech I'd given to their photographs. I'd been offered the opportunity to face the nightmares that wouldn't rest. Yet, as unbelievable as it was, I couldn't help but wonder whether this opportunity was truly a gift or if it would end up being nothing short of a curse.

To give up everything positive that had come into my life these last ten years was practically inconceivable. Chase's family had taken me under their wing, allowing me to belong in this world again. What would they think if I were to suddenly remove myself from their lives? My fingers caressed my neck, clasping the familiar golden chain with the heart charm attached. It had been an heirloom in Chase's family and one of his mother's most cherished possessions. He'd given it to me on our first anniversary. At the time, I hadn't realized just what a grand gesture his presenting it to me had been. After I found out, I'd sobbed like a baby.

Chase. It killed me to think that I would be responsible for a decision that could have such a profound effect on him. If I chose to leave, would he understand or would he hate me? Never had I felt like I deserved someone as kind, intelligent and devoted as him. In some ways, I felt as though he'd been a gift from my parents; he was sent by them to look out for me.

Try as I might, it was all too much to take in. I checked my schedule and confirmed that I had no further appointments. Given the circumstances, I then decided it would be best for me to go home "sick" for the rest of the day. After leaving a message with the Human Resource Department, I packed up my things and changed my voice mail message before walking out the door. On my way out, Veronica came up from behind me, concerned.

"Are you all right?"

"Yeah. Just a bad case of food poisoning, I think."

"That figures. All the good food usually screws you over in the end. Do you want me to walk you home? You look like you're about ready to pass out."

"No… no. I'm fine. Thanks, Veronica, but I think I can make it from here."

"All right." She looked at me with disbelief in her eyes.

"I'll see you tomorrow."

"Not if you're contagious, you won't. I have a date this weekend, so if you think it's something more than just food poisoning, you'd better keep that keister of yours in bed."

"Understood."

She smiled at me, disappearing back into the building. And I was almost to the sidewalk when I heard Veronica shout, "Mind your own business, *Weiner.*"

I would miss her.

# 9
# THE CHOICE

I LAY IN bed staring at the cracks in the ceiling, following their journey until it abruptly ended where the ceiling met the wall. Everything seemed surreal to me to the point where I wasn't entirely certain that what had transpired today had actually happened. There had to be some sort of catch to all of this. Had they ever seen me run or throw a punch? Those acts alone were more of a comedy routine than an action sequence when I performed them. What did they think I could offer them?

Why was I so hesitant to run after vindication when it was being handed to me? After all, if Chase wasn't in my life, would I even need to contemplate Blake's offer? I knew the answer to that question was a resounding "no". In my mind, there was no doubt that I would have accepted the new life I'd been offered on the spot had it not been for Chase.

My body was like dead weight as I rolled over to check my clock. Two hours had gone by since I'd arrived home. Chase would still be at work, but he would soon call, sense the confusion in my voice and invariably ask me whether I was all right. That was a question even I couldn't answer at the moment.

My fingers drifted to the knob of my nightstand drawer, reaching for the photo album I kept locked away inside. I hated looking at it, knowing that if I did, my mind would be made up, but I did it anyway.

Their lifeless images stared up at me almost as though they were pleading with me. They were begging me to bring them justice. Would they forgive me if I chose to ignore the one chance I may have to deliver it? Better yet, would I ever be able to forgive myself? Even attempting to answer the questions flashing through my head was pointless; for I knew that, in order to answer them, I must first make a choice.

If ever I needed advice, it was now. Lucy. I needed to talk to Lucy. She was always the dispenser of common sense, advising people on the solutions to their problems. It was her job, after all. I forced myself up from my bed and retrieved my purse, rummaging through its contents until I located my cell phone. Old Faithful Lucy picked up on the first ring.

"Hey, pretty lady, I was just thinking about you," she answered.

"Must be our ESPN," I giggled as convincingly as possible.

"Yeah, I always suspected we were twins separated at birth. So, what's going on?"

"Well, I was hoping you could give me some advice."

"Sure. You're on the clock. That'll be one hundred twenty-five dollars for the first hour."

"Bill me."

"Well, I usually take the cash up front, but for you I'm willing to look the other way. What is this all-important advice you seek? Does it involve a certain male friend of ours?"

"Amazingly, no."

"Whoa. You mean to tell me you have a life outside of him? Hold on a second, let me sit down for this."

"When did *you* become such a smart ass?"

"What do you think keeps me from jumping out of the window each day after never-ending day of listening to people piss and moan about their lives?"

"Touché."

"So, what can I do you for?"

"Let's just say, theoretically, you have two choices. Two doors if you will…"

"Oh, oh, like that one show where all the people dress up in silly costumes for a chance to choose blindly between different doors, giving up what they have for something that may or may not be better."

"Stick with me here, Luce. Wait…you mean *Let's Make A Deal?*"

"Yeah, that's the one."

"As much as I hate to admit that my life has been reduced to a pathetic game show analogy, that's actually not a bad comparison to what I'm theoretically up against right now."

"That's why I make the big bucks, sugar."

"Okay," I say, rolling my eyes. "Imagine you have these two doors. One door leads you to the status quo; a good, some may say even perfect, life where you're happy, modestly successful and the future looks promising. It may even get a tad better for you but, basically, nothing changes. The second door leads to a path filled with twists, turns and uncertainties that may or may not lead to a dead end. If by chance it doesn't lead to one, it will ultimately take you to the single greatest moment of your life and the fulfillment of every promise you've ever made to yourself and those you care about. Faced with this scenario, which one would you choose?"

"Can I take a rain check?"

"Not if you value your life."

"This must be important to you if you're resorting to death threats."

"You have no idea."

"Let's analyze this for a minute because that's what I do and all. What you're looking at is a question of how bold you are and what you're willing to gamble. You, Celaine, have always been a play-it-safe kind of girl. Always playing it safe hasn't made you rich, but it's profited you enough to where you're able to stay in the game. It's made you content, if you will. Now, there's an opportunity presenting itself that may give you the chance for a windfall. But, in order to win, you have to bet and, in this case, they're asking you to go all in. If you win, immense wealth will surely be yours. But if you lose, then what? If your life is only a smidgeon less enjoyable than it is now, would it have been worth it? If the answer to that question is "yes", then by all means put your chips in. Are you going to lose yourself in the process? Are you going to lose something that can't be replaced? If the answer to those questions is also "yes", then you may want to think about cashing in and going home. But, to give you my own personal point of view, contentment gets you nowhere."

"When in this conversation did we travel to Vegas?"

"Sorry. I just love analogies. They make me sound like I know what I'm talking about. Did that help you at all whatsoever?"

"Actually... yeah. It sort of did."

"Good, good. Listen, I have an appointment coming in about five minutes, but I can talk until then if you want."

"Thank you, Luce, but I think you've given me something to think about."

"Are you sure?"

"Yeah."

"By golly, I did something right today. I'll talk to you later, then?"

"Always. Thanks again, Luce."

I ended my call with Lucy, stumbling around my apartment aimlessly in the wake of our conversation. Lucy was the one to turn to for the dispensing of brutal wisdom and honesty. However, I couldn't help but think that if she knew what she had just advised me to do, she wouldn't have dispensed it so readily. Just as I set my phone back down, it rang. It was Carrie again. She was most likely worried that I hadn't returned her call. Carrie and I always had our weekly talks about life and whatever else came up in between. I'd often pictured what a great mother-in-law she would make and felt thankful that she may well be *my* mother-in-law someday.

"Hey, Carrie," I answered, trying to mask the tsunami that was churning in the sea of emotions spinning through my head.

"Hi, sweetie," Carrie answered in her usual pleasant tone.

"Sorry, I haven't had a chance to call you back. I had to leave work early. Something came over me at lunch, and I haven't felt well since."

"Oh, honey. I'm sorry to hear that. Is everything all right? Do you need me to bring you something? I made some homemade vegetable soup and can bring some right over if you like."

"Carrie, you live an hour away."

"Your point is?"

"No... no. I'm feeling better, but thank you anyway. I appreciate the offer."

"Well, tell that son of mine to take care of you."

"He always does."

"That's good to hear. The reason I'm calling you is because MaKayla's choir group is competing at the Met next week. I know it would mean a lot to her if you and her brother were able to come."

"I will definitely let Chase know."

"I know you will, doll. You've always been good at keeping his head on straight. You're exactly what he needs." My grip on the phone tightened with her last sentence; my stomach twisted into painful knots. "I'll let you go so you can get some rest. Give me a call when you feel better, and I'll give you more details about the performance."

"Sounds like a plan."

"Bye. Take care of yourself."

"I will. Goodbye, Carrie."

I almost didn't make it through the last part of our conversation before the tears began running down my cheeks. Before speaking with Carrie, I hadn't realized how my sudden absence would affect her, Chase's father, or his sister. They were the parents and sibling I'd lost ten years ago.

MaKayla had never liked any of Chase's girlfriends until I came around. Much to Chase's relief, she and I had bonded instantly because I wasn't–as she put it–as "hoity-toity" as the others had been. She was the little sister I never had, often calling me to talk about her boy problems and anything else she didn't care to share with Carrie.

I was just as much in love with Chase's family as I was with him and nearly as much as I'd been with my own flesh and blood family.

A knock on my door a short time later startled me, forcing me to wonder whether Blake had changed his mind and followed me home, expecting an answer now. I debated whether or not to answer it before deciding that, if it were indeed Blake, he would probably already know that I was in here and wouldn't leave until I answered it anyway. It was better to get this over with now than delay the inevitable. When I opened the door, to my surprise, there stood Chase, complete with a bouquet of daisies and a thermos of soup.

"Let me guess," I said. "Carrie called you, and you came dashing over to save the day?"

"Something like that," he said. "You never get sick. It's like an eclipse, only happening once in a blue moon. I just had to witness it for myself."

"Thanks."

"It's amazing, though."

I raised my eyebrow. "Exactly what is so amazing about it?"

"Even deathly ill, you're still the most beautiful woman I've ever laid eyes on."

I blushed. I wasn't sick, and I felt guilty for lying to Chase and Carrie. But what was I supposed to tell them? *I'm sorry, but some strange man made me an offer at lunch today that I don't think I can refuse, meaning that I'm going to have to leave you guys forever with little explanation.* Right. That would go over well.

"You're too good for me," I said with a half-hearted smile.

"There's no such thing as being too good for you. Are you hungry?"

"A little," I lied.

"Good. Get back in bed and I'll get your soup ready."

I smiled and nodded at Chase, turning my back to him before a single tear could roll down my nose. My hand reached for the box of tissues on my coffee table. No way could I let Chase know that I was upset. If he even so much as suspected it, he would ask me what was wrong and I would–I was pretty sure–tell him the truth.

While he stumbled through my poor excuse for a kitchen, I changed into my sweat clothes to give the whole sickness excuse the full effect. He came into my bedroom a short time later with the soup in a bowl and the daisies displayed in one of the many vases I'd accumulated from the virtual greenhouse he'd purchased for me over the last two years.

"Thank you. You're just so…. great," I uttered without looking him in the eyes.

"You're pretty great yourself." He kissed my forehead, setting the bowl on the nightstand. "I have to go back to the hospital for the start of my next shift. They're doing a repair on a baby with a hole in her heart, and I'm going to sit in and observe. I'll be available after midnight tonight if you need me."

"I think I'll survive."

"You better. We have our big date at Angelo's on Saturday night. Unless, of course, you plan on bailing on me."

"Not a chance. I'll be there with bells on."

He smiled, kissing my forehead again. "I'll give you a call tomorrow."

"Good luck on your observation. Thanks for taking care of me." I ran my finger along the petals of one of the daisies, still unable to look him in the eyes.

"Celaine, as long as I have breath in me, I'll keep all harm from coming to you. I promise you that."

"I love you."

"And I love you."

Then, as fast as he came, he was gone, and I was left alone again with my thoughts. Why did this have to happen now? Why not three years ago when I had nothing to lose by making the decision that had been placed upon me? It wasn't fair. Why would I be given the gift of Chase and his family only to not be allowed to keep them in my life? To give me my soul mate, only to take him away, was cruel. This choice was beginning to look like more of a lesson in torture.

My eyes drifted in the direction of the bowl and vase of daisies. Carefully, I picked up the bowl, placing it on my lap. I took the spoon, collected some of the soup, and put it to my lips. It was good, but I wasn't very hungry. The events of the day had washed away any semblance of an appetite I may have had.

It had been five hours since I'd been presented with the decision to change my life forever. And in those few, short hours, I'd made a choice that many would need five years to make. I took a deep breath as I sat on my bed holding a daisy I'd plucked from the vase. My fingers glided over each individual petal, pulling them out one at time. At that moment, as I watched each petal fall one by one, I decided that no matter what the consequences, I would take the path destiny had cleared away for me.

# 10

## THE AFFIRMATION

SLEEP EVADED ME that night. Morning came, bringing with it the promise of a beautiful day, the likes of which would excite those who didn't already have a dark cloud looming over their head. Over the night, I contemplated how I was going to quit my job. Normal procedure would be to give at least two weeks' notice, but nothing about what was occurring in my life was remotely normal. Around four in the morning, after I'd been tossing and turning for several hours, I decided that I would quit today, hopefully leaving before anyone had a chance to notice anything was amiss. People would talk. They would speculate about the emergent nature of my departure and where I was heading off to. If she were to find out, Veronica would have numerous questions which I would have to find a way to blow off. That would be no easy feat.

When I rolled out of bed, I wondered if Blake Cohen was watching me; I wondered if he knew what I was about to do; I wondered if he would see me leaving work early again today, toting a box of my belongings back to my apartment. Would he expect me to report early? Would I at least get the chance to say goodbye? The questions were again coming at me a mile a minute as I slipped my blouse over my head.

The warm summer air filled my lungs within seconds of stepping out of my building. My walk to the bank seemed to go in slow motion today with every step only appearing to take centimeters off my journey instead of feet. My expression, I was sure, had no life left in it. When I reached the bank, I stopped at the steps, where I took a deep breath before beginning the ascent into the building. Climbing up those steps for the last time felt like scaling Mt. Everest, and the door leading inside felt like dead weight on my weakened being. This had to be quick and discreet.

My heels clicked on the floor with ferocity as soon as I stepped foot inside. Every step seemed conspicuous, resounding like rumbles of thunder each time one of my heels touched the marble floor. I bypassed my office, heading straight to William, the bank manager's office, near the back of the building. Veronica, Travis, and a few others were already gathered around the table in the break room. They looked up at me as I walked past them.

"Hey, Cel...Oh," Veronica started calling to me, but was abruptly cut off by the realization that I would not be joining them for the usual Friday morning doughnuts. Behind me, I could hear the hurried *click-clack* of her heels as she rushed from her spot at the table to the break room door to peer around the corner at me. Without looking back to acknowledge her, I knocked on the door of William's office.

William was a workaholic and, to put it bluntly, just plain didn't have a life. He was a single man, never married and without any prospects in the works to change that. I knew he would already be typing away in his office.

"Come in," he called.

My stomach turned in time with the brass knob between my fingers. Slowly, the door opened, and I stood standing in the doorway face-to-face with my soon-to-be former boss.

"Oh, Celaine," he said, confused. "What's going on?"

I was going to throw up; I could feel it. Nervously, I sat down on the red velvet chair in front of his desk in a vain attempt to counteract the dizziness and nausea I felt, tapping my fingers on one of its oak arms. William stared at me.

"There's no easy way to say what I'm about to say," I began.

He looked up at me, a wave of concerned realization spreading over his face.

"I want to start out by saying that this has been a great... no, a wonderful company to have worked for. You have been a wonderful boss, and I highly respect you and al... most... of my co-workers. This company has opened many doors for me in the field of finance, and I can't thank you enough for having given me the opportunity to be a part of this amazing team of brilliant people." He knew what was coming. By the look on his face, it appeared as though he was contemplating what he would–or even could–say to change my mind. "With that said, today will be my last day. Something has come up in my life, and I'm afraid that I'll have to leave town indefinitely. It's a wonderful opportunity, one that I've wanted for several years. The catch is that, in order to be eligible for it, I have to leave this weekend. This means that I can't give you two weeks' notice like I know I should do and that you most definitely deserve, and I apologize for that."

William looked at me for the longest time, readjusting his glasses. I wondered if he was contemplating whether or not I was being serious or whether I was just trying to get a rise out of him. Finally, he spoke, "As sorry as I am to hear this, I trust your judgment. I've always trusted your judgment. It's made you one of the better loan officers this institution has ever had. Your departure will be a great loss to us." He scratched behind his ear and sighed, knowing that my leaving would put an even bigger burden on his already hyper-extended shoulders. "Although, I'm not thrilled with the fact that today is your last day and that you couldn't have given me just a few more days' notice, I understand that opportunities are precious and don't present themselves at the most convenient times for everyone. I wish you well, Celaine. I know you will succeed in whatever endeavor you decide to undertake. We'll miss you here. If you need any kind of letter of recommendation, let me know. I will be more than happy to provide you with one."

I fought back the tears as professionally as I could. "Thank you for being so understanding with my situation," I answered.

"Thank you for doing the work you did for us." I nodded, stood up, and shook William's hand the same way I had done at my interview just three short years ago.

I turned the knob to William's door and quickly disappeared into the supply room down the hall to find a banker's box for my belongings. It was in the supply room that the dam broke and the tears came. If this kept up, I would have permanent paths etched down my face from the course of travel my tears always seemed to take. The boxes were in the back of the room, and I stumbled over random piles of office supplies on my way to retrieve them. Dusty from months of inactivity, the supply room was the perfect metaphor for my life: disheveled and dark. Once in the back of the room, I bent down to pick up a box from the corner, climbing back over the chaos again. I stood by the door for a moment to regain my composure before presenting myself to my curious co-workers.

With the hope that I would slip back to my office undetected, I treaded lightly down the hallway. It was wishful thinking. The whispers started then. They started with the teller booths, moving on down to everyone whose office I passed clutching the empty box. By the time I reached my office, the whispers were almost deafening. I knew they were speculating on the reason for my meeting, the empty box, and exactly what was going on with me.

Before entering my office, I passed Veronica who was returning inside from a smoke break. Her eyes widened almost comically when I passed her without saying a word. Behind me, her heels once again clacked the floor with a vengeance to catch up with me. Stepping into my office, I placed the box on my desk to begin the task of gathering my possessions to fill it. Pictures; there were lots of pictures. Pictures of Chase, Lucy, Carrie, Chase's father, Jim, and MaKayla all adorned my office, along with my degree and various knick-knacks given to me throughout my time here by co-workers and clients.

"What's going on, Celaine?" Veronica's voice was riddled with concern.

"I've had an opportunity presented to me that I can't pass up and, unfortunately, it means that I'm leaving today."

I could see the tears forming in Veronica's eyes as she walked closer to me. I looked down at the floor, unable to make eye contact with her anymore. Her arms wrapped around me.

"You could have at least given me a heads up."

"I'm so sorry. I just found out about it myself and made the decision to leave this morning."

"You and Chase are leaving then?'

I looked back up at her, throwing more items into my box. "Not exactly," I mumbled.

"Oh, Celaine. I really hope you know what you're doing and that you're all right."

"I know what I'm doing. Whether or not I'm all right, well, that's always been up to interpretation."

"That it has. That it has. What is this opportunity, anyway?"

"A job at another bank out West."

"Out West? I didn't know you were looking for another job or one out West for that matter."

"It just kind of found me."

"Oh… okay. Well, keep in touch…okay?"

"I will." I hated lying.

Veronica hugged me again, drying her eyes on her sleeve. "Goodbye, Celaine. You're one of the few good ones left."

"If only that were true." With a final sheepish smile, I picked up the half-full box from my desk, walking out of my office for the last time.

"Celaine," Travis said from behind me.

"Goodbye, Travis," I said back to him without turning around.

I walked out the door, down the steps and onto the sidewalk without looking back. They were watching me leave, I knew it. And I'm sure they were all wondering whether I'd lost my mind. Perhaps, I had.

While walking down the street to my apartment, it seemed as though the box was holding the weight of my decisions from the last twenty-four hours in it along with my possessions. Though, as hard as today was, it would pale in comparison to tomorrow. I would take a million todays over tomorrow. Chase would be far more inquisitive, far harder to convince. And as well he should be. He'd just invested two years of his life and his whole heart into a relationship that ended up leading him nowhere.

The key clicked in the lock of my apartment. I entered my living room, balancing the box on my free arm, setting it down on my coffee table before I collapsed onto my couch. What was I going to tell Chase? Lucy?

My desk, a mahogany remnant from my parents' home, sat in the corner of my living room, giving me inspiration. Like a beacon, it beckoned me to stand up and walk over to it. In the top drawer, I found a notepad and pens in a coffee cup. I grabbed the notepad and sat down at the desk to think about what I wanted to say. What would I want Lucy to know? I sat for a minute before scribbling out a letter to her in my nearly illegible handwriting; a trait I blamed on having a doctor for a father.

*Luce,*

*I'm so sorry for not having the chance to tell you this in person. I've been presented with an opportunity that I couldn't pass up. Don't think that your advice drove me to it. I would have come to this conclusion no matter what you would have said to me. I just wanted you to know that you've been the best friend anyone could have ever wished for and I'm sorry. I'm so, so, incredibly sorry that I had to leave like this. Just know that what I'm doing is something I've dreamt of. I'm finally fulfilling a promise I made to myself a long time ago. If I can contact you, I will. Just know that I'm well and taken care of. I hope you achieve everything you ever dreamed you would. I know you'll be great no matter what you do.*

*You will be my best friend for life,*

*Celaine*

I would mail the letter tomorrow. It would reach Lucy well after I'd left. She would freak out and try calling me. When she couldn't reach me, she would call Chase and the two of them would compare notes.

I couldn't leave my second family without saying goodbye. To Carrie, Jim, and MaKayla I wrote:

*Carrie, Jim and MaKayla (a.k.a. my other family):*

*Words can't describe how much I love you guys. You've accepted me as your own and have brightened my otherwise dim existence. I'm sorry that I had to leave so abruptly, but I was given an opportunity that's only offered once in a lifetime and I had to take it. Please understand that I never wanted to hurt any of you, but I know that my decision has rendered that fact unavoidable. Chase was and will always be the love of my life. Believe me when I say there will be no one else. My heart simply will never allow it.*

*Carrie–Our talks were amazing. You took me in as a daughter-in-law even though I never truly was. You are a wonderful mom and your guidance and the love you have shown me these last two years will stick with me for the rest of my life. For this, I am thankful.*

*Jim–Your sense of humor and quirkiness are irresistible. I will always remember the laughs you extracted from me every time I visited your home. I'll look upon our time together fondly.*

*MaKayla–You will always be my sister. I'm sorry I left the way I did. I will never forget you. You are an amazingly talented singer and beautiful woman to boot. I'm sure your talents will take you far. Please look after your brother for me as I have a feeling he'll need a shoulder to cry on in the next coming weeks. In my mind and heart you will always remain.*

*Love,*

*Celaine*

I wrote one final letter to Chase even though I knew I'd be seeing him one final time before I left. Somehow, I didn't think I would be in all that great a shape to completely express my feelings when I see the look of sheer pain in his eyes. More than likely, my goodbye to him would consist of a hug and me running away before I changed my mind about this whole thing.

*Chase:*

*Right now you're probably experiencing a whole slew of emotions. I just hope that the negative ones don't supersede the positive. I love you more than I can ever express and more than you'll ever get to know. Meeting you was the best thing that ever happened to me. You were my only light, my only love. My time with you was the happiest time of my life. I wish with all my heart that I could tell you where I was or what I was doing, but it's impossible for me to do so. I know this must sound like complete BS or even a cop-out to you, but it's not. You will always have my heart but, with that said, I also want you to be happy. For that to happen, you must move on with your life. As much as it pains me to think about it, please do so. I wish you nothing but the very best that life has in store. I always knew you'd make an excellent doctor, one my father would have been proud to have on his staff.*

    *Please don't hate me for what I've done.*
    *I Will Love You Forever,*

*Celaine*


    When I signed my name to that letter, I ran to the bathroom and threw up. The thought of Chase moving on was a little more than I could bear right now. I reached up from my position on the floor and flushed the toilet. Still sick to my stomach, I picked myself up from the floor to rinse out my mouth and wash my hands. The sickness didn't go away nor did I picture it leaving anytime soon. Although not complete remedies, fresh air and solitude would do me some good. And In this city, I knew there was only one place I could get both of them.

    It was late in the afternoon when I walked through the menacing steel gates surrounding the grounds of the cemetery. A basket of flowers in various shades of pink–my mother's favorite color–dangled from my fingers. I passed the parade of headstones, mausoleums, stone angels, a virtual garden of flowers and a plethora of ferns in all different sizes and shapes. A moment later, I reached the familiar rosette and sichuan marble stones situated in the shade of an elm tree. On a near regular basis, I visited their gravesites. As painful as it was, being here also gave me a strange sense of peace. To be able to touch something tangible associated with them again was strangely comforting. A wilted basket of flowers that I'd brought on my last visit hung precariously on a hook between my parents' and brother's stones. I unhooked the wilted flowers and replaced them with the basket of fresh ones I picked up from a local market.

Although it was hot outside, the shade the elm provided was somewhat of a welcome oasis. I took a seat on the grass, staring at each stone, at each blade of grass, at nothing at all. For what seemed like hours, I sat in the grass running my hand along the stones, wanting nothing more than to speak to them but coming up short of words. Only after I forced myself to speak did the words begin to flow with ease.

"I can't express to you how much I miss you. If you're listening now, I want you to know that I've been given the opportunity to keep the promise I made to you ten years ago. I just hope that I can make you proud of me, that I'm able to stop that monster so this doesn't have to happen again. So that another daughter doesn't have to sit and stare at the headstones of her family while making the same promises to them. Thank you for bringing Chase and his family into my life. They almost accomplished the impossible; they almost replaced you. This wasn't fair; it never should have happened. Not only were your lives destroyed but, now, so is mine. I'll make it right again… for the both of us. I love you."

With the wilted flowers in hand, I walked back through the cemetery gates, disposing of them in a trash receptacle before walking back out onto the sidewalk. If I hadn't already made up my mind, that visit would have been my final affirmation. This was the path my life needed to take. It was the one I'd always been destined to take. The path would be a rough, unpaved path filled with bumps and unforeseen turns, but it was my path to take and no one else's. I strolled down the sidewalk almost without purpose before realizing that I still had one last place left to visit before heading home.

Erected on the site of the parking ramp was The Lakes Remembrance Memorial Park; a beautiful homage to those whose lives had been lost there. It was elaborate, to say the least, featuring a man-made river running through its entirety, surrounded by weeping willows, evergreens and ferns. An abundance of rose bushes and other species of flowers, the likes of which I couldn't even begin to identify, flourished throughout the park everywhere I walked.

I wandered through the splendor of the park, admiring the beauty around me, thankful that not too many other people had picked tonight to come here. Crickets were chirping their nightly lullaby signaling that dusk was fast approaching. Ahead of me stood a bridge, bowing over the river in an arc. I walked over to it, stopping in the middle, and leaned against the railing to watch the water lazily flowing by, wishing I could stay in the tranquility of the moment forever.

In the center of the park stood a black marble memorial wall etched with the names of all 104 victims of The Lakes tragedy. I walked up to the wall, gingerly running my fingers over the names of strangers until coming to those of my family: Dr. George Stevens, Carol Stevens and Jacob Stevens.

Despite the fact that the park was ripe with esthetically pleasing tributes, the *pièce de résistance* of the park, in my opinion, were the 104 eternal flame candles scattered throughout it. One for each victim of The Lakes explosion. The candles' glow kept the memory of them burning in the minds of all who visited. With the fall of dusk, the glow of the flames lit the way for me as I exited the park back to the street.

Stars appeared overhead, a sight that I would never tire of. Even before Chase came into the picture, I would lay in the grass staring at them, pondering the reason for my existence. Within the first five minutes of meeting the Matthews, I thought I'd found it. But, after the events of the last few days, I was beginning to realize that my whole life had been just a stepping stone leading me to it.

My cell phone rang. It was Chase. Had it been a week ago, I would have jumped at the opportunity to speak with him. Now, given what I had to do, the thought of hearing his voice was too painful for me. How was I going to look in him in the eye and lie to him by telling him that I didn't want him anymore? I knew that telling him that was going to be the only way he would ever accept me breaking up with him. Chase would follow me to the ends of the Earth if he knew it would make me happy. The only way to prevent him from following me would be to make him think I would be happier without him. He wouldn't understand. His heart and mine were going to be broken tomorrow night with the damage, at least to me, being irreparable.

I walked down the long hallway to my apartment, finding a note from Chase taped to my door. It hadn't surprised me that he'd stopped by. When he wasn't at the hospital or studying, he was at my apartment. Honestly, I had no idea what his fixation was with me. I was mediocre at best; clumsy and the average form of pretty that couldn't be mistaken for beautiful. I slumped in my chair, checking the voice mail he'd left for me on my phone. A hint of worry was evident in his voice as he enquired about my whereabouts and whether or not I was all right. It wasn't like me to not answer my phone.

The familiar sickness returned to my stomach, making me aware that whatever strength I could muster to speak to Chase would be lost upon hearing his voice. No, texting him was the safest form of communication.

*Was at the cemetery. Sorry I missed your call. Going to bed. See you tomorrow. Love you.*

A few seconds later I received his reply message:

*If you need to talk, call me anytime. Sweet dreams, beautiful. I love you more than you can fathom.*

My eyes began to water; my strength was gone. Tomorrow would be the second worst day of my life.

# 11

## THE UNFORESEEN GOODBYE

THE DAY OF contradictions was here. Questions poured relentlessly through my head like a steady rain. Would I get to bring anything from my apartment? What would become of my belongings? What about my lease? I had another six months left on it and, knowing how management was around here, I knew that they wouldn't let me out of it early.

In the ten years since my family's death, there hadn't been a moment in my life I hadn't been in complete control over, and this inability to steer my life didn't set well with me. I preferred being the pilot, not the passenger. With a sigh, I looked around my apartment, resigning myself to the fact that Blake or his superiors probably had everything already figured out for me and there was nothing I could do about it either way. All I had to do was make a choice and then sit back and enjoy the ride.

Tonight, I would be putting on the performance of a lifetime. In a haze, I sat on the edge of my bathtub, turning the steel knob with a shaky hand until water began flowing out of the faucet. My apartment complex's plumbing wasn't exactly up-to-date in that its water heater was grossly inadequate in supplying hot water to every unit. In essence, it was a toss-up whether or not your bathing experience was going to be an enjoyable one. I ran my hand under the faucet realizing, as warm water flowed over it, that I'd won the toss today.

I lay in the tub with my head resting against its fiberglass backing, eyeing the black dress I'd selected to wear to tonight's dinner at Angelo's. It was one of the very few dresses I owned and, from this day forward, it would be forever known to me as the symbol of the end of my relationship. In my head I attempted to contemplate the right words to use to break someone's heart. Were there *right* words? My guess was that I already knew the answer to that.

I raised my arm out of the tub, watching as the droplets of water cascaded down my skin, journeying toward my shoulder. At that moment, I was in a hypnotic state. It was as though the world stood still and my mind was left to wander to the mysterious Blake Cohen. I wondered where he was, whether or not he was waiting for me outside my apartment, and if he would follow me to the restaurant.

Time ticked away in slow motion as I dried off and slipped the dress over my head. Chase loved this dress on me. I could tell by the way his eyes fell out of his head every time he saw me in it. It would be his last vision of me, and I wanted to make it as memorable as possible. I looked at myself in the mirror with the knowledge that, after tonight, it would be a sight I wouldn't be able to stomach anymore. I would be a shattered soul whose pieces would never again fit together as solidly as they once had. Chase was the only person out there who could make me whole. Without him, I would only be half alive, and that was a reflection of themselves that no one should have to see in the mirror.

The necklace, my precious Matthews' family heirloom, lay on my night stand. To see the look on Chase's face when I slipped that necklace off my neck would be devastating. Until the necklace came off, he would probably think my breaking up with him was just some kind of twisted joke. The minute he saw the necklace in my hand, however, he would know that I was serious. Returning it would destroy him.

I grabbed the letters to Lucy and the rest of the Matthews family and headed out the door. With an unsteady hand, I placed them in the archaic, bronze mail slot in the lobby of my apartment building. When I heard them hitting the bottom of the box, a sickening feeling overcame me, making my knees weak. This was really happening, and there was no turning back now. My thoughts turned to Lucy and the Matthews as they read those letters. Carrie, Jim, and MaKayla would likely already know of the breakup beforehand, but the letter would still shock them nonetheless.

I took a deep breath before stepping outside. Angelo's was five blocks down the street from my apartment, but it may as well have been five miles. The further down the block I walked, the more I thought my legs would give out. With every step I took, I felt as though I would collapse to the sidewalk. So, it was nothing short of a surprise to me when I looked up and realized that I was standing with both feet firmly planted on the ground in front of the entrance to Angelo's. My eyes stared at the door for what seemed like a half century before my weakened, jelly-like hand clasped the handle, and I allowed myself to walk into the building.

He would already be in there waiting for me. Knowing Chase, he'd arrived ten minutes prior. We were polar opposites in that respect. More often than not, I was late for appointments, dates, or whatever else had a set arrival time attached to it.

Angelo's was positively gorgeous. A virtual diamond in the rough, it was out of place in the sea of abandoned buildings, cracked sidewalks and graffiti-covered concrete. I stood for a moment admiring its opulence before taking in a deep breath and striding across the marble laden floor to the front desk.

"Welcome to Angelo's, Madame. How may I assist you this fine evening?" asked the portly man behind the desk, whose uniform probably cost more than my entire wardrobe.

"My name is Celaine Stevens. I'm here with Chase Matthews."

"Ah, yes. The young doctor. You're just as beautiful as he made you out to be. We have a special table set up for you this evening. Right this way." He motioned for me to follow him, and I couldn't help but think that he was leading me to my doom. Perhaps it was all in my head, or maybe it was because the employees get paid extra to slather on the butter to appease the egos of their usual clientele, but I could swear I saw an extra glimmer in the maitre d's eyes and an I-know-something-you-don't smile on his face as he led me to the table.

I'd never been inside Angelo's before. My finances ensured that from happening. Now that I finally had the chance to admire it from the inside, I couldn't help but notice the elegant, distinctly regal theme it exuded. When I walked into the dining hall, I found myself encased in dark purple, the color of royalty. From the table cloths to the curtains, from the wall treatments to the carpeting, the theme prevailed. In the middle of the restaurant's cathedral ceiling hung a beautiful crystal chandelier adding to the holier-than-thou attitude permeating the atmosphere. Why Chase chose to bring me here was beyond my comprehension.

It seemed like a lifetime before we reached the table where Chase was seated near the back of the restaurant. The table donned a beautiful setting complete with candelabras and fresh flowers in various shades of violets and deep pinks. I stole a quick glimpse at the other tables nearby and couldn't help but notice that our table was more put together than the rest. He'd really outdone himself, but why? It wasn't our anniversary or my birthday. Maybe he received a promotion and this was his idea of a celebration. The way he was dressed was also very unlike him, and he made me look like somewhat of a bum. Rarely did Chase dress up. He always said that the only thing ties were good for was for hanging yourself. But here he was, in a suit coat *and* a tie, looking as though he'd just stepped out of the pages of a magazine.

"You look absolutely stunning tonight," Chase said with a noticeable quiver in his voice.

"Chase, you're shaking, what's wrong? Did something happen?"

"No, I'm fine. Amazing, really."

"But, you're shaking. You're not fine, Chase. What's going on?"

"Celaine, I'm the best I've ever been. Everything is perfect. More perfect than I ever thought it would be for me."

"Okay." I picked up the menu, searching for something that would be gentle on my weakened stomach.

Something wasn't quite right with Chase. I had never seen him like this before. He was so...nervous. What was there to be nervous about? His face was flushed, and he stared at me as though seeing me for the first time. The intensity he projected began to make *me* nervous. After some hesitation, he broke the silence. "I was going to wait until after dinner for this, but looking at you, it's kind of hard to keep quiet any longer."

"Huh?" I looked up from my menu, puzzled.

"Celaine, you are the most beautiful woman I have ever met. Aesthetically, mentally and emotionally. From the moment I first saw you, my soul has ached to be by your side. I can't imagine anyone more perfect for me than you. You are my better half, and I can't picture my life without you." Chase looked into my eyes as he paused, resuming again with a slight tremble in his voice. "I don't think there is life without you. Before I met you, I was a hollow shell of a man stumbling around in the dark, barely able to make it from point A to point B. When you came into my life, you brought the light to help me see the way to destinations I didn't know existed. You picked up the pieces and made me whole again."

My eyes began to water as my body trembled from the impact of his words. I looked up at Chase with a look I was sure projected the absolute guilt I felt.

"Your eyes...they shimmer like topaz. They're so beautiful."

I couldn't make the tears stop; my eyes were burning, and wiping them with my fingers just wasn't cutting it. I looked down and saw the Angelo's trademark napkin folded in the shape of a swan resting on my plate. Chase's eyes lit up as I reached down to unfold the napkin in order to blot them. An audible *clunk* startled me as something fell from inside the napkin and onto the plate. Averting my eyes from the napkin, I gasped when I realized what the source of that sound had been. In the middle of the plate sat the most beautiful ring I had ever seen. It was an emerald cut, two, maybe three carats, with a prismatic rainbow of colors radiating off it creating the most amazing sparkle. I was speechless.

A hand grasped mine, bringing me back down to reality. At my feet knelt Chase, his eyes watering. My heart pounded in my chest with the realization of what was happening. Around us, diners looked up from their tables, their eyes wide with the anticipation of what was one of the happiest moments in any normal couple's relationship.

"Celaine Elizabeth Stevens, you have made me the happiest man in this room thus far. Now, would you please make me the happiest man in the world by doing me the honor of being your husband? Will you marry me?"

Time stopped as I stared blankly at Chase's anxious face. This wasn't the way it was supposed to happen. Not only would I be breaking his heart, I would be humiliating him too. I was sick and I knew I was only going to get sicker when I finally spoke, saying what I'd come here to say. "Chase, I love you. I do. You're perfect for me. You're perfect for anyone, really. Believe me when I say that there will never be anyone else who'll have my heart."

He looked up at me and smiled his gorgeous smile, the dimple on his chin standing out. His eyes were as bright as sapphires, making me want to dive into their intoxicatingly blue depths to drown. "But," I began again, "there's no easy way to say this. I came here to tell you that…that…" I hesitated. Not sure what to say, but knowing I needed to say something to remove myself from his presence as soon as possible, I proceeded. "I'm going away. I've gotten a job across the country. Chase…I can't marry you. I'm leaving tonight. I don't know when or if I'll be coming back. I'm sorry. I'm so very sorry."

Behind us, a slew of gasps erupted. I glanced back to see the house band readying themselves to play as soon as I'd accepted Chase's proposal, staring at me in horror. This had obviously been a first for Angelo's. My eyes trailed off to the other tables, only to be met with the same shocked and stunned expressions. Then came the most painful of all: Chase's expression. His brow was furrowed in a look of pain mixed with confusion, coupled with the expectation that I was going to say *gotcha*, and accept his proposal after all.

I had to leave and fast. My unsteady legs felt like gelatin as I stood up, walked around Chase, and took off in a dead sprint past rows of tables to the front of the restaurant. I burst through the door, narrowly avoiding taking out an Angelo's employee who'd stepped out for a smoke break.

"Sorry," I said, choking back tears.

My eyes drifted up to the marquee in front of the restaurant. In big, bold letters that screamed *read me* was the announcement, *Congratulations, Chase and Celaine.* He'd gone all out, and my bolting out of the restaurant with little explanation would be all he'd remember. Winded, I stopped to catch my breath, leaning against the building for support, my legs feeling as though they were about to give out on me. My head scraped against the coarse brick wall, and I wished it would swallow me up right then and there, forever burying me, shielding me from the world and the unbearable pain I felt. Next to where I stood, the door flew open as Chase emerged from the restaurant. He looked at me for several seconds, the pain and disbelief still evident on his face.

"After two years, don't you at least think I deserve an explanation," he demanded, his face bright red. "You know, like an explanation of what exactly this job is and...oh...I don't know...when you were going to tell me about it?"

No explanation short of the truth was going to appease him, and even the truth would be a stretch. "I didn't know how to tell you. I didn't want to tell you. Hurting you was the last thing I ever wanted to do, but I didn't see any way around it. Chase, this is the last thing I wanted. Had I had even the slightest inclination that you were going to propose to me tonight, I would never have let you take me here in front of all those people."

"I just don't understand. Where is this job, and why can't I come with you? Why does this have to tear us apart? When did you start even looking for another job and...and why couldn't you at least have given me some sort of heads up?"

"Chase, I don't want you to give up your life for me. I'm going to be working for a bank on the other side of the country. It's an increase in pay and a fresh start. Living here has just brought back too many bad memories of my family, memories that I just can't live with anymore. I thought I'd be strong enough to handle them, but I was wrong."

"Celaine, *you* are my life. There will be other hospitals. Trust me, there's no shortage of employment for pediatricians out there. I love you. Whatever is going on, whatever it is that makes you feel like you need to run away, we can work it out together."

I sucked up every last bit of the agony I felt before looking at him to deliver the final blow. "This is something that I'm going to have to go at alone. You can't be a part of my life anymore. I don't know that I want you to be a part of my life anymore. My feelings for you have changed, and I see my life going in another direction. I'm sorry. I just hope that there will be a day when you can forgive me." My eyes met his, witnessing the absolute defeat in them. I'd broken him to the point where I swore I could hear his heart stop beating.

"I'm sorry I couldn't be what you needed," his voice cracked.

I had to leave before I changed my mind and ran back into his arms to beg for forgiveness. But, as I began to turn around, I remembered the necklace. I put my hands around the back of my neck and grabbed the clasp holding the chain in place. When Chase realized what I was about to do, he rushed to stop me before I could unclasp it.

"Please, don't," he pleaded in agony. "Returning that would be like twisting the dagger buried in my heart. Keep it. I can't imagine there's a woman more worthy of it than you were out there. Besides, I promised my mother that I wouldn't give it to just anyone so...keep it." His eyes were beginning to water, and I wanted to crawl into a hole and die. "Maybe once in a while it will remind you that you are deeply loved, and it will be enough to bring you back home again...back to me."

It felt as though the world had crashed down around me. I was short of breath, dizzy, with my heart on the verge of stopping. With a broken heart, I looked up at Chase, avoiding direct eye contact. "I will cherish it for the rest of my life," I barely squeaked out between tears.

He nodded and, for the last time, I wrapped my arms around him to embrace him. He hesitated for a moment, unsure whether or not to reciprocate, but his hesitation didn't last long. Wrapping his arms around me, he squeezed me tighter than he ever had, knowing that once he let go it would be the end. I broke away from his arms, keeping my eyes focused on the pavement. "Goodbye," I blurted.

I left him there on the street as though he were nothing but a piece of garbage, as though it weren't the last time I would ever see him.

My feet flew across the pavement so swiftly that I could barely feel my heels striking its hard surface. When I reached the door of my apartment building, I blew through it, keeping pace through the lobby, drawing inquisitive stares around me. With a loud crash, I barreled through the door of the fire escape and began the long climb up the several flights of stairs to the rooftop. Surprisingly, I scaled the ten floors of my building effortlessly until I reached the top of my ascent where my body buckled and I collapsed to the floor. My legs burned, my lungs struggled to take in air. Through the door, just a few short feet away, life as I knew it would change forever.

Angelo's? What would possess her boyfriend to take her to this yuppie infested, petulant, purple nightmare? Blake Cohen sat in the corner of the restaurant, blending in seamlessly with a bachelor party assembled at a nearby table. This was too easy; one of the easiest assignments he'd ever been given.

He pretended to stumble while on his way to the bathroom, feigning as though he were bracing himself for support against the table where his target's boyfriend was sitting. The boyfriend, sounding genuinely concerned, had asked him if he was all right. He'd made small talk with him, assuring him that it had just been a lapse in coordination, while secretly placing a microphone underneath the table. Barely the size of a pinhead, it would be undetectable, more than serving its purpose. It would be obvious now, when she showed up, if this night were going to work in his favor or take a more sinister turn. He sat back down at his table and removed an ear piece from his pocket as he waited patiently for his target's arrival.

A moment later, the door opened and in she walked. He did a double take. The dress she was wearing was form fitting, and she had all the right forms to fit it. Her legs were bare, their length accentuated by the stilettos she wore. She was dressed to kill or, if things went wrong, to be killed.

"This is going to be interesting," he mumbled.

He looked at his watch. They would be expecting a resolution to this mission soon. Just what the resolution would be remained to be seen. The look on her face didn't scream happy, but the boyfriend was beaming so much he swore the guy was farting sunshine. As she took her seat, the conversation started, and he cupped his hand to his ear to listen.

*Geez, this guy is sappy*, he thought, taking a sip of ice water. Much to the disdain of his waitress, an annoying blonde, the water grazing his lips was going to be the only thing he was going to consume here, but that didn't stop her from trying. For the third time, she approached his table.

"Sir, is there anything I can get for you?" she asked, attempting a polite tone as her customer's affinity for only ice water had steadily worn through her perkiness.

"I told you I would call you if I needed anything," he said without looking up. The waitress walked away in a huff, angrier with his obvious disinterest in *her* than in the menu.

A clanging noise echoed in his ear piece followed by a sharp gasp at his target's table. He looked up to see the horror etched on her pretty face. It all made sense to him now. The ambiance, the boyfriend beaming with pride and expectation; it was blatantly obvious. The bastard was going to propose to her.

"Oh, crap," he muttered loudly enough to draw the attention of some members of the bachelor party at the table next to him.

"What's your problem?" he asked the intoxicated groom-to-be.

"Nothing, man, nothing at all," he replied, barely coherent.

*The poor sucker*, Blake thought as his attention refocused on the impending disaster unfolding in the back of the room. The boyfriend was down on one knee, garnering the attention of those around them. *Wow, this guy really must have it bad for her. It's too bad he is going to lose her one way or another tonight.* He moved his hand into the pocket of his overcoat over the barrel of the revolver. If she said "yes", it was going to be all over. He would draw the gun, shoot, and be out of the restaurant before anyone had a chance to look his way. Speed and agility were just one of the many perks of being a couple of notches above humans on the evolutionary chain.

Silence fell between them for what seemed like an eternity until he heard the words he'd been waiting to hear: "I can't marry you" and "I'm sorry." With those words, she ran out of the restaurant, eliciting commotion in her wake. He had the answer he'd come for. In relief, he removed his hand from the revolver. It was time to make contact with the target.

I forced myself to pick my body up from the floor of the stairwell. After taking in a deep breath, I struggled to push the door to the rooftop open. It was a door I'd opened several times before but, for some reason, tonight it seemed to weigh a thousand pounds more than I remembered. With the opening of the door, I fully expected to see Blake Cohen standing before me, ready to take me to places unknown. To my surprise, the roof was vacant except for a ray of light from the rising moon. Where was he? Had this been all some kind of sick, twisted joke? A rush of anger flooded through my body.

"Where are you?" I yelled. "What more do you want from me? I have nothing left to give." My body shook from the gravity of the entire evening.

"Don't you think that was a little over the top?" Blake Cohen's voice asked from behind me.

I turned around to see him leaning on the door of the stairwell, his cocky smile illuminated by moonlight. "You weren't here a few seconds ago. How did you get up here so fast?"

"That's my little secret."

I wanted to smack that smug smile right off his face. "Look, I believe you. I've done everything you asked me to. I've given up everything I could possibly give up. I'm a broken person ready to be pieced back together in any way you see fit if it helps to bring The Man in Black down."

"You act like you're the only one who's ever given anything up in their life. I hope you get over this melodramatic, whining thing quick. It doesn't suit you very well." He strode over to the edge of the building, looking over the edge as though he were unimpressed by the view below. "Not to mention it makes you more vulnerable. They'll eat you alive where we're going."

"Well, are we just going to stand here, or are you going to take me to your secret lair?"

"Someone better lay off the superhero flicks. Go back to your apartment and grab anything and everything you want to take that can fit into this." He threw a small backpack into my arms. Not much was going to be able to fit into its inadequate canvas interior. Thankfully, I hadn't planned on taking much of anything.

"What about my other things and my lease?"

"Already taken care of. Now, I suggest you hurry. That boyfriend of yours doesn't take no for an answer. You probably have about five minutes before he comes knocking on your door begging you to take him back."

"So, you saw everything at the restaurant?"

"Did you expect me not to? Meet me back up here when you're done."

"Aye, aye, Captain."

"I can already tell this is going to be the start of a beautiful relationship," he said, smiling.

In a rush, I scrambled back down the stairwell to the floor of my apartment. The last thing I wanted to see was Chase. I couldn't face him again. He'd been hurt by me in every way conceivable, and I knew that if I were to see him and the hurt in his eyes again, I would cave and I wouldn't be able to rejoin Blake.

I was going to miss my apartment. The eclectic mix of mismatched furniture; the lack of hot water; the memories Chase and I had made there. Already knowing what I wanted to take, I ran to my night stand drawer and grabbed my photo album. Ironically, I knew that the family photographs that had caused me so much pain were going to be the incentive I would need to get me out of bed each day. Quickly thumbing through the remaining photographs, I found one of Chase and I that had been taken at the beach. Regardless of how painful it was going to be to look at, I grabbed it along with a few others.

What else? My closet door was open, prompting me to rummage through it, grabbing a shirt, a pair of blue jeans and a pair of tennis shoes. I figured that packing them was a smart bet considering I wasn't exactly sure what I would be required to wear wherever we were going. With the photographs and clothing being all I could fit into the minuscule backpack and, remembering what Blake had said about Chase, I made a dash for my door.

On my way out, I glanced at my desk, remembering the letter I'd written to Chase. In my emotionally wrought state, I hadn't given him the letter at dinner as I had planned. Without hesitation, I ran over to the desk, tore off a piece of tape from the dispenser, and retrieved the letter. Once I was outside my apartment, I taped the letter to the door. If Chase was coming, there would be no way he would miss it there.

A short distance away, I heard hurried footsteps on the main stairwell. I knew whose footsteps they were. My time had run out. In a mad sprint, I raced to the fire escape as the footsteps continued drawing steadily nearer. Just seconds before the source of the footsteps came into view, the door to the fire escape slammed shut. Crouching down against the wall, I waited.

After several minutes had passed, I summoned the courage to stand up and peer out of the doorway window overlooking the hallway of my unit. Blake had been right. Chase was standing in front of my door with the letter in his hand. It was too much. With a heavy heart, I trudged back up the stairs to meet the fate I'd accepted.

Blake stood looking over the edge of the roof in sheer contemplation. He turned his head as I appeared from the stairwell, inspecting me thoughtfully. "Not that I care or anything, but are you sure you want to wear that?" he asked, eyeing me up and down.

I was still wearing my dress from the night, and the thought that I should change my clothes had been the furthest thing from my mind. "It's not like I had a chance to change," I said, more emotional than I would have liked.

"You saw him, didn't you?" he asked, his voice laced, curiously, with concern.

"You already knew the answer to that question."

"You catch on quick."

"That's what they tell me."

"Okay. Let's get this party started."

"I can hardly contain my excitement."

"That's the spirit."

I walked over to Blake's vantage point on the edge of the roof. "What are we going to do?" I mused. "Jump?"

"You already know the answer to that question."

I looked at his face and realized he was serious. "Are you kidding me? Maybe *you're* not breakable, but *I* am."

"For the time being, anyway."

"Huh?"

"Just hang onto me and be sure to not let go. They're expecting me to bring you back in one piece."

"How exactly do you want me to hold onto you?"

"Wrap your legs around my waist and your arms around my neck. It's a position I'm sure you're familiar with." I felt my face begin to burn. Blake let out an amused chuckle.

"I'm going to die tonight, aren't I?"

"If you let go of me, then...yeah...probably."

"Swell."

Blake stepped to the edge of the roof so that his toes were hanging just slightly off it. He had incredible balance. I walked up behind him and, hesitating, I put my arms around his neck. Instantly, his arms swung around, grabbing my legs, securing them tightly around his muscular frame. "Have you ever been on a roller coaster?" he asked.

"Yeah."

"Well, I liken this experience to that, except we're higher and our fall isn't as controlled. Standing on the edge of a building is like the pause before going down the track. You know what's coming and you prepare for it, but even though you know what to expect, it's still one hell of a ride."

"So, it's like skydiving?"

"Oh, no, that's just suicide."

"I'm glad to see that even you have your limits."

"Just hang on, close your eyes and enjoy the ride." I clutched Blake tight enough to cut off a normal person's air supply, but he said nothing. It was as though he weren't carrying a fully grown woman on his back. My heart was pounding, my stomach was in knots. I looked down at the rooftop, refusing to look over the edge of the apartment building. Then, after taking one final breath before bending his knees, Blake prepared to jump. Right as I closed my eyes, he dove off the roof.

The wind whipped viciously through my hair. And even though I knew we were careening towards the pavement, I could have sworn my stomach was still cowering back on the roof. A scream made its way from my mouth as the thought of us falling and ultimately splattering against the pavement ran through my mind. Much to my dismay, my eyes flew open and all I could do was watch the ground drawing nearer and nearer. This was it; this was how I was going to die.

It was during my panic that I felt Blake's body snap upright as if it were meeting resistance from somewhere. The jolt nearly loosened my grip from around his neck, forcing me to reposition my legs around his waist tighter in order to stabilize myself. When I looked up, I noticed the jolt had been caused by some sort of harness attached to a band around Blake's wrist. I followed the trail of rope leading from it, finding it secured to a billboard promoting a new sports drink. Instead of free falling, we were safely gliding into a darkened alleyway.

Blake's feet skidded on the floor of the alley. Once he regained his footing, he flicked his wrist, releasing the rope–which resembled more of a cable upon further inspection–from its hold on the billboard.

"You can let go now," he said, prying my legs from around his waist. This night kept getting better and better for him.

"Sorry," I trembled.

"You act like you've never jumped off a building before."

"What gave you your first clue?" He smiled before proceeding down the alleyway. I took in a deep breath, happy to be back on land. I'd just done pretty much everything I'd been told repeatedly all my life never to do. Hurling myself off a building, following a mysterious stranger down a dark, damp alleyway to destinations unknown; Carol would be so proud of me right now.

"Here," Blake called out to me as he tossed a helmet in my direction.

"You didn't see fit to give me this *before* jumping with me on your back off the roof of my building?"

"Trust me, had you let go, whether or not you were wearing a helmet wouldn't have mattered."

"Good point."

We continued our walk down the dank alleyway until we reached a pile of cardboard propped up by a dumpster near the end of it. Blake bent over the pile of cardboard, throwing pieces of it into the dumpster. "I draw the line at dumpster diving," I added, watching as Blake tossed aside yet another piece of cardboard.

"Beauty, brains, *and* a smart ass. How did I ever get so lucky?" My cheeks burned again, only serving to fan the fire of Blake's amusement. When he lifted the final and largest piece of cardboard I gasped as a large, black motorcycle was revealed. Motorcycles were not in my area of expertise but, from what I could tell, this particular machine was built for speed. The front end was pointed in a design I'd never seen before but appeared aerodynamic in nature. The chrome features on the wheels and gears shimmered in the sliver of moonlight shining down into the alleyway.

"Great," I choked out. "Another way to die tonight." Blake rolled his eyes, moving the motorcycle from out against the building. I had to admit it was pretty, even for a death trap. "What model is it?" I asked.

"You aren't going to find this cycle at any dealer," he said.

"So, this is where my tax dollars are going, eh?"

"You're stalling."

"Perhaps."

"Just get on and hang on."

"Where are we going?"

"You'll find out when we get there."

I shot him a dirty look before slipping the helmet over my head. Never before had I ridden a motorcycle. This was shaping up to be a night of firsts for me. Awkwardly, I positioned myself behind Blake, placing my feet in what I thought were the appropriate footholds and again wrapped my arms around him. He kicked the motorcycle to a start, gripping the throttle, sending it racing ahead through the alleyway and back onto the roadway within seconds. Petrified, I held him close while he tore down the road at speeds that didn't seem possible. Buildings became streaks, insignificant blobs dotting the horizon. Within moments, we were outside the city limits. I craned my neck, forcing myself to look back at my former home. *Goodbye, Chase,* I thought.

The motorcycle tore through an exit ramp and, before I knew it, we'd merged onto the highway. It was vacant due to the impending curfew. I wasn't sure where we were headed and, at that point, I didn't care. My life was in the hands of whoever had sent Blake to me and as long as I was the one who got to do away with the Man in Black, I wasn't going to look back. Without Chase, my former life meant nothing anymore.

Moonlight lit a path for Blake, making a trail for him to follow as he sped down the highway. The moonlight was a beacon lighting the way home to the beginning of my new life; to my new destiny.

# BOOK TWO

# MY NEW LIFE

# 12

## THE EPICENTER

FOR CLOSE TO an hour–or so I estimated–the motorcycle roared eastward down the dismal interstate. I found myself grateful that the backpack Blake had given to me hadn't allowed for too much of anything since my shoulders were already sore from what little I'd been able to stuff into it. My body slid back as Blake propelled the motorcycle off the roadway and up a ramp that lead to an even darker path. For someone who'd never ridden a motorcycle before tonight, I had to admit it was growing on me. It felt as though we were flying down the road, untouchable and free.

Blake turned down a hidden dirt road masked by a line of evergreens. In the daylight, I assumed it made for a beautiful sight but, being as dark as it was, it took on more of a macabre appearance. As we barreled through the trees, I peered over his shoulder and saw to my horrified surprise that we were approaching a steel gate at a high rate of speed. My body tensed at the sight of the approaching obstacle, causing my grip on Blake to tighten like a vice. Surely, he had to see it. At any moment, I expected him to veer off to the side of the road or, at the very least, to slow down, but that never happened. The gate was drawing closer but, instead of slowing down, he only seemed to speed up faster.

"What are you doing?" I yelled.

I knew he'd heard me, but still he said nothing. In my mind, I was already taking drastic measures, debating what scenario would hurt more: bailing off the motorcycle and slamming into one of the numerous pine trees or crashing head-on into the steel gate. Blake wouldn't be able to stop in time. The cycle was going too fast and the gate was just a couple of yards away now. I shut my eyes and prepared myself for impact, knowing that bodily injury would be inevitable.

One second slowly turned into twenty before I realized that we should have already made contact with the gate. I opened my eyes and looked ahead, peering over Blake's shoulder. The gate was gone and there was nothing but wide open road ahead of us. Had I been seeing things? I looked back to see the gates closing behind us. How had those doors opened so quickly? In disbelief, I shook my head. Absolutely nothing tonight had made any sense and, at this point, I shouldn't be shocked by anything that happened.

We proceeded to travel further down the road when I heard Blake bark a command into what I observed to be some sort of microphone-like device built into his helmet. "Main hatch open. Cohen. Serial number, two-four-five-seven-nine."

My eyes widened as the earth in front of us began to rise. Steel doors such as those that composed the gate behind us opened up to consume the motorcycle. With a deafening roar, we accelerated into the earth, moving down a ramp that seemed to be just a few inches shy of a complete ninety-degree angle, and my stomach sank right along with the practically free-falling motorcycle. At the bottom of the ramp, the floor leveled out as lights embedded within the concrete walls around us flickered on. Bright lights encased us on both sides of the motorcycle, moving forward in the direction we were traveling, lighting the way to our final destination. I wondered how far down below the surface of the earth we were but figured that was probably an answer I really didn't want to know.

The dull, gray concrete walls surrounding us reminded me of those comprising an overpass. Mounted on these walls, about every fifty feet, were devices that looked like cameras. When our motorcycle passed by them, they sprang into action, following our every move. It was then that it all hit me. This was real. In my heart I'd known it all along, but now all the cynicism in my mind was being put to rest.

Ahead of us appeared a large opening, signaling the end of our journey. A massive, garage-like structure greeted us as we sped through it. Motorcycles, similar to the one Blake was operating, were parked in tight rows ahead of us. Off to the right, automobiles, the likes of which I deduced were not available to the general public, were parked. *So much for being inconspicuous*, I thought as I loosened my grip around Blake.

Suddenly, with an expertise that only extreme sports enthusiasts would envy, Blake wheeled the motorcycle sharply, spinning it into a gut wrenching skid. Unable to control myself, I felt a scream escape my lips that continued until we came to rest next to the other cycles. Able to breathe again, I patted my body down to ensure that I was still in one piece. Satisfied with my inspection, I clumsily dismounted the motorcycle, tearing off my helmet in disgust. "Was that necessary?" I asked.

"What?" Blake asked, the annoying smugness returning to his face. I chucked the helmet at him but, to my dismay, he caught it before it could slam into his face. "Temper, temper," he chided, shaking a finger at me in admonishment. "No one told me there was a little spitfire hidden beneath that beautiful exterior."

My teeth gritted together and I was fully aware of the fact that my complexion was turning all shades of crimson. This further prompted Blake to let out a bellowing laugh that echoed off the concrete walls around us.

"I see you've already made a great first impression on your new partner," a voice sounded from somewhere nearby. "A dress? You made the trip in *that* dress? Oh boy, you're one lucky man, Blake."

I turned around to see a young man with a boyish appearance that, in high school, I would have likened to being that of a Poindexter type. He reminded me of the times when Chase would take me into the only hobby shop left in town to pacify his comic book interest. Every time I went with him, there would be the same group of guys all sitting at card tables set up in the back, playing games that I wouldn't have been able to understand if my life had depended on it. Whenever I would walk in, they would all look up simultaneously with a unanimous holy-crap-it's-a-girl look etched on their faces. That same look was perfectly illustrated on the face before me now. He was skinny, sickeningly so, with unkempt red hair and a shirt that had some sort of lingo I assumed only a true geek would understand.

"Hello, my dear." He sauntered over to me, his eyes refusing to leave mine. "My name is Cameron Lake. It's nice meet you, Celaine. Is that how it's pronounced?" He extended his hand toward me. I hesitated before finally taking it.

"Yeah...uh...yeah...that's right," I looked over at Blake, who had an almost apologetic expression on his face which made me nervous.

"I've read a lot about you," Cameron blurted out.

"Wow...creepy," I replied.

Blake howled with laughter. "Yup, that's Cameron to a tee," he mused.

Cameron rolled his eyes and spoke again. "It's late and you no doubt had a very interesting day to say the least. Follow me. I'll take you to your room so that you can get settled in." He turned to walk down a hallway leading out of the garage.

I looked back at Blake, my eyes ravaged by indecision.

"Don't worry, Cameron's harmless. He won't bite."

Cameron swung around. "Unless, of course, you're into that sort of thing," he said with a wink.

I shuddered, eliciting a snicker from Blake. "Yup, pretty much the same reaction he gets from most women," he said, laughing.

"Shut up, Frank," Cameron retorted. Blake's face tensed, letting me know that last comment had hit a nerve with him.

"What does that mean?" I asked him.

"Nothing. Just the ignorant words of a jackass."

A short distance down the hall, Cameron held his thumb out against a plate adorning yet another steel door. The plate did a quick scan of his thumb which allowed the door to slide open, revealing another hallway comprised of a thinly carpeted floor, fluorescent lighting and the standard concrete walls made a tad homey by a coat of beige paint.

"Are we in school?" I asked.

"Wait until you see your room," Blake muttered.

We turned down another hallway containing numerous doors ornamented with name plates. Flashbacks of college dorm life invaded my thoughts at the sight of them. Five doors down, Cameron stopped in front of a door bearing my name.

"Home sweet home," he announced. "Hold out one of your thumbs, please." I held out my hand, allowing Cameron to take my thumb. He placed it onto a plate resembling the one that had granted us access to the maze of hallways. The plate scanned my thumb while Cameron imputed some sort of code on the keypad underneath the plate. Once the code was accepted, the door slid open. "Congratulations. You are officially in the system," he said.

"Great." I looked down at the freckled hand that still held steadfastly to mine. "I'm assuming that means you can let go of my hand now."

Cameron smiled, removing his hand from mine. Blake shot him a dirty look as though chastising him for his inappropriate actions with his newly inducted co-worker.

"There's a button on the wall next to the door," Blake said. "To close the door, you will need to push that button or, after a moment, it will just close on its own."

"Thanks."

"Well, I hate to leave all this fun and excitement, but I have a long day tomorrow and so do you, Ms. Celaine," Cameron said. "Goodnight, ladies and gents."

I nodded in Cameron's direction. Blake shook his head, turning to me. "We're not all like...that," he said, nodding towards Cameron. "You'll have to excuse him. He's not used to being around women. There's no computer program available to teach him how to talk to them."

"What is this place called, anyway?" I asked.

"Well, that all depends on who you ask. Some would say home, some would say work, and, if you were to ask my opinion, I would say it's called the seventh circle of Hell. But, technically, they refer to it as The Epicenter."

"So, it's basically headquarters."

"Yeah, but for what, I don't even know."

"What's going on tomorrow?"

"Your orientation, or so they call it."

"Wonderful."

"Yeah. You'll see why I call this place Hell tomorrow." He hesitated, and for the first time since I met him, I swore I could see an actual human in those stone cold brown eyes of his. "If I were you, I would get myself settled in and try to fall asleep. After tomorrow, the very act of sleeping will be more of a luxury for you than a necessity." I gave Blake a look of confusion, causing a smile to appear on his surprisingly vulnerable face. "Goodnight, kid," he sighed.

"Goodnight."

Blake's room was a couple of doors down from mine. I watched him until he disappeared inside, then turned and walked into my room for the first time. When I entered the room, I scanned the wall next to the door until I found the button that closed it. The second my fingers hit the button, the door slid shut, leaving me alone in my new home. Like the rest of The Epicenter thus far, there was nothing too spectacular about my living quarters. The walls were painted a nondescript blasé neutral color; the carpet was an even more quintessential neutral Berber. In the far corner stood a glorified cot for a bed with a dresser, closet, nightstand, lamp, small television and bathroom completing the ensemble. "Well, that's a plus," I muttered to myself, eyeing the bathroom.

On the wall was some sort of speaker system which only added to the whole scholarly feel of the place. Being underground, there were no windows in the room, a fact which made it that much more dreary and undesirable.

A sense of loneliness overtook me as I stood in the silence, gazing upon my essentially bare cube. I tried to shake it off by opening my backpack and spilling its contents on the bed. There were empty hangers in my closet, allowing me to hang up the few items of clothing I was able to bring with me, and I figured I'd better get started making this room my "home".

I opened the drawer to the dresser, listening to it creak in protest as it struggled against me. To my pleasant surprise, it contained clothing. I pulled out a pair of pajama pants. They were larger than what I would have worn and in just as neutral a color as the walls of the room. Underneath the pajama pants was a tank top just as plain as the pants, but adequate nonetheless. With clothes in hand, I headed to the bathroom. It too was just as dreary. Was there a crime against color in this place? Apparently, aesthetics weren't important in the superhuman industry. The bathroom counter was large and held a numerous supply of toiletries. Their presence served as a hint to me that there may possibly be another feminine presence in the sea of testosterone I found myself swimming in.

Desperate to return to a sense of normalcy, I spotted a toothbrush amongst the bathroom supplies, wet the bristles, and brushed my teeth while sitting on the edge of the bathtub. My fingers gripped the faucet, turning on the water for a shower. Warm water flowed freely. Another plus. I slipped my dress off and removed the heels from my throbbing feet. As I stepped into the shower, I closed my eyes, letting the warmth envelope me like a security blanket. It was weird being able to take a shower and actually enjoy the process. That fact alone inched this place to a notch just slightly above my former apartment.

I stepped out of the shower and wrapped myself in a towel, my gaze drifting to the mirror situated above the sink. It was the first time I'd seen myself since breaking Chase's heart, and the reflection in the mirror was unrecognizable. Before me stood a broken woman; a woman who had nothing left to lose; a woman with no hope of being pieced together again. Quickly, I got dressed, leaving the stranger in the bathroom mirror to her misery.

I sat on the edge of the bed, knowing that getting to sleep was going to be none too easy. This became especially true after feeling the stiff, hard as a rock mattress beneath my body. Theorizing that it must have been filled with gravel, I figured getting comfortable would be a challenge to say the least. On top of that, the sheets were thin and the pillow was barely big enough to hold my head. They spared no expense here. Hopefully, Blake had been right about sleep not being a necessity as, if I really did need it, I would be out of luck because I wouldn't be getting it on this thing.

My photographs were still sitting on the bed where I'd removed them from the backpack. I reached for them and placed them on my lap. Gently, my fingers glided through each picture, causing memories to flood through my brain. There were memories of holidays and vacations spent together filled with laughter and celebration. Life had been near perfection. My parents, although not always perfect themselves, had done the best they could with raising two demanding children. They didn't deserve to have it all come to an end the way it did. What they deserved was a chance to be able to retire, to spend their elderly years together traveling and reveling in the joys of grandchildren while swinging on porch swings. Of all the decisions I had made in my life, I knew without a shadow of a doubt that I had made the right one this time. It was the most unselfish yet painful decision I'd ever made.

The photographs became more current the closer to the end of the stack I came. Loose photographs fell onto my bed. Photographs of Chase; photographs of me. My face had been blissful, the polar opposite of the girl back in the mirror. Chase and I had had a wonderful relationship. I turned to the few photos taken during our camping trip. A little over a year ago, Chase, Lucy, her boyfriend, Luke, Chase's best friend, Trey, and I had all gone camping in upstate New York. It had been one of the best weekends of my life and the first time Chase and I had made love. That night was the first time I'd allowed myself to tell a man that I loved him. It'd been a big step for my commitment-phobic self, and I knew that it had meant the world to Chase, too. My eyes began to water as I leaned over to put the pictures in the nightstand drawer. I dried my eyes with my tank top as I forced myself off the bed to shut the lights off, stumbling in the dark on the way back.

With Chase on my mind, sleep wouldn't be an option. All the wonderful memories we'd shared were now nothing but memories. Only devastation remained in the wake of our once picture perfect relationship. I wondered what he was doing right now. Where he was, what he was thinking. Did he hate me for what had transpired tonight? He'd never know the truth, and I'd never be able to explain it to him. The tears once again traveled down my cheek, sluggishly dripping onto my pillow. It was all I could take. I let all of the pain that had accumulated over the last few days loose. Silent tears turned into an outright sob. "I'm so sorry, Chase," I said, muffling my cries with my pillow.

Quite unexpectedly, I fell asleep during my crying fit. But, in my restless slumber, my conscious thoughts invaded my dreams, and all I saw were images of Chase's devastated face.

"What the hell happened?" Trey's message reverberated on Chase Matthews' cell phone. "Give me a call when you can, I'm worried about you, bro."

Chase set his cell phone down next to his fifth bottle of beer. He hadn't known what else to do, so he'd called his best friend, Trey, leaving a message when he hadn't picked up. Now, he didn't feel like talking to anyone. What was he going to tell them when he didn't entirely understand what had happened tonight himself? Everything had gone so perfectly. She was the one he'd waited for his whole life. Life with her had been surreal.

He pulled out the ring that was burning a hole in his back pocket. It was such a minuscule piece of metal and stone for such a large sum of money. Months had been spent picking it out, making payments on it. Months had been spent planning when, where and how he would present it to her along with his whole heart and soul. All of this tedious planning was spent just to have her run out on him with little explanation. To leave him there with everyone's eyes gazing upon him in pity. Why did she do this to him? He thought he knew everything about her, but now it appeared as though she was nothing more than an enigma to him, a puzzle that couldn't be solved.

He paid his tab and stepped out into the night air, noticing the stars as he walked toward his apartment. The Big Dipper was prominently displayed in the heavens before him causing him to stop in the street. From its position in the sky, he traced out the ladle until he reached the handle where he then followed its path, stopping at the last star. It was his and Celaine's star. They'd claimed it one night while on the roof of her apartment. It was their reassurance that whenever one of them was lonely for the other, all they had to do was look up at that star and know that the other was somewhere under the same sky. The star had been christened, "Hope", a metaphor not only for their relationship but for the future of society as a whole. Even now, after their relationship's devastating collapse, he couldn't help but wonder whether Celaine was staring at that same star at that same moment, too.

He climbed the stairs to his apartment, discovering Trey propped against the door to his unit.

"About time you showed up," Trey said, agitated.

"I'm sorry, man. I should have answered my cell phone. I just needed a few minutes to myself."

"Do you want to tell me what happened tonight, and why you were blubbering like a crazy man on the message you left me?"

"It's over."

"You're making no sense. How much have you had to drink?"

"Enough to dull the pain, man."

"Would you stop being such a drama queen and explain to me what pain you need to dull so badly. You have a great life. I've never seen you sulk like this. It's kind of pathetic, really."

Trey stood up, allowing Chase to open the door of his apartment. Once open, Chase threw his keys aside on the bookshelf just inside the doorway. "Well that's just it, buddy. I *had* a great life," he muttered.

"That's right. You were going to propose to Celaine tonight. What? Did she say no? If that's the case, I'm sure she'll come around eventually. You know I love Celaine, but that girl has always had commitment issues."

"That's just it. She didn't just say 'no', she said, 'hell, no', and bolted out of the restaurant. She's gone." He took the note that had been left for him out of his pocket and tossed it to Trey.

"What? She just left?" Trey asked while unfolding the note.

"Yeah. She got some new job and left town tonight."

"You don't find that just a little odd?"

"Of course I do. But what am I going to do about it? Track her down? Follow her to god knows where?"

"How about calling her?"

"I've tried. Her cell phone has been disconnected."

"Wow. That was fast."

"Tell me about it."

"So, do you think she had…you know…been planning this for a while?"

"Of course I do. It was so perfectly orchestrated that there was no way she just decided to leave on the fly."

"Maybe, she'll realize that the grass isn't greener and come back."

"I don't think so. I think she's gone for good. Tonight…I'm almost positive…was my last time ever seeing her. She's made up her mind, and once Celaine has her mind made up there's no going back."

"You don't think there's someone else, do you?"

"No." He shook his head definitively. "Celaine is the most honorable woman I've ever met. If there was someone else, she would have been honest with me. What took her away from here…from me…had to be greater than anything we could possibly think of."

# 13

# THE ORIENTATION

*BEEP...BEEP...BEEP.* It felt like I had only been asleep for ten minutes when the tone went off. Startled, I shot up out of bed and looked around the room. Was it some sort of alarm? Should I be concerned? I stumbled to the door in a daze, fumbling around its surface in search of a knob before I remembered that there was a button for that. My hand felt around the rough exterior of the wall until I felt the smooth circular button. The door obediently slid open, allowing me to wander into the hallway, stopping when I reached Blake's door.

After noticing it was steel, I decided not to knock on it and began searching for an alternate way of alerting him. My eyes scanned the door. A plate similar to mine was mounted next to it, but I doubted that it would open for my fingerprint. I sighed as I leaned against the door, allowing it to support the weight of my frustrated body. Considering there was no smoke in the hallway, the alarm probably wasn't signaling any kind of dire emergency.

Then, in an instant, the door I'd been leaning on disappeared. With a crash, my body fell forward as I lost my balance. A deafening squeal escaped my mouth the moment my elbow violently struck the floor. "Ouch!" I exclaimed.

"Funny," Blake's voice bellowed above me. "I've always dreamt of women falling at my feet, but somehow this just isn't as hot as I thought it would be."

"Have I told you how charming you are?" Embarrassed, I reached my hand up toward Blake. He grabbed it, helping me to my feet all while never losing the amused smirk painted on his face. "Let me guess. This is their sadistic way of waking us up to greet the day each morning?"

Blake laughed. "You catch on quick."

"This is an everyday thing?"

"Correct again."

"Swell."

"Isn't it, though? It's our own little slice of heaven. If I were you, I would get ready. You have about five minutes to report."

"Report? What is this, the military?"

"Worse."

"So, what does one wear to orientation?"

"Well, for me, what I have on. For you, whatever they give you when you report."

From what Blake had on, it was obvious he was going to be working out or doing some sort of physical labor and, from the looks of his physique, it must be something he did a lot. Before now, I hadn't noticed how impressive his biceps were. They were unnatural. I imagined him as being able to pick up a car and hurl it through a brick wall. He began to flex when he noticed my obvious admiration. "Yep, these bad boys always get the ladies' attention," he said, smirking. A wave of heat overcame my face. "On second thought, follow me," he said, making his way down the hall. "It's not like you need to make yourself presentable for what you're going to be going through today."

Confused even more than I already was, I followed him down the hall. It had pained him to say that last statement. I wondered what he meant by it and what I had gotten myself into.

"Oh, by the way," he called out. "The next time you want to come into my room, just put your thumb to the finger plate. Since you're in the system, it will announce your presence and the door will open to the inside of each of our cells. Unless, of course, you like fainting in my presence."

"You could have told me that last night."

"I suspected you'd figure it out for yourself."

"I'm here, aren't I? Apparently, there isn't much I can figure out on my own."

"Isn't that the truth."

We reached a set of double doors; steel, just like the rest of the building. He walked over to a pad on the wall to the right of the door and began inputting a code of some sort into it.

"You'll be assigned various codes for all of the entrances and exits in and out of this place that you will be expected to memorize."

"Wow, this place is secured tighter than Fort Knox," I marveled.

"This place houses value greater than that of Fort Knox."

"Why? Is there gold, diamonds, artifacts…scandalous government secrets?"

"No. It houses us."

I followed Blake through the double doors into far more inviting quarters resembling more of a five star hotel than an underground dungeon. The granite floors shone in the light coming through the windows. Windows; there were windows. This place may be more tolerable than I thought. Before us appeared a sitting room complete with a television bordering on being the size of a movie screen. High on the vaulted ceilings, a chandelier was displayed over the array of leather furniture dotting the room. For an added touch, fresh flowers bloomed throughout the entirety of the room, adding a much appreciated touch of feminism to this fortress of steel.

"Don't be fooled by the windows," Blake commented. "They're fake, and so is the daylight you see coming through them."

"So, we're still underground?"

"At least a good seventy feet."

"Way to burst my bubble."

He guided me down yet another corridor to the right of the sitting room. Along this corridor were even more rooms with even more steel doors.

"That door," Blake began, "leads to the gymnasium and simulation room. In a few days, you will be spending a lot of time in that room."

"Why in a few days?"

"That's something they'll explain to you," he said grimly.

"Wait. What's going on?" I stopped following him down the hallway. "You've been nothing but pessimistic about everything since we arrived here last night. Coming here was your choice. It's what you wanted to do, right?"

"Sometimes an obligation is masked in the guise of a choice."

"Cryptic."

He forced a half smile, commencing his walk down the corridor. "These smaller doors," he gestured, "lead to the rooms of some of the other employees here. Composed mainly of scientists, doctors, chefs, counselors, scouts, computer technicians, and other choice governmental hostages, they, like us, are so dedicated to the Cause that they've opted to give up their identities just to come here, blend in and have their work go unrecognized."

"Some people don't need the recognition."

"Yeah, dead ones. Trust me, when recognition is the only thing you can't have, you begin to crave it. It becomes a necessity, like air. The same goes for human contact."

At the end of the corridor stood an even larger set of double doors, much thicker than the rest.

"What is that – ground zero?"

"It's the nerve of The Epicenter. So, in a sense, yes, it could be considered ground zero. That is where you will be spending your time for the next few days."

"That's where an ordinary human becomes a superhuman?"

He shot a sideways glance in my direction. "Yeah, super," he grumbled. We turned left down another corridor where I could hear other voices echoing throughout the hall. "We're going to the dining hall," he announced without missing a stride. "Everyone has gathered for breakfast, and you're going to be the honored guest."

"Honored guest? Look at me. I literally just rolled out of bed."

"Like I said, you won't need to look presentable for what you're going to be doing today."

"But still...you know, first impressions and all."

"Trust me, this isn't the first time any of them have seen you."

"You've all been stalking me...good to know."

"Here goes nothing," he said, entering the dining hall.

The dining hall was just as elaborate as the sitting room. A ridiculously long oak table filled with people sat prominently in the middle of it. Every five feet, a candelabrum was displayed on the table with flames dancing from each of them, putting on a show for their captive audience. Curtains framed the faux windows with daylight streaming in, adding a touch of normalcy to a place that was anything but. Busboys and waiters blew past me, carrying trays of food. My stomach let out a sigh of approval. It had been a while since I last ate anything.

"Good morning there, Celaine," a familiar voice called out. My eyes scanned the table, taking in all of the unfamiliar faces until one familiar one caught my gaze. "You're...looking...well...uh...you're *really* looking," Cameron said.

"Cameron, geez," a fair haired woman with a peaches and cream complexion said in obvious disgust. "Have you no couth?" She looked at me apologetically. "The rest of us really do have some class."

"It's okay," I replied. "I had a younger brother once." I couldn't take my eyes off her. Aside from being pretty, something was familiar about her. Her face was one I'd definitely seen before but couldn't quite place where I'd seen it and, from her expression, I could tell the same was true for her about me.

Sensing my confusion, she spoke again. "My name is Kara, and I'm a nurse here. I'm sure you're a little overwhelmed as there is a lot to take in here. I wish I could tell you that it gets easier and that things start to make more sense, but as any one of these men and women could tell you, it doesn't. You just have to take everything one day at a time and just know that, if you ever need to talk to someone, we're all in the same boat as you." She paused, trying to gauge my expression. "I guess what I'm trying to say is, my door is always open."

"Yeah, you better leave it open, too," Blake muttered.

"Thank you, Kara," I replied.

Blake motioned for me to follow him, leading me around the table to two empty seats facing Kara and Cameron. He gestured to each person at the table, giving me a formal introduction. "Seated next to Cameron are Edwin, Lars and Marcus, our scientists. Next are our physicians, Dr. Harris and Dr. Martin and therapist, Dr. Lin. Then there are the tech guys, Kyle and Drew. Finally, there are our researchers and inside intelligence officers including Lana, Brian, Inez and Caine. Our kitchen staff you see running around here consist of Henry, Colby and Becca."

"Is everyone going to wear name tags for the new girl?" I asked him under my breath.

He rolled his eyes; a gesture I was sure I was going to receive quite frequently from him. Everyone around the table took the time to give me a friendly smile and "hello".

Inez, at least I think it was Inez, spoke next. "Celaine, I trust you'll find our accommodations fitting."

I wondered if that was a question or a statement. "They're great, thank you," I replied.

"Actually, I think they suck, but that's just my opinion," Drew offered.

"Always the pessimist," Brian muttered.

Kara spoke up again. "We all really get along much better than this. It's just been an off day and, well, quite frankly, we're still trying to figure out how to act in front of you. Testing the waters, so to speak."

I could tell that Kara was trying her best to make me feel welcome and a part of the group. "Well," I offered, "just act the way you normally would."

"In that case," Cameron interceded.

"Oh, god," Kara sighed.

"I'm Cameron, I'm single, and my room is just a couple of doors down from yours, so if you're ever lonely and want to engage in a nice long…" A collective gasp, intermingled with chuckles, emanated around the table. Kara's face turned bright red with her horrified expression still evident even after she backhanded Cameron over the head. "Ouch! What? I was going to say conversation," he said.

"Well, you have to admit, she left the door wide open on that one," Lars said.

"Yeah, that's Cameron. Our brilliant yet socially inept walking hormone," Lana chuckled.

I looked over at the head of the table, noticing that the seat stood empty. Curious, I caught Blake's eye and nodded towards the empty chair.

He leaned in and whispered into my ear, "That's Victor's seat. He'll be joining us shortly."

"Is he the head honcho here?"

"Unfortunately."

I shot a look of disbelief at him, wondering what in the world would elicit such an unenthused response from him. It'd become increasingly clearer to me that Blake was none too happy with the life he had chosen for himself, and I found myself wondering what had brought him here in the first place. A sudden clang at the table jolted me back to reality. Becca and Colby were arranging various platters with what I could only assume to be breakfast on them. The aroma was almost too much to bear, and I was dying to rip the covers off the platters right then and there but didn't think that would go over too well.

"Oh, Celaine," Kara's voice pierced through my anticipation. "We never asked if you had any food allergies or preferences in food choices."

"Believe me," I replied, "even if I *did* have allergies, I would look the other way right now and, as far as preferences are concerned, I have the sinking suspicion that a few of you may already know what those are. It's become pretty obvious that there are no secrets around here."

A few uncomfortable glances were exchanged across the table. Kara looked at me with a twinge of guilt etched on her face. "I'm sorry," she said. "We really should have tried to make you feel a little more comfortable. We just didn't want to smother you right away with all you've been through so far."

I realized then that I'd been a bit rude. "I'm sorry," I said, looking around the table. "This isn't like me. I've just had a rough few hours."

"That's completely understandable," Edwin spoke up. "As much as I admire the task placed upon your and Blake's shoulders, I don't envy you."

"Me neither," Blake grumbled.

"Well, aren't we just big balls of sunshine this morning. How about we just eat and let Victor catch up later?" Kara announced.

"Oh, thank god," I said.

An eruption of laughter reverberated across the table. "Hey, at least this one has personality," Edwin said. Blake shot him a dirty look.

"Well, on that note," Becca giggled, lifting the covers off the various platters.

"Dig in, Celaine," Kara offered.

She didn't have to tell me twice, and my plate filled up fast with scrambled eggs, toast and waffles, anything to satisfy the hunger pangs in my stomach. It was breakfast heaven. I looked over at Blake. His plate appeared scarce as he sat in his chair looking bored, rolling a scrambled egg around its perimeter with his fork.

"Is it like this every day?" I asked, trying to lighten him up a little.

"Pretty much." It grew quiet around the table while everyone ate. I wasn't sure if it was the norm around here or if it was just because no one knew how to speak to the new girl.

"We're not usually this quiet," Lars broke the silence after a moment. "It's just that we're all still pretty somber as, I'm sure you've heard, we lost Blake's former partner, your predecessor, Liam, a few days ago."

"I had heard something about that." I set my fork down and looked at Lars. "I'm sorry about your loss...all of your losses." Everyone shook their heads collectively. "How, if I may ask, did he die? I didn't think that could happen to people like him and Blake."

"Science isn't perfect," Lars answered. "As much as we believe we've perfected something, there are always exceptions. We just haven't found a way to keep people from dying – yet. In fact, we came pretty close to losing Blake too that night."

I looked at Blake. For someone who'd been on the brink of death only a few days prior, he didn't look half bad. "What are my odds of dying, too?" I asked. I noticed that no one at the table would look me in the eyes except Cameron, who saw it fit to offer an answer to my question. "Well, I guess it all depends on whether or not you survive today."

Kara's face turned an instant shade of crimson, more from anger than embarrassment this time. A loud snap sounded next to me. When I turned to find the source, I noticed that Blake's fork was broken in half next to his plate.

"That was uncalled for, Cameron," Inez spoke up.

"Exactly what is going to happen to me today?" I asked.

"She needs to know," Edwin piped in.

Dr. Martin added, "I know she needs to know. I just figured that we were going to have Victor explain it to her like he did with the others."

"And he will." A voice boomed from the doorway, startling everyone but Blake.

"Good morning, Victor," Cameron called cheerfully. The same greeting from everyone but Blake followed.

"Good morning, everyone," Victor greeted us.

He appeared normal for a man of his power, with only a hint of menacing sprinkled in. Tall and broad in stature, he was pale, almost deathly so. Despite it being summer, he was clad in a way-too-warm-looking turtle neck paired with dress slacks. He scoured the table until his eyes met mine, a smile spreading across his pointed face. It reminded me of the wide-eyed hungry look of a cat preparing to pounce on an unsuspecting mouse. My heart began pounding, my stomach sinking as he made his way to me. At that moment, my head told me that the proper thing to do was to stand, so I did, an act which seemed to please him. Cordially, he took my hand and bowed.

*"Enchanté, mademoiselle."*

Oh, great, not only did he scare the shit out of me, he was a charmer as well. This was going to be interesting.

"I trust, Celaine, that everyone here has made you feel welcome?"

"Yes," I said. "They've all been trying." Kara gave me a sheepish smile.

"That's good to hear. I apologize for the lackluster sleeping quarters but, as I'm sure Blake already pointed out to you, you won't be using them much." Victor made his way to his seat at the head of the table.

"He mentioned something about that," I said, sitting back down. "I'm not going to be able to sleep much? I think my body will beg to differ."

"I think not." Victor loaded his plate up as if he hadn't eaten for a month. "You'll be amazed by what your body is going to be able to do."

"With all due respect, I honestly don't know why you picked me of all people. There's nothing strong about me. I'm not fast, agile or even graceful for that matter."

"A mere formality. Trust me, after today, you will think differently."

With that, Blake excused himself, standing up to leave the table. His demeanor had changed substantially since Victor's appearance.

"Really, Blake," Victor interceded in his retreat. "You should eat more. You need to keep up your strength."

"I'll work on it," he said, annoyed.

Victor shook his head, mumbling something inaudible. I must have still been stunned by the sheer amount of food on Victor's plate as he caught me staring at it and chuckled. "Eat up," he said to me, breaking my trance. "After you're done eating, Celaine, please accompany me to Dr. Harris and Dr. Martin's office, and I will brief you about the events of the day."

# 14

## THE TRANSFORMATION

THE DOCTORS' LAB was unlike anything I had ever seen before even in all my meanderings through the halls of Hope Memorial as a child. It was a mixture of a mad scientist's lab with a dash of high tech trauma bay included for appearances. There were books scattered about one corner of the room as though it served as some sort of research center. Medical encyclopedias, some of which I recognized from my father's den, along with computers and other monitoring devices, dotted the room, encircling what resembled an operation table of sorts. Tubes led to pumps, the likes of which I'd never seen before; cords led to monitors and other large, unfamiliar devices. Surgical tools were dispersed throughout the room, ready to report for duty at a moment's notice.

Despite all of the obvious technological anomalies in this pseudo-hospital, one common link remained: the smell of sterility. In a strange way, this familiar smell set my mind a little more at ease, creating an odd sense of comfort. I searched the room some more. Alongside one of the walls stood a sink, wash basin and counters. But it was the peculiarity situated directly above the sink that caught my eye. Upon further examination, I deduced that it was probably a window to what was most likely a viewing room like the viewing rooms the interns and residents used at the hospital to view surgical procedures. *Great, if I die today, I'm going to have a captive audience*, I thought.

"Impressive, isn't it?" a voice from behind me enquired in a tone meaning he meant it to be more of a statement of fact than an actual question. I turned around and saw that Dr. Martin had entered the room.

"Yes," I replied. "I spent a good share of my childhood following my father around in the hospital he practiced at and, I must say, I'm ashamed to admit I couldn't tell you what most of this equipment does...or... really what it even is for that matter."

"That's because you've never come across some of this equipment. It's not available in modern hospitals and won't be for another ten to fifteen more years."

"I'm going to be a guinea pig, then?"

"Nope. Blake was our guinea pig. We've thankfully worked out all of the kinks just in time for you."

"Well, that's reassuring. So, tell me, will this surgery cause me to develop the same sparkling personality Mr. Cohen so exuberantly displays?"

"Afraid not. He came off the assembly line with that one. It wasn't one of the after-market parts we installed."

"What do you mean by 'install'? I'm not going to wake up with a third eye or something, am I?"

Dr. Martin glanced up at me with a sly grin, returning to his notepad to scribble down more notes.

"Don't let him worry you." Dr. Harris entered the room with Victor following close at his heels.

"Marty here just needs to work on his bedside manner," Dr. Harris chuckled, patting Dr. Martin on the back. "We won't let anything too bad happen to you."

"How about we start with what's going to happen to me." I felt a twinge of concern.

"Gentlemen," Victor interceded. "If you will allow me, I will explain it to her." The doctors nodded while Victor moved to face me, looking at me with an icy glare so piercing that it sent chills through my body. "The human body is an amazing creation as I'm sure you're aware." Something about Victor made me uneasy. His half-smile exacerbated this uneasiness.

"You see, unlike the rest of the living organisms in this world, our kind can think and feel. We learn and we improvise. We develop meaningful relationships with each other that blossom into love. However, with all the exceptional natural abilities we possess, we are also fatally flawed with our sheer physical limitations. We're weak…slow when compared to most animals, lacking a measurable amount of agility and strength. Physically, we are essentially at the bottom of the food chain when compared to our opposable-thumbed deficient friends." He braced himself against the operating table as though the very act of standing and lecturing were too much for him. "Fortunately for us, though, there is a feature that unites us with the rest of the pack, whether they are a denizen of the land, sea or air. Have you ever heard of the fight or flight response, Celaine?"

"Sure. It's where your body senses the presence of danger and prepares itself by releasing adrenaline through your system."

"Good. The fight or flight response is one of the most primitive defense mechanisms that we humans possess. The hypothalamus sends chemical signals to the adrenal glands, activating the sympathetic system, causing the adrenal glands to release adrenaline and noradrenaline from the amino acids phenylalanine and tyrosine." At this point in Victor's lecture I wished I'd actually read one of George's medical encyclopedias. "These hormones create a state of readiness that aid us, as humans, to confront challenges head-on, making us more agile and giving us the ability to exhibit astounding strength."

I remembered the stainless steel fork Blake so effortlessly broke in half and shuddered.

"I'm sure you've heard the story that tends to go around of the mother who miraculously picked up a car that had fallen onto her child. Well, what if that kind of strength could be controlled…or harnessed? What if a person could be in a constant state of readiness with the capabilities of producing that kind of strength at the drop of a hat?" Victor stood up and proceeded to walk around the room.

"That very question was one that was posed here by the minds you see present in this very room; and has been a question of which we've made and continue to make numerous attempts at answering. Until Blake came along, our attempts almost always failed. We were starting to get discouraged, to say the least. You see, Celaine, there aren't too many people whose bodies can handle the stress placed upon them by a constant river of adrenaline flowing through their veins. We simply had to learn more about adrenaline, including its effects on the human body, and counteract those effects the best we could."

"When a person has adrenaline flowing through their system, their muscles contract more than they normally would when their body is in a state of calmness. In a state of tranquility, our blood flows easier throughout our muscles. Additional oxygen is, in turn, carried to them by this extra blood, allowing the muscles to function at elevated levels. Our skeletal muscles, however, are activated by electrical impulses from the nervous system. When stimulated, these muscles contract. It is the same contraction that occurs when one lifts an object or throws a punch at someone. However, in a state of calmness, we only use a very minute percentage of our muscles' capabilities. It's only when we're confronted with the danger that precipitates the fight or flight response that we can transcend our perceived limitations and simply act. This fact is illustrated after a person is electrocuted, wherein they experience a sudden and violent contraction of the muscles, throwing them an impressive distance from the source of the electrocution. Many people assume it's the blast that catapults them through the air when it's their muscles' response to the immediate danger that actually does this."

"Okay," I interrupted. "From what I'm gathering, I'm going to be electrocuted in some fashion to produce adrenaline?"

"Yes. In a sense."

"Would you mind explaining to me how it is I'm *not* going to die from that?"

"It's a crap shoot," Dr. Martin chimed in.

"Yes," Victor agreed. "That is a good description for it."

*Well, that's just beautiful*, I thought. Knots began to form within the depths of my stomach, making me wonder whether the fight or flight response would allow me to get the hell out of here. After deciding that, no, it probably wouldn't and determining that, after I was caught by Blake that I would most likely be snapped in half like some defenseless fork, I decided to stay put. Nonetheless, it irritated me to think that everything I'd given up would have been for nothing if I died here today. This would mean that I'd devastated the people I dearly loved just to fulfill a pipe dream.

"However," Dr. Harris interjected, taking me away from my morbid thoughts, "we haven't lost a single person since before Blake. We've refined our technique and have thus far been able to control the side effects."

"Side effects?" I asked. Obviously, I was in for more than I bargained for.

"An increased amount of adrenaline raises your blood pressure, increasing your heart rate. Many of our failures sustained fatal heart arrhythmias when their bodies simply couldn't handle the adrenaline rush any longer. However, with that being said, we have been successfully able to counteract the effects of it with a cocktail of daily medications including beta blockers, antidepressants, ADHD medications, antihypertensives and multivitamins. Plus, you will be asked to wear a heart monitor at all times so we can constantly monitor your heart functions to determine if you're in danger of going into cardiac arrest."

"You said I wouldn't need to sleep anymore. Is it because of the adrenaline rush?"

"It's not that you won't need sleep anymore. Your body, although much more resilient, won't be invincible, and sleep will still be the only real way it can repair and recharge itself. You will be given sedatives to take to calm you down enough to get to sleep when necessary. Blake usually sleeps around three days a week and always seems well rested. Our bodies are all different. Only time can tell how yours will react."

"What does this procedure entail?"

"We will be performing an operation wherein we will insert this into the base of your brain stem." Dr. Harris held out a small metallic rod in his hand. My best estimation put it to be around an inch in length. "This transmitter emits enough electrical waves to keep your brain stimulated, producing adrenaline."

"Again, how does this not limit my body in other ways or make my essential organs fail. I mean, this can't possibly be good for a person's body." I looked at the transmitter, bewildered. The prospect of brain surgery rendered me extremely uncomfortable.

"Blake and the others have done exceedingly well. The pharmacological therapy we have been able to come up with has stabilized their bodies, preventing the severe limitation of essential functions while still maintaining the same exceptional physical level of performance."

"Others? Do you mean that Blake had another partner aside from the one that was recently killed?"

"Yes. He had two others, in fact," Victor chimed in. "But don't worry, their demise had nothing to do with the surgery or the subsequent effects it will have on your body. Just because your body is being enhanced to an almost impervious state doesn't mean you're going to be immortal. You still need to maintain your wits about you and not be so cavalier with your newfound abilities. Your predecessors didn't see it that way and decided to play hero instead of working together as a team."

"How did the public not know there were others?"

"All of Blake's partners were men of the same build, and it's not like we hold press conferences here. No one speaks of this place, where it's located or what we do. As far as the public is concerned, we don't exist."

"Why are there just two people at a time? Wouldn't an army be a little more successful and ultimately fulfill your purposes?"

"Do you think that would be wise, Celaine? Let's say, theoretically, we build an army. A few of them start having delusions of grandeur or simply go off the deep end and decide to revolt. Do you know what kind of mayhem we would have on our hands? It could be a catastrophe in and of itself the likes of which not even The Man in Black could produce. We'd lose everything, our integrity, our funding...not to mention the impact it would have on the public."

"Funding? So, this is a government project after all?"

Victor let out an amused chuckle. "Oh, Celaine, you're too smart for your own good. What do you say we get started now as poor Blake is in desperate need of some help? Particularly, if the Man in Black shows his face around here in the near future."

"Don't you think his existence is kind of odd in a way?"

Victor raised an eyebrow. "Pardon me?"

"Doesn't his mere existence beg the question of how?" How was he created? Is there another place churning out super villains just like this place is churning out super humans?"

"Those are answers we won't know until The Man in Black is dealt with, which we can only hope will be soon." Victor picked up a scalpel and proceeded to check out his appearance in its reflective surface. Satisfied, he set it back down. "The surgery will take approximately three hours to complete, but you will be out of it for a good day thereafter. When you return to consciousness, you will be exceptionally sore and will regret ever coming here or perhaps even being born for that matter. But, in a few days, you will notice a difference in your body. We will begin conditioning you at that time." Victor looked up at me with an eerie twinkle in his eye. "Unless you've changed your mind about going through with this?"

I glanced at him. "There is no way I'm going to back out now. I made a promise a long time ago, and I'm not one to break my promises. Besides, something tells me that even if I wanted to back out, I wouldn't be able to."

A look of surprise briefly came over Victor's face but was quickly replaced with the same snide chuckle he exuded a moment ago. "Like I said, you're too smart for your own good. Well, Celaine, I will leave you to the capable hands of these fine gentlemen. When I see you next, you will literally be a new woman."

"I can't wait."

Victor turned and left the room. I looked over at Dr. Martin expectantly while butterflies threw a party in my stomach.

"Well," Dr. Martin began, "it's now or never. In the room next to the wash basin are a couple of hospital gowns. I don't think I have to explain to you what the drill is with the gowns. Once you've changed, hop up on that table over there and we'll proceed."

Though only a few feet from me, the journey to the changing room seemed like it took forever plus an eternity to complete. Upon entering the room, the door shut behind me with a loud thud, making me jump. The events of the day had taken their toll on my nerves as well as my body. I felt dizzy and sat down on the floor. In my mind, I knew I was doing the right thing by being here. After all, hadn't this been everything I'd prayed for during the last ten years? Still, my nerves were shot at the prospect of what this surgery would do to me. Would I still be me? If I were to defeat The Man in Black, allowing me to be able to resume my normal life again, would Chase still want the new woman that I was going to become? Chase. The thought of him sent a wave of sadness rushing through my body. I wished he could be here with me now, to hold me and tell me it was all going to be all right.

Not wanting to delay the inevitable anymore, I stood up and began undressing. The gowns were neatly folded on shelves in the back of the room. I folded my clothes, swapping them out for one of the blue-striped gowns. The thin sheath did nothing to shield the chill in the air. After taking a deep breath, I grabbed the back of the gown and held it as I made my way back out of the room, being careful not to accidentally give a show to whomever may be sitting in the viewing room. Drs. Martin and Harris were outfitted in their surgical attire and were ready for me when I walked out. I nodded at them, climbing up onto the table.

"Okay," Dr. Harris said, "lay back, close your eyes, count backwards from one hundred, and then sweet dreams."

I reclined on the table, taking in a couple of breaths to sooth my nerves. Dr. Harris put the mask over my face, reaching over to turn on the anesthesia. Just when I could feel myself starting to drift off, I looked over in the direction of the viewing room. Sitting on one of the chairs watching over me was Blake with a look of pity etched upon his face.

# 15
## THE THEORY

IT HAD BEEN three days since Chase Matthews last saw her. They say that time was supposed to heal all wounds, but to him it was like treating a laceration with a band aid. The damage had been done; a deep cut through the skin covered up by a more appealing shell. He sat in the audience of the packed Met Theater, trying to put on a front that pronounced more strength than hopelessly damaged. He was failing miserably, as anyone and everyone could tell. Even complete strangers looked at him with empathetic glances. Seated next to him were Carrie and Jim. For the last two days they'd comforted their son, making futile attempts at lifting his spirits, trying to bring him out of his virtually comatose state.

Exactly forty-eight hours ago, Carrie received an unusual letter in the mail. Within five minutes after having read it, she was on the road to his apartment to be with him. He'd missed work the past couple of days, which was unusual for him, and only got out of bed when nature called. Carrie sat with him at his apartment, forcing him to eat and drink, trying her best to console him in his endeavor to find the reasoning behind the events that had transpired.

Carrie, Jim and MaKayla had all known about his plans to propose to the woman they'd all grown quite fond of over the years. MaKayla always wanted a big sister and was thrilled that her brother had chosen a candidate that met with her stringent standards. Celaine and MaKayla had clicked right away, often engaging in girl talk and shopping trips.

Needless to say, they were waiting impatiently by the telephone on the night he was to propose, growing restless as the hours went by, and then ultimately becoming concerned when their phone calls went unanswered. Concern grew into alarm after receiving a message that Celaine's phone had been disconnected when they attempted to reach her. They'd been seconds away from making a call to the police when Carrie received the letter in the mail, and it all began to make sense. She looked over at her son with a half-hearted smile. Despite the obvious attempt at being all right, he wasn't even remotely there. Her son was no stranger to break-ups. He was handsome, having had several girlfriends. However, none of those girls struck him the way Celaine had. Just a mere three weeks into their relationship, Carrie knew that she was the one for her son. He'd never looked at any of them the way he looked at her.

A hush fell over the crowd, forcing Chase to concentrate on the stage instead of his own misery. MaKayla was so devastated by Celaine's unexplained departure that her choir teacher, Ms. Appleby, asked her if she wanted to back out of performing tonight. After putting some thought into it, and with the help of Jim's insistence, she decided to proceed as planned. Now, she stood on the stage, facing the audience. It was her first solo performance. On top of being nervous, Chase could tell that his sister's heart just wasn't into it like it had been the week prior. MaKayla had always had a beautiful voice but had been far too shy to let others in on that fact. It had been Celaine who'd been able to bring her out of her shell by encouraging her to try out for the choir. In fact, it was during one of Celaine's motherly interactions with his sister that he'd first realized he'd fallen deeply in love with her, knowing without a shadow of a doubt that she'd been put here specifically for him.

MaKayla was singing "Evergreen" from the *Phantom of the Opera*, channeling Christine Daaé to perfection. He listened to his sister nervously, knowing that she had reservations about being able to hit the last note of the song. She'd been practicing it for months, prompting Carrie to invest in a pair of ear plugs after the one hundredth run-through. All the worry was all for naught, though. At the end of her solo,

142

MaKayla hit the last note with such expertise that applause unanimously exploded from the audience, eliciting a smile of brotherly pride over his face. It was the first time he'd smiled in the last seventy-two hours. After the concert, Chase searched the crowd until he found his sister, sneaking up on her and wrapping his arms around her waist in a bear hug.

"I take it you were impressed with my performance," she beamed.

"You were amazing. I never knew you had those kind of pipes on you."

"I have Celaine to thank for that. She really brought them out of me." The mere mention of her mentor's name made her appear sullen. "Have you heard from her yet?"

"No," he replied.

"You will. You'll see. She'll come back to us. I mean, what's not to love about us, right?" she said, choking back tears.

"I hope you're right, kiddo."

"Just do me a favor, okay?"

"Anything."

"Take a shower. You're starting to smell pretty rank." Chase forced a laugh, tousling her hair. "Hey, don't mess up the do."

Carrie and Jim appeared from the depths of the mob with the bouquet of roses they'd bought in honor of their daughter's newfound superstardom.

"We're so proud of you," Jim said, hugging his daughter.

"Hey, something good had to come out of this week, right?"

"I suppose you're right."

Chase returned home two hours later after convincing Carrie that her presence, although appreciated, wasn't necessary and that he'd be returning to business as usual tomorrow. Nonetheless, the apartment seemed empty without her. It emanated a lifeless, cold feeling that made him long for Celaine's presence. In the middle of his living room, he stood motionless in a state of contemplation until deciding to scour the apartment for a box. *Let the healing process begin*, he thought, unconvinced.

After emptying cupboards, searching through closets, and even overturning couch cushions, he located a shoe box buried under a pile of dirty laundry in his bedroom. He took the box to the couch and sat down as though a moment of contemplation would change what he knew needed to be done. For several minutes, he sat on the couch in the middle of his sparsely decorated living room, staring at the box, wondering whether he had the strength to do it and live up to his promise to Carrie.

After several minutes, he stood up and proceeded to walk around the perimeter of his apartment, gathering all of the photographs and mementos that had defined his life over the last couple of years. With the box overflowing, he located some room in the back of his closet and shoved it, along with the memories it contained, away. Out of sight and out of mind. Perhaps, for more fickle-minded people, that concept held water, but to him it was full of holes.

With all of the photographs, trinkets and notes gone, his apartment seemed even more barren and desolate. Task completed, he once again plopped down on the couch, staring off into space before forcing himself to snap out of it by turning on the television. He'd never been much of a drinker, but still kept some alcohol in his refrigerator as, every once in a while, he and Celaine had used it to unwind. Trey also appreciated a good drink every now and then, usually raiding his kitchen whenever he came to visit. These days, it seemed like he was only buying the beer to keep Trey happy. For times such as this, he was happy he did. A distinct urge to escape from reality overcame him as he stood up and headed to the kitchen, where he opened the refrigerator in the hope of finding something to do the trick.

Opening the refrigerator, however, revealed a gallon of expired milk and a tub of butter. This discovery made him appreciate Carrie's visit even more as he would have surely starved to death had she not come to see him. He let out a disgusted sigh, deciding that was probably his cue to go to bed instead, but when walked back into the living room he heard a knock at the door.

"Hey, man." Trey greeted him.

Chase's eyes darted from Trey, switching focus to the case of beer gripped firmly between his fingers.

"Man, you're a life saver," he said, lunging for the case and whisking it off into the kitchen.

"I'm happy to see you, too."

Chase cracked a can open and chuckled. "Sorry, you just have no idea how badly this is hitting the spot right now."

"Well, it's good to see you up and laughing a little. I was starting to wonder whether I was going to have to drag your sorry ass out of bed and beat you back to reality."

"Funny, my mom said the same thing."

"Really? I always knew Carrie and I were perfect for each other. It's too bad your dad got in the way."

"Hey, man, not cool."

"What? Your mom's hot."

"Would you shut up?"

"Okay, okay, but seriously, it's good to have my best friend back, even if he is turning into a raging alcoholic."

"You're funny."

"Wow," Trey said after noticing the apartment's barren walls. "Did your mom take all of your pictures with her?"

"No, I took them down just before you got here."

"Well, that explains the beer craving."

"Yep."

"So, do you think she's still around here?"

"You know, it's funny because a part of me still feels that she's close, even though she told me she was moving to the other side of the country. You can't be as close to someone as her and I were without developing a sort of sixth sense about them. I always felt like our souls were connected...that we always knew what the other was thinking. I just know there was something she wasn't telling me. The pain in her eyes was so real. I think it was even worse than mine."

"Was your mom upset about the necklace?"

"The strange thing about that is...no, she wasn't. I expected to be all but disowned by her after I told her. I mean, you know that necklace had been in her family for a couple of generations, but, she wasn't even concerned about it. It's like she loved Celaine so much that she felt like the necklace belonged to her...like it didn't belong around anyone else's neck but hers." Chase placed the empty beer can on the coffee table where it made a sharp *clang* as it struck the surface. Standing up, he headed back to the kitchen for round two.

"Pace yourself, man. This isn't a drinking marathon," Trey mused.

"I'm just grabbing one more, then I'm done. Besides, I have to return to the hospital tomorrow afternoon. And I'm pretty sure my patients wouldn't appreciate their doctor being hung over while he's examining them."

"Yeah, that would put a whole new meaning to the term turn your head and cough." Trey repositioned himself, resting his feet on the coffee table. "You're going back? I thought you were out on sick leave the rest of the week?"

"Actually, it's called mental health leave or, in layman's terms, 'get your sanity back and don't return until then, you poor, crazy bastard' leave."

"Ouch."

"Tell me about it. You wouldn't believe the looks I received in the break room after I told the chief about it. Everyone was whispering and looking at me like they weren't sure whether or not to pat me on the back, offer their condolences, or leave me the hell alone to sulk in my own sorrow. Not to mention, I'm now known as the crazy resident."

"I think that nickname will go away once they've seen how far you've come in only a matter of a couple of days. Which, speaking of, how about you and I hit the bar up next weekend? We could find us some girls to dance with and have a good time like we used to."

Chase looked up from his can of beer. "No, I don't think I'm quite *that* healed yet."

"Your loss."

Another knock at the door startled them.

"You expecting a hot date or something?" Trey asked.

"Not that I'm aware of. Maybe it's my mom coming back to check on me."

"Well, in that case, send her over my way. I'll make her comfortable."

"Don't make me hurt you." Chase looked through the peephole which revealed Lucy standing nervously on the other side of the door in her oversized jogging pants and her long, blonde hair pulled back in a tight pony tail. She'd been out jogging, and it appeared as though coming to his apartment had been an afterthought.

"It's Lucy," Chase called to Trey in a hushed tone.

"Really? Is she still with Luke because if not, you can send her over here, too."

"Down, boy." Chase shook his head and unlatched the door.

"Hey, Chase," Lucy greeted him, giving him a hug as she stepped into the apartment, where she spotted Trey sitting on the couch."

"Hey you, too, Trey," she said.

"Hey, Lucy. What's up?"

"I was just out and about for my nightly jog and thought I would drop by to see how you're holding up." She looked sheepishly at Chase.

"Lucy, it's past curfew. What are you doing out?" Chase asked.

Lucy extracted her badge from its perch, tucked in her shirt on a chain around her neck. "I'm a doctor," she announced. "Curfew doesn't apply to me."

"I thought you were a psychiatrist?" Trey asked in a confused tone.

"Same difference. I can prescribe medications, I just can't perform surgery. Although, I would like to do some mean work with a scalpel on some of the whack jobs I have to deal with."

"So, what's your excuse when you're stopped on the street by the law? 'Oh, I'm sorry officer. I just had to go out and talk a guy out of throwing himself off a bridge'."

"I've used that one before, and you would be surprised by how effective it is."

Trey laughed. "Man, I am in the wrong profession."

Lucy turned to Chase. "How are you holding up?"

"I'm better than I was three days ago."

"Wow, you're going through the stages of grief faster than a lot of individuals I counsel. Have you hit anger yet? Because I see it in a lot of my patients who've recently separated with their..."

"Please don't use any of your psycho-babble bullshit on me, Lucy."

"I'm sorry, Chase...it's...it's just that *I'm* not holding up well and my psycho-babble bullshit is the only way I know how to cope with it."

Chase sighed, placing his hand on Lucy's shoulder. "Sorry, Luce, I didn't mean for it to come out as harsh as it did."

"It's okay." Tears cascaded from the corners of her eyes.

"Luce, look, I didn't mean to offend you. Don't...don't cry, please."

"Chase, it's not you. Look, the reason I came over is two-fold."

"What are you talking about?"

"It's guilt, Chase. I feel so incredibly guilty. Ever since I received that letter in the mail, I've done nothing but beat myself up." She looked up at Chase's confused face with tears past the realm of controllable. "Before she left, Celaine called me. It was obvious she was very conflicted about something. She mentioned some sort of opportunity…she was vague about it. She said that this new opportunity may or may not give her everything she's ever wanted and I told her to…to…" She could barely make out the last words. "I told her to go for it. Trust me, had I known she was talking about disappearing from the face of this planet, I never would have told her to go ahead with it. On the contrary, I would have done all I could to talk her out of it, to tell her she was crazy and that she already had everything she ever looked for or wanted right here. I would have told her to stay here with the people who loved and cared about her."

Chase slumped down onto the couch with his head in his hands. "It's funny. I always thought the only thing she ever wanted was me. I guess I wasn't enough. Now, I feel stupid for proposing to her."

"Wait. You what? Oh, my God, Chase. I'm sorry. I had no idea."

"That's okay, neither did she."

"What happened? What did she say?"

"She said 'no' and ran like hell."

"Gosh. I never in a million years would have thought it would have ended like this. Heck, I never in a million years thought it would ever end, for that matter. I thought I would be putting up with you for the rest of my life."

"It's nifty how life works out sometimes, huh."

Lucy's eyes caught sight of the beer cans on the coffee table. "You have any more of those?"

"He sure does." Trey sprang from the couch to fetch Lucy a drink.

"What's his deal?" she asked.

"He's a lonely, lonely man."

"I guess I can relate. Luke broke up with me about a month ago."

"Aw, that's a shame." Trey re-appeared from the kitchen, beer in hand, and placed an arm around Lucy's shoulders.

"You have no shame, do you?" she retorted.

"None whatsoever."

She took a seat on the couch. "Well, aren't we just a sad, sad trio."

"You can say that again," Chase replied.

"Speak for yourselves," Trey said, lifting his shirt up to reveal his sculpted abs. "I'm not sad. A little sick, perhaps, but certainly not sad." Lucy choked on a swig of beer and began coughing relentlessly.

Chase rolled his eyes. "Man, put those away before you hurt someone."

"I'm going to find her," Lucy began after reclaiming her composure.

"How do you purport to do that?" Chase asked.

"Our government. I'm sure you've noticed how everything went to hell as soon as President Brooks took over. Unfortunately, no one else seems to."

"What are you getting at?"

"I don't think Celaine is on the other side of the country. In fact, I don't think she's even on the other side of the state for that matter." Chase's eyebrows perked up. "This new job that Celaine supposedly has...I think it has something to do with the Brooks' Administration. That's why she was so secretive. I mean, think about it, Chase. She just left everything and everyone. I'd like to think I know Celaine better than anyone, and the Celaine I know would never agree to do that unless she had no other choice or was threatened in some way."

"As crazy as your conspiracy theory sounds, it does make an iota of sense, I suppose."

"Thanks. I think."

"I'm thinking the alcohol has already kicked in," Trey announced.

Lucy gave Trey a dirty look. "Oh, it's already past midnight," she said, glancing at the clock. "I have to get going. I have a couple of early morning nut bags...I mean patients coming in." She slammed down the rest of her beer, setting the can down on the table. Trey stared at the empty can in disbelief. "Just know that I will do what I can to find her and try to talk some sense into her for you."

"Thanks, Lucy. I appreciate it. It was good seeing you again."

"I'm just happy you don't hate me," she said, opening the door to Chase's apartment.

"I wouldn't go that far," he said with a wink.

"I'll keep in touch." she said, a small smile forming across her face.

The door shut with a thud and she was gone.

"Has that girl gone crazy?"

"I don't know, Trey. I think she's grasping at straws. After all, she and Celaine have known each other for over ten years. Lucy's the type who always has to find reasoning and hidden meanings behind the way people think and how they act. That's what makes her one hell of a psychiatrist."

"Well, she should be careful taking on President Brooks. The second she starts becoming vocal with questioning his motives is the second we can say sayonara to her."

"I didn't know you were such a Brooks detractor."

"Dude's crazy like a fox. But, he's doing what he can to keep us safe, I guess."

"Sure. Safe."

# 16

## THE ROAD TO RECOVERY

FROM THE MOMENT the anesthesia wore off, I was in pain. My muffled, internal screams of pain were actually what brought me back into semi-consciousness from the depths of an unconscious darkness. Never had I been so sore. From the tips of my toes to the roots of every hair in my scalp, it was as though I'd been run over repeatedly. But, although intense, it wasn't the pain that worried me as much as the rapid beating of my heart within my chest. If I hadn't known better, I would have thought I was going into cardiac arrest.

"Give her another dose of the beta blockers," Dr. Martin ordered. A hint of concern was present in his voice.

I felt the prick of a needle piercing my skin, followed by the rush of liquid flowing into my arm. A couple of minutes later, the pounding in my chest subsided to just a slightly more faster-than-normal rhythm. However, just as my heart was pacified, a far more intense pain overtook the rest of my body. *Is this what it feels like to die*? I wondered.

"Damn it," I recognized Dr. Harris' voice. "Why did we have to pick a woman? They're much more susceptible to cardiac arrest."

"What Victor wants, Victor gets," Dr. Martin answered, sticking another needle into my veins. "Although, you have to admit, she's done well despite the slight heart issues. Blake didn't even do this well."

"My guess is that she'll be up and around in the next couple of days." Dr. Harris agreed.

"Definitely, if not sooner. Her vitals are fantastic."

It was all too surreal, hearing people talk about you while they prodded your body without you being able to do anything about it or speak up in your own defense. I felt them examining my body, pushing on my limbs, tapping my joints. Being treated like a lab rat was not something I was too fond of. With each tap, I could feel my irritation increasing exponentially, growing with intensity when they reached my legs. *Tap – tap – tap.* My irritation grew into outright rage, rendering me powerless in controlling my body's response any longer. When Dr. Martin tapped my knee once more, suddenly and without hesitation, my leg sprang up and struck him. His face impacted my knee, causing him to grunt in pain. Seconds later, I heard the thunderous crash of his body impacting with the floor.

"Holy!" Dr. Harris exclaimed, eyes wide in amazement. My eyes fluttered open to survey the damage I'd created. I expected to see Dr. Martin lying at the base of the gurney and was confused when he wasn't on the floor where I thought he should be. "Hold on, let me help you," Dr. Harris called out next to me. "Don't try to get up on your own. You may have broken something."

I followed Dr. Harris with my eyes across the room until he reached Dr. Martin...on the opposite side. No...that wasn't possible. My simple kick couldn't have thrown him across the room.

"She has one hell of a reflex," Dr. Harris remarked, pulling Dr. Martin from the table of surgical equipment he'd landed on.

"Reflex, my ass," he yelled. "She meant to do that."

"Are you injured?"

"Just my pride, and I think my nose as well." Blood trickled out of Dr. Martin's left nostril, dripping onto the collar of his lab coat.

"Absolutely remarkable." I looked up and saw Victor standing over me. A strange look of triumph adorned his face. He looked down at me, noticing that I was conscious. "Ah, you're awake. How are you feeling?"

"I'm in pain," my voice was barely audible. "Lots of pain."

"Yes, well, that's to be expected until your body gets used to the effects of the adrenaline and medications invading your system. With the progress you've displayed thus far, I would imagine you to be up and around and feeling just fine within the next couple of days."

"I heard."

"See, I told you she meant to almost kill me," Dr. Martin grumbled, limping his way back to the gurney.

"Sorry." I said, unconvincingly. "I guess I don't know my own strength."

"Indeed you don't," Victor laughed. "Indeed you don't."

I attempted to sit up, but my entire body felt like dead weight in my efforts and it took me a couple of attempts until I was able to sit up straight enough to see around the room. Once up, I felt myself become overwhelmed by dizziness. Behind me, a machine went off.

"Take it easy, Celaine," Dr. Harris said. "That noise you hear is your heart monitor. We never want to hear it go off like that. From now on, you'll be wearing monitors so we can ensure that you aren't going into cardiac arrest."

"Like I did just a few minutes ago."

"You came close, but the medications were able to regulate your body."

"Will it happen again?"

"It's always a possibility."

"Good to know you turned me into a walking, ticking time bomb."

Kara appeared, pushing a wheelchair. A smile blazed across her perfect alabaster complexion when she saw me. "It's good to see you awake," she said. "I hear you're making outstanding progress. I guess we women really are stronger than men in every way." She smiled at Dr. Martin, who mumbled something inaudible under his breath.

I forced a smile for Kara's sake. Her attempts at making me feel welcome had been very much appreciated. Plus, I still couldn't shake the I-know-her-from-somewhere thought that repeated over and over again in my head like a broken record. Dr. Harris and Kara helped me off the gurney and into the wheelchair. As much as I hated the thought of someone helping me that way, I was still feeling dizzy and would've probably fallen flat on my face if I'd tried to do it myself.

"I don't know why you think she needs the help," Dr. Martin fumed. "It's not like she's weak or anything." Kara gave him the look of death.

"Kara here will wheel you to your room," Victor said, "and she will assist you with anything you need. Rest up, and we will assess your condition tomorrow morning to decide how best to proceed next." I nodded at Victor as Kara wheeled me out of the room into the hall.

"You know," she said once she'd wheeled me a safe distance down the hallway, "I respect what you're doing and what you had to give up in order to do it."

"Thanks. How come you're not doing it?"

"They never asked me to. I guess I don't meet their requirements."

"They actually have requirements for this?"

"Well, health-wise, yes. I have a heart murmur and diabetes so all of the drugs I have to take coupled with the added strain it would have on my heart would make it more of a death sentence to me than anything else."

"Oh...geez, Kara. I'm sorry. I didn't know."

"Don't be sorry. I'm still working for the Cause. That satisfies me enough."

We entered the sitting room where Cameron, Kyle and Edwin were watching the massive movie screen of a television.

"It's alive," Cameron announced in his best Dr. Frankenstein imitation.

"Can it, kid," Kara grumbled.

"Hey, Kyle. I guess you owe me fifty big ones."

"I swear, Cameron," Kara began. "I've had about enough of you today. Don't you dare think I won't snap, because I will."

"Oh, come on, Kara. You know I'm just kidding. Besides, I have to say, Celaine, you look a heck of a lot better than Blake did."

"I'll take the credit for that, thank you," Edwin stood up in the middle of the room, beaming. "If it weren't for my new design concept with its more efficient control of the electrical impulses on the brain, she would still be unconscious."

"Wow," I began. "So, when are you going to find something to control the pain because, quite frankly, right now I could care less about how your transmitter is keeping me conscious enough to endure it."

"Dang, Edwin, she told you," Cameron said, amused.

"Yeah, we're still working on that," Edwin replied, deflated.

"Well," Kara chimed in, "I'm going to wheel Celaine to her room. You'll have to flirt with her another night."

"Can do," Cameron winked. Kara rolled her eyes. Something told me this was the only way she knew how to deal with Cameron civilly.

"Does everyone have to stay here?" I asked after Kara wheeled me through the steel doors that lead to my room.

"No, that's the funny thing. The only ones who have to stick around here are you and Blake. The rest of us are free to come and go as long as we stick to the stringent levels of confidentiality required here. But most of us stay anyway. Only Lars, Marcus, Inez, Henry and Becca are married with families or have any semblance of a life. Of course, their families have no idea what it is they do for a living, and I know that, especially for Lars and Marcus, all the secrecy has caused quite a few rifts in their marriages. We work long hours and, although it compares nothing to what Blake and you are doing, we receive free boarding and meals if we choose to utilize them on top of our annual salary. You can't beat that anywhere else."

"I suppose not."

"Besides, Cameron shouldn't be unleashed upon the outside world."

"I'm not going to argue with you there."

"We're all pretty committed to this place. You could say that most of us are a little too committed. Heck, I haven't had a date in five years. But I figure that my sister will never have an opportunity to live her life, let alone date, so I have nothing to complain about."

We arrived at the door to my room. Kara picked up my hand and placed my thumb against the plate. After a quick scan, the door slid open. "Why didn't you just open the door with your thumb?" I asked.

"That would only work if you were in the room."

"Are you saying that the room senses when I'm there?'

"Kind of. It logs you into the system when you enter and when you leave. When you leave, it logs your departure and doesn't allow anyone access unless you've given them permission in the system. When someone wants to enter your room, they press their thumb to the name plate and their presence is announced. You can either say "yes" or "no" to let them in. However, in the case of you and Blake, being who you are, you're automatically allowed entrance into the other's room in case of an emergency. It's nice in a sense. At least you can rest easy knowing that you have some sort of privacy."

She wheeled me to my bed, grabbing me around the waist to help me to my feet. I was a little more wobbly than I'd been back in the lab. With my hand, I searched behind my back until I found the sheet on my bed and allowed myself to plop down, jolting my neck forward, sending a wave of pain through my body. My hand moved up the back of my neck until I hit bandages, locating the surgical incision.

"The stitches should be able to come out in about a week," Kara said reassuringly.

"Did they beat me while I was out, too?"

She smiled. "No. But I would watch my back if I were you around Dr. Martin."

"He doesn't scare me. I can take him."

"I'll give you that."

"Can I ask you a question?" I asked while slowly lifting my feet from the floor to the bed.

"Sure."

"What happened to your sister?" She looked surprised, but not shocked that I'd asked her that question. "I mean, if you don't mind. You don't have to answer that if you don't want to."

"No, it's okay." She spread a thin sheet over my body, rubbing the stiffness out of my arms and legs. "Well, like most of us here, my life was torn apart by all the devastation created by The Man in Black. My sister, Hannah was her name, was driving home from a trip to Annapolis when the bridge she was stuck on during rush hour traffic was bombed. They searched the river and the wreckage for weeks. In the beginning, we prayed they'd find her alive, trapped in her car with only minor injuries. But, as more time passed, we came to the realization that wasn't going to happen. In the end, they never found her body, just pieces of her car."

She'd grown solemn, making me feel guilty for having mentioned it. "I'm sorry, I shouldn't have brought it up," I said.

"It's all right. Besides, I've heard you're no stranger to tragedy yourself."

"I was basically orphaned at the age of seventeen when The Lakes mall was bombed."

"The Lakes? I was there after that happened. Well, I should say I was assisting with the injured in transporting them to Hope Memorial. I'm a certified EMT."

"Hope Memorial? My father was the head of the pediatric unit there."

"Oh, yeah, I'd heard that a doctor from that hospital had been killed. Dr. Stevens. Wow, I don't know how I didn't put two and two together with your last name being Stevens and all."

"You know, it's funny because the moment I first saw you at breakfast I thought you looked familiar." It was then that a moment of clarity struck me like a rogue bolt of lightning. As I looked up at Kara, I realized that I remembered where I'd seen her face before. The memory was blurred, but I remembered the face perfectly. "You said you were an EMT. This may be a stupid question but…did you, by chance, work solely out of an ambulance or did you pretty much stay at the scene of the explosion to assist with the injured?"

"I treated the injured via ambulance from the scene until their arrival at Hope Memorial. I was also interviewed on the news later that night about the need for more volunteers and blood donors. Perhaps that's where you recognize me from. All I know is that…that day was horrible. It was the second worst day of my life outside of my sister's death." Her gaze focused on nothing in particular within the room as though becoming overwhelmed by the memories from that day. "I treated patients from ages two to eighty-two. That day, I learned that pain, suffering and death don't discriminate, nor do they take any prisoners. Aside from all of the chaos, though, I think my most vivid memory from that day has to be when we took in the girl who rescuers plucked off a ledge created when the parking ramp imploded in the blast. I remember her being different. She was different than the rest of the injured, so innocent and fragile, and darn near catatonic. It was like all her life had been sucked out of her…like she had nothing left to care about anymore. To this day, I've often wondered what became of her after we dropped her off at the hospital. She's been in my thoughts since that day quite a bit."

If I'd had any residual doubts, there was now no question why I'd recognized Kara from the get go, nor why I'd felt such a strange connection to her since my arrival here. A lump developed in my throat, rendering me almost unable able to squeak out, "Is your last name Topper, by chance?"

Kara sat stunned, staring at me intently. "Yes. How did you know that?'

"It was the name on the badge of the EMT who cared for me after I was plucked from the ledge of the parking ramp at The Lakes Mall."

Kara gasped, cupping her hands to her mouth. "Oh, God. Of course..." she said as I reached my sore arms out to her. With tears in her eyes, she wrapped her arms around me, and we both sobbed hysterically. On that day, Kara adopted me as her sister.

# 17
## THE MAKING OF A SUPERHERO

AFTER KARA WENT to bed, I discovered that my revamped body made sleep pretty close to impossible. I felt uneasy, at edge even. Following the deaths of my family, I'd begun experiencing severe anxiety and panic attacks. I likened the feeling I was currently experiencing to what I went through with those attacks. My skin felt as though it were crawling, all but forcing me to get up and down out of bed numerous times, unable to sit still. Throughout my chest, my heart was pounding like a bongo drum, and I was uncomfortably short of breath. If I wasn't able to calm myself down soon, I'd surely be paid a visit by either Martin or Harris. To add insult to injury, the back of my neck was still throbbing as if broken glass had been implanted into it.

Thankfully, Kara had been able to sneak a sedative into my room. She knew I would be on edge, in pain, and probably unable to sleep on my own. I'd consciously decided that I wouldn't touch it unless absolutely necessary. After the one thousandth time of getting out of bed, I decided that necessity had taken over, and I took the pill with the hopes of being able to relax enough to put myself out of my misery.

With one final thrust, the door to the parking ramp squealed open. The cold air rushed through my body chilling me to the bone. I took off, running toward my parents' vehicle because, like in all my other dreams, they were inside, trapped. Jake was kicking the back passenger side windows with both feet in a vain attempt to break through the glass. Carol was screaming. George wore a blank expression, staring straight ahead at something my eyes could not yet see. It was only after I approached them that I saw what was catching George's attention. It was him. As in all the other dreams, I couldn't make out any distinct features because his face was always hidden by a dark fog, but I knew what was to happen next. It was inevitable, but I wouldn't allow myself to accept it. I was much closer than I had been before and I wasn't going to fail them this time, or so I thought. In a split second, my body was flung back through the familiar door of the department store that I'd once again fought so valiantly to open. The parking garage imploded and then they were gone.

I shot up in bed, my heart racing, sweat dripping down my body. My hand drifted to a night stand that wasn't where it should be when I then remembered where I was. There would be no comforting call to Chase this time, or ever again for that matter. Dejected, I slumped back down on my bed, knowing that I was wide awake and, barring another sleeping pill, I was not going to be able to return to any form of measurable slumber.

The tone sounded then, signaling morning, meaning it was probably between six and seven o'clock. My body still felt like it'd been used as a punching bag the night before. I knew that I didn't have to get up, that they wouldn't be expecting me to show my face at breakfast, but I figured since my resiliency had already impressed them up to this point, why let them down now?

My body screamed in pain as I pushed myself up and headed toward the bathroom. Upon passing the mirror, my eyes did a double take at the sight of the strange girl staring back at me. I hadn't looked at myself in the mirror since the night I arrived, and already the difference between the two reflections was marked. A hint of devastation and anguish was still present in the expression worn by the woman before me now. However, a new sense of strength and determination was also present in her eyes, something that hadn't been there during our last encounter.

My eyes trailed down from my face to my arms. Something was

distinctly different about them. Already, I could see a noticeable difference in the structure of the muscles composing them. They were toned, appearing as though I'd been pumping iron for at least a good six months. I ran my fingers down them, feeling every taut muscle. With the way they poised themselves, I imagined them propelling my body forward in a series of hand springs. I assumed this had to be some supernatural side effect of the adrenaline coupled with another substance that they purposefully neglected to tell me about. Jitters, a less ideal side effect, invaded my body as though I'd downed a couple of dozen cups of coffee. I turned on the cold water, splashing my face. It didn't help much, but it was something.

The hallway was empty when I stepped out into it on my way to the dining hall. Before this morning, I hadn't noticed how long it was and, in my assessment of its length, I couldn't help but think about how it would serve as the perfect human runway for me to utilize all of the pent up energy that pleaded for release. Was I really stronger? Was I faster? Well, there was one way to find out. Stopping in the middle of the hallway, I took a deep breath and began running as fast as I could to the end of it.

It felt as if I hadn't taken more than a couple of steps when I felt my body smash into something solid, instantaneously hurtling me to the ground with such force that I lay stunned on the cold linoleum floor, the wind knocked out of me. Once I could breathe again, I raised my head up to see what I could have possibly run into in an open and empty hallway. What I saw when I lifted my head sent shock waves through me. I was at the other end of the hallway and the object in front of me was the wall I'd been trying to run to. I gasped at the sight of the damaged cement. Not only had I run into it, but a noticeable dent had appeared in the area where my upper torso had struck it. The dent resembled a crater of about two inches in depth and was permanently imprinted into the cement wall.

Still in shock, I looked behind me to the point where I began my run; that point was probably a half a football field away. How was any of this possible? I patted my body down to see if I sustained any damage upon impact, finding nothing out of sorts. *This can't be real*, I thought.

Still unconvinced, I knew there was only one way to find out. As I began to stand I decided to add a little extra spring to my step to test the waters. With my arms steadying my body, I pushed myself up from the floor as hard as I could. To my amazement, the added spring I was shooting for turned into a full blown catapult propelling my body six feet into the air before I landed on my feet. *Okay, one more test*, I thought.

Never in my life had I been able to do a cartwheel, let alone a front handspring so, since I was doing the unbelievable anyway, I figured why stop now. I stood up straight, held my arms out in front of me and allowed my body to fall forward. It was like riding a bicycle. I did, one…two….eight handsprings, landing on my feet at the end of the adjoining hall. Maybe this new body wouldn't be so bad after all. For the first time since my arrival here, I smiled out of satisfaction.

Blake left the codes to each of the doors on my dresser. I memorized most of them and keyed them in, successfully unlocking each set of doors on my way to the dining hall. Upon approaching the dining hall, I could hear various conversations echoing from the room, most of which were centered on me. What struck me as odd, though, was the fact that I could delineate who was speaking and what was being said even from the opposite end of the hall. Everyone's voice was crisp and unnaturally amplified.

"How was she feeling when you left, Kara?" Dr. Harris' voice was the most recognizable amongst the commotion.

"Great. I can't believe how well she's doing, actually."

"That's good to hear." Victor was speaking now. "You two seem to be getting close."

"Well, we have a lot in common," Kara said.

"Dr. Martin, when do you think it will be safe to begin her training?" Victor asked just as I walked into the room, causing disbelieving stares and gasps to emanate from around the table.

"I'm pretty sure I'm ready now," I answered.

Blake looked at me with an expression that screamed *shut up and sit down, you don't know what you're getting yourself into.*

"This is utterly astounding," Marcus said. "Edwin, I guess congratulations are in order. Your new design has proven to be pretty effective." Edwin beamed. Something made me guess that he wasn't the usual recipient of recognition around here.

"How are you feeling?" Lana asked. Her curly red hair was tucked into a neat bun at the base of her neck.

"I'm still sore, but I'm no worse for wear than that wall is out there." I pointed in the direction of the hallway, explaining to everyone my activities of the morning.

"Oh, I have got to see this," Cameron said as he, Kyle, Drew and Colby took off down the hall.

The smell of French toast caught my nose. My stomach screamed in an anguished response. "Eat," Victor grinned. "As always, we have plenty."

I took my seat next to Blake, helping myself to the daily variety of breakfast food. For some reason, everything tasted better than it ever had before. The textures of the food and their individual flavors hit my palate, creating a virtual samba in my mouth.

"I can already see the increased hunger has affected you," Victor observed. My face burned as I set the plate down. "Oh, don't be embarrassed," Victor began again. "Your body is burning off much more energy and is trying to regain some of the fuel it's losing."

"What about my senses? How does this thing you implanted in me affect those? Is it supposed to?"

"Yes. Elevated levels of adrenaline can have a profound effect on your vision, hearing and sense of touch. If you look in the mirror, you may notice that your pupils are dilated. This is your body's way of naturally enhancing your vision. It's a defense mechanism used by your body to escape the invisible danger the adrenaline is telling your body exists. Your hearing is also enhanced for this reason. The only sense not enhanced is your sense of touch. This sense has been decreased to the point of numbness. The numbness lessens your feeling of physical pain and ultimately increases your overall stamina."

Upon hearing Victor's explanation, there was no wonder why hitting a cement wall hadn't seemed to faze me. "I guess I'm a regular force to be reckoned with."

"Indeed you are. With Blake, you'll be all but invincible."

I looked over at Blake. He was eating in silence, staring outside the faux window, oblivious to the world around him, and I doubted he wanted to be made aware of anything.

"You must have one hard head," Cameron announced, entering the room from his assessment of my damage. "I guess I shouldn't be surprised. Don't most women?"

"How would you know?" Becca sneered, clearing empty plates

from the table. "Have you ever even talked to a woman for more than five minutes without having given her your credit card first?" Cameron went to speak, but Becca cut him off. "Oh, and your mother doesn't count."

"Oh, dang, she got you," Drew proclaimed.

"You always hurt the ones you love, Becca." Cameron shot a sly wink in her direction.

"Excuse me; I think I'm going to be sick." She picked up a pile of dishes and disappeared into the kitchen.

"She wants me."

"Who wouldn't," Inez added. "You're ninety-five pounds of pure romantic fury."

"One hundred twenty, thank you very much. I've been working out." He rolled up his sleeves and kissed his nonexistent biceps.

"On that note," Victor scooted his chair back and gestured down the hall. "Care to join me in our science lab, Celaine?"

"As long as you're not going to be inserting more objects into my body…sure."

I heard a muffled laugh coming from Cameron's direction to which Kara muttered, "Shut up", between her teeth.

Like the medical room, the science lab was filled with technology I couldn't even begin to comprehend. Beakers, vials, books and machinery dotted a room illuminated by fluorescent lighting that seemed almost archaic in comparison to the technology it shone upon. Like every other room here, the ambiance was nondescript, reminding me of a high school chemistry lab.

When I did a quick scan of the lab, something peculiar caught my eye. In the middle of the room stood what appeared to be a mannequin. I walked closer to the oddity, studying it and taking notice that its height and dimensions were very similar to my own. The figure wore a suit the likes of which I'd never seen before. It was black, smooth and very tight fitting on the form it covered. I extended my fingers to feel its material. It was like none I'd ever felt before, hard, but flexible. With the whole suit encased in such a hard, shell-like material, I wondered how heavy it would be if it were worn.

Around its waist lay a belt, utility-like in nature that I speculated served as a holster for a gun or other weapon. At its base sat a pair of boots resembling the same material as the suit. I picked up one of the boots and, to my surprise, assessed it to be rather light, even though it felt harder than a rock in my hands. Curious, I placed the sole of the boot to the bottom of my foot and realized that, like the suit, it, too, seemed to be my size.

"The size should be dead on. They took the final measurements before you came out of the anesthesia," Victor confirmed my suspicions.

"Good to know I had people feeling me up in my sleep."

"Oh, Celaine, always with the sarcasm. Although, I suppose it's a good quality to have, especially with the monotony that exists around here."

"How does she like the uniform?" Marcus entered the room.

"I've never seen anything like it," I answered him.

"That's because there's only one other one like it in the world. It's one of my crowning achievements."

"It feels so solid. How am I supposed to wear it?"

"Looks are deceiving. It's actually remarkably lightweight. The materials used in it are to thank for that. It's not only ballistic proof, but also made from one of the most impenetrable substances available."

"What is it? Some form of Kevlar?"

"Yes. Kevlar that's had its molecular structure spliced with that of diamonds."

"Diamonds?"

"Diamonds are the hardest substance on earth, as I'm sure you already know. In this lab, we have been able to bind the molecules from Kevlar and diamonds together to form a super material. This suit is more than just bulletproof; it's a virtual force field. You can get hit and feel like you haven't even been touched."

"So, what's the dry cleaning bill run on this thing?"

Marcus looked at me perplexed as if he were contemplating what I'd just asked. "Well...well, there's really no dry cleaning involved...I mean."

"There, there, Marcus," Victor interceded, amused. "You see, Celaine, humor isn't something that can be cultivated in a science lab."

"Be that as it may," Marcus interceded. "This is a multi-million dollar piece of equipment, and I ask that you treat its condition with the utmost seriousness."

"You have my word." I glanced at Victor as if to say, "Is he serious?"

"How about you try it on to see if we have the measurements correct," Victor again saved the moment from turning awkward.

Marcus peeled the suit off the mannequin. I speculated how comfortable it would be as it gripped my body. "Grab the boots and follow me," he ordered.

"Yes, boss," I replied. Marcus glanced at me in pure annoyance. "I'll bet it's a barrel of laughs in your household."

"Yeah, my wife's laughing all the way to divorce court."

"Oh, I'm sorry, Marcus. I didn't know."

"It's all right; just a natural part of devoting yourself to the Cause, right?"

My thoughts turned to Chase, and the pain I'd banished down to the deepest depths of my mind returned with full force. "I guess it is."

Marcus led me to a small room used as more of a storage closet than any other functional purpose. I set the boots down on the floor as he handed me the suit. "I don't think I need to tell you how to dress. Victor and I will be in the training room with Blake. It's the one right before the dining hall. Meet us down there after you've changed."

I stood there suit in hand, running my hand down its contours, trying to figure out how it'd been pieced together. It didn't seem indestructible to me. In fact, it seemed downright fragile. Thinner than it had appeared on the mannequin, I wasn't sure how it would be able to stop a bullet and was terrified at the prospect of it even being used for that purpose.

Further inspection revealed a meticulously hidden zipper in the back. At least one mystery had been solved. I slipped out of my clothes, uneasy over donning the form fitting suit, but guessing that modesty was a foreign concept here. While standing on one leg, I slipped my foot into the first leg of the suit. Given how tight the legs alone felt on my body, I theorized that I would need the jaws-of-life to get out of this thing if I managed to even get into it in the first place. When both legs were in, I sucked in my stomach, cutting off my air supply in the process, in order to pull the suit over my torso. Once covered, I fought my way through the sleeves with my arms until my hands poked through the cuffs.

Even without being zipped, the suit secured itself to my body, gripping it in a chokehold. I wondered if it was supposed to be like this or if the measurements taken had been just incredibly poor guesstimates instead. Straining against the material of the suit, I struggled to get the zipper zipped in the back all while thinking that whoever made the suit must either be a sadist or that this was some twisted, sick joke. Inch by inch–although it felt more like millimeter by millimeter–I managed to zip up the back.

"Well, the hard part is done," I said to myself.

Thankfully, the boots slid on easily since the material didn't seem to be quite the same as the rest of the getup. Perhaps, they figured the boots didn't need to be quite as secure as the rest of the suit as, aside from Achilles, no one ever died from a wound to the foot. And since I was no mythological being, I figured I'd be safe.

To top off my new look, I snapped the utility belt around my waist. I had to admit that even though the whole getup wasn't my style, I still felt pretty bad ass. The suit was entirely black in color. Coupled with the utility belt, it resembled an outfit a person would wear to a rock 'n' roll funeral. Still, despite the thin material, I did somehow feel as though I was encased in steel. The adherence to my skin gave me a sense of security. I was both sleek and unstoppable. In slow, awkward movements, I took my first steps in the suit and, although stiff at first, my body became accustomed to it.

I walked down the hallway to what was referred to as the training room. Once outside, I heard Blake's guttural gasps resounding through the steel doors as though he were being tortured. Perhaps, going in there wouldn't be such a good idea after all. With a deep breath, I opened the door to find out what horrors awaited me on the other side. Oddly enough, when I opened the door, all that was there to greet me was a darkened viewing room containing a console filled with gauges, buttons, levers, and monitors illuminated with a virtual rainbow of lights. Cameron and Drew sat at the console. Marcus and Victor were standing off to the side watching what I suspected to be Blake and the source of his discomfort through the viewing window. I walked in Victor's direction, joining him in watching Blake.

Blake was running, jumping, dodging and punching at invisible objects around the entire perimeter of a padded room that I estimated to be the size of a small stadium. I marveled at the speed at which he was executing his movements. They were remarkable and, until this morning, were speeds which I would have thought impossible. His jumps appeared as though he were taking flight. When he landed, he did so with such coordination and grace he appeared almost poetic. Some unseen force in that room was provoking him. Whatever or whoever he was fighting was giving him quite a workout, so much so that I couldn't tell if he was winning or royally getting his butt kicked. My eyes traveled from the viewing window up to Victor, who was watching Blake as intently as a proud parent whose son was on the verge of scoring the game-winning touchdown.

"I take it he's doing well?" I broke the silence, studying Victor's unflinching expression.

"Quite. He's working through a new simulation with a few added twists that Cameron threw in. He seems to be one step ahead of them."

"Simulation?"

"In that room, a series of events is being played out that are invisible to us in this room, but are as real as you and I to whoever is in there. It's an optical illusion. He's wearing special glasses attuned to Cameron's computer and is reacting to each scenario being displayed before him. If he were losing this particular one, the scenario would be shut down and he would be asked to repeat it again." He turned to me and smiled. "At the risk of sounding redundant, that suit really does suit you well."

I felt so uncomfortable with the way his eyes were piercing through me that I decided to divert the course our conversation was heading in. "Is the helmet a part of the whole simulation thing?" I asked, gesturing towards Blake.

"No, you will be fitted with a helmet as well. You will need to wear one at all times while you're out. Of course, the obvious reasons for this are to protect your head from injury, but, when you go out in public, you will need to have your face hidden to prevent your recognition not only for your safety but for the safety of those you left behind."

I was taken aback by that last statement. I hadn't considered the thought that Chase would actually figure out who the new "superhero" in town was, and I most certainly didn't see his life as being in jeopardy because of any decision I had made. As if sensing my sudden apprehension, Victor reassured me, "Don't worry, The Man in Black would actually have to recognize you or know you first to have any way to use them against you. The odds of that happening are slim."

Victor was right, but his statement did little to quell the concern creeping into my mind. If anything happened to Chase or his family because of me, I would never be able to live with myself. It would never happen. I would fight to the death to prevent it from ever happening. From out of the corner of my eye, I saw Victor's body stiffen, possibly indicating that the simulation had reached a pivotal point.

"It's the true test. We'll see how good he really is," Cameron muttered.

"Right, it's now or never," Drew concurred.

I walked over to check out what was being displayed in the monitors Drew and Cameron were staring at so intently. The picture painted in the monitor told a whole different story than the one taking place in the padded room. In the middle of a simulated scene, depicting a city in chaos, stood Blake, muscles rigid, glare visible through the mask he wore. He was the definition of every warrior I'd ever seen in the movies before they prepared for their final battle charge. I couldn't tell what was getting him so riled up, but I knew it must be something big. Effortlessly, he leapt onto an overturned car in the middle of the crumbled remnants of a city street surrounded by hallowed out buildings and a bright orange sky as a backdrop.

"A little melodramatic, don't you think?" I turned to Cameron.

"Hey, this is the only entertainment I have so..." He'd turned his chair around to look at me, finding himself speechless. "On second thoughts..."

"Wow," Drew added, turning around. "Remind me to send a nice "thank you" note or fruit basket or something to Marcus."

"Okay, boys. How about we keep our eyes on the monitor?" Annoyed, I gestured back to the monitor.

"Smoking hot *and* bossy, just the way I like my women." Cameron didn't know when to quit.

"I hear Blake is making a mockery out of your new simulation." I smirked.

"The beginning of my program was all just child's play. The true test of his abilities are yet to come."

I didn't have a chance to ask Cameron what he meant by that as, at that moment, a sickening thud rang out from the simulator, followed by a deafening scream of agony from Blake. I diverted my attention back to the monitor to see the image of the figure that had burned itself into my subconscious over the last ten years. The Man in Black was here.

# 18

## THE ROPES

BLAKE BARGED OUT of the simulator looking ragged and worse for wear. In frustration, he ripped off his helmet, wiping away the sweat that had accumulated on his brow. "Damn it," he grumbled.

"You came close until the end there." Cameron inadvertently poured salt into Blake's wounds. "Don't worry. You'll get another crack at it tomorrow." Blake muttered something that sounded like another expletive under his breath. He glanced briefly at me, doing an instant double take which only supplemented Cameron's amusement. "It fits her well, eh?" He smirked. "Maybe she doesn't even have to learn to fight. We can just use her as a distraction. I mean The Man in Black is still a *man*, right?"

My face burned. Catching Cameron's eye, I mouthed "shut-up" in his direction.

"Blake, you did very well." Victor walked toward our little group. "You almost had him. It's too bad that almost will get you killed here in the real world."

"Understood, Sir," Blake replied.

Victor smiled as though he took an acknowledgement from Blake as being a sort of twisted victory. "Well, what do you say to testing out Celaine's new wardrobe?"

"What does he mean by that?" I muttered to Blake.

"I hope you enjoy getting smacked around," he answered.

"Sounds like one swell afternoon. Although, I have my concerns as to how this thing is supposed to protect me. It feels like steel, but it's almost as thin as a sheet of paper."

Victor laughed. "This is a clear case of looks being deceiving." He turned to Blake, gesturing towards me. "Blake, would you oblige?"

"Here? Right now?"

"Why not?"

Blake sighed, facing me. "You heard the boss," he shrugged. "Stand still, don't move. This may hurt you more than it hurts me."

Before I had a chance to protest, he had his hand balled into a fist that was heading with a vengeance directly toward my stomach. I shut my eyes, bracing myself for its impact and certain bodily harm. A loud grunt, followed by several sharp cries of agony, erupted a second later. Strangely though, they hadn't come from me. When I opened my eyes, I saw Blake on the floor. He was writhing in pain, alternating between holding onto his hand in pain and shaking it profusely. His fingers were misshapen. Marcus, Cameron, and Drew stood behind him, their jaws practically touching the floor.

"Did he miss or something?" I was standing close to a wall and assumed that Blake's fist must have run off course.

"No, he was dead on," Cameron pronounced.

"Unbelievable. He didn't even budge her," Drew said. "Either the transmitters are working more efficiently or Marcus here has finally perfected the fusion for the suits."

"Both," Victor declared, happy with himself. "It appears as though Celaine is the strongest one yet."

In shock, I looked back down at Blake, who was still cradling his deformed hand. With one stomach-churning crack after another, he grasped his bent fingers, snapping each bone back into place. Blake looked up at me in amazement, somehow managing to stand back up. His hand was bright red and clearly swollen.

"That's impossible," I said in awe. "He hit me with enough force to almost break his hand and I felt nothing. I didn't even move."

"Exactly what we were aiming for," Victor inspected Blake's hand. "It appears as though Marcus' research and refinement has paid off. You and your suit are even more indestructible than Blake here is. Don't

172

worry, Blake. I'll have Marcus commence work on a new suit for you immediately." Marcus nodded. Victor patted Blake on the back. It was a gesture which I could tell was more irritating than reassuring to him.

"So, is it me or the suit?"

A grin crept over Victor's face. "A little bit of both. I'm sure you remember what I told you about the effects the implantation of the transmitter would have on your body. You've already witnessed the various possible feats of wonder for yourself in both Blake and your little science experiment in the hallway this morning. The physical integrity of the suit coupled with your enhanced physique have combined to create quite the force to be reckoned with. With a little training, you may well be one of the most powerful fighters we've ever had."

"I'll say. I've never seen anything or anyone take a punch from Blake and still remain standing, or breathing for that matter," Cameron said, still in a state of shock.

"Blake, why don't you take Celaine to the gymnasium and start showing her everything you know? Tomorrow, we'll test her out in the simulator. Marcus, Cameron, Drew, accompany me; I have a little project for you." They obediently followed Victor out of the training room, leaving Blake and I alone.

"This place has a gym, too?" I asked.

"Does that really surprise you?" Blake rubbed his injured hand again.

"No, I can't say that it does. Look, I'm sorry about your hand. I guess I don't know my own strength." I stuck my arm out and flexed my muscles, but my lighthearted attempt at lightening the mood fell on deaf ears as Blake shook his head and walked away.

With me following closely behind him, Blake led me to a set of double doors at the opposite end of the training room. He pushed the doors open, revealing an elaborate display of weights and equipment. Off to the side of the room sat a large, padded wrestling mat which took up half of the space available in the gym. In the middle of the room, anchored to the ceiling, was a large television tuned into a cable news station featuring President Brooks' recent trip to Japan. Blake led me to the mat, bypassing the equipment.

"Do they expect you to show me how to exercise or something? It's kind of insulting if they think I don't know how to use a treadmill."

"That equipment isn't for us. Trust me, you're physically well beyond what that equipment could help you with. Your muscles are constantly working out, so to speak. The effects of the adrenaline are far more profound than what any machine could do. My job is to teach you how to fight."

"Excuse me? I can fight."

"I'm not talking about slap boxing."

"Very funny for a guy who just got his butt kicked by a girl." Blake winced as though my remark had wounded his hand all over again. He rubbed it, flexing his fingers. "Well, sensei, show me what you got."

He shook his head. "Okay, grasshopper," he chuckled.

"Hey, at least I got a laugh out of you."

"All right," Blake began, looking serious again. "You have the body, you have the armor, but you don't yet have the skills. You're running into walls, for Christ's sake."

"That was *one* time."

This is serious, Celaine," Blake sighed. "I don't think I have to tell you that the life you've chosen requires more dedication than you could ever have imagined. We have to be on top of our game physically and mentally at all times because those who oppose us will most certainly be on theirs." I must have had a confused expression on my face as Blake continued. "Although, the vast majority of the population is grateful for our existence, there are still those who loathe us. They view our existence as some sort of conspiracy. To them, we are the catalysts behind the new order instituted by President Brooks. We're more symbols of oppression than peace."

"That's ridiculous."

"I used to think that, too."

"What do you mean?"

"Nothing. Let's get started with teaching you how to fight, shall we?"

I was struck by Blake's last statement. Obviously, a tremendous amount of tension existed between him and Victor, leading me to wonder where the source of it originated. "Learning to fight," I said out loud. "I never thought I would say that and have it be a reference to something that *I* was going to do. Aren't we going to use weapons? We're just supposed to rely on our own physical prowess?"

"We have guns, but it's not like they're all that effective against The Man in Black. His armor is more advanced than our own. I have my doubts that there is much of anything short of nuclear warfare that could take him out."

"If that's the case, how are we supposed to stop him? Aren't we too weak for him?"

"No, not quite. Liam and I came close a couple of times. He's powerful, but like us, he's not invincible. He wasn't quite prepared for two of us. One of us, sure. However, two of us posed a challenge. We..." Blake trailed off for a moment as if he was deciding whether or not to relive that day, ultimately deciding that it was better that I know than not. "Liam hated The Man in Black...hated him more than I think anyone I'd ever met before. That hatred made him one of the best of our kind; until, as hatred often does, it rendered him blind to anything else but his own agenda. He wanted to be solely responsible for taking out The Man in Black just as that monster had taken out his three-year-old daughter. The night Liam died, we had him cornered on the roof of a warehouse in Dover. We'd run him down; he was weak. In his weakness I noticed a flaw in his armor, a small but nonetheless vulnerable tear, and took advantage of it. I fired one shot, striking him."

"I saw the blood dripping onto the concrete when he took off running. Liam and I had devised a plan before that night that if something like that were ever to occur, we would flank him and bring him down together. If we chose to bring him in alive, so be it. If not, then he resisted and we were defending ourselves. But, instead of sticking to the plan we'd gone over, Liam decided to take him down himself without waiting for me. I'd been injured in a blast that night which ripped a hole in the leg of my suit. A beam shot into my leg, coming close to the femoral artery. I was losing a lot of blood which obviously slowed me down, royally irritating Liam. And The Man in Black, even with only half his strength, was still too much for Liam to handle on his own. Before I could stop him, Liam charged him, attempting to knock him off the roof of the warehouse. Instead, it was Liam who was thrown from the roof, and The Man in Black managed to escape."

I walked over to Blake, placing a hand on his shoulder. A sort of solemn state had overcome him, making me suspect that he blamed himself for not being able to save his partner. "Teach me what you know, and I promise you I won't let you down."

He sighed. "Just don't do anything stupid."

"I'm afraid it's too late for that. I'm here, aren't I?"

"I guess so." He changed his stance on the mat, shaking off the memory he recounted. "So, Celaine, do you know anything about Judo?"

"Do I look like I know anything about Judo?"

"Do you always have to be such a smartass?"

"Go on."

"Judo is more of an art form than a form of fighting. It requires discipline, self-control, poise and concentration. It keeps you mentally focused, allowing your body to move fluidly, and rendering your target..." I didn't have time to blink before I found myself flat on my back on the mat with Blake's arms around my neck in a chokehold. "Defenseless."

"Okay, okay, I get your point." I gasped to fill my lungs back up with air, rubbing my throat. Blake released me from his grasp, leaping up into the air to what must have been close to twenty feet before gracefully landing back on his feet at the opposite end of the mat. Upon landing, he executed a series of thrusts, jabs and calculated kicks at such remarkable speeds it gave me whiplash just watching him. Not to be outdone, I sprung to my feet, landing on the opposite side of the mat, facing him in my best martial-arts-wannabe stance. Again, I ended up finding myself hitting the mat after having been taken out by Blake. "You're just showing off now," I grumbled, rubbing my back. "I thought Judo was the gentle form of martial arts."

"Should I tell Victor that you've given up?"

"Hardly."

Determined not to let him get the best of me again, I shifted my undivided attention towards him. He was like poetry in motion in the way he moved. My muscles stiffened with the anticipation of his next attack, my eyes catching every subtle movement of his limbs until the subtleness dissipated and I found my body reacting to his fast-as-lightning ambush. I flew into the air and twisted my body, thrusting my right leg forward until it made contact with his back. The force of my kick was enough to throw him off balance, causing him to do a series of somersaults on the mat. He jumped up and, after regaining his composure, prepared himself for another attack. On the other side of the mat, I landed awkwardly on my left foot, turning it in slightly. Pain shot through my leg, and I tried my best to ignore it and regain my focus.

When I landed, he charged and, like before, I was able to dodge him, throwing him off his game. He made a sharp jab at my chest as he backtracked and, even though I was able to fend off his fingers from making contact with my body, I didn't quite anticipate the kick to the abdomen he delivered next. My body hurtled across the mat, rolling to a stop against the wall. Sensing another assault, I hopped to my feet, throwing out a jab that struck Blake's shoulder. He retaliated with a series of jabs of which I was able to block with precision, throwing in a few of my own.

I detected a familiar movement in Blake's right leg and sprang into a back flip, narrowly avoiding a kick to the shoulder in the process. Upon landing, I returned to my defensive stance. There he and I stood, staring at each other, our eyes beckoning the other to make a move as if we were in a live-action game of chess. Who would be the first to checkmate?

After deciding to go for it, I charged. Blake reciprocated by delivering a flying kick that came within centimeters of hitting my jaw. I'm sure, from the spectator's point of view, our training looked like a choreographed routine, but it was anything but that. Our battle went on for fifteen minutes, then twenty-five minutes, with neither of us relenting or forcing the other to the ground in defeat. We catapulted ourselves into the air simultaneously, spinning around, trying to derail each other.

Finally, after one in-air spin, I made the mistake of miscalculating his next move and, before I knew it, his foot was impacting my shoulder, slamming my body down on the linoleum floor a foot away from the mat. He pinned me down, glancing at me from above with his wide-toothed grin. I hadn't noticed it before, but he really did have a nice smile.

"You're pretty good for a first-timer," he commented. "I'm impressed."

"I'd be more inclined to believe your attempt at sincerity if it weren't for the fact that you seem entirely too pleased with yourself." He knelt down offering me his hand but, instead of holding out one hand for him to take, I took it with both hands, throwing him over my back. He landed with a crash on the weight bench twenty feet away. *Sucker*, I thought.

Blake sat stunned where he'd landed with his back propped up against the weight bench. "Was that really necessary?"

"Why, whatever do you mean?"

He rolled his eyes as he stood to pick up the weights that had fallen onto the floor. My muscles ached with such intensity that I wanted nothing more than to curl up in the fetal position on the cold linoleum floor to soothe them. But I refrained as I figured they would frown upon something like that here and proceeded to pick myself up from off the floor. As soon as I put pressure on my right shoulder, I heard a pop that was immediately followed by intense pain, the likes of which I'd never felt before. Its intensity made my arm give out, forcing me to smack my body back down against the floor. I moaned in agony. In a flash, Blake was by my side.

"What is it? What's wrong?" he asked, inspecting me.

"My shoulder. It feels like my arm is being ripped off," I said between gritted teeth.

Blake ran his hands up my arm to examine my shoulder. "You probably tore your shoulder from its socket. It's pretty common to over extend your muscles with the science experiment they're conducting inside our bodies. I've done it a few times myself." He reached down to pick me up, but his attempt to help me was met with sharp resistance. "Celaine, you have to let me help you up. I can't pop your shoulder back in place with you writhing in pain on the floor."

My heart was racing, and I felt as though I was going to pass out from the pain. Nonetheless, I managed to push myself up to my feet with my other arm. "Just make it quick."

"I've never had a woman tell me that before."

The pain was too overpowering for me to even attempt any form of a witty retort. Blake gently took my arm from behind my back and proceeded to rotate it until a final pop indicated that it had been relocated back into its socket. By now, I was trembling. I could feel my pulse begin to race. Sweat formed in my hairline, my eyesight began to fade. With dizziness beginning to overtake me, I turned around to thank Blake.

"Celaine…"

My name was the last thing I remember hearing before everything went black.

# 19

# THE MAN IN BLACK

REMOVED FROM SOCIETY, sheltered by the abyss of darkness, he remained. Society was a joke with a punch line he didn't find humorous; a travesty that needed to be erased from publication. And since no one else was up to the task, he'd be the one to do it. He was the entity they'd dubbed The Man in Black. To attach an identity to one based purely upon their physical attributes was a cliché. After all, he'd killed countless people. Surely, they could do better than bestowing him with a moniker based upon his gender and choice of attire. Then again, they were nothing more than mere mortals, and he shouldn't expect too much.

He stood from his vantage point atop the Piedmont Tool and Die building, steadying himself for his descent. Without fault, he leapt between both it and an abandoned warehouse on the opposite side, using his feet like a spring to bounce between the two buildings until he landed on the crumbled, concrete sidewalk. In the last ten years, he'd made a profound impact upon humanity. Single-handedly, he'd instilled enough terror to make them abandon their livelihoods. They were afraid of him and he loved it. He'd been called a serial killer, deranged, a monster even. These references annoyed him. No rhyme, reason, or pattern existed to his killings and, therefore, he was no serial killer. The monster label, on the other hand, he somewhat agreed with as he knew he'd ceased being human long ago.

From the neck down, he was no longer organic. The injuries he'd sustained over the last ten years of being pursued had rendered him more robotic in nature. His last injury, a gunshot wound to his abdomen, still throbbed with the bullet having come close to striking his spleen. He'd almost succumbed from the blood loss but, as always, he managed to pull through. Years of cheating death made him quite oblivious to mortality. There was no one who could stop him no matter how badly they were able to mar his body. After all, there were always replacements. In fact, quite a few of his organs were organs he had not been born with. Portions of his arms and legs had been rebuilt with titanium steel, replacing the original bone. Skin grafts covered areas of his back and chest. No one ever saw him without a shirt on, nor would they as, most certainly, a slew of annoying questions would surely follow.

He adjusted his mask, allowing the cool air to brush against his face, drying up the sweat accruing under its confines. His victims were relying too much on their government to protect them. They were looking to their beloved leader for answers, reassurance, and safety. But, instead of coming to their aid, this government was using his existence as a platform to benefit its own agenda. The curfew they'd enacted not only spat on the foundation their country had been built upon, but was as big a joke as society itself. Sure, it kept throngs of people out of potential target locations at night, ostensibly keeping them safe. However, in allowing such legislation to pass, the people had in essence turned a blind eye to the fact that their chief had been able to herd them into their homes. They were sheep who'd made not so much as a *baa* in protest to this new order. President Brooks had almost as much power over the masses as he did, and that did not set well with him.

Then there was the matter of those so-called superheroes. Give someone an ability that overshadowed most of the population's and, suddenly, they were considered a superhero when, in reality, they hadn't done anything super at all. They hadn't been able to stop him. To the contrary, a few of them had met their maker in confrontations with him. Only the one they called Blake still remained, and it was only a matter of time before he was dealt with as well.

It had been too long since he'd been responsible for the spilling of human blood, and the urge was welling up inside him like an out of control brush fire that no amount of water could extinguish. He needed the perfect target. Not just any one would do. And now, as he stalked the streets, he believed he'd found it. It was perfect, too perfect. There were hundreds if not thousands of people there…all helpless. People who not only worked within its confines, but who were laid-up in beds, and hooked to machines. People who were immobile. Sitting ducks, so to speak.

The Man in Black cracked a smile as he glared at Hope Memorial Hospital and pondered his next move.

# 20

# THE STORY OF BLAKE

MY EYES FLUTTERED open, taking in the fluorescent lighting and familiar blasé atmosphere comprising my room. I felt as though I'd been through a war zone where I'd been a casualty. Pain still pervaded throughout my shoulder, running down my back. Slowly, I lifted my arm out from under the covers and noticed fresh needle marks on the skin of my forearm.

"It's alive." I turned my head to see Blake sitting in a chair near my bed, his feet propped up on my open dresser drawer.

"How long have you been sitting there?"

"About three hours."

"What happened to me?"

"Your heart. Apparently, it's made of ice, after all. Imagine that."

"You're a funny man."

"You came close to suffering cardiac arrest. It's a pretty common scenario with us along with our joints falling apart at the seams at the most inopportune moments."

"Am I out of the woods? Shouldn't I be in a hospital or something?"

"You have one doctor five doors down and another monitoring your every bodily function in a laboratory at the other end of this place. I think you're better off here. Not to mention, conventional medicine would be of little help to you now."

I looked down at my body and couldn't help but notice that I was in a tank top and sweat pants.

"Don't worry, Kara dressed you, not me. Your suit's hanging up in the closet." I nodded, a bit relieved. Blake pushed in the dresser door and stood up.

"Where are you going?"

"To my room. You're conscious, so there's no need for me to be here anymore."

"How sweet of you."

"What? Do you want me to crawl in bed and cuddle with you?"

"Totally not where I was going with that." I sat up in bed. The ache from my shoulder returned, causing me to wince. "What's your story, Blake?"

He looked at me, confused. "I have no story."

"Sure you do. We all have one. I'll help you out. Where are you from? Why are you even here if you hate it so much? Put those answers together and you have some semblance of a story."

"Okay, let's see. I've gone through almost a handful of partners since I've been here. If anything, that fact alone has taught me that sharing a story with someone means you've somehow bonded yourself with them." A solemn demeanor overcame him. He stared at the floor, rubbing his fingers down the folds of his training shorts. "And this sense of attachment inevitably leads to feelings of devastation and guilt when you look over the ledge of a fifteen story building and see their remains splattered on the pavement below."

"What if I promise not to die?"

"If only that were possible. Our existence is a lonely, thankless one, and I guess it would be nice to be able to care and be cared about." He heaved a deep sigh, reclaiming his seat next to my bed. "When I first came here, I was like you. Optimistic, determined, and vengeful. I was brought in right on the cusp of my best friend's murder at the hands of that bastard, and I didn't think twice when I was approached by Victor with the promise of being able to spill the blood of the thing that so callously bathes in the agony of others. I didn't think twice about leaving my life, my job as a fire fighter for the city of Cambridge, my apartment, my family, my girlfriend. I didn't think twice at all, until a year later. After I'd grown so listless and disenchanted with sitting here by myself not knowing how those I'd left behind were faring. So, I went back to Cambridge and learned that life really does go on quite well without you."

"She moved on?"

"She didn't just move, she strapped on a rocket pack and blasted away. When I went back there, I saw her. She was married...and pregnant."

"I'm sorry, Blake."

Blake ran his hand through his thick, disheveled hair. "You aren't a prisoner here, Celaine. You can go back as long as they don't see you in the outside world. We're given pagers that they use liberally to notify us. However, even though you can go, I wouldn't recommend it to you. Like me, there will be a day when you look through one of their windows only to wish you hadn't. That fact is an inevitable one. You'll give up on love, on life and then, five years later, you'll just be bitter, looking forward to death as a way out."

"Blake, it doesn't have to be like that. The Man in Black will fall one day and we can both return to life as normal. We'll be able to reclaim what we lost."

"Always the optimist."

"Why do you hate Victor so much?'

He smirked. "You'll see for yourself someday. Victor has an agenda. I haven't figured out what it is, but I'm pretty sure it's politically motivated in some form."

After putting some thought into it, I decided to ask him the question that had been on my mind from the moment I made the decision to leave my life as I knew it. "I've wondered how we're selected. Out of the billions of people in this world, why us?"

"You're full of questions tonight."

"What else do I have going on?"

"Honestly, I don't know how we're selected. I mean, I know what I was told when I asked that same question. But, what the actual truth is, I have no idea. They say it's random, based upon our social security numbers. If the person whose number is selected is able, qualified, and willing, then so be it. The kicker is that every person selected has had someone they loved tragically killed by all this madness. That's no coincidence if you ask me." "That's why they've never had anyone turn them down."

Blake looked at me, clearly troubled, as though he wanted to tell me something but couldn't. "Yeah, no one's turned them down," he replied.

The charm from Chase's mother's necklace slid down on the chain around my neck. I reached for it, feeling its coarse exterior between my fingers as I guided it back to its position down the center of my neck. Blake watched me, a frown forming on his face. "You should take that off, you know," he said.

"Over my dead body."

"I'm just trying to help you out. Over time that charm will feel heavier and heavier. Its presence will begin to mess with your mind."

"I appreciate your concern for my mental well-being." Blake stood up, fiddling with a controller of some kind on top of my dresser.

"What is that for? Do I have some sort of hidden television in here?"

"No one showed this to you yet?"

"Not that I can recall. Then again, electronics aren't my thing, so I could very easily have tuned them out while they were explaining it."

"This little contraption has given me the added dosage of sanity I've needed to get me through long, sleepless nights when I've had nothing to do but lie awake in bed while the whole world sleeps with their dreams still intact." He pointed to a dial at the top of the control. "This just regulates your room temperature." He pushed a button adjacent to the knob. Music appeared, flowing throughout the room. "I don't think I need to explain that button further." He hit it again and the music disappeared. "Do you remember when I told you that the windows you were admiring in the sitting room were nothing more than holograms?"

"How could I forget? That completely ruined my day."

"Well, watch this. Lights off."

My room became pitch black. "Let me guess, Cameron came up with this."

"No, if that were the case the lights would just slightly dim and Barry White music would be playing from the speakers. In actuality, I came up with the idea and bet Drew that he couldn't pull it off. That's all it took. A week later, I had what I wanted and Drew had the satisfaction of proving me wrong. Two birds with one stone, I guess you could say."

"Blake Cohen, I'm impressed. There is a sense of humor lodged in that thick skull of yours."

"Okay," he said without missing a beat, "here it goes."

The ceiling illuminated, displaying the image of a serene waterfall, but it wasn't just the pictures that struck me, it was the realism. I heard the water rushing over the falls, felt the wind on my face, and smelled the fresh earth churned up by the rushing water.

"Blake, this is amazing."

"There's more."

The scene changed to one of a field of wildflowers. Vibrant purples, blues and oranges intermingled with the tall grass. I heard the wind whipping through the surrounding trees, the birds singing in the background. The smell of spring air invaded my nostrils, ushering in a sense of serenity.

"At the risk of emasculating myself," Blake began, "I'd have to say that the meadow is probably one of my favorite ones. For a split second, I always forget where I am, where I came from, or why I'm even here. There's nothing else that brings about that same type of quiet meditation for me quite like this. I feel almost like I'm me again."

I looked up at the ceiling, admiring the meadow, thankful for my newfound vision of Blake.

"Lights on," he said. The meadow disappeared into the depths of the ceiling. I looked up at Blake, noticing that he was looking at me, too. "Thank you," he said.

"For what?"

"For making me feel, for the first time in a long time…like I'm not alone anymore."

"Don't mention it." I gave Blake a half smile. "Thank *you* by the way."

"For what?"

"For beating the crap out of me and almost forcing me into cardiac arrest…oh, and fixing my shoulder, too."

"Don't mention it." Blake stretched, allowing a yawn to escape his lips. "Well, I've been up for four days straight, so I think I should try to rest a little."

"That's probably a good idea. More training tomorrow?"

"Always."

"Goodnight, Blake." He nodded, disappearing out the door.

"Lights off." It again became pitch black in my room. I reached for the controller Blake had left on my bed and pushed the bottom button. The image of the meadow reappeared. I hit the button again, greeted this time by a forest of snow covered trees, pure and untouched by humanity. Cold air invaded my room, making me shiver. Another push of the button revealed a beach scene; another push revealed an apple orchard; another one caused a city party scene at night, clearly before the institution of curfew, to appear. A couple more presses revealed what I had hoped my search would uncover. Above me, as though I were lying outside in the grass, was a starry night sky. I closed my eyes, breathing in the slightly humid, but nonetheless refreshing, summer air while listening to crickets chirping around me.

My eyes opened, staring at the starry scene unfolding before me. I scanned the sky until I located the constellation I'd been looking for. The Big Dipper and the special star contained within it, the last star at the tip of the handle, was directly above me. I stared at this star for the remainder of the night, imagining Chase running toward me, hurtling over the constellations in the night sky.

# 21

## THE SIMULATION EVALUATION

I DIDN'T SLEEP at all. Despite the rejuvenated sense of calmness I felt, it still wasn't enough to settle my body down to accommodate rest. The funny thing was that I didn't even feel tired at all. It was as if I'd gained a second wind that was far from ready to blow over. For what seemed like an eternity, I lay there motionless, ready to start my day before deciding to beat the tone.

"Lights on."

The room lit up, stinging my eyes, causing me to rub them in response. My shoulder was still sore, but the pain was more manageable. My fingers grasped the shower curtain, pulling it aside as I turned on the hot water in the hopes it would alleviate the rest of the pain. When I stepped into the shower the near-scalding water enveloped my body, caressing every inch of my skin. My muscles loosened up and I was provided with a brief sense of comfort. I moved my afflicted shoulder in semi-circles to stretch the muscles further.

Wrapped in a towel, I padded back to my room and opened the closet door. Hmmm…superhero costume or civilian clothes? Decisions, decisions. I grabbed the suit, figuring that I should continue to try to break it in with the hopes that perhaps, like a new pair of shoes, after a few fittings it wouldn't be quite as uncomfortable. As it was, it was so tight that I was afraid to eat for fear that another ounce of weight gain would cause a mass explosion within its molecularly-engineered, Kevlar, diamond-encrusted structure.

The hallway was quiet as I trekked down it. Everyone was probably still asleep. At Blake's door I paused in an attempt to determine whether or not I could hear any rustling, but not so much as a snore emanated from his room. I opted not to push the plate next to his door to disturb him, remembering what he'd told me last night about not having slept in four days.

When I traveled down the hall through the double doors, I noticed that the television in the sitting room was already on and tuned in to the five o'clock news. I surmised that someone must already be awake before confirming that notion by detecting a whiff of sausage and eggs in the air. The kitchen crew must already be busy in the kitchen as cooking breakfast to suit each individual palate at The Epicenter surely took some time. Curious, I ventured toward the dining hall to investigate.

Ever since the implantation of the transmitter, I'd been non-stop hungry and, as I approached the dining hall, I heard the clanging of pots and pans accompanying the sizzle of food in a skillet. I peeked in just in time to see Colby cracking an egg on the side of an oversized pan then expertly dropping it in along with probably half a dozen others.

"Good morning, Celaine."

I turned my head to see Becca mixing pancake batter in a large stainless steel bowl. "I swear I'm not staking out the food." My face flushed.

She laughed. "Oh, that's all right. Blake comes in early all the time. That's why you hardly ever see him eating much when everyone gathers together for meals. We know how hungry you guys can get."

"Yeah, it's a little overpowering."

Henry stepped out of the freezer with sausage patties in hand. "We have some eggs and sausage links made up if you're hungry."

"Oh, no...no...I'll wait. I'm just more or less walking around out of sheer boredom more than anything else."

"Yeah," Henry began, "it has been quite a while between attacks."

"Maybe the bastard has finally met his maker," Colby added between egg cracks.

"No, he's preparing himself for something big," Henry interceded. "This next one won't be just some tiny bonfire where maybe a handful of people are injured. If you look at his track record the worst attacks always come after a period of relative dormancy. It's almost like his homicidal lust builds to overflowing. I predict that, in his next attack, hundreds, if not thousands, will die."

I shuddered. Becca paused her mixing to look at me, gauging my reaction. "Blake and I will be ready. We have to be," I said unconvincingly.

"That you do," Henry agreed. "You two are the only hope we have of regaining relative normalcy around here again." I nodded, feeling the urge to leave the room.

"Celaine, are you sure you don't want anything?" Becca called after me. "Really, I can make you anything you want. It's no trouble."

"No, I'm fine," I said without turning around.

When I was out of view, I heard a slap and Becca's voice saying, "Good job, Henry," in a disgusted tone.

I walked down the hall with Henry's words replaying in my mind. "Hundreds, if not thousands, will die." He was right. The death tolls in the larger attacks had been escalating. The Man in Black was getting bolder with his targets, selecting those more frequented and heavily populated. Was I going to be ready for the next attack when it came or would I be more of a burden to Blake? Would I be just another one of Blake's former partners later identified only as "Blake's successor" instead of by name? No. I wouldn't allow that to happen. If I was going down, I was going to take that monster with me.

The training room appeared in front of me. I needed to be there; I needed to learn everything I could to survive long enough to fulfill my promise. Through the closed doors, I heard the familiar clanging of fingers on a keyboard. Yet another person was awake at this unholy hour. I debated whether or not to go in, but figured there was no reason why I shouldn't.

"Good morning, sunshine," Cameron turned from his work with the simulator to greet me.

"Morning, Cameron."

"It's Cam to you," he said with a wink.

"Okay, Cam. What are you doing up already?"

"Genius never sleeps."

"Of course. How silly of me."

"You look like you're feeling better." He'd turned back around to resume his typing.

"I'm alive. That's all that matters."

Cameron feverishly typed numerous characters into a program, then minimized it to reveal, in the foreground of yet another screen, the same orange sky and demolished buildings that were in the program he'd been working on the day before, except, in this screen stood a male character decked out in fatigues, a t-shirt, and a bandolier.

"Another character for your life-sized video game?"

"You betcha'. The opening act before the finale starring The Man in Black. Blake likes to warm up first."

Goosebumps appeared on my arms at the mere mention of that name. Cameron hit a couple of keys and the character sprung to life, leaping from one pile of concrete rubble to another. The push of another key prompted the man to ball his fingers into a fist and, with fury, he punched the concrete, causing it to rupture in two. I imagined my body under the force of that fist, which sent a sickening chill to course down my spine.

"When do I get a crack at this?" I asked without taking my eyes off the screen.

"Are we talking about the simulator or me?" Cameron smirked.

"You don't miss a beat, do you?"

"I'll wear you down one day."

"Today? Would it be possible for me to try it out today?"

"I don't see why not. I'll have to clear it with Victor after he gets in first."

"Victor doesn't live here?"

"He has a room here, but he pretty much comes and goes. I don't think any of us know where he lives, to tell you the truth. Blake will have to go in with you for your first time in the simulator for training purposes. You'll need your helmet, too."

"Don't I have to be fitted for one?"

"We did it after you almost died on us the second time. Since you're prone to passing out, we figured we at least ought to have something made for you to protect your head."

"How very considerate of you." I glanced back up at the screen, searching for the main event. "When do you think he's going to strike next?"

"That's a question you'll have to ask either Lana or Brian. I deal with facts, not variables."

"You're saying that they don't even know when or where it's going to happen?"

"They rely solely on the information they receive from their informants on the outside. Most of the time, the information they receive is valid. Sometimes, we're led on a wild goose chase."

"Nice use of governmental resources."

"It's the government, not rocket science. Besides, thanks to President Brooks' tax hikes, the pit our funding comes from is darn near bottomless."

The doors opened with Blake emerging looking well-rested, a first since I'd met him. He was suited up, a helmet on his head and another in his hands.

"Victor wants us to hit the simulator." He looked at me. "He also says to go easy on the first timer here." My hands shot out from my sides just as Blake unexpectedly pitched the helmet to me. Pain from my shoulder struck my body like a bolt of lightning, almost forcing me to drop the helmet.

"Nice reflexes," Cameron said.

"Yeah, they take her straight to the floor."

"Ha, ha." I sneered. "If I remember correctly, I believe I was keeping pace with you rather nicely yesterday."

"Blake is getting his butt whipped by a girl," Cameron said, all but giggling.

"I wouldn't talk if I were you," I said, crouching down face-to-face with Cameron. "After all, I think I can take you, too."

His eyes grew wide with excitement. "I'd let you wipe the floor with me any day." I arose disgusted, and followed Blake into the simulator.

"Blake," Cameron called behind us, "have you had Marcus check out your suit yet?"

"I haven't gotten around to it."

Cameron muttered something about suicide.

"What was that about?" I asked Blake after we entered the simulator.

"Cameron is being a little on the anal side. He seems to think that our suits are like tires and need to be replaced after so many uses. I'm not too worried about it."

"Brave man."

"There's a fine line between being brave and just not giving a shit anymore," he sighed. "You better put your helmet on."

I fumbled with my helmet, pulling it over my face like a ski mask. The top portion was perfectly contoured to my skull. However, unlike the usual helmet, this one was made out of the same material as the portion shielding my head. The material came down through the back of my head, covering my ears. It masked my eyes, extending down to the tip of my nose. On each side were solid black metallic straps. I grabbed the straps, snapping them in place under my chin. Cameron's voice blared over the loud speaker, subsequently echoing throughout the empty, padded room.

*"Simulation will commence in sixty seconds."*

"Just follow my lead." Blake's muscles tensed as he positioned himself in front of me to protect me from the invisible threat.

"Who said chivalry was dead?"

*"Thirty seconds."*

"If this is the one I think it is, it will be a piece of cake," he reassured me.

I braced myself, trying to project an air of confident vigilance while I waited to be encased by the unknown. The tension was mounting in my body, and I felt as if I were going to leap out of my skin.

*"Ten seconds."*

"Get ready to jump to the left and keep low." Blake's voice came over an ear bud on the side of my helmet.

*"Let simulation commence."*

In an instant, the padded room before me changed into a scene straight out of a post-apocalyptic movie. I found myself standing amidst rubble with felled wires, bricks, tiles, tires, and bits of motor vehicle parts rusted from their exposure to the elements at my feet. An orange hue illuminated the sky. Fires burned in the distance from the mountains of debris.

"Now!" Blake commanded.

I leapt to the left, overshooting Blake, coming to a landing on my side in the rubble. Regaining my bearings, I sought refuge near a concrete pillar. Blake was on the opposite edge of the pillar, motioning for me to join him. Carefully, I crawled over the rubble. There were personal effects strewn about over the ground that I hadn't noticed before, adding an extra touch of eeriness to the scenario we were in. Books were scattered about as though a library had exploded. Chairs were overturned along with multitudes of broken glass and porcelain from once priceless heirlooms. However, what struck me the most were the stuffed animals and dismembered dolls intermingled in the chaos. Cameron was one sadistic bastard.

When I crawled over the rubble, it evoked a feeling in me I hadn't felt in years. From what I remembered from my years of therapy after The Lakes bombing, what I was experiencing was the post-traumatic stress I'd been diagnosed with. Despite being covered by gloves, my hands felt clammy. Sweat poured down my forehead, and my breathing was becoming shallower as I made my way towards Blake. I could feel myself becoming dizzy, making me fearful of passing out before I made it to him. "Snap out of it, Celaine," I told myself, continuing my crawl. Once I was beside Blake again, I was able to regain my composure.

"Look ahead; off to the right to about two o'clock," he said.

I followed Blake's instructions, but wished I hadn't, for what I saw made every hair on my body stand on end. Before us, standing about ten feet tall, was the same character I'd watched Cameron upload.

"Funny, he wasn't so menacing on Cameron's monitor."

Blake laughed. "That's because he was only four inches tall then."

"Details, details."

The graphics were unbelievably realistic. Even from a distance, I could make out every feature on the giant that stood before me, from the wrinkles in his clothing to the distinct markings on his face, including the large scar across his right cheek bone; a feature I hadn't noticed before. But what struck me the most were his eyes. They weren't vacant like I would expect from a programmed apparition. Instead, they appeared contemplative – evil. Almost as though life was flowing within them. I shuddered to think that this thing before me may actually have a soul.

"Get ready. Show's about to start." Blake ordered.

"I was born ready."

"That's funny because you look and sound terrified. Remember, I have an ear bud, too, and I can hear every gasp you utter."

"I always breathe like this."

"Uh-huh. Just copy everything I do and try not to get too overzealous again." Blake had no sooner spoken those words when Mr. Big and Ugly took charge with strides that could be measured in meters. "Jump!" he ordered, leaping into the air.

I followed suit, trying to give it less "oomph" than I had before which proved to be an even bigger downfall. Not only did I not keep stride with Blake, but the jump itself wasn't quite enough to clear the giant I was trying to evade. And realizing that I wasn't going to leap over him, I swung my leg out in mid-air where it made contact with the bridge of his nose, barely throwing him off balance. I landed in the rubble behind him, tumbling to rest next to a rusty sedan door. Dazed, I tried pulling myself back up when I heard Blake shout. "Celaine, run!"

I looked up to see my pursuer looming over me. In a haste, I scrambled to my feet in an attempt to leap away from the gargantuan hand heading toward me. In mid-leap I was jolted back and then slammed down into the ground by a pair of hands grasping my waist. I felt my body being pulled upward and, before I knew what was happening, I was face to face with the monster. His grip tightened around me, which caused a sharp increase in pressure around my abdomen and ribs. He squeezed my body tightly like a sadistic anaconda with its newfound prey until my air supply became compromised and my ribs began to crack. Gasping for breath, I struggled to free myself from his death grip before losing consciousness, but the more I struggled the tighter his grip became, squeezing more and more air out of my body.

As I felt myself begin to black out, the giant suddenly released me from its clutches. I looked up to see what had caused him to let me go, noticing that Blake now stood where the monster had been with the cement pillar we'd taken refuge behind earlier gripped firmly in his hands. The monster rolled through the rubble, striking his head on bricks that had broken loose from a simulated building.

"I totally had him," I said, catching my breath.

"I could tell."

With a subhuman growl, he got back to his feet, stumbling a little in the debris beneath him. "Charge him," Blake yelled, running in the direction of the monster. I ran next to Blake, keeping my body and movements in sync with his. "Flank him," he ordered.

I branched off, taking aim at the monster's right side while Blake approached from the left. The monster, understanding what we were about to do, took steps to defend himself in response. He swiped at me, but this time I was able to dodge his outstretched fingers and, with a flying kick, made contact with his body just as Blake did the same. Big and Ugly moaned in obvious pain as his body was thrown through the air. With a blood curdling shriek, he was silenced forever, his body impaled on a steel beam. The gore was all so graphic and real that I had to turn my head for fear I would get sick at the sight of the blood that was pouring out of the monster's wound.

"Cameron spares no expense when it comes to the realism, does he?"

"No. He's a morbid little bastard. Brace yourself; we're far from being done."

"Fantastic."

In a split second, two more monsters appeared before us. They were just as big and just as ugly as their predecessor except with a hint more anger in their eyes. It was as though they realized they'd journeyed here to avenge their friend's untimely demise.

"More spawns," Blake mused.

"Looks like I get my very own this time."

"Do you think you can handle him before he handles you?"

"Very funny. Don't worry, I can keep a man's hands off me."

"On my mark," Blake commanded. "One, two, three, go."

Side by side, we took off towards the offenders. In unison, they crouched down in a defensive stance to await our blows. Blake struck first, hitting his monster in the chin with his fist and knocking him back a couple of steps. It was my turn. Determined, I whirled my body around in a spin kick and struck my target with the heel of my right boot just as he reached out to grab my other foot. My kick was just enough to knock him sideways, enabling me to twist my body around in a backwards flip where I landed on my feet. However, I didn't have long to celebrate my feat of gracefulness when Big and Ugly, Jr. took charge. I leapt up into the air, landing behind him where I delivered a series of blows to his back until I forced him to fall forward. Triumphantly, I looked over at Blake only to see him casually resting upon his already slain opponent.

Angry, I made one last flying leap at my monster, sending him crashing into the windshield of a pickup truck, silencing him forever.

Blake gave me a nod of approval as he stood up from his resting spot atop his kill. He motioned for me to join him as he ran behind the shell of a dilapidated building. Behind the building, he regained his stance of readiness, which meant only one thing. Seconds later, three more spawns appeared.

"I've got the two on the right," Blake announced.

Again, I took off after him, repeating the scenario that'd unfolded with my last successful kill. For the next hour it played out like this. Blake and I worked as a team to take down our unwitting challengers. He stepped in when I needed him to and there were a few times where I landed the blows that allowed Blake enough room to make the kill shot to his opponents. I was thrown, kicked, punched and shoved into the rubble, but never for an instant did I feel like I was getting tired, nor did I feel as though I was in too much pain to continue.

With every opponent we felled, more appeared to take their place. Until, at one point, we had ten of them to contend with. After the final one fell, I turned to Blake and held out my hand for a congratulatory high five. He looked at me and shook his head.

"That was just a warm up," he said.

"A warm up?"

I'd remembered my conversation with Cameron earlier that morning when I heard a disgusted grunt coming from Blake. I didn't need to look up as I knew what was coming. Swift booms and clangs approached us as The Man in Black sprinted through the rubble from across the simulated city. Instantly, I felt myself being transported back to The Lakes, my nightmares overcoming me. The Man in Black drew closer, but I was frozen back in time.

"Celaine," Blake called my name frantically.

My body was in such an overwhelming state of shock that I couldn't budge. Two things happened next: first, I stood mask to mask with The Man in Black; then, I was sent flying through the air into the rubble as an alarm rang throughout the simulator.

"Congratulations, Celaine," Cameron's voice came over the loudspeaker, "you're dead."

# 22
## THE RUMINATIONS OF LUCY PIERCE

BLAKE HELPED ME up from my point of impact on the padded floor. We were within the sanctity of the dull, boring simulation room again.

"What happened back there?" he asked.

"I don't know other than I choked." Victor's voice boomed over the loudspeaker. "Okay, you two, break time. Get ready for breakfast. Celaine, you will have another chance to redeem yourself later today."

I looked at Blake, dejected. "Is that his way of saying I sucked?"

"Pretty much."

We walked out of the simulator, Blake taking off his helmet and I following his lead.

"What the heck hap…," Cameron began.

"Not now, Cameron," I interrupted him.

He slunk back in his chair and whispered something I couldn't make out to Drew, who'd joined him.

Victor stared at me, wearing a clear look of disappointment. I averted my eyes as I headed out the door into the hallway, knowing I hadn't performed up to par. After we'd gotten a safe distance down the hall, Blake asked the obvious. "So, what did happen in there?"

"I don't know." I really didn't care to talk about it, but I figured I owed my partner an explanation. "You never had a personal experience with The Man in Black, right?"

"If by personal experience, you mean have I ever physically come in contact with him outside of here then, yeah, you're right." Blake said, offended.

"I'm sorry. I didn't mean to short change the fact that your best friend was killed. What I meant by that was, you've never personally been in the middle of the carnage and, with that in mind, I'm also assuming that you've never been plagued by the nightmares that wait in the shadows to haunt your dreams on any random night of their choosing. I've never seen The Man in Black personally like you have. I've only had witness descriptions and newspaper accounts to aid in my mental picture of him. Seeing him today live and in color, even though it was just a simulated version of him, brought back all of those nightmares. I was once again that broken teenage girl who was plucked from the ruins of The Lakes Mall. So, I'm sorry to have let you down, but unless you've ever been in my shoes, you wouldn't understand." I was shaking as we entered the hallway containing our rooms. I'd vented in a way I'd never been able to before, not even with Chase. Blake stopped me in my tracks and took me by the shoulders, forcing me to turn towards him, forcing me to look him in the eyes.

"You're wrong," he began. "True, your experience was far more traumatizing than mine was. But if you think for an instant that I haven't stayed awake at night thinking about Hank even before it was physically impossible for me to fall asleep, you're wrong. If you think that I've never thought to myself over and over again repeatedly like a broken record what, if anything, I could have done differently in my life to have possibly saved him, then you're also sorely mistaken. You see, he wasn't taking a joyride over that bridge because it was a nice day out and he needed some air. He was coming to help me, to give me strength to face my addiction. He was coming to my house to participate in an intervention put together by my family because I refused to do a thing to help myself and give up that damn bottle. He died because of *me* and *my* choices. Don't think I'm not haunted by that. The only difference between you and me is the fact that instead of letting my nightmares consume me, I look them in the eye and fight right back. I fight, not for me, but for Hank." He was stern without raising his voice, but I noticed a slight tremble in his speech. "I want you...I want you to go back...go back to that day when your family was taken from you. Go back five minutes before it happened and you're now suddenly face-to-face with that bastard. Only now you *can* do something about it. You can save them. Channel that the next time you're in the simulator and let's see if you back down then."

Blake placed his thumb to the plate next to his door, charging into his room. After a moment of hesitation, I attempted to follow him, but the door shut, beating me to the punch. Defeated, I slumped down on the floor next to his doorway. Selfish, I was being incredibly selfish. To think that I'd experienced more pain in life than any other person, especially here, was naïve. Blake's pain was obviously not something he let show very often. Only after an ignorant comment on my part was it brought to the surface. I knew I'd revealed a part of me that should have remained veiled. Determined to make amends, I stood up and pressed my thumb to the plate, watching as the door slid open.

Even though he was anticipating my retort, my appearance still rattled him. He was sitting on the corner of his bed with his head in his hands. He'd taken the top half of his suit off, revealing a sight I would never have expected to see. The ripped, muscular frame I'd been training with was marred with more scars than I'd ever seen on a living human body before. There were the obvious surgical scars around his navel and his breast bone, encircling his heart. But, besides the surgical scars, there were also combat scars that appeared to be inflicted by anything from a gunshot, burn, blunt object or something serrated; a knife or a piece of glass, perhaps. From his left shoulder, cutting through his nipple and journeying on down to his mid-abdomen, was a long, bright pink, newly healed scar. I knew I should turn away, but I couldn't. It was like a car accident, a morbid curiosity.

"You know," Blake said, "the funny thing about the technology here is that, more often than not, it fails in comparison to a nice deadbolt."

"Look, Blake, I'm sorry. I can go."

"Why? You're already here. Might as well stay and get comfortable." Blake stood up and tugged the rest of his suit down. Flushed, I turned my head towards the door.

"Geez...Blake," a surprised squeal escaped my mouth. "Just because we're partners doesn't mean I need to know *everything* about you." I heard the doors of the dresser open, some fumbling around, and then the sound of it shutting again.

"It's nothing you haven't already seen before on some other guy."

I looked back in his direction, making sure to keep my eyes above the equator in case the pants that I assumed he retrieved from his dresser weren't already on. Thankfully, they were, and I caught him just as he was pulling a t-shirt over his head, covering up the wounds on his abdomen. Against my better judgment, I asked him what I believed to be the obvious. "What happened to you, Blake?"

He looked at me puzzled, prompting me to make a gesture with my eyes towards his chest. "Oh, you mean the work of modern warfare that's overspreading my body like some form of masochistic graffiti?"

"If that's how you want to put it."

"Let's just say that I'll try my damnedest to not let it happen to you."

"None of those scars were there before you came here?"

"I hadn't had so much as my tonsils taken out before I arrived here. Since, I've had two kidney transplants, a new liver, my gall bladder removed, my spleen repaired, a portion of my intestines re-sectioned and removed as well as my heart operated on more times than I care to think of. Like I told you before, we're veritable human science experiments in this place. It's like a mad scientist's lab here."

At that moment, a realization hit me like a rogue lightning bolt. "Oh, my God."

Blake looked up at me. "What?"

"Is that what Cameron meant when he called you Frank?" Blake glanced back down again, verifying my observation. "It is...isn't it? Frank means Frankenstein, doesn't it? Wow, that little weasel."

"Don't be too harsh on Cameron. His social skills were developed during conversations with imaginary friends."

"I know, but still, that's harsh."

"That's life. They had to do whatever it took to keep me alive, spare parts and all." He looked back up at me with eyes more intent than before. "But I promise you, Celaine, as long as I have life left in me, I will not let this happen to you." He made a gesture to his abdomen, putting his hands back on his lap.

"I don't understand. What about our suits? Are they not supposed to prevent that kind of damage from happening to us?"

"Like all forms of technology, they aren't perfect. Obviously, if they hadn't worked at all, I would be dead instead of a walking horror movie. After a while, though, the suits start to wear down. Weaknesses develop in their structure. They become vulnerable. Plus, don't forget, I was the lab rat they used to test every theory they ever had."

"Blake, your life, your body. Have you ever wondered why you sacrifice so much for an uncertain future? Don't you have your regrets every time you look in the mirror and see what they've done to you?"

"No. My actions inadvertently took a life and, though it wasn't grounds for a murder trial, it is grounds for me to sacrifice my life to make up for the one that was lost because of me. I have no regrets. Do you?"

"No. At least, not yet, anyway."

"You should probably go and change."

"Actually, this suit has kind of grown on me."

"Well, then, we'd better get down to the dining hall. Our warden is waiting for us."

Lucy Pierce was on a mission, one which she wasn't going to stop until she'd obtained the answers she was looking for. No matter how many eyebrows she raised or whispers she provoked in her wake, she was determined to find out what had happened to the woman whose name meant nothing to anyone else but her: Celaine Stevens. Predictable, reliable, Celaine Stevens. The Celaine Stevens who'd lived in a bubble of conventionalism and, aside from a propensity for crude humor that tended to go over Lucy's head, never did anything unconventional.

After utilizing all of the resources available to her through favors owed by indigent clients, Lucy had done the research she hoped would turn up answers and result in the closure she needed. Closure, not only for her, but for Chase as well. She'd called in a few favors to Mr. Jackson, a dowdy old man and former patient of hers who happened to work for the Social Security Administration. Earlier in the year, she'd assisted him by offering free sessions when his wife, a lifelong manic depressive, committed suicide. Now, in her time of need, she felt it was time to cash in even though she felt guilty as, if caught, he would undoubtedly be terminated. However, this prospect didn't even seem to faze Mr. Jackson as, when she contacted him, he agreed to do whatever was in his power to help her.

She provided him with what information she knew about Celaine, asking that he track her activity by using the Social Security number she'd obtained from Celaine's worried Aunt Tasha. Even though she hadn't known what to expect from Mr. Jackson's findings, the information she received from him was unexpected, raising her suspicions to the hilt. No record existed of there ever having been a Celaine Stevens matching the information of her missing friend. Dejected, but undeterred, Lucy thanked Mr. Jackson for his efforts and resumed the search on her own.

As disappointing as it was, the news didn't surprise her. She suspected there was something fishy about the way the government had been operating since President Brooks took office and, although she was back at square one, she felt as though she'd made some headway. Little doubt remained in her mind that Celaine's new job somehow involved the government. After all, who else could erase all trace of a person's existence?

On a rainy afternoon, Lucy pounded the pavement in Washington, D.C., flyers in hand, searching for the friend who'd been gone for nearly a month. Hundreds of people saw the brightly colored flyers depicting Celaine's image. Most of them glanced at it for no longer than a millisecond, shook their heads, and promptly refused her pleas to take the flyers and distribute them amongst their friends.

Despite her umbrella conspiring against her, bending out of shape in the strengthening winds, a soaking wet Lucy continued her mission, seeking refuge underneath the awning of an office building. While waiting under the awning, she stopped every employee who came in and out of the building, inquiring as to whether their employer was government operated and if they'd ever had anyone disappear on them like her friend had. This inquiry was met with several frightened expressions and eventually got her kicked out from the shelter of the awning back into the pouring rain by a security guard who'd muttered, "That kind of questioning is bound to get you killed." Undaunted, she blew off his comment and continued down the street.

Towards the end of the day, with only a few flyers remaining after posting them in store windows, on light poles and in telephone booths, she ran into a man who took particular interest in her and her mission.

"Can I ask what it is you're doing?" he asked, stopping her on the street.

"I'm looking for my friend. She disappeared a month ago with the story that she was moving out West to start a new job. The problem is that, upon doing a few background checks, I was told that she basically doesn't exist and has actually never existed, which leads me to believe she's here somewhere."

"Hmm…interesting concept. Are you implying that it was a governmental job of sorts and that stripping her of her identity is a form of cover-up?"

"I know it sounds far-fetched, but I believe the only way she could have disappeared off the face of this planet is with a little governmental assistance."

"May I take a look at one of those flyers?"

Lucy handed the man a flyer and couldn't help but notice the marked change in his expression as he gazed at the photograph on it. It was an eerie expression she couldn't quite decipher; a cross between anger, worry and shock.

"May I keep this?" he asked, recovering quickly.

"Sure, that's what I made them for." She eyed him suspiciously.

"Very well." He neatly folded the flyer, tucking it into the pocket of his rain coat and, just as soon as he turned to walk back down the street, he paused to turn back around. "I'm sorry to hear about your friend but, if I were you, I would disregard the conspiracy theory you've concocted and consider the possibility that your friend disappeared because she wanted to. Whoever fed you the information you have was misinformed."

"I appreciate your thoughts, but in my heart I know what the truth is."

"So be it." The man nodded as he headed back down the street, traveling a couple of store windows down the block before Lucy called out to him.

"Hey."

"Yes." He turned around to face her again.

"May I ask what your name is?"

"Certainly. My name is Victor."

"Nice meeting you, Victor. Thank you for taking a flyer."

"Nice meeting you as well...Lucy. Right? The name on the flyer?"

"Yes. Lucy."

"Well, Lucy, thank you for the riveting conversation."

She nodded, and he turned to walk back down the street. After rounding a corner, he saw another flyer taped to a lamppost in front of a small family-owned diner. Promptly ripping it down, he balled it up and tossed it into a trashcan on the sidewalk. He then reached into the pocket of his khakis, removing his cell phone.

"Yeah," the voice on the other end answered.

"We have a problem; a potential security breach."

"You know how to handle those, so handle it," the irritated voice replied.

"Very well. Consider it handled."

# 23
# THE DAY AWAY

IN ONE SWIFT move The Man in Black crumbled beneath my feet, all signs of life leaving his digitized shell. I looked down at his body in disbelief that quickly gave way to a sense of accomplishment as the simulation room flickered back into less foreboding territory. Blake took off his helmet, beaming with pride as a teacher would at a student who'd finally gotten it. He held out his hand for a high five.

"And that's how it's done," he looked at me proudly.

"Did you ever have any doubts?" I asked, feigning disbelief.

"Umm…"

"Don't answer that."

"Do you want to get out of here for the day?" he asked in a hesitant tone.

"Of course I do. How are we going to make a break for it?"

"We just go." he said. "We put our time in today. Let's go."

I looked at Blake in disbelief at the level of defiance he was exhibiting and, together, we exited the simulator. Cameron, as always, was there to greet us.

"I'll set everything back up for you guys to have another run-through. I made it easy on you this time. Next time, you'd better watch your backs and…"

"We're done for the day," Blake announced.

"But...but...Victor says you need to keep practicing. She's not ready yet," he gestured toward me.

"Is Victor here right now? Blake asked.

"Well...no."

"Then we'll be back by curfew."

Cameron proceeded to follow us until we left the training room, blubbering the entire time. We ignored his pleas and, instead, walked to our rooms to change for our day of indiscretion.

I rummaged through my closet, pulling out the one outfit I'd managed to bring with me and placed it on the bed. After I peeled my suit away from my body, I stuffed it into my backpack and then slipped into my blue jeans, which were looser than I remembered. My fingers down the length of my stomach, discovering the abs that had formed since my arrival. I'd never had abs before, and feeling them underneath my fingers was like discovering a hidden treasure.

While kneeling down to pick my shirt up from off the bed I heard Blake's name announced through the speakers in my room as he pressed the thumb plate to gain entry. "Just a second," I called. It was too late. The door slid open revealing Blake in the doorway. In a hurry, I grabbed the shirt, pulling it over my head. "You know, just because you're cavalier about your nudity doesn't mean I am about mine."

I'd expected some smart aleck comment from him, but instead witnessed an uncharacteristically speechless Blake, who stood staring at the floor. "So...sorry. I should have waited for you out in the top...hall...the hall," he stammered.

"Are you all right?"

"I am now."

"Where are we going?"

"I thought I'd drive the cycle to the ocean for a day." He held up his backpack. "I snuck some sandwiches out of the kitchen."

"Well, Mr. Cohen, who would have thought you'd turn out to be such a deviant. A picnic on the beach, eh? You must have been really popular with the ladies."

"I can't complain."

The wind whipped past us as Blake weaved the motorcycle in and out of traffic down the highway. Even since my transformation into the super human world, Blake's suicidal break-neck speeds still made my stomach turn. Cars honked their horns at us in our wake, their occupants flashing us looks of pure annoyance which I was sure only made Blake drive with that much more reckless abandon.

In less than an hour, we pulled up to the parking lot facing the Atlantic Ocean. I'd always loved the ocean, a fact of which had made me go stir-crazy when I lived in Iowa. I found something enchanting about staring out at a large body of water. It always had a way of making me feel free, as though it could whisk me away to destinations only attainable in my dreams if only I were to close my eyes and hold out my arms.

We removed our helmets, taking them with us onto the sand, where Blake took two small rolled-up blankets out of his backpack and tossed one to me. I spread my blanket on the sand where I sat down and took my shoes off to let my bare toes explore it uninhibited. Blake sat down next to me, closing his eyes, allowing the salty, sweet ocean air to overcome him.

"Thank you," I said to him.

"For what?"

"This." I made a gesture towards the ocean and my surroundings.

"Don't mention it," he said. "I needed the break myself. They seem to forget that we're human beings, not robotic slaves."

"What exactly are they, Blake?"

"What do you mean?"

"You know, the cause, The Epicenter. What are they? Do *they* even know?"

"Unfortunately, we're not privy to that information," he said as though he'd contemplated the same unanswerable question before. "From what I do know of it, The Epicenter was instituted shortly after President Brooks took office; shortly after the attacks began. The public demanded action. So, in order to save his hide and his approval ratings, Brooks sought solutions from a collective group of individuals. One of those individuals was Victor, who touted himself as a human engineer."

Blake picked up a handful of sand, spreading his fingers apart as he allowed each grain to sift through them like a human hourglass. "In reality, Victor's more of a doctor with dreams of becoming a scientist who uses humans as test subjects. He had this grand idea of turning the ordinary into the extraordinary and possessed the research to back it up. Along with Dr. Harris and Dr. Martin, he plugged his idea to Brooks. Long story short, they were given the equipment and a time frame to make their idea for their new race of super humans come to fruition."

"It was like a 'you scratch my back and I'll scratch yours' kind of thing?

"Sort of. Brooks retained the faith of the nation, and Victor received the funding he needed to play God. He was able to hire the best of the best for his staff and thus, both The Epicenter and we were born."

"I'm not too sure about the whole best of the best part. I'm nothing special. Why I was chosen, I'll never understand."

"I don't know. I think you're pretty amazing."

"I have to say, you've surprised me, Mr. Cohen," I replied, trying my best to mask my embarrassment. "You're not nearly the hard ass you make yourself out to be."

"Yeah, well, that's our little secret."

"How about we break out those sandwiches you acquired from the kitchen."

We sat on the beach enjoying our impromptu picnic and each other's company in comfortable silence, which spoke volumes for our newfound friendship. Being with each other and enjoying the company that only another person of our kind provided was enough conversation for the both of us. We were true partners. Blake and I were the only two people in the world who could possibly understand what the other was going through.

"Come on." I stood up, grabbing Blake's hand.

"What?"

"Are we just going to sit here all day? We're at the beach, let's take advantage of it."

"I thought we were."

"Oh, geez, Blake. Live a little."

I tugged at his arms harder, pulling him to his feet, much to the amazement of the other beachgoers around us.

"You need to be a little more discreet, you know," he muttered.

"Wow, who says white guys can't jump," I replied with a wink.

He rolled his eyes. "Great cover."

"I thought so, too."

We walked to the shoreline where I ran up to my calves in the ocean; the waves splashed droplets of water that attacked my jeans. I looked up at Blake to see that he was watching me with an amused grin. With my foot, I splashed him with more water than I meant to, soaking the front of his pants.

"Oh, really," he replied playfully. "You've just started something here that I don't think you're going to be able to finish."

"Bring it."

Challenge accepted, he kicked his shoes off and raised his leg as though readying himself to splash me, but instead of kicking water, he barreled at me, knocking me off my feet and into the waves. Before I could fall over, I grabbed hold of his arm, pulling him into the depths of the ocean with me. When I surfaced, I sat up in the water. Blake was sprawled on my lap, laughing.

"I'm…I'm sorry," he stuttered, removing himself from my lap.

"Why? Do you think I've never had a man in my lap before?" I splashed him once more before standing back up to head to our spot in the sand. "I needed this," I told him when we were seated back on our blankets. "I just wish I had extra clothes to change into."

"You'll air dry just fine," he said with a laugh.

Looking around the beach, I noticed a group of people staring in our direction as if they were studying us for signs of recognition. "Do you know those people?" I asked.

"What people?"

I nodded in the direction of the gawkers. "The ones over there who keep looking over here as though they're getting ready to walk over at any minute to introduce themselves."

Blake glanced at the group out of the corner of his eye. "No, I can't say that I do."

"It's strange how they keep glancing over here and talking amongst themselves."

"They probably just think they recognize one of us. I wouldn't worry about it unless they actually do come over here." He ran his fingers through his hair, which caused water droplets to free themselves and run down his back. "I'm thirsty. Do you want anything?"

"An iced tea would be great. If you don't mind."

"Not a problem." He stood up to venture to the concession stand a short distance from where we sat.

I knew that I shouldn't concern myself with the people who still kept looking over in my direction even after Blake had left, but there was just something about the way they were looking at me that made me wonder. It wasn't a look of curiosity anymore, but a look of fear.

It had been a while since he'd had as much fun as he'd had today. It had been a while since he felt so alive, or that he actually wanted to be alive for that matter.

"One iced tea and one water, please." He placed his order at the concession stand, still sopping wet from the ocean. His t-shirt, skin tight from the water, clung onto his biceps, which generated stares of admiration from the women who passed by him while he waited for their drinks. Strangely, he didn't notice any of them. He'd only noticed one woman all day, and he only wanted one woman to notice him.

"That will be $2.75."

Blake handed the concessionaire the money and took the drinks. On his way back, something posted on a light pole caught his eye, causing him to do a double take.

"Oh, crap," he said.

On the light pole was the same beautiful, vibrant woman he'd spent the last few weeks training as his partner. In shock, he dropped the drinks on the sand encrusted pavement and ripped the flyer down from the pole, balled it up and threw it onto the ground.

When he looked back in Celaine's direction, he noticed that one of the members of the group of people who were staring at her so intently was cautiously making his way over to her. Hurriedly, he sped towards her, making it just in time.

"We've got to go, now," he said.

"What? Why?

"They need us back at The Epicenter."

# 24

# THE ROOFTOP

A MONTH HAD passed since my arrival at The Epicenter and, for the most part, I seemed to be getting the hang of things. The initial shock of having been thrust face-to-face with the virtual Man in Black had worn off, enabling me to focus on my training in the simulator. And like any overzealous coach, Blake kept me entrenched in an arduous conditioning schedule. From dusk until dawn, I learned to evade, block, and master my newfound abilities.

Over time, I began getting the best of Blake–much to the amusement of Cameron and the crowd of Epicenter inhabitants who'd taken to gathering at the gym, throwing heckles from the sidelines whenever I managed to one-up my teacher. Oddly, though, Blake didn't seem to mind. We were becoming as one in our movements, as one in our attacks. In the simulator, we attacked in sync, bringing down our targets in virtual choreographed perfection.

Since our day at the beach, we'd become closer, developing a friendship I wouldn't have thought possible only a month prior. On our sleepless nights, Blake regaled me with tales of his heroics during his former life as a firefighter. I, in turn, confided in him about my family's death; my own near-fatal encounter with The Man in Black; my subsequent move to Iowa; and my life with Chase. We'd both sustained losses that had changed our lives irrevocably, breaking us in half, bonding us together. If misery loved company, then our partnership was the picture of perfection.

"You're one tough broad," Blake turned to me in the sitting room one night after everyone had gone to bed.

"Yeah, I'm a regular Wonder Woman," I laughed. A cheesy romantic comedy I'd seen at least a dozen times emanated from the screen. It had only been on for twenty minutes, but to Blake, those few minutes might as well have been an eternity; a fact made evident by the grimace etched upon his face. His silent protest entertained me more than the movie itself.

"No, really," he continued. "With all you've been through, and you've managed to take care of yourself and pick up your life. You're strong, Celaine. Most people would have waved the white flag of defeat. You've met life head-on, accepting the cards that fate dealt you. I admire that."

"Thanks, Blake," I said. "That means a lot." I grabbed the remote and switched the channel from Hugh Grant to Vin Diesel. "You've been punished enough for tonight," I said, laughing.

When we weren't training, Blake managed to keep me busy in a vain attempt at keeping my mind off Chase. During the day, it worked fairly well, but it was a different story at night. The darkness of a still Epicenter night had a funny way of shedding light on those thoughts I chose to keep locked away. When I did manage to sleep, I dreamt of nothing but Chase. The dreams were vivid. I could feel every strand of his hair on my face, the warmth of his breath upon my neck, taking me back to a time I'd never again relive. The next morning, I'd awake depressed, and no matter how hard I fought it, its impact wore heavy on me.

My depression was becoming so obvious that I was sent down to Dr. Lin's office more than once for an evaluation of my emotional state.

Our sessions usually ended with me spilling my guts like a sinner in a confessional while Dr. Lin sat in her leather desk chair, scribbling some notes on a pad with the occasional *holy crap* look on her face. At the end of our sessions, she gave me more pills in the hopes that I would be too drugged-up to think of much of anything other than what Victor wanted me to. I'd flushed a multitude of prescription pills of various colors and sizes down the toilet. Not because I had anything against pacifying my emotional instability, but simply because my emotions were the only thing I had left tying me to my former life.

Dr. Lin cautioned against me venturing out of The Epicenter before I was emotionally ready, but I couldn't take it any longer. He was beckoning me like a beacon in the night, leading me away from the dark uncertainties ahead. I couldn't stay away any longer. For the last couple of weeks, besides training with Blake, I'd enlisted his expertise in learning how to operate a motorcycle. Apparently, my learning to ride a motorcycle was considered entertainment in his eyes, though I didn't care if he laughed at me. If all my spills, bruises, and humiliation lead me to him, it would all be worth it in the end.

"Why don't you just take one of the cars?" Blake asked me after I'd dumped the cycle for about the tenth time.

"You and your mad cycle skills got me hooked the night you brought me here. That and I think I'd look pretty badass on one." Blake had a smirk on his face that I knew meant he had something he was keeping bottled up inside. "Go ahead, say it. You know you want to."

He turned into a kid at Christmas. "You just want to feel all that power between your legs."

My resulting blush added to his enthusiasm. "Cameron must be rubbing off on you." That comment didn't set well with him.

In two weeks I'd mastered, as well as I could, the basic principles of motorcycle operation, including how much twist to give to the throttle for the perfect acceleration; braking smoothly without locking up the wheels; disengaging the clutch before shifting; and turning without ending up with a massive amount of hot metal on top of me.

"Remember," Blake said after he deemed me road ready for cycle operation, "wait until nightfall and ditch the bike in a safe location at least a couple of blocks from your intended destination." A hint of concern laced voice like he wanted to tell me to stay put, to not venture off, but he knew that such advice would be a waste of time and would only go unheeded. "Keep the pager and the cell phone on you at all times in case you're needed back here."

I nodded at Blake. Giddiness coursed through my body as I secured the helmet on my head. The motorcycle started with a thundering *vroom*, causing a wide grin to spread across my face. With a wave goodbye, I took off towards the tunnel leading to my freedom. Just before entering the tunnel, I stole one last look behind me, noticing that Blake was still standing there staring back at me, a dejected look reflected on his face.

The feeling of the open road, the asphalt against my tires, was exhilarating. Whatever inconsequential reason I had for shying away from motorcycles in the past eluded me. The cycle was equipped with a GPS. Directions sounded over a speaker built into my riding helmet. It was a godsend considering I had no idea whether or not I would be able to locate the entrance to The Epicenter amid the maze of pine trees without it.

About thirty minutes into my joy ride, the surroundings whizzing by me started appearing more and more familiar until, finally, the cityscape appeared in my field of vision like a glorious panoramic picture. I always loved overlooking the city at night, admiring the few remaining lights that still adorned the skyline like multi-colored stars.

Within minutes I rode into the city limits. The lump forming in my throat confirmed it all the more. In response, I rubbed my throat to counteract the tightness, but just as soon as that problem was resolved, I had a whole new one to contend with. Butterflies migrated back into my stomach and my nerves took hold. I hadn't felt like this since the day I first met Chase. A part of me couldn't help but wonder what Chase's feelings toward me were now. Did he think of me? How much? Was there still love for me or just nothing more than well-deserved hatred?

In an alleyway, five blocks from his apartment, I ditched the motorcycle in the same fashion Blake had done the night he'd whisked me away. Strewn about the concrete were large chunks of cardboard and garbage, which I used as makeshift camouflage to cover the bike. When I was satisfied that it had been concealed enough, I surveyed my surroundings, knowing that I shouldn't walk down the street.

I located a fire escape ten feet above my head and leapt onto the landing, where I began my quick ascent up the stairs, taking multiple steps at a time. At the top of the stairs, I took one last flying leap onto the rooftop. While running up fifteen flights of stairs would take the wind out of most people, it only served to invigorate me more from the sheer excitement of seeing Chase again. In a flash, I darted across the rooftop, springing from its ledge to the roof of an adjoining building. In my head, the spectacle resembled a scene from almost every action movie I'd ever seen, making me feel like a bona fide action hero.

I sprang across three more rooftops before arriving at St. Helen's dance studio, where the uber-coordinated conjugated to flail their limbs from here to there. Dancing was a sore subject to me. When I was a little girl, Carol pushed me to take it. I'm pretty sure it was more for the frilly dresses—which I refused to wear and of which she was desperate to photograph me in—than the actual dancing itself. After a couple of months of downright begging and bribery, Carol had worn me so far down that I relented to taking the class just to make her shut up. Needless to say, it was every bit as traumatizing as I'd imagined it would be. I was a tall, pink, frilly train wreck.

Regardless of that, I had to appreciate the irony that I was, at this moment, beaming at the thought of having arrived at the very building I'd once loathed and vowed never to return to. The rooftop was close to being level with the tenth floor of Chase's apartment building across the street. I counted over five windows from the left, locating the one belonging to Chase's bedroom. It was all too surreal to be staring at the darkened window of his bedroom, to be on the outside looking in. Although it'd only been a little over a month since I'd last been there, it felt more like a lifetime.

I crouched down near the ledge, making sure I stayed undetected in the shadows. Chase's schedule at the hospital fluctuated, ensuring that I would never fully be sure when and what shift he would be working. When we were a couple, that fact alone had made events such as date nights and vacations nearly impossible to plan. Tonight, I was relying on the hope that he was working second shift, which would make him due home any minute. Regardless of when he appeared, now that I was here, the thought of being this close to him without getting to see him was inconceivable. So I vowed to wait until I got what I came here for. And I didn't have to wait long.

Just minutes into my stake-out, I was rewarded with the sight I'd longed to see in my first month of captivity. Light appeared in Chase's bedroom, drawing my eyes into its glow. There he was, arriving home from work just as I hoped he would be. He was in his scrubs which he hated with a passion, and he must have had no clothes in his locker to change into after his shift. As if not being able to take them touching his skin anymore, he pulled the blue scrub shirt over his head, replacing it with a white undershirt from his dresser.

A familiar, moist burning sensation formed in my eyes. I turned my head, taking in a few deep breaths to counteract the tears streaming down my face. Seconds later, a high pitched squeal diverted my attention back to the bedroom window. To my surprise, he'd opened his window and was leaning out of it, eyes closed, drinking in the night air. At that moment, it took all I had not to reach out to him, to let him know I was here with him, and that he wasn't alone.

He opened his eyes, glancing in my direction. For a moment, our eyes seem to lock, enabling me to feel reconnected with him as though I'd never left. From my vantage point in the shadows, I knew he couldn't see me. A smile spread slowly across my face. Smiles were like a reflex that could only be triggered by Chase's presence.

The wind whipped through his hair as he leaned out of the window, continuing his gaze off into space, until his glance was diverted upwards towards the sky where it seemed stuck as though being pulled by some unseen force. With the skilled hands of a surgeon, he lifted a finger up toward the night sky, moving it around as if tracing an invisible path. Confused, I looked up to steal a glimpse of what had captured his undivided attention. The sky was crystal clear, revealing an ocean of stars, and I couldn't remember the last time I'd seen so many of them in a non-artificial setting. It was a breathtaking sight to behold. My eyes then followed the imaginary path Chase had drawn, leading me to the Big Dipper.

While lying together on my rooftop, we would often trace the different constellations with our fingers, drawing pictures of what we thought we saw. I pointed my finger up towards the sky, tracing the Big Dipper until I reached our star at the end of its handle, the tears running down my face like a raging river. Chase still loved me. I was sure of it. Sure, there may be some resentment and anger sprinkled into that love, but love was still present nonetheless.

I couldn't take it anymore.  Screw the rules.  After all, they were made to be broken.  Slowly, I raised myself up, starting to walk towards a beam of light coming from a light source that originated from a light post on top of the dance studio's rooftop stairwell.  My body was shaking as I contemplated what I would say to him, what he would say to me.  My boots clanked softly against the concrete roof closer and closer to the light when, mere feet away from the beam, I felt a vibration coming from the holster on my utility belt.  For a moment I stood perplexed, unsure as to what was causing the strange sensation, then I remembered the pager.  *Why now?  Why on my first night away must something go wrong?*  Angry, I tugged at the holster and freed the pager, nearly dropping it before regaining my composure long enough to read the message it displayed:

## GET BACK HERE ASAP

Great.  I angrily shoved the pager back into its holster, looking behind me to take one final glance at Chase's now dark, empty window.

"Goodnight, Chase."

With a running start, I leapt from building to building, diving face first into the alleyway concealing the motorcycle, my head careening towards the pavement.  Halfway through my freefall, I snapped my wrist to release the hidden cable tucked away in the arm of my suit.  The cable whipped out in the direction of its intended target: the landing of the fire escape.  I reeled some of the cable back to avoid impact on the pavement below.  It was the first time I'd tested the cable out in a true freefall and I prayed my training had paid off or it would be the last test I would ever do.  Success. Eight feet from hitting the ground, the cable tensed, allowing me to swing safely underneath the fire escape.  When I flicked my wrist again, the cable gained slack so that my feet gently touched the ground. I then unhooked the cable from the fire escape and proceeded to uncover the motorcycle.

His day at the hospital had been grueling.  Not only had he assisted in the amputation of a six-year-old boy's leg, but he also had to tell the parents of a nine-year-old girl that their daughter had leukemia. As a doctor, he tried not to become too consumed with his patients, but when your patients are doe-eyed children, that was impossible. Until a month ago, whenever he had a bad day, Celaine had always been there to lift his spirits, often breaking curfew to do so. Now, he had no one.

His emotions had waxed and waned during the last month. As to be expected, he had experienced both good days–though sparse–as well as his fair share of hard ones. On the outside, he appeared to be the same old has-it-all-together Chase. Whispers circulated around the hospital and, pretty soon, he found himself surrounded by several admirers consisting of young nurses and new interns, all vying for a date with the handsome young doctor. Hardly was there ever a time when he could walk down the hall without one of them flashing him a smile or trying to strike up a conversation about the most trivial of matters. The man in him enjoyed the new attention, however, his heart wouldn't let him betray his memory of her. It had been over a month since she'd left him, and he still held tight to the engagement ring tucked away in a safe in his room. Allowing himself to part with the ring would be like admitting she was never going to come back to him.

The light in his room flickered on as he flipped the switch. When not at work, all he wanted to do was sleep. It was the only way he could escape reality. Exhausted, he tore off his scrubs, pulled an undershirt on over his head, and sat down on his bed, his head in his hands. At that moment, an urge was overcoming him; an urge that he couldn't quite understand. Something was drawing his attention to the window as though he were being watched.

"Wow, I really must be going crazy," he muttered.

Nonetheless, this strange, new feeling was strong, strong enough that he found himself giving into it and, rising from his bed, he opened the window. The warm breeze flowed through his hair. He leaned out of it, closing his eyes, letting the air consume him. Still, the feeling that he was being watched didn't subside, in fact, as he hung his head out of the window it only intensified.

A glance down at the street didn't reveal anyone. Scanning the roof of the abandoned dance studio across the street, his eyes focused on a particular section of the rooftop directly across from his window.

Something was drawing his eyes to this particular spot. Something was there that wanted to be seen. He shook his head. No, there couldn't be anyone there, the building was boarded-up shut.

Outside, the breeze intensified, making the warm air comforting. The moon shone brightly upon him, diverting his attention towards the one thing that just may be able to salvage his night. In the sky, providing the moon with celestial company, were more stars than he could ever recall seeing in his existence. But it wasn't just any star he wanted to see. Chase guided his fingers across the sky until he found the Big Dipper. He outlined the ladle and curved his finger up the handle, easily locating their star. *Hope*. How that name rang true now.

*Come back to me, Celaine*, he thought, his finger lingering on the star as though it had the capability to grant his one wish.

Overcome with exhaustion, he closed the window, turned off the light and crawled into bed, where a single tear streamed down his cheek as he fell into a restless sleep.

# 25

# THE PLAN

I NAVIGATED THROUGH the pine trees, traveling at speeds that shouldn't be possible for a motorcycle, especially in the woods. Veering off the path, I flew over branches that had broken off and fallen to the ground in haphazard piles.

"Main hatch open. Celaine Stevens serial number two, four, five, nine."

The motorcycle thundered down the hatch and into the tunnel to the familiar interior of The Epicenter. I'd learned that the serial numbers were nothing more than a mere formality, kind of like a password given to us to gain entry through those entrances that didn't or couldn't feasibly house thumb plates. You had to love the efficiency at this place.

I entered the garage, encountering Blake who seemed to be waiting patiently for my arrival. He wore a look I hadn't seen on him before. A look of worry, not the cocky smirk I'd grown accustomed to. This was my first clue that a true emergency was brewing. My nerves on edge, I glided the motorcycle to a halt in front of him and killed the engine.

"What's going on?" I dismounted the motorcycle, removing my helmet.

"Our informants believe they know The Man in Black's next target."

"How do they know where he's going to strike?"

"We employ private investigators whose sole job is to tail him. They do the best they can but, for some reason, they can never stay less than two steps behind him. He moves around, finding new hideouts. Our investigators recently found one of those hideouts and gathered some of the information he left behind." He stopped walking, turning to face me.

"Celaine, he toys with us. That bastard wants us to figure out his next step, he wants the attention. He thrives on it. It's like he's taunting us with the hope that we confront him. He purposely leaves behind clues for Caine and Inez to decipher." Blake's nervousness rubbed off on me. "What was it they deciphered?

He shook his head, walking ahead of me again at a faster pace this time. This wasn't going to fly with me. He was purposely keeping something from me, and I was going to figure out what that something was even if it killed me. I picked up my pace to walk in time with him, becoming more aggressive. "Tell me, Blake. I'm your partner, and I have a right to know what I'm going to be facing. It's pretty obvious that you think I can't handle it and, quite frankly, I find that somewhat offensive considering the poundings I've been able to inflict upon you." My words had no effect on him, a fact that boiled the very blood that ran through my veins. I stopped dead in my tracks before giving into my urge to tackle him. "Damn it, Blake," I yelled. "At least have the common decency to tell me what's going on."

He whirled around to face me again. "All right, but you need to promise me something first."

"Okay." I walked closer to him, coming to the realization that I already knew why he was being so secretive. I hesitated, "This attack is going to hit close to home for me, won't it?"

"It never ceases to amaze me how astute you are," he laughed half-heartedly. "You need to promise me, Celaine, that you won't pull a Liam on me. Keep your emotions in check. Don't let passion get the best of you."

"Oh, my God." My body trembled.

"Promise me, Celaine," Blake pleaded. "I don't know what it is about you that makes me crazy, but I won't lose you like I did the others. You're different than they were. You're the first genuine person I've met in a long time. So, I beg you, please."

I braced my body against the wall to keep from collapsing, my stomach sinking to a low I hadn't felt in ten years. "It's Hope Memorial, isn't it? It was more of a statement than a question as, in my heart, I already knew the answer, but looked up to Blake's face for confirmation regardless.

"Promise me."

Tears blurred my vision. "I promise."

"They want us in the training room to go over the information that came in."

He put his arm around me, a gesture I appreciated since I wasn't entirely sure whether I could walk on my own at this point. Everyone was gathered in the training room, their conversations coming to a stand-still once Blake and I entered. Perhaps, it was just my nerves that made me perceive all eyes being on me as I entered, particularly Kara whose red eyes gave away the fact that she'd been crying.

"Does she know?" Victor asked.

"Yes," Blake answered, "she does."

"Very well."

Victor approached me, placing his hands on my shoulders in what I assumed he meant to be a comforting gesture. But, despite his show of concern, something about Victor bothered me. Something that created a feeling of coldness that consumed me with his touch. "Celaine." My name on his lips sent a shudder down my spine. "This could potentially be the most devastating attack yet. Blake will be depending on you more than he's ever depended on anyone before. I need to know that you'll be able to handle this. If not, you need to tell us as, if you can't, you'll only be dragging him down."

"I can," I uttered. "I won't let him down."

Victor let go of my shoulders and returned to the group. "Inez," he said, "would you be so kind as to brief Blake and Celaine of our anticipated plan of action?"

Inez nodded. "The information we've received is, as always, sketchy to say the least. We have strong reasons to believe that Hope Memorial Hospital is the next target for the simple reason that the casualties could reach catastrophic levels. His intended victims would be, based upon the note he left for our investigators, 'sitting ducks'. The Man in Black's combination of genius-like intelligence and unpredictability makes him particularly deadly. There's no way to know when he's going to attack, so we're going to be sending the two of you near the hospital to scout it out and try to peg down with more certainty when and if the attack will take place."

"Why are we not having the hospital evacuated?" I asked. "This doesn't make sense. What are we supposed to do, wait until a bomb goes off and a couple of dozen people are killed before we swoop in?"

"Celaine," Victor jumped in, "there is simply no way we can alert the hospital on a hunch. Sure, we can have the hospital evacuated, but when it's cleared and nothing happens, then what? They file everyone back in and The Man in Black chooses then to attack? We can't ask the hospital to remove their critically ill patients. By doing so, not only would they be posing a risk of their patients' conditions deteriorating in the evacuation process, but it's just not feasible to move a couple of hundred people when we have no concrete evidence to go on."

Caine cleared his throat. "Our best guess is that the attack will take place sometime during the day between late morning and midafternoon when there are more patients, staff and visitors in the hospital. Historically, daytime attacks have been the case. We're sending you both out tonight to stake out the hospital. There are several abandoned buildings within a block of it that you can set up camp in if you choose to do so. Blake, you know the drill here and can answer any questions Celaine may have. Given Celaine's history with the hospital, we recommend that she stay put at camp until confirmation of The Man in Black is made. You are both to wear your suits at all times, with your helmets within arm's length of you. Blake, if you are going out during the day, please wear street clothes over your suit."

"You are dismissed," Victor declared. "Don't forget your medications and to keep us apprised as to your statuses. I would also advise that you take one of the cars and not the motorcycles."

I couldn't believe how coy they were being about all of this. I was fuming on the inside. All of the lives that could be lost was a devastating thought. What if the pediatric unit was the intended target? What if Chase was on staff when the explosion occurred? Nothing could happen to Chase, I wouldn't allow it. If it meant taking my last breath, I would keep him safe. If it meant breaking my promise to Blake, I would keep him safe. A hand appeared on my shoulder. I turned my head in its direction only to meet eyes with Blake as he motioned me to leave with him.

"Oh, and Blake," Victor called after us, "be sure to brief Celaine on the procedure in the event things don't go according to plan."

This last statement struck a particularly bad chord with Blake. "What did he mean by that?" I asked.

"Don't worry about it, I'll explain later." We trekked down the hall toward our rooms, Blake entering his and I, mine. I grabbed my helmet, flying back out of the door, practically running Blake down in the process. "Wow, you pack lightly for a woman." I wasn't in the mood to joke around and continued my unwavering mission down the hallway at such a pace Blake had to run to keep up with me. "Hey, I'm sorry. I know this is all a big shock to your system. I guess I was just trying to lighten the mood a little."

"I think I hate him."

"Excuse me?"

"Victor. There's something about him that makes me want to rip his head off."

"I'm right there with you."

We entered the garage, walking down each row, examining the cars.

"Which one do you want to take?" Blake asked.

"Whichever one will get us there the fastest."

"You're my kind of woman."

He walked to the end of the pack, keying in a code on the door of a sleek, black, coupe with an aerodynamically shaped exterior. It was obvious to even me that this machine was built for speed. The windows were tinted, ensuring that there was no possible way for anyone who happened to be observing the car to see the passengers it contained. In awe, I opened the door and crawled into the passenger seat next to him.

"Get your helmet on," he ordered, "just in case we have to make a quick escape."

Before I knew it, he took off, slamming me into the passenger side door. I angled my arm up, grabbed my seatbelt and secured it around my body. "You could have given me some kind of warning."

"Yeah, I could have, but what fun would that have been?"

The car sped through the tunnel, blaring through its entrance into the pine forest. I glanced at the dash, noticing that it wasn't laid out the way a normal car dashboard was, which, by now, really shouldn't have been a shocker to me. Blake pressed a button, lighting up a screen in the center of the console between him and I. In the screen was an image from the training room where everyone was still assembled. Inez walked over to the camera.

"Inez," he began, "we're en route to the target. We've taken vehicle number 445A. Please keep us informed of any new developments while en route."

"Roger, Blake."

He turned off the screen just as the car emerged from the trees and onto the roadway where he punched the accelerator. I watched the speedometer: 40...60...85...110... After 123, I focused my attention on the roadway hoping that, if he were to lose control, our deaths would be quick and relatively painless.

"You look like you're going to be sick."

"No, I drive 123 miles per hour all the time."

"Actually, we're going 154."

"Stupendous."

"At this rate, we'll be in the vicinity of Hope Memorial within twenty-five to thirty minutes."

"It's comforting to know that you fully anticipate getting us there in one piece."

He laughed. "Don't like my driving, do you?"

"When my eyes are closed, it's perfectly fine. By the way, do you really intend on me staying back at whatever hideout we establish?"

"Nope."

"Didn't think so. So, you're totally okay with defying Victor, too?"

"Yep."

"Glad we're on the same page."

"The way I see it, you know more about this hospital than any of us. You're our best asset for this mission. It would be stupid for me to leave you completely out of the equation when your knowledge could solve it before our time runs out."

"Are you going to tell me what Victor meant about things not going as planned?"

He grew sullen. He'd been avoiding an answer to this question, and I could tell he'd hoped I wouldn't bring it up again. His brow was furrowed with concern sprinkled with defeat. "I don't suppose you're going to take 'no' for an answer on this, are you?"

"Not a chance."

"What Victor means by that is if…if we were to confront The Man in Black, and in all likelihood we will, if one of us is injured, we can't seek treatment from anyone outside of The Epicenter. It would be a huge breach of security, compromising our entire program. Our funding would be cut and everything we've gone through would have been for nothing."

"If one of us is injured, and it's a survivable injury only if action is taken in…oh…let's say five minutes…that doesn't matter to them?"

"No, it doesn't."

"We're supposed to die as opposed to being treated by a third party?"

"Yes."

"Well, I guess the only solution to that is to not get injured at all then."

The familiar smirk returned to his face. "That's the spirit."

Our car turned down Blossom Street, the surroundings becoming more and more recognizable, telling me that we were less than a mile from Hope Memorial. As we turned down the street, a police car pulled out of a dark alleyway, coming within inches of our bumper. A red beam appeared from the windshield, a sign that our license plate was being scanned and read.

"Government plate?" I asked.

"Yeah, he won't dare try to pull us over." Blake prophesied. As though agreeing with him, the officer, appearing satisfied with the information he received, pulled into the lane next to us, nodding at Blake as he drove by. We continued down Blossom Street, eventually passing Hope Memorial, my former home. A shiver ran throughout my entire body, and goose bumps prickled my skin.

"What if he's watching us this very second?"

"Let him watch us then. The sooner he attacks, the sooner our job is done."

"And the sooner we catch him, the sooner we can return to our lives."

"Yeah. Our lives." The tone in Blake's voice seemed less than enthusiastic.

"You don't seem too thrilled with that premise."

"That's because I have no life to return to. The Epicenter and the cause are my life now. To be honest with you, I'm not too sure what I would do if I weren't there. I guess I never thought about it before." He turned down the alleyway of an abandoned building two blocks from Hope Memorial, angled the car behind a weathered dumpster, and killed the engine.

"Let's cover her up, then develop our plan of attack," he announced as we emerged from the car. I peered in the dumpster, where I spotted some cardboard. Once the car was covered, Blake and I, donning our masks, made our way down the dimly lit street to the doorway of a dilapidated building. From the looks of the weathered advertisements on the window, our chosen hideout had once housed fine antique furniture. With a swift kick, the boards covering the doorway were reduced to splinters by the force of Blake's foot.

"Show off," I said.

"Ladies first." He gestured for me to enter.

"Who said chivalry was dead."

"Chivalry? I'm sending you in first to make sure this place really is abandoned."

"You're using me as a human shield. How sweet."

"Only the best for you, babe. Don't say I never gave you anything." I stepped inside the pitch black building, allowing my eyes to adjust to the infinite darkness that encapsulated the room. A hint of moonlight shone through a space in the boards that crisscrossed the window, creating somewhat of a lunar light source. In the light of the moon, I saw a figure facing me at the far end of the room. My body stiffened as a surge of adrenaline overcame my being.

"Calm down, Cujo. You're looking at a mirror," Blake said, amused.

"I knew that." My body relaxed, and I was happy that it was too dark for Blake to see the crimson on my flushed cheeks.

"Uh, huh." We wandered around the cluttered building, avoiding pieces of broken furniture and whole pieces of perfectly good furniture left in the previous owner's hasty retreat. Buildings like this were common place around here. Once the frantic mortgagee left town, ultimately defaulting on their loan payments, the banks took over. Having worked at a bank, there were a few times when I was called in on weekends to help clear away the possessions of the former tenant of a building we were in the process of repossessing. Most of the time, the bank, after failing to locate the whereabouts of the tenant, would just send the confiscated items to auction and pocket whatever money was made. Then again, sometimes we employees would benefit from the cleanups, getting first dibs before the items were hauled away. The kitchen table in my former apartment came from just such a repossession.

I located a mattress amidst a pile of discarded dresser drawers. After clearing the debris away from it, I lay down, enjoying the feeling of an actual bed underneath my back instead of the board-like imposter mattress my room at The Epicenter offered. Blake walked over and sat down beside me. The mattress shifted with his weight. "Are you worried?" He asked, a hint of compassion reflected in his voice.

"Of course I am. I'm not worried for me, though. I'm worried for all of those patients, those physicians, nurses, visitors and…"

"Chase?" Blake interceded.

"Yes. As selfish as it may sound, I'm worried about him most of all."

"You aren't going anywhere near the pediatric unit, you know."

"What if that's where the action is?"

"We'll cross that bridge when we come to it."

"Some plan that is."

"Speaking of plans, we should probably come up with one of those."

"That's probably a good idea considering daylight is only a couple of hours away."

He dusted off the side of the mattress and laid down next to me, staring up at the ceiling. I shifted to my side, my head resting on my arm, spinning my finger around an indentation in the mattress, following one of the stripes that made up its pattern like an imaginary roadway. Blake turned his head to watch me, obviously amused. "I plan on putting street clothes on over my suit while I scout around the hospital using the map you're going to draw for me based upon your memory of the hospital's layout."

"You know, I'm not an expert. They've added an entirely new wing for the cancer center that I'm not at all familiar with."

"Do the best you can."

"What do you want me to do? It's not like I can just walk around there without being noticed."

"I need you to scout around the outskirts of the building, letting me know if you see anything that appears out of place to you. Also, do the best you can to break into the ventilation system. That seems to be a popular place for him to set up explosives." He rolled on his side to face me. "But...most importantly...I need you to keep your head on your shoulders. Whether Chase is there or not, don't let your emotions get the best of you."

I nodded without looking him in the eye, rolling back onto my back. His eyes were still on me. He was deep in thought. My guess was that it had nothing to do with the impending confrontation. "Celaine," Blake's voice cut through the silence, "do you think you'll ever be able to move forward in your life without him?"

"If by that you mean will I ever be completely over Chase...well...no. I can't see that ever happening."

"Kind of what I thought." A touch of disappointment infiltrated his voice. "How long has it been since you've slept?"

"A couple of days," I replied.

"Why don't you try now? I need you in top form tomorrow. I'll do a preliminary patrol of the streets and the buildings surrounding the hospital."

"The chances of me falling asleep right now are slim to none."

"Yeah, but the chances of there being any attack for a few more hours are also slim to none, so you might as well rest up while you can."

"Okay. You're the boss," I conceded.

"Don't worry; I'll wake you if there's any action."

"You'd better." The mattress shifted again as he stood up to leave me alone with my restless thoughts.

Blake paced the sidewalk, feverishly taking drags from a cigarette out of the pack he'd managed to keep stashed away from Victor's prying eyes. Smoking–especially when it pertained to someone of his kind–was not exactly smiled upon back at headquarters.

"Damn it."

He threw the half-smoked cigarette onto the ground, stomping it out against the cracked concrete. There'd only been one other time when a woman had made him feel the way he felt now and that had ended miserably. So why was he considering changing his entire philosophy for this one? Was she so different? Yes, he already knew she was. Never before had a woman been able to both intrigue *and* terrify him. Try as he might, he couldn't deny his feelings for her even though he knew he had to. For the sake of the mission, and his pride, he had to.

But that was easier said than done. The way she smiled that crooked smile of hers; the way her eyes seemed to penetrate his soul; the impeccable, smartass retort she always seemed to come up with even to his most audacious of comments. She was the complete package, one of which he'd been incredibly protective of since her arrival at The Epicenter. Surely, her feelings for Chase would grow cold, especially when he found some other broad to shack up with to take her place.

Blake ran his hand through his disheveled hair. Nervous, he pulled out another cigarette, stuck it in his mouth, and lit it behind his cupped hand. Nerves always had a way of bringing out the chain-smoking pacer in him, and tonight was no exception. Ash poured down, falling to the ground slightly behind his footsteps. "Just tell her, you idiot," he muttered.

Yes, he would tell her. At the very least, it would give her something to think about and, who knows, maybe someday she would look at him with the ability to reciprocate those feelings burning within him. He took a final drag from his cigarette and tossed it to the pavement, watching it roll into an awaiting storm drain. It was time to man up.

He shuffled up the sidewalk to the door of the furniture store, where he hunched over to crawl through the remnants of the doorway, making his way back to the mattress where she lay –sleeping. He'd only been gone twenty minutes and she was already sleeping. Blake sat down at the foot of the mattress, doing his best to avoid disturbing her. In the silence, with his head in his hands, he listened to the melody of her breathing, knowing that this was as close to perfect as he was going to get tonight.

*Tomorrow*, he thought. *I'll tell her tomorrow.*

In that instant, she began stirring in her sleep, mumbling unintelligible words he couldn't quite make out, until a single, undeniable name escaped her lips, tearing through him. "Chase," she moaned.

*Damn it.*

# 26
# THE INCIDENT AT HOPE MEMORIAL HOSPITAL

I AWOKE AS the sunlight broke through the horizon. Blake was nowhere in sight, still patrolling, perhaps. My muscles ached. I stretched them, eliciting a charley horse in my right calf. Frantically, I jumped up, putting pressure on the afflicted leg in the hopes of gaining some relief. Instead, I managed to further exacerbate the matter by tripping over one of the many piles of junk congregated throughout the building. One thing was for sure, no matter how much science intervened, it still couldn't eliminate my propensity for klutziness. It was as though it'd been infused in my DNA somewhere.

From my vantage point flat on the ground, I saw a pair of boots entering the building. My eyes trailed up from their leather exterior to the figure they belonged to: a blue jean-wearing, sweater-donning Blake complete with coffee and doughnuts to start the day. His expression changed from one of exasperation to one of curiosity as he cocked his head.

"It was the strangest thing," I mumbled, half embarrassed. "I got out of bed to start my day, minding my own business, when this random pile of junk just jumped out of nowhere, taking me out."

"Yeah. You have to watch out for those rogue bed posts; they've been known to take unsuspecting bystanders out by their knees."

I stood up, dusting myself off. "You've had a pretty productive morning already. When did the transformation to Mr. GQ occur?" His face flushed, a sight of which I didn't anticipate.

"Well, you know, have to go incognito and all," he murmured, his face reddening. "Here." He held out one of the styrofoam cups of coffee. I took the cup, eyeing the box in his other hand. "I didn't know which one you'd like," he said, noticing my fixated gaze, "so I bought a variety." He smiled, handing me the box, which I opened, finding myself greeted by an assortment of brightly colored, heavenly confections. My stomach voiced its approval.

"Thank you, Blake. This is exactly what I needed."

"Don't mention it, kid."

With the approaching daylight, I was able to locate a partially complete sofa. I motioned to it, grabbing Blake's attention. "Shall we?"

"Lead the way," he said. "Just watch out for those vigilante footstools. I've heard they've been causing all sorts of mayhem lately. Got caught up with the wrong crowd – sad, really."

I feigned a gasp. "No. Not the footstools. Alas, what is this world coming to? And to think they used to be such good kids. I blame those hedonistic barstools. Horrible influences they are."

The couch seemed smaller than I'd initially thought. And as I sat down, I found myself gripping the edge of the cushion to allow for enough room for Blake to sit. His larger, muscular body took up more room, causing our bodies to press together, his becoming noticeably tenser.

"I know you're digging the very retro floral design on this bad boy," I teased. "I wonder what they'd think about me moving this into the chic sitting room back at headquarters."

He smiled. "Kara would have a stroke."

"I don't know," I replied, patting the cushion. "She has character." I balanced the doughnut box on my lap, selecting one that appeared to encase some sort of jelly.

"Don't you want any?" I asked. The flustered visage returned to his face. "Blake, are you all right?'

"Wha…yeah. Super."

He was keeping something from me, a secret was being betrayed by his nervous demeanor. Nervous about what? Potentially having to face

The Man in Black with me as his new partner? To tell the truth, I was nervous as hell over that prospect, too. No. It had to be much bigger than that. Something was swirling around inside his head, and I wondered whether I should try to pry it out or mind my own business. I decided that the latter seemed like the best option for the time being.

Blake grabbed a powdered sugar doughnut. He took a bite as he stared off into oblivion. "I have a wig," he uttered between bites.

"Really? I never noticed before."

"No," he said, laughing. "Not me. I bought a wig for you to wear along with street clothes for you to put on over your suit. You're going to be a blonde today, if you don't mind."

"I hear they have more fun."

"No. They're kind of a drag, actually."

"Not your type, are they?"

"You could say that." I felt his gaze drift over to me as I swirled my coffee in my hand before taking a sip. Still feeling his gaze upon me, I turned my head to meet his stare. In his eyes, I saw something I hadn't seen before. A look of confusion, frustration, and a sort of – longing. It was the same look I used to see in Chase's eyes. His body tensed further, and I averted my eyes, prompting him to respond by practically jumping up from the couch.

"I'm going to go get your disguise," he announced, frustrated. His footsteps fell heavy on the floor as he all but ran out of the building. What the hell had just happened? Better yet, what the hell had *almost* just happened? I finished my coffee, gazing out the doorway. Intermittent cars traveled down the street in the direction of Hope Memorial. It was probably close to seven in the morning, which meant that the shift change was about to take place. Blake re-entered with a plastic bag in his hand.

"Let me guess, this isn't a headquarters-approved disguise?"

"Not exactly."

I walked over to him, taking the bag from his grasp and opening it to inspect its contents. A long, lustrous blonde wig greeted me.

"Who am I, Lady Godiva?"

"It was the best I could do. I figured it was the furthest thing from your present appearance."

"I'll have you know that under this mass of auburn lies a blonde waiting to be revealed." I pulled the wig over my hair, blowing the loose strands from my eyes. "Well? Do I look unrecognizable?"

"You look like Celaine in a blonde wig. But I think you'll pass if you keep the bangs down and avoid making any direct eye contact with anyone. We just need to keep you away from the pediatric unit as much as possible."

I removed the clothing from the bag and slipped the oversized sweatshirt over my head. "This thing could house a small country."

"You're carrying a gun. It's not like I want you to be in something skin tight."

I fastened the two-sizes-too-large jeans over my waist and tucked my helmet in the holster hidden entirely under the sweatshirt. "Are we ready?"

"As we'll ever be, I guess."

We exited the building, walking amongst the few who dared to venture out into the streets. The further we traveled down those two short blocks, the more nervous I became. And those nerves intensified with each familiar landmark we passed, coming to a head as we rounded the corner of the flower shop Chase frequented, until we beheld Hope Memorial in all its glory. The sprawling three story hospital was a Mecca of technology comprised of various wings separated by multiple breezeways. It was going to be next to impossible to anticipate where The Man in Black would attack first. In contemplation, we strolled up the shrubbery-lined sidewalk, following it as it led the way to the main entrance.

"My guess is that I'm going to have to enter the ventilation system from some access point in the boiler room," I mused, keeping stride with Blake.

"I'm betting that would be a good guess."

"Any guesses as to where he may strike?"

"He thrives on shock values and death tolls, so my guess is either the intensive care unit or the maternity ward."

"They're on opposite ends of the building."

"That's why there are two of us. My guess is that pediatrics is near the maternity ward?"

"We have a winner."

"Well, then, I'll scout around the maternity ward and you can take the intensive care unit." Blake reached into his pocket, from where he retrieved a small steno pad and pen. "Map, please," he said, handing them to me.

"Don't hold any of what I'm about to draw against me."

"We'll see about that."

"Okay, but you may be sorry," I said. With Blake looking on, I roughed out a cross-section of the pediatric unit as I recalled it and handed it to him, watching as he folded it and tucked it into his pocket.

We entered Hope Memorial, where we purposefully avoided making eye contact with those among us. Once in familiar territory, I directed Blake down the hall towards the elevators. "I guess this is where we split?"

"It would seem that way. Try not to miss me too much," he said with a wink, pushing the 'up' button on the elevator.

"I'll try to contain myself."

"Are you nervous?"

"A little. Okay...a lot."

"Just keep in contact with me through your ear bud."

*Ding, ding.* The elevator door slid open, allowing Blake entry. Before it could close, he blocked the door with his arm and called out to me as I began to make my way down the hall. "If it's any consolation, there's been a couple of times where the information they've gathered has been less than perfect."

I nodded, giving him a half smile as he moved his arm back inside the elevator and allowed the door to close, leaving me alone in the hallway. When I looked around, I felt as though a piece of me was home. Sure, there had been changes in the décor; namely, the inclusion of an unfortunate flowery ambiance that bordered on gaudy. For the most part, though, it was still the same old Hope Memorial that I remembered from my childhood, complete with the same familiar odor of sterility and sickness.

Almost instinctively, I headed in the direction of the Intensive Care Unit, trying to avoid drawing suspicion while looking for those whose actions warranted my suspicion. Not surprisingly, there was nothing out of the ordinary around me. Surely, The Man in Black wouldn't make an impending attack too obvious as it would trim down the shock value, and, as such, I had a feeling that my investigation would prove to be fruitless. I wasn't disappointed.

Everything appeared very 'business as usual'. There were the contradictory feelings of hope intermingled with tremendous grief, flowing in unison throughout the halls. Visitors paced the linoleum wearing looks of relief, sadness, and anticipation, the only things on their minds being their loved ones either in surgery or recovering in the rooms by which they paced. The last thing in their thoughts was the idea that their own lives may be in jeopardy.

A frazzled nurse nearly ran into me as she rushed out of one of the patient rooms. I glanced at her, immediately recognizing her as being one of the nurses who'd worked in close proximity to my father. Madison was her name. When I came to visit my father at the hospital as a child, she would take me by the hand and guide me to a secret stash of candy that she kept hidden in a desk drawer. As I grew older, she'd stop me in halls to chit-chat about current events and to *ooh* and *ah* over my having *grown up so fast*. After my father's death, she would occasionally call Tasha to check up on me. When I moved back to Maryland, she couldn't have been happier, and she was downright ecstatic when I began dating the new, premier pediatric surgeon in town.

Madison wore a look of uncertain recognition as she stopped dead in her tracks. And I quickly averted my eyes, hanging my head down towards the floor as I made a beeline out of the Intensive Care Unit, ignoring her when she called out my name.

I wasn't going to be able to adequately search the rest of the hospital without drawing additional looks of recognition from the staff and compromising the entire mission. The jig was up, signaling to me that it was time to head to the boiler room.

Blake Cohen drew looks of admiration from the young nurses as he strolled down the hall, using the hastily drawn map as his guide. He was used to being stared at, and the stares he was receiving were the standard reaction he'd received from women his entire life. The flattery, however, bounced off him as though he were made of Teflon. He was on a mission and he was focused solely on that mission.

The Man in Black would make nothing obvious, for anything amiss in a hospital would most certainly draw attention and foil any prospective plan. If he were a betting man, he'd put his money on there being an outrageous attack, a taboo attack, even for the likes of him. An attack on the pediatric ward would inspire feelings of shock and outrage if it were struck while full to capacity. However, its inhabitants were sparse.

As throngs of people began removing themselves from the larger cities, many of the more populous locales had become virtual ghost towns, a fact which screamed throughout the halls of the pediatric unit. Usually, he would have been happy to see so few sick children in need of hospitalization, but now he was confused. Why here? Surely, there were busier hospitals to attack. Perhaps the Intensive Care Unit was teaming with the injured and sick, putting Celaine right in the thick of it if anything were to unexpectedly occur.

He walked past the maternity ward. That, too, was more desolate than usual. At a viewing window, he stopped to watch a handful of newborns. So fragile and innocent, there was once a time in his life when he would have loved to have brought one of them into the world. However, now that the world was in utter chaos, introducing innocent life into it seemed cruel.

"Which one is yours?" A cute redheaded nurse asked him, pausing by his side.

"None of them," he replied without throwing so much as a glance in her direction.

"Oh. Well, is your wife about ready to give birth?"

"Don't have one of those either," he said. A glimpse at the young women's reflection in the glass revealed a transparent look of interest on her face. He rolled his eyes and decided to put her out of her misery. "If you'll excuse me," he said as he proceeded to walk back down the hall.

"Dr. Matthews," another nurse called out.

Blake whirled around to see Chase Matthews do an about-face back to the triage near the entrance of the pediatric center.

*What is he doing here now?* Blake wondered, knowing that he couldn't volunteer this information to Celaine. The knowledge of Chase's presence would only add that much more weight onto her overly burdened shoulders. Just the thought alone of this Chase guy being in any kind of danger would throw her over the edge.

Blake studied Chase. Sure, he was a good looking guy if you liked that clean cut pretty-boy kind of look. Obviously, he also had to have some iota of intelligence to be a doctor and, to be with Celaine, more than likely he also had wit to boot. Still, he couldn't help but wonder how much the poor sap could bench press and what the heck she ever saw in him anyway. Chase looked up and the two men locked eyes for a moment until Chase broke their gaze with a half-smile and nod of which Blake reciprocated. Flustered, Blake had begun to make his way to the Intensive Care Unit when a frantic, middle-aged nurse blew through the double doors, barreling towards Chase.

"There you are," she said, breathless to the point that Blake wondered if she was having a heart attack.

"Geez, Madison, what's wrong?" Chase put his hands on her shoulders, trying to calm her down.

"She…she…"

*What, is this chick having an asthma attack or something? She looks like she's seen a ghost*, Blake mused, attempting to be less than obvious about his eavesdropping.

"She's here…in the ICU."

"Who's here?"

"Celaine. I just saw her," she huffed. "She's blonde, but she's here."

*Oh, shit*. Blake could feel a resurgence of adrenaline in his body.

"What? Blonde? Madison, I can assure you that there's no way you saw Celaine. Especially not a blonde Celaine."

"Listen, I've known Celaine ever since she was barely able to walk; and as sure as I am standing here, that was her I saw just now in the ICU. Unless you want to let her walk away from you again, I would suggest that you–pardon my French–get your ass down there."

Chase had a stunned look on his face as he turned back toward the paperwork he was blindly scribbling on at the triage center. Unable to concentrate, he shook his head, tossed the pen aside, and ran through the double doors at speeds that made even Blake's head spin. Stunned, Blake sped through the double doors after him, cupping his hand over his ear bud.

"Celaine." To his disappointment, he received no response in his ear bud. He sped up, jumping over obstacles, dodging all persons who crossed his path. Up ahead, Chase was waiting at the elevator to go down to the first floor. Blake ran past him in the hopes of finding a stairwell. When he looked back, he briefly locked eyes with Chase again as he entered the elevator.

"Celaine, where are you?" Again, nothing but silence greeted him.

Success. A stairwell appeared before him as he rounded a corner. Instead of taking the stairs one by one, he leapt from the top step with his feet making contact on the landing separating the two stairwells. Looks of amazement followed him. He shrugged off the inquisitive stares.

"Celaine, if you can hear me, you need to leave the intensive care unit immediately. That's a direct order." He made a flying leap from the landing, flipping through midair to the first floor. Just as he was about to take off running again, he was halted by a voice ringing from his ear bud.

"I'm one step ahead of you, boss."

He smiled, feeling his body begin to relax again in time to look up and see a couple of children staring at him, mouths open wide in amazement.

"I'm healed," he said, jumping up and down with a sly smile projecting towards them as he walked towards the Intensive Care Unit.

"What's the emergency?" Celaine's voice came through the ear bud again.

"False alarm. Where are you?"

"The vents, and I must say I have to thank you for giving me this absolutely wonderful assignment. I'll have to return the favor someday."

Of course, now it made sense why she wasn't responding to him. The signal strength in the ventilation shaft was surely less than ideal. People were entering the hospital in clusters, in time for prime visiting hours. A thought stuck him as the groups of well-wishers nonchalantly passed him by. It was just after noon, and people were using their lunch hours to visit relatives and friends. In response to the time of day and the influx of people, the kitchen crew would all be present and accounted for to fulfill patient orders and maintain the snack booths for the visitors. If ever there was a time to strike, it was now. Blake scanned the crowd, still finding nothing amiss. Was the information headquarters' outside sources gathered wrong?

"Blake…" Celaine's concerned voice came through his ear bud

once more.

"Yeah?"

It had been a long time since I'd used my feminine charm to my advantage. For the most part, I used to jeer those women who did what I had just done to the poor, unsuspecting maintenance man who just so happened to be at the wrong place at the wrong time when I entered the boiler room. After playing dumb, confusing the boiler room for the ladies' room, something that was pretty much impossible to do, and complimenting "Pete" on his cute smile and abilities with a wrench, I was granted admission. Heck, if I'd wanted it, I probably could have had full access to almost anything I wished in the boiler room. Pete guided me through the massive room. 'The heart of the hospital', he'd called it. It supplied all the energy needed to run any and all pertinent equipment. When he gave his spiel, it took all I had to act as if I were interested in everything he was telling me, including his rant on why his job was probably the most important one here, as he gave me a tour of the room. I maintained a smile on my face the entire time, sifting through the bull. After all, I was only partially paying attention as my main focus was on locating an entryway into the ventilation system.

Finally, after what seemed like an eternity, I found what I was looking for in the far corner of the room. In a haste, I tried to think of a diversion to allow me to gain entry into the vents, asking Pete to explain the inner workings of the boiler. A terrified look sprang across his face as, I was sure, he was hurriedly attempting to think of a way he could fudge through this one while still maintaining my interest. He turned his back to examine the boiler and started speaking again but I didn't hear a word of what he said as I was already in the vent by the time he ended his first sentence.

For something that was supposed to supply air to a sterile facility, the ventilation system was by far one of the most unsanitary environments I'd ever been in. Dust covered my hands during my crawl through the tunnels of cold steel that also served as some kind of mortuary for bug carcasses and a lone rat.

Blake's voice blared through my ear bud, "Celaine, if you can hear me, you need to leave the intensive care unit immediately. That's a direct order."

A direct order? There had to be something going on since that was a very un-Blake-like thing for him to say. "I'm one step ahead of you, boss," I replied. I continued crawling through the vents, thinking about what Blake had just said. "What's the emergency?"

"False alarm". His tone was more relaxed, which calmed me. "Where are you?"

"The vents, and I must say I have to thank you for giving me this absolutely wonderful assignment. I'll have to return the favor someday."

I came across a fork in the vents, deciding to take it to the left in the direction of what I believed to be angled towards the Intensive Care Unit. The vents clanged underneath my body while I navigated through them, trying to catch a hint of something sinister. One thing I knew for sure was that I was going to have some major difficulties finding my way back out of this thing, and I wondered how The Man in Black had managed to traverse these metallic caves without raising suspicion. Surely, someone at the hospital had to notice something amiss. When I shifted my body to turn and continue down yet another pathway, something caught my eye in the tunnel ahead of me.

The closer I came to it, the more I realized that what had caught my attention didn't belong here. My stomach twisted into knots upon confirmation of my suspicions. It was the first time I had ever seen a bomb, but just as in many action movies I'd seen, making a positive identification was not difficult.

*Oh, God, Chase, please, don't be here*, I thought. Upon further inspection of the bomb, I could make out a slight ticking noise coupled with another barely audible electronic sound. Carefully, I angled my body around the apparatus, trying to get a better view of it as well as a possible idea as to when it was set to wreak its deadly vengeance. That's when I saw it.

The green animatronics ticking away before my eyes revealed a sight that I was beyond unprepared for: 00:02:43. Does that say two minutes? If so, how many others were there set for the same time, if not sooner? Was there a way to dismantle it? My mind was swirling, clouding both my vision and thought processes, at once rendering me near useless.  Please, Blake, be able to hear me now. I pressed my hand to my ear bud.

"Blake…"

"Yeah," his voice sounded from the other end.

"We have a little problem here."

# 27
## THE ENCOUNTER

"GET OUT OF there now!" Blake commanded.

"Is there nothing that can be done to stop this? Cutting a wire…anything?"

"Not in two minutes, there's not, and when there's most likely more than one, there's most definitely not. Celaine, just get out of there…please, get out of there…do anything and everything possible to do it. I need to start evacuating the hospital, although I fear there's not much of an evacuation that can be done in two minutes."

"All right, I'll be joining you soon."

"Okay."

In a frenzy, I pulled my sweatshirt and pants off, exposing my suit. *Don't fail me now*, I thought, unclasping my helmet from its holster, securing it into place on my head. I knew I wasn't going to be able to crawl through the vent back to the boiler room before the detonator went off. My only means of escape would come by breaking through the vents. Frantic, I forced my legs against the metal and pushed as hard as I could until I felt it give a little. There wasn't much time left, probably close to a minute now. My pulse increased, forcing a resurgence of adrenaline through my body. With this sudden burst of energy, I forced both of my feet down in a stomping motion. The vent groaned as it started breaking apart.

"Come on," I groaned, thrusting my legs down harder against the metal. With a sharp creak, a portion of the ventilation shaft broke loose and swung down like a trap door, nearly taking down other sections of it in the process.

I peered down to see that I was atop the fluorescent lighting fixtures. With time ticking away, I lowered myself down from the broken vent and kicked one of the fixtures, breaking it. Shards of glass and bits of metal and wire struck the floor of the commons area. People were strewn about, already in a panic. Thankfully, they'd scattered before the debris crashed down from above. But the loud crash it made when it fell to the floor only exacerbated the utter mayhem that had taken control of them.

"It's now or never," I said to myself.

I positioned myself and jumped the forty feet from the site of the broken fixture to the floor of the commons area. Though I'd braced myself for a hard landing, I was pleasantly surprised when my feet landed gently and without incident on the linoleum. In front of me, hoards of people were streaming from the interior of the hospital, many skidding to an abrupt halt upon seeing me.

"Get out of here now," I ordered. "There's a bomb!" I rushed in the direction of the Intensive Care Unit, running upstream against the tide of terror. While pushing through the crowd, I couldn't help but hear the surprised exclamations from the individuals within it.

"Is that another one?" a woman's voice asked.

"A woman? Is that a woman?" an older man asked in disbelief.

Finally, finding a break in the crowd, I took off towards Blake, who I was sure was located at the origin of all the chaos. I didn't make it far.

A bomb. She'd found a bomb. Never had he cared so much about the welfare of one of his partners, and the thought of her up there with an explosive sickened him. He knew she was smart, that she was capable of taking care of herself. After all, she'd already been one of the most promising partners he'd ever had, not to mention annoyingly beautiful. Of course, it also helped that none of the others had been able to uncover the feelings he'd managed to keep buried away for the last several years the way she had.

Very little time remained to be secretive as he ran full tilt down the hallway, throwing off his sweater and snapping his helmet into place. An orderly appeared around a corner, eyes widening at the sight of him.

"Evacuate the building," Blake ordered, barreling past him without so much as a glance in his direction.

Without questioning him, the frightened orderly nodded as he rushed down the hall. Blake continued his mission, eyes searching the rough exterior of the wall until he found a fire alarm, abruptly setting it off. Crowds filtered into the hallway, their faces changing in expression from sheer annoyance to pure terror when they recognized who it was who had pulled the alarm.

"Evacuate the building!"

Just as in the case of the orderly, there were no questions directed towards this masked man whose identity they'd attempted to decipher in the countless stories contained within the local newspaper. Instead, only gasps exuded from the scattered groups. While some began to weep, others ran to the nearest exits, their self-serving acts leaving only a select few to head toward the patient rooms to assist the patients to safety. Blake shook his head in disgust. The selfishness of others never ceased to amaze him. Emergencies had a strange way of bringing a person's true colors to light.

An unwritten rule existed at headquarters that, over the years, had been drilled into his head. This rule roughly stated that it didn't matter the death toll, the main focus was apprehending The Man in Black. In Blake's mind, that rule basically meant that it was completely acceptable for tens of thousands of people to die if the vile monster was apprehended, but not at all acceptable if lives were spared and he was to escape in the process. This rule had never set well with him, and was the one cardinal rule he always seemed to break. Just allowing people to die went against the very grain of his soul. His true colors always remained the same shade.

From what he'd witnessed today, he was certain that the Intensive Care Unit would be the wing that would take the brunt of the action. He knew The Man in Black had cased the joint just as he had done, inevitably reaching the conclusion that it wouldn't be worth it, body count wise, to waste his resources on the pediatric unit. Not to mention, just as in every other attack, he suspected that the vile monster was waiting somewhere in the wings in order to witness the devastation he was about to create. He ran on grief, drank in the destruction. It fueled him, providing him with the sustenance he needed to thrive.

Chaos was in full force in the Intensive Care Unit, and Blake's sudden appearance fanned the flames. His appearance was likened to that of the angel of death. It was something he thoroughly resented, but nonetheless had learned to deal with. Panic was thick in the air, and there was nothing the flustered doctors or nurses could do to alleviate the situation, making an already stressful event that much more unbearable for those incapacitated patients.

The evacuation process was underway, but it wasn't moving along well amidst the confusion. For Blake, it was time to take action; it was time to earn the superhero title they'd branded him with. But, as he was about to join in to speed along the evacuation process, a large explosion, originating from the vicinity of the commons area, reverberated throughout the Intensive Care Unit.

Instinctively, Blake's thoughts turned to Celaine, making it all he could do to hold himself back from taking off down the hall to find her. He shook his head to clear his thoughts, knowing he couldn't let his emotions get the best of him. Where there was one explosion, others were sure to follow.

In the Intensive Care Unit, the panic stricken had taken to violent desperation, shoving and, in some instances, trampling over each other like savage animals in their attempts to escape. They ignored the pleas of the staff to allow all critically ill patients priority over everyone else, choosing instead to save themselves. Blake shook his head in disgust, diving into the center of the chaos. Grabbing patients, along with any and all medical equipment that may be attached to them, he searched for an exit out of the hospital, kicking doors off their hinges in the process. The Man in Black was here; he could feel his presence strongly.

After securing an exit, he ran back inside, scouring each of the patient rooms for those left behind. All had been emptied until he came across a room housing a man who was either a John Doe or a person whose family had very limited contact with him. Either way, he was easily overlooked in the midst of the horror that was occurring. He was heavily sedated with bandages covering the circumference of his head and arm. Not wanting to worsen his condition, Blake located a gurney that'd been hastily abandoned in the hallway and wheeled it into the room, where he lifted the man from his hospital bed and positioned him on it. He then maneuvered the man into the hallway and ran in the direction of the exit.

Time seemed to stand still during his run to safety. Every movement appeared as though it was being performed in slow motion. And these slow movements did not hasten the closer he came to the sanctity of the outside; they did not quicken as the second explosion rang through the Intensive Care Unit, burying him and the patient under a pile of debris.

I laid in the hall amongst the rubble, several feet from the remains of the commons area of Hope Memorial. Like the dozens of people scattered around me, I should have been killed. My body had been flung into the air as though it had been shot out of a cannon, crashed into a wall and was partially buried by a couple of hundred pounds of steel and concrete. At the very least, I should have been rendered an invalid. But, as I pulled myself from my sepulcher, dusting myself off while checking my body for injury, I was shocked to find not so much as a scratch on either myself or my suit. In fact, there wasn't even a visible scuff on its exterior. If there were ever a time I would kiss Marcus, it was now.

While I was well protected physically, emotionally was a completely different story. Around me, through the dust, smoke and approaching sirens, the scene that unfolded was a hellish flashback to The Lakes with the moans of the agony of impending death cutting through my head. Anxiety cut through my system, causing me to gasp for breath. *Keep it together*, I thought.

I climbed through the rubble, where I checked each lifeless body hoping that one of them would contain some semblance of life. No such luck. My breath hitched in my throat as I continued my journey through the debris. It was still early in the day, too early for Chase's shift. With any luck, he wouldn't be anywhere near the vicinity of Hope Memorial until all the action came to a head.

I climbed only a few more feet when I heard a muffled cry mere inches from my feet. My heart raced as I crouched down and lifted chunks of drywall half my size, throwing them aside until I uncovered the source of the cry I'd heard. In a crevice, deep within the debris, lay a badly injured, barely conscious little boy. I put my hand near his mouth, feeling the air caress my fingers, proving that life was still left in his limp body. Although this little boy was several years younger than Jake had been, I couldn't help but think of how similar in appearance he was to my brother, shaggy hair and all. My eyes were burning from the dust that was able to seep into my helmet, making the tears I shed that much more painful as I lifted the tiny body from its resting place. There would be another bomb, I suspected; and I couldn't allow mini-Jake to be in the building when that second wave of terror began.

I leapt over piles of concrete, moving my legs as fast as they would carry me as I ran toward what used to be the front entrance of the hospital. It'd been rendered to nothing more than a giant road block in my path. Carefully positioning the boy over my shoulder, I cleared a pathway to the outside world, coughing on the dust and smoke that rushed into my mask, burning the back of my throat. Fearing that the boy's frail body would asphyxiate on the smoke overtaking us, I worked faster, flinging remnants of Hope Memorial in all directions until the sunlight from the outside poured in to signal the end of my excavation. A virtual mob had formed outside, consisting mainly of the staff and those patients they were able to evacuate. Already, doctors were setting up makeshift hospitals in the parking lot in the hopes that the critically ill patients' conditions wouldn't deteriorate before they could be transferred to another hospital. In the distance, I could hear sirens approaching. The local news crew would soon follow suit. Military personnel were already at the scene donning breathing masks so that they could enter the building.

I ran several feet before finding a doctor to turn the boy over to. The balding, bespectacled man took the boy from my arms, nodding his approval. All eyes were on me despite the utter devastation unfolding before them. Most were curious while some, I sensed, felt that my presence was all too convenient. However, a common thread united the two divisions: their overwhelming fear of me. People tend to fear the unknown and the incomprehensible. To them, I was all of the above.

When I ran back into Hope Memorial, the second explosion

occurred, rocking the hospital and the people near it to their cores. Screams emanated from the crowds. Without further hesitation, I took off back in the direction of the source of the blast, for I knew that Hope Memorial would not be able to withstand any further assault, and I wasn't going to let her go down without a fight.

The second blast had blown a hole in the corridor that lead to the Intensive Care Unit. With a running start, I leapt the five feet into the newly minted doorway, choking on smoke from one of the many small fires that surrounded me. "Blake, can you hear me?" I asked, tapping my ear bud. Silence. With my vision blurred by the veil of smoke, dust and debris, I worked my way down the corridor, hoping to hear from him. *He must be all right*, I thought. *He's had to have done this several times by now.* This all should be like clockwork to him. Nevertheless, pangs of worry began eating away at my stomach. And although it had only been minutes since my last attempt at communication with him, it felt more like hours before he replied.

"I'm in the ICU. Meet me in here so we can regroup. Our informants have spotted The Man in Black. The excitement here was too much for him. They think he's keeping shop in an abandoned warehouse across from the hospital, a couple of blocks over on Spruce Street."

My heart pounded in my chest. The Man in Black was only a couple of blocks away. This was the closest I'd been to him live and in person since that day at The Lakes. Today was turning into everything I'd waited for in the last ten years. At last, my chance to bring down the man who'd brought my world to a screeching halt was upon me. Soon, I would finally be able to fulfill the promise I'd made to my family when they were laid to rest in the hardened, dark earth that cold, December day.

"Dr. Harris says to calm down. Your cardiac readings are all over the chart," Kara's voice came over loud and clear in my ear bud.

In hindsight, it made perfect sense, but before hearing her stern voice booming in my ear, correcting me like a stern parent, I hadn't entertained the notion that whatever Blake and I said to each other could be heard throughout headquarters as well. "Tell the good doctor that I'll try, but I can't make any promises."

I entered the ICU, smoking and in shambles from the second blast. Thankfully, it appeared to be empty, for the most part. Further down the hallway, I found myself relieved to see Blake. He was draping a blanket over a body next to a mass of metal that looked to be the remnants of a gurney or hospital bed of sorts. Blake looked up at me, regaining his composure. "We'd better get out of here before another one goes off," he said, a coldness present in his voice.

"Aren't we going to stay here and try to help the people who haven't gotten out of here yet before they're blown to bits? There are three whole floors of rooms. Surely, they couldn't have all been evacuated."

"I don't like it any more than you do, but saving them isn't part of our mission. Capturing The Man in Black is."

"That's ludicrous. Sure, our ultimate goal is to catch him, but we're catching him to save lives, to prevent death, not to just turn our backs on it."

"If catching him means that a few dozen have to die in the process, then so be it. Capturing him will save countless others."

"You don't honestly believe that," I fumed. "This whole thing disturbs you just as much as it does me."

"You're letting this mission become too personal for you, Celaine."

"Screw you."

His body stiffened in anger, but he remained silent. I felt guilty for having gotten angry with him. This hospital had been my refuge, my life for so long. How could I not take it personally when told that I had to let it and the people within it die?

"Blake...I'm..."

"Let's go," he said as he trudged through the rubble. "Before another blast rips through this place and makes it harder for us to get out and find that bastard." He took a flying leap at a nearby wall, his foot caving it inward as the foundation stubbornly refused to give way. I followed suit as I brought my leg up and struck the wall. It crumbled and gave way beneath my foot, revealing the world outside once the dust settled. "Show off," he muttered.

"You got it started for me."

"Uh-huh."

We climbed through the hole in the wall. Outside, the dust and smoke swirled in the wind. Half of Hope Memorial stood ablaze. A news station helicopter swirled overhead, churning up the air. The side we were on was not as busy as the front of the building, which housed all of the evacuees and news crews. It allotted Blake and I a sort of secrecy in our departure. "Run," Blake commanded.

We took off through the field behind Hope Memorial toward the abandoned sector of town, but we didn't get far before another, even more potent explosion ripped through the sky, shaking the ground like an earthquake. My heart sank into the depths of despair when I looked behind me and saw what had been the epicenter of the explosion as flames shot through the pediatric unit.

"Son of a bitch," Blake's voice bellowed behind me, enraged.

I began to shake; the air left my body, deflating me. My knees buckled, taking my body down with them. Blake's arms wrapped around me, keeping me upright. A moan involuntarily escaped my mouth like a reflex. And that was all it took for the uncontrollable sobbing to start. He pulled me up to face him, but instead of telling me to calm down, he pulled my body into his, embracing my limp being.

"I'm sorry," he said softly in my ear. "This is why it's more important that we get the bastard when the opportunity presents itself."

I pulled my body away from his, realizing that I hadn't taken a breath yet. "Let's find him...now."

He smiled. "Now you're talking."

After taking one last glimpse back at the near-decimated Hope Memorial Hospital, I turned my attention straight ahead and started running. With Blake hot on my heels, we tore through the field, the world going by us in a blur of color. Bending my knees, I made a flying leap over the chain link fence, landing on the other side. "Spruce Street?" I asked Blake.

"Yeah, at a former office supply warehouse that apparently went out of business during the recession and subsequent mass exodus from this dump."

"This dump was my home."

"That must have sucked."

"No, actually it was peaceful, having an entire city to yourself at night." I looked over at Blake, his face bearing a stoic expression.

"What's the plan?" My question didn't seem to surprise him.

"We check it out. See if it all jives."

"And if it does?"

"Then you apply what you've learned in the simulator."

"And?"

"Stick with me, don't…"

"I know, I know, don't play the hero."

"I was going to say 'don't get yourself killed' but that works, too. Kind of goes hand in hand, I guess."

Formerly the home of Steinbach's Office Supplies, Inc., the abandoned warehouse had once been a lucrative metropolis of efficiency. Many school districts from the area had furnished their classrooms with furniture and supplies from Steinbach's. With several locations statewide, the small family-owned business managed to turn into a corporate empire seemingly overnight. Unfortunately, corporate-sized expansion generates corporate-sized mentality, masking a familiar face, making it a complete stranger to the public. Thus, an expanding ego coupled with an expanding recession worked together perfectly toward the devastation of a once great company. Several stores closed their doors, making way for strip malls, which forced the former bustling warehouse into bankruptcy. Now all that remains of the Steinbach legacy is a boarded-up, empty concrete cocoon. Its only means of recognition to the outside world consists of half of a dilapidated sign on its concrete exterior that read: Steinb.

As we neared the building, I could almost feel his eyes watching my every step. I knew he was in there. I didn't need any corroborating evidence to confirm that in my mind. He was in the air, in my bones. My body felt his presence. It was so profound that I could almost hear them —my family —calling me from inside the building, their faces peering out of the cracks in the boarded-up windows, motioning for me to come to their rescue. An intense rush of adrenaline, the likes of which I'd never felt before, wound its way through my veins. At that moment, I wanted nothing more than to explode through those concrete doors and take care of business. Whether or not I was taking care of myself in the process, I didn't care.

Sensing a change in my demeanor, Blake took my arm, guiding me towards the alleyway that ran parallel to the warehouse. "I know they say you should meet your challenges head on, but I think we can make an exception in this case."

"He knows we're here."

"Maybe, but that doesn't afford us room for recklessness."

"I've never wanted to do such bodily harm to another person in my entire life," I uttered. Concern spread across Blake's face. "What is it?"

"That's exactly what Liam said."

"I'm not Liam."

"Liam wasn't even Liam until the last thirty seconds of his life."

"You don't trust me at all, do you?"

"No, I do trust you. I just don't trust myself. You scare the hell out of me."

I smiled. "Well, let's hope The Man in Black shares that sentiment." Blake assessed the building before us. The side we were standing before was solid brick, perfectly vertical and lacked any noticeable footholds.

"I say we scale it." Blake flicked his wrist, propelling his grappling hook out towards the heavens. His line met resistance when the hooks gripped the roof. He jumped, positioning his feet horizontally against the wall, the wire reeling itself back into its source around his wrist with each step. One flick of my wrist and I, too, was scaling the warehouse at a right angle, quickly catching up to Blake until we were climbing in sync. I unhooked the grappling hook and folded the metal bars inwards, allowing them to fit back into their pouch around my wrist.

Blake proceeded to walk around the perimeter of the roof until his attention was caught by a skylight in the center of the building. I walked over to him to peer over his shoulder.

"See anything?"

"Sure do. Empty pallets, shelves, garbage…"

"Sadistic psychopaths?"

"No, haven't come across one of those yet. Of course, he's not going to roll out the welcome wagon for us. Give us a firm handshake and offer us a plate of brownies and whatnot."

"Darn. I really like brownies, too. So, we're going in, then?"

"You bet."

He grabbed a small blade from his utility belt and held it against the glass as he guided it along the edge of the pane. "Jab this into the section I just cut," he ordered, tossing a rubber wedge-like object to me. Following his instructions, I jammed the wedge into the sliver he'd cut into the glass. A distinct cracking sound creaked through it. Blake continued running the blade along the edge of the pane until he made it the rest of the way around the perimeter of the square. "Okay. Lift the wedge up and grab the glass as it pops." I pulled on the wedge, bringing the top of the window up with it, effectively shifting the window downward toward the floor of the warehouse. Blake grabbed the other side of the glass and, together, we lifted it from its frame and set it down on the rooftop.

"Ready to go spelunking?" I asked.

Blake chuckled. "Let's just hope this cave doesn't have a bear in it."

"Oh, come on. Where's your sense of adventure?" We stood with our backs toward the edge of the empty window frame and flicked our wrists to release our grappling hooks, making sure they had a firm hold on the window frame.

He looked at me, smiling his rugged grin. "Let's go hunting." Without hesitation, he jumped backwards into the warehouse, disappearing within the darkness below. With a deep breath, I allowed my body to fall backwards into the abyss, my wire securing me like a puppet on a string, gliding me safely to the concrete floor where I found myself surrounded by pallets. Blake stood next to me, an aura of heightened concern emanating from his body.

"I must say this place is rather charming."

"Stay close," he ordered. "Keep your eyes open. His eyes never give up their vigilance." Blake walked across the concrete floor with me following in tandem. It was the last place I would have ever thought an evil mastermind would have as a hideout. Of course, that may be the exact reason why he chose it. We were surrounded by pallets. Empty pallets, pallets containing boxes of unshipped and abandoned supplies encased us, watching our every move. The dust billowed off their wooden exteriors, blowing in my face.

We passed forklifts, work benches and desks, none of which were willing to give up their secrets to us. But despite finding nothing out of sorts, I continued to feel like a very evil set of eyes were burning deep into my soul. Perhaps I was going crazy, but if there was one thing I'd learned about myself, it was that my intuitions were hardly ever mistaken.

Just as I leaned in to say something to Blake about this whole thing being some perverse wild goose chase, something caught my attention as it blew past my peripheral vision. I spun around, expecting to see a bird that had flown through our freshly made entrance. Instead, I was greeted with a hand lunging forward, firmly gripping my throat, lifting me up until I felt my feet leaving the ground. Shaken and gasping for air, my eyes met the image that had haunted both my dreams and consciousness. Finally, I was living face to living face with The Man in Black. The invisible evil whose presence I only just suspected was boring a hole into my very being. Those eyes, those evil eyes were staring directly into mine. Unrelenting and with zero empathy, they were hollow, soulless.

It felt as though I had no air left in my lungs. I tugged on the unrelenting fist around my neck in a vain attempt to pry it open. Unsuccessful in my attempt, I began to feel dizzy, the world around me growing darker. At the very moment I thought I would pass out, I saw Blake's body, a blur in my eyes, ramming into the side of The Man in Black, throwing him off kilter just enough for him to let go of my neck, flinging me into a pallet behind him.

After crashing into the wooden pallet, I lay motionless on the concrete floor, watching helplessly as The Man in Black pinned Blake against a wall, pressing the sharp edge of a splintered piece of wood against his jugular.

# 28

# THE TWIST OF FATE FOR CHASE MATTHEWS

IT PLAYED OUT just as she'd described to him during one of the many nights she'd been abruptly arisen from her slumber because of the images plaguing her mind. An explosion emanated with a roar so powerful his eardrums felt as though they were about to implode. Then the smoke raced into the room, followed by the screams of the terrified and the moans of the injured, dying, and the trapped. And just as he was beginning to recover from the first explosion and regain his bearings, a second one threw him from his feet into a wall. Dazed, he picked himself up from the linoleum floor of the Intensive Care Unit.

Evacuations had commenced but he'd ignored them in the hope that he would be able to catch her before she left the building, walking out on him yet again. Madison wasn't one to exaggerate, nor was she easily excitable about many things. Those facts alone led him to believe that she'd in fact seen Celaine. But instead of the answers he was hoping to gain by a chance encounter with her, he was left with even more questions. Why was she in the ICU? Why did she alter her appearance? Was it because she didn't want him to recognize her? Did she even want to talk to him at all?

The floor beneath him shuddered, forcing him to make the decision to call off the search for his lost love. He just hoped that she was among those who'd managed to escape Hope Memorial before the devastation began. For the most part, the second floor had been emptied. However, there were still those patients who were too weak to leave their beds and thus had not been evacuated yet. There were also those family members and physicians who were too devoted to leave their posts even in the midst of the chaos and confusion transpiring in the wake of the explosion.

Smoke, heavy and black, seeped in at a million miles a minute, forcing Chase back onto the floor for fresher air. The emergency stairwell, he knew, was in the thick of it and most likely blocked by debris that made escape from certain suffocation seem impossible. His lungs were filling up with smoke, causing him to cough uncontrollably. Around him, he could hear the screams and persistent coughing of others, those like him who were trapped.

It had never been in his nature to lie down and accept defeat. Before Celaine came along, he'd never accepted "no" for an answer, nor had he let the possible become impossible. Death was not an option for him. He would not die on the second floor of Hope Memorial today. Near him, he saw people crawling, frantically looking for a way out, only to become increasingly more frustrated with each failed attempt. Like himself, they too failed to accept an alternate fate. With a new resolve, he scoured the halls for an exit, an idea occurring to him as he crawled in front of an empty patient room. It was a thought of which he despised himself for thinking, but one of which he knew would work. *There's no reason for those who are healthy to die today.*

"Everyone," Chase shouted through the panic, "gather around me."

A voice came up from behind him. "Do you know a way out of here that I haven't tried yet?"

Chase turned his head to see a large framed, balding man in a gaudy Hawaiian-print shirt crawling in his direction.

"I think I might."

"I'm all ears," the man said, wheezing.

"Are you all right?"

"Yeah…just…kind of hard to…breathe in…in here."

Those left who were still able to crawl appeared around Chase, their eyes pleading at him in desperation.

"Okay," he began. "We're all going to gather in this room." He pointed to a patient room a couple of feet from their positions on the floor.

"I want the last person in to shut the door behind them. We're going to break the window and the door needs to be shut as the excess oxygen will attract the smoke, bringing it into the room with us. Once the door is closed, we will stick a bed sheet under it and break the window open with whatever we can get our hands on inside the room. If you stand up, hold your breath. Rescue departments should be here by now and the best case scenario is that they see us and extend the ladder up to our window, rescuing us."

"Yeah, well, what's the worst case scenario?" A young woman chimed in amidst a barrage of coughs.

"Worst case scenario is that we jump."

"I'm not jumping out of a window," one of the men from the group retorted. "Are you crazy?"

"What," the balding man chimed in. "Do you want to stay here and suffocate to death? Well, that's your choice, as I sure as hell don't. Come on, Doc, let's break that window."

Chase led the group of a dozen into the patient room, where the door was promptly shut.

"What about our families?" one of the women asked, jamming a sheet under the door. "We're just going to leave them here to die?"

He looked at the salt and pepper haired woman. A look of sheer guilt was reflected on her face.

"No…" he said, trailing off. "I promise you I will do what I can to get them out of here."

The balding man stared at him in both admiration and disbelief before adding, "As will I."

Chase looked at him and smiled. "Does anyone here know an exact head count of those still in their rooms?"

"There are three of them," a resident answered. "All three are towards the end of the hallway."

*Of course they are*, Chase thought. He turned to the balding man, who seemed even paler than before. "Are you up to it?"

"Do you know who you're speaking to? Of course I'm up to it."

"Well, in that case, what do you say to us breaking a window?"

Chase took a deep breath, stood up and grabbed a chair in the corner of the room. Together, he and the balding man secured it up in the air and, using it as a modern battering ram, shattered the window. The smoke that had collected inside the room rapidly escaped into the air outside. Collectively, the group gathered around the open window to take in the fresh oxygen.

"How far of a drop would you say that is, Doc?"

"Somewhere between thirty and thirty-five feet, I guess." Chase scanned the horizon, locating emergency personnel who were already engaged in battling small fires all over the hospital. "They aren't going to notice us here. One of us is going to have to make a jump for it and tell them to get a ladder."

"Is that possible?"

"Sure. If you land right."

"I'll do it," a man around Chase's age volunteered. "I'm into BASE jumping and the like. I've broken a few bones in my day. It doesn't faze me much anymore. Besides, it's not like I'm not surrounded by doctors, right?" Chase moved away from the window, allowing the young man to draw near. "Just make sure to land on an extremity, right?" He shot Chase a smirk.

"You're an expert in injury."

The self-proclaimed daredevil stepped onto the empty window frame, balancing precariously over the edge.

"See you on the other side," he said, letting go of the ledge, allowing his body to free fall to the ground below.

Afraid to look out the window, but knowing he should, Chase glanced down to see the man lying motionless on the cement.

*Oh, God, get up*, he thought as to not instill panic in the room.

After a couple of seconds, the man slowly began to stand up in noticeable pain. Chase observed an obvious injury to the man's leg and wondered, as the man looked up at him, shooting him a "thumbs up" while proceeding to hobble towards rescue personnel, whether or not the government would give out a purple heart for valor and injury outside of the military.

"I'm Paul, by the way," the balding man extended a hand to Chase.

"Chase," he said, taking the man's hand.

"Well, Doc," Paul said in a hushed tone as to not alert the others of what he was about to say. "I hate to say this, but if we don't get those patients out of here soon it may be too late. Heck, chances are that it is already too late."

"I know, but we still have to try."

"You're the Doc –" Paul said through a cough, the wheezing in his chest becoming more audible.

"Are you sure you're all right?"

"I'm fine." Paul brushed his question off in favor of putting on a strong-man front.

With relief filling her voice, another resident exclaimed, "They're coming!"

Cheers erupted from the room.

"Thank you, doctor." The young woman wrapped her arms around Chase.

"Yes, doctor. If you hadn't thought of this, we'd probably all still be lying out there in that hallway, dead."

Chase blushed. "Don't thank me until your feet hit the pavement."

A loud clang sounded through the room, signaling that the firefighters' ladder had struck the window frame.

"All right," Chase ordered. "Everyone line up single file." He turned to Paul. "Once the last one is on the ladder we'll head down the hall. Just remember to hold your breath and hit the floor when it's necessary to breathe again."

"Can do, Doc."

Single file, they headed down the ladder to the safety and fresh air below. Chase stood looking out the window, ensuring everyone made it down without incident. Paul locked eyes with him.

"It's now or never."

He nodded, and together they dislodged the sheet from underneath the door, took a deep breath and ran out into the hall in the direction the resident had indicated the remaining patients were located. Flames were fanning out across the second floor, creating even more of a hazard for Chase and Paul while they struggled to ration the precious oxygen they'd stored in their lungs. Near the end of the hall, Chase glanced in room after room, hoping to catch a glimpse of those who'd been left behind. Chase motioned to Paul to take a room while he ventured a few feet down to another one, turning around when Paul spoke, his wheeze far more profound now than it had been.

"What…if they're hooked…to machines?"

"Unhook them."

"Won't that...kill them?"

"Either they die here from smoke inhalation or they die outside where they at least have a fighting chance."

Paul nodded, and the pair entered their respective rooms. The smoke stung Chase's eyes, his lungs burned in his chest. He hit the floor, but the air down there was becoming too saturated with smoke that what little oxygen that had clung there before was swiftly becoming depleted. While trying to suppress a coughing fit, Chase crawled to the side of the hospital bed where he unhooked the arterial line, catheter and ventilator from Ms. Branigan, the elderly widower whose fall down the stairs had landed her in Hope Memorial's Intensive Care Unit two weeks ago. Even though he knew that unhooking her now would cause her condition to decline resulting in her demise, he couldn't bear knowing that a person had perished in such a cruel and inhumane manner under his watch. He lifted Ms. Branigan from her hospital bed and ran back into the hallway. The heat from the flames rising up from the floor below all but scorched his exposed flesh in the process.

Chase breathed a sigh of relief when he entered the empty patient room and found rescue workers making their way back up the ladder. "Doctor, you need to get down here. The whole building is about ready to collapse," one of the rescuers commanded.

"I will as soon as you take her." Chase leaned out the window with Ms. Branigan, transferring her into the rescuers' arms. "Did the other two make it down all right?"

"What other two? Do you mean the group that came down earlier?"

Chase's heart sank to his stomach. "No, there should have been two more right after that. A middle-aged man carrying another patient."

"Haven't seen them."

"I'll be right back." Chase inhaled fresh oxygen into his lungs before running back out into the hall. Behind him he could hear the rescue worker shouting, "Wait. It's suicide going back in there."

Ignoring the encroaching flames, he ran down the hallway, praying he'd find Paul with a pulse. He held his arm out as he ran past each room, counting the door frames. The smoke was growing thicker and blacker, making visibility next to nothing. If he remembered correctly, he figured he'd been about fifteen rooms down, which would mean Paul was in room fourteen. Chase knew this would be his last trip back. In the back of his mind, he knew that if he made it back from this second run, it would be a miracle. It was a thought he continued to shrug off even as he entered the fourteenth room. The window in the room cast enough light inside that he could make out the hospital bed with the form still lying in it. Just as he began to wonder where Paul had gone, he tripped over something on the floor, falling elbow-first into the hospital bed. Dazed, he guided his hand along the floor, searching for the object that had tripped him. After scouring about a foot of linoleum, his hand felt a familiar texture. Skin.

He couldn't leave Paul there to die. Paul had been brave enough to put his life on the line just as he had. With great difficulty and using the last ounce of strength he had, he lifted Paul, positioning him onto his back. In doing so, dizziness overcame him. Almost dropping Paul, he crashed into the wall, a cough escaping his burning throat. If he didn't get out of here now, he was sure he would die. Time seemed to move slower as he entered the hallway with Paul's dead weight weighing him down with each footstep. His coughs were increasing in frequency and the dizziness was almost too much to bear, but on he went. He mustered up strength he didn't know existed, swearing that, at times, it felt like he had left his body and was watching the figure of himself trudging down the hall.

"Come on," he told himself. "You won't die here, not now." But he knew there was only so much smoke a person could inhale before dying was completely out of their control. With lungs blazing, Chase entered the escape room.

"You're damn lucky," the rescuer yelled. "We were about ready to pull the ladder away."

Chase coughed, leaning down to prop Paul against the window frame. "Here," he said between coughs. "Take him down. I'll follow you."

"You'd better. It doesn't sound like you'd make it much longer in there."

The rescuer motioned for assistance from the crew on the ground and, once the other crew member joined them, Chase lowered an unconscious, limp Paul into the arms of the awaiting rescuers. Then after taking one last look at the inside of Hope Memorial, Chase proceeded down the ladder. He was shaky from the lack of oxygen in his blood, a feeling he knew would pass.

When he reached the ground, he went over to Paul to assess his condition. Paul's skin was ashen, his lips blue, a sign that he wasn't breathing. Chase hastily examined him, feeling his wrists for signs of a pulse, finding nothing. Frantically, he opened Paul's mouth and realized why. Suet had caused Paul's throat to swell shut, making an impasse for air and ensuring that CPR would be fruitless.

"Help me take him to one of the tents," Chase ordered one of the rescuers. He grabbed Paul's midsection while the rescuer grabbed his legs. A tracheostomy was the only thing that could save Paul and he needed it done now. They placed Paul on a surgical table from equipment that was both salvaged from Hope Memorial and brought over from nearby Grace University Hospital, where Chase made a quick assessment of his surroundings and available resources.

"What do we have here, doctor?" A nurse rushed over to him to offer her assistance.

"I need a scalpel – fast. He needs a tracheostomy or he's not going to make it."

The nurse scrambled to locate a scalpel on a nearby tray. "I'll get the trach tube from Grace." She hurried across the tent area in search of a tube.

Chase took a deep breath and made a horizontal incision across Paul's neck directly above the sternum, dissecting the skin and exposing the trachea. The nurse appeared with the trach tube. "Good timing," he said amidst an incision to the tracheal ring. Without taking his eyes from his work, he asked the nurse to find sutures, dressings, a ventilator and a d-fib.

"The sutures and dressings are already on that tray," she said, pointing to the small stainless steel freestanding tray. "But I think they're using all of the heavy equipment," she announced, dejected.

"Just see what you can come up with."

The young nurse nodded and ran off to go foraging through the tents. Chase inserted the tracheostomy tube into the incision. He then located the sutures on the tray and proceeded to weave them through Paul's wound, closing up the incision surrounding the tracheostomy. It was an operation performed under less than perfect circumstances with the risk for infection being high but, for what it was worth, he'd made do with the available resources. Even though, despite his best efforts, he knew that if the right equipment could not be found, Paul was as good as dead.

"Doctor Matthews," the nurse came rushing back with another doctor following hot on her heels. Chase noticed a cart being pulled behind them and did a double take to confirm that he saw what he thought he was seeing. On the cart being pulled by the nurse and pushed by the Grace University physician was a ventilator and defibrillator, both of which Paul's life depended upon.

*He may have a chance after all,* Chase thought. Chase grabbed the cart from the nurse, pulling it the rest of the way to the surgical table, where he hooked it up to the tracheostomy tube while the other doctor started it in motion. He rechecked Paul for a pulse and was relieved when he was able to locate a weak one in Paul's carotid. After several minutes of working on him, the color began to return to Paul's face, replacing the blue-grayish hue.

"Good job, doctor. It would appear that you have saved this man's life," the doctor from Grace University proclaimed.

"He's not out of the woods yet. It's hard telling how long his brain was deprived of oxygen." Dizziness had resumed its battle with him and was overtaking his body even more so than before. He stumbled to a folding chair, sitting down with his head lowered to try to counteract its effects.

"Don't be so modest, doctor," the young nurse joined in. "Without you, he never would have had a chance."

Chase held his head in his hands as the voices of the doctor and nurse became nothing more than mere mumbles in his ears. Instead of breathing normally, his breaths came as wheezes just as Paul's had been.

With concern in her voice, the nurse asked, "Are you all right, Dr. Matthews?"

Chase nodded, knowing full well everything was far from all right. Before today, he'd passed out two times in his life and he knew the feeling very well.

"Dr. Matth…" Chase looked up at the nurse and then slumped from his chair to the ground. "Someone grab an oxygen mask," she shouted.

As he drifted further into unconsciousness, his thoughts traveled back to Celaine, her radiant smile as beautiful as he remembered, a trail of blonde hair flowing from her while she motioned for him to join her in her run through the halls of Hope Memorial.

# 29

# THE IMPOSSIBLE

BLAKE WAS STRUGGLING as I'd never seen him before, as I'd never thought possible. He wasn't going to die in front of me. Not without a fight. In pain, I picked myself up from the pile of splintered wood comprising the remains of the pallet that had disintegrated when I landed on it. Then, with the full force of my body, I charged at The Man in Black, only to be met with solid resistance as soon as our bodies made contact. It was like slamming into a brick wall, and it caused me to end up flat on my back without having even budged him. Instead, I just barely succeeded in jostling him enough so that Blake was able to wriggle free, escaping the wrath of the wooden spear.

Furious, The Man in Black turned his attention to me, lifting his enormous arm like a sadistic mallet. Mesmerized by my first time ever having seen him outside of the simulator, I couldn't help but notice the most striking characteristic about him: the disproportionate size of his extremities. His arms were massive. In the few seconds I had to analyze them, I came to the conclusion that they weren't organic in nature.

His arm swung at my head, prompting me to counter in defense by rolling my body sideways, coming within milliseconds of being struck by his battering ram of a fist. Before The Man in Black could realize that I'd escaped his wrath, I sprung to my feet and sprinted over to Blake.

"Are you all right?" Blake asked.

"Just splendid. You?"

"As far as I can tell, I am. That was amazing, by the way. I've never seen him outrun like that before."

The Man in Black turned around, angrier than before.

"He's out for your blood now."

"Let him bring it on. I'm out for some blood of my own."

"Remember your training; flank him. Don't try to go all Wonder Woman on me."

As much as I wanted to abide by Blake's orders, there was a storm brewing inside of me that, after ten years, had just about reached its climax. The calm before the storm was beginning to pass and the dark clouds were starting to roll in. And it was a matter of time before I let the lightning strike.

"On my mark," Blake's voice resounded within my ear piece.

My body tensed, each muscle making its presence known. I trained my sights on The Man in Black, contemplating my plan of attack.

"Now!" Blake ordered.

Together, our feet left the ground, zeroed in on a common target that few had attempted to hit but of which all had wished they could. Even though I was running faster than humanly possible, it still felt as though time was standing still. My mind was racing with a myriad of thoughts and emotions. Would the last image my eyes captured be of this despicable monster? What does death feel like? Was I capable of killing another living being? Unlike most questions in life, these had answers which I would soon discover, ready or not.

"Jump!"

I followed Blake's command. Simultaneously, we struck The Man in Black just as he was about to propel himself into the air to dodge our assault. The force of our blows hurtled him through the air into a shelving unit filled with pallets, snapping it in half. An avalanche of wood and steel greeted him seconds after he impacted on the concrete.

"Stand back," Blake ordered. "He's going to be really pissed now."

"Do you think we've injured him?"

Blake chuckled. "Hardly, though I'm sure he's rattled a bit."

Seconds later, I felt something strike me, throwing me off my feet as it slammed me violently onto the floor. Intense pain erupted along the right side of my body. When I looked up, I saw The Man in Black throwing bits of jagged steel like javelins. "It appears as though we've given him ammunition," I said to Blake, jumping back to my feet, narrowly avoiding a piece of sharpened steel as it flew just inches from my head.

"If you can't beat them, join them. Grab a piece of debris and let's take care of business."

I grabbed a broken piece of pallet while Blake opted to fight fire with fire with steel. Through his mask, I could detect a hint of a sneer on The Man in Black's face as though the violence provided some sort of sick excitement for him.

"Time for another run. He'll be expecting us this time, so be prepared." Blake took off with me trailing just inches behind him. Like he predicted, The Man in Black was ready for us, swinging a broken board. A sickening thud arose as it made contact with Blake, sending him rolling. With his attention diverted, I made my move, swinging the splintered pallet and knocking him off his feet. Satisfied with myself, I turned to Blake, expecting him to capitalize on my minor success but, instead of launching an assault, he remained balled up on the concrete where he'd come to a rolling stop. With The Man in Black still down, I dashed over to him. He was clutching his side in obvious pain.

"Blake...Blake..." I crouched down next to him. "Are you all right?"

"I'll be fine."

His hand fell down from his side, revealing a tear in his suit. Blood was dripping from a small gash to his abdomen.

"How is that possible? I thought these things were indestructible."

He winced. "They are. With regular maintenance and replacement for wear and tear. Nice shot, by the way."

"Thanks."

Blake stood up, doing his best to shake off the sudden loss of his invincibility, making me question just how protected we were. On his feet, he checked out his wound, his eyes widening when he glanced in my direction. "Celaine, jump." he yelled.

I turned just in time to see The Man in Black charging toward me, a look of pure demonic evil burning in his eyes. In swift response, my feet left the ground. However, it was a second too late, and I found myself being tackled by him, his massive form crushing me into the ground.

With a swift kick, I knocked him from me, but not before he landed a crippling blow to my chest, taking my breath away. Re-energized, he took full advantage of my sudden handicap, and I felt my body levitate as he picked me up by my leg. Before I had the chance to fight back, he'd flung me through the air with my back striking the wall of the warehouse, sending me to the floor writhing in pain.

I lay on the ground where I landed, my head telling me to get up and fight, my body not allowing me to move anymore. Near my head, I heard the *clunk, clunk* of his feet approaching me. Dizzy, I looked up to see his ugly, masked face staring down at me in triumph. It was then that he did the unexpected: he spoke.

"This new one is more pathetic than the last partner you had. Surely, you didn't think she would make a formidable opponent for me," he said, smirking. "I'm going to take great joy in disposing of her."

His voice, an almost mechanical one in nature, made more of an oddity with his helmet in the way, sent me into a state of shock. It shouldn't have surprised me, but it did. To actually hear his voice, to hear intelligible words come from him, gave him a more humanly quality. Never before had I considered The Man in Black to be in the category of "human". This revelation paralyzed my mind along with my battered body.

"Over my dead body," Blake said through his teeth.

"Is that an invitation?"

"Take it as you will."

"With pleasure." He glanced back down at me. "I'll be back to deal with you, sweetheart." He put his hand up to the mouthpiece of his helmet, blowing me a kiss.

That voice resonated in my mind, echoing throughout the crevices of my cranium. Had it been the last one my family heard before the blast? Did he blow them the same kiss goodbye as he'd just blown to me? Did he laugh as he witnessed the parking ramp crumble before him? Did he enjoy the fear in his victims' eyes as the life left their bodies? Each thought entering my head fueled my anger more, bringing my blood to a rapid boil. A surge of adrenaline coursed through my vapid veins, invigorating them as it put my body and brain back on the same page. Energy renewed, I picked myself up from the ground while ignoring the horrendous pain emanating in my chest.

Blake threw a punch at The Man in Black, knocking him back a couple of steps, where he retaliated with a swift kick to Blake's sternum. Unmoved, Blake performed a flying kick that, despite his best efforts, The Man in Black could not dodge. Blake's boot blasted the side of his helmet, throwing him into a pile of broken desks and garbage. Although I was glad that Blake had knocked the evil bastard down a few pegs, I was miffed that I hadn't been the one to do it. A strange feeling was beginning to overtake me. Pure rage, like none I'd felt before, consumed me. Their faces appeared in my head, the scenario with him standing outside their window knowing the fate that beheld them, and them powerless to stop him.

"Are you all right?" I nodded my answer to Blake's question. "When he gets up, wait for my mark. No matter how much he may trash talk you, I know you caught him off guard a few times. You're a threat to him. He would have toyed with you more had he not seen you as one."

I heard the words that Blake spoke, but I didn't take them in. My mind was made up, his words were inconsequential to me now. It would be insubordination to the extreme, but I had to do it. The images from my dreams had haunted me for too long, and I wasn't going to give him the chance to get away again.

He emerged, brushing garbage off his suit, metal bar in hand. Blake's posture stiffened, his eyes scanning his opponent for any signs of weakness.

"On my mark," Blake's voice fell on deaf ears.

Spread before me now appeared the scene inside the parking ramp with just seconds left before the blast. It was me and The Man in Black with my parents' vehicle in the background, their voices barely audible behind the metallic structure. With my anger consuming me, I charged at The Man in Black of my nightmares.

"What the hell are you doing?" Blake shouted in my ear piece. I ignored him. He was mine, and I was going to claim him before he could claim them again. With my nightmares as my guide, I lunged at him. A massive force wound its way around my neck as he met my advance, but instead of choking me, he twisted my neck in a direction that necks could not normally bend. He was going for the kill. By breaking my neck, he would most likely succeed. I had failed them. I would die without having kept my promise, allowing him to take something else from my family.

"I'm sorry," I sputtered to the image of their car in the parking ramp.

Suddenly, his grasp was broken, causing me to fall to the ground with my neck throbbing in pain. When I sat up, rubbing my neck, I saw Blake tousling with him, jabbing him from left to right, missing some blows but landing most while dodging the metal bar he brandished. The Man in Black stumbled, falling to the floor in the debris heap. It was the most vulnerable the monster had been. He was going to do it. Blake was going to defeat him. This nightmare would be over once and for all.

"Put your hands where I can see them," Blake ordered.

The Man in Black sneered. "As you wish."

It's funny how one second's time can alter the future for an eternity, how one moment can change one's perception indelibly. One second it appeared as though Blake had prevailed, that good had been able to overcome evil with the downfall of The Man in Black. But, in the next second, it became apparent that a different fate had been written in the stars altogether. The Man in Black removed his hands from behind his back, revealing the broken metal bar still clutched in his right hand and, although the action only took an instant to complete, time seemed to move in slow motion from my vantage point. A scream escaped my mouth as I witnessed the metal bar's jagged edge thrust like a harpoon from the hand of The Man in Black into the exposed flesh of Blake's abdomen. Blake exhaled a sickening gasp, collapsing to his knees, clutching his wound.

My horror turned rapidly into fury as I picked myself up to face the devil himself. Pleased with himself, he moved towards me with a swagger that screamed superiority. "Now that he's out of the way, I can finish what I started with you."

The sound of his voice served to fan the flames of the inferno that was manifesting inside me. "Your arrogance will be your downfall," I replied, facing him.

He laughed. "Your tenacity is amusing. I may just regret snapping your neck."

I took a defensive stance, analyzing his every move. Physically, there was no question he dominated me. But what he had in sheer bulk, he lacked in speed. Although he could move much faster than the average person, he was no match for my lighter, adrenaline-enhanced body. When it came to making the first move, I would leave the ball in his court, surveying every move he made in an attempt to find a weakness. We walked in a large circle, staring at each other, daring the other to make a move.

After practically wearing a trail on the concrete floor, he lost his patience and broke down. I studied each step he took as he ran at me; the way he held his arms with each stride, the slight arch of his back, the exaggerated armor he wore. When he was within ten feet of plowing me over, I flipped up into the air, landing on my feet several feet behind him.

Enraged, he charged at me again like a bull to a matador. I visualized his eyes reddening, his nostrils flaring. And when he came within a couple of feet of impaling me, I sprang into a back flip, kicking my leg out, successfully making contact with the side of his head. *That's for you, Jake*, I thought. The blow to the head knocked him off kilter. Clearly, he hadn't expected that out of me.

"Am I formidable enough for you now?"

He emitted a deep, guttural noise that could only be described as a growl. At that moment, I wondered whether he was part beast, after all. Steadfast, he took off, pounding the pavement with more purpose than before. I held my ground and tried to guess what tricks he had up his sleeve, but when it appeared as though he planned on doing nothing more than running me down, I bent my knees to prepare to leap over him. When I was no more than two feet in the air, he leapt up, launching his fist at me, striking me in the only unprotected part of my body: my neck. I fell to the floor, struggling to take in air. He stood over me, pinning me down, his foot firmly planted on my chest.

"You will never be worthy enough for me."

He pressed down even harder on my chest until I could hear my ribs cracking underneath his weight. Moments later, after figuring I was too incapacitated to be of any danger to him, he removed his foot from my body, allowing my lungs to fill back up with air. Though as I expected, the reprieve didn't last long as, once again, I felt myself being lifted off the floor as he grabbed me by the legs and proceeded to spin me furiously, my body gaining momentum.

Never in my life had I thought I was truly going to die. Not even during the assault on The Lakes did I believe my life would end. But now, as I flew through the air across the warehouse, I knew that today would be the day. After all I had been through, the assault my body would take upon impact would be too devastating to live through. I had a lot of faith in the suit that encased me, but it couldn't perform miracles. My eyes closed, I braced for myself for impact as my body flew into a shelving unit filled with empty pallets. The force of the impact shattered the unit and knocked me to the floor. I looked up from the concrete to see a shower of steel and wood raining down on me. Within seconds, I was covered, buried alive in the remnants of the shelving unit.

The familiar sound of The Man in Black's feet pounding against the floor drew closer. Undoubtedly, he would try to succeed at what the impact had been unable to do. Around me, I could hear bits and pieces of wood and steel being lifted off where I landed and thrown to the side. It was only a matter of moments before I was uncovered. All I could do was wait.

At last, he picked up a sheet of steel, revealing my head. I struggled to free my legs, but was met with nothing but resistance. My arms were relatively free, allowing me to run my hands up and down my body in a vain attempt at finding something to deliver me from certain demise.

"It's time to join your partner." He drew his arm back, revealing my fate to me. I braced myself, praying that death would come swiftly. In nervous anticipation, I ran my fingers down the side of my body, where I felt something strike my right hand. At that moment, a revelation struck me. I have a gun.

As his armored hand rocketed toward me, my fingers gripped the holster, unclasping my hope for salvation and, with lightning accuracy, I gripped its handle, my fingers grasping the trigger. When his fist came within inches from crushing my head, I pulled my hand from the debris and fired.

I expected a lot of things to happen as the bullet left the barrel of the gun. For instance, I expected it to throw him off his game, giving me an opportunity to attempt an escape. I expected it to throw him back down the pile of wood and steel, giving me at least a few more seconds of life. I expected it to piss him off even more, making my death quicker and, perhaps, relatively less painful. However, I *didn't* expect the bullet to enter through a slight defect in his armored suit, and I most definitely did not expect the bullet to pierce his flesh.

An agonizing groan erupted from him as he stumbled down the pile. He removed his hand from his wound, revealing a stream of blood. To say that I was stunned was an understatement but, just as Blake's suit had proven, nothing was perfect. Flaws existed everywhere. It was the length of time it took between looking for that one imperfection and finding it that gave one the false perception of perfection.

He lunged for me again in an undecided manner, knowing that if he sustained one more direct hit, he could be done for, effectively ending all of the destruction and chaos he'd worked so hard to sustain. In the distance, I heard a siren approaching, which meant more guns and even more bullets.

"Until we meet again," he said with a snarl.

"I'm counting on it."

I heard his boots running across the pavement as he took off like the coward he was, leaving a trail of blood droplets in his wake.

I tugged on the wooden plank and freed my legs, pulling myself out of the debris. With the adrenaline winding down, I started feeling the effects of the beating I'd just taken. My body, particularly my neck, throbbed and burned as though I'd been lit on fire, and I lay in the mountain of debris, uncertain whether I would be able to pull myself to my feet. That uncertainty was vanquished when a soft moan erupted in the distance. Blake.

My body searing with each step, I ignored the excruciating pain and limped toward Blake. He remained lying in the same spot where he'd been brought down. It had been obvious at the time that the shard of metal he'd been stabbed with had caused serious injury, but it hadn't dawned on me just how serious it really had been until I saw the pool of blood settling underneath his body.

"Blake," I called his name, crouching down on my knees beside him, cupping his head in my hands. "Blake, speak to me."

He groaned, clutching his wound. Slowly, I took my hand and ran it down his body to the hand that clutched his side and removed it, prompting a new stream of blood to pour from the hole in Blake's abdomen. I gasped aloud. Despite having dated a doctor, my knowledge of survivable traumas to the human body wasn't all that extensive, but it didn't take a medical degree to know that the wound I was looking at wasn't compatible with life. Devastated, I kept my hand on Blake's wound as tears formed in the corner of my eyes.

"I'm so sorry," I said, trying to suppress them.

"Hey, stop the waterworks. These things happen." His voice was strained as though the very act of speech took every ounce of his being. "Please...take off my mask. I can't breathe in this thing."

I removed Blake's mask. His face was drained of all color and, despite the sweat that was running down his forehead, he was trembling. I removed my mask so that I could look at him face to face, for I feared that mine would be the last face he'd ever see. He moved his hand down his body, cupping it over the hand I was using to suppress the bleeding. With tears rolling down my cheeks, I stroked his hair with my other hand as I really wasn't sure what else to do; I was paralyzed with dread. Blake knew his fate, and my blubbering like a baby wasn't helping matters.

In an attempt to regain my composure, I turned my head away from his gaze, trying to will my tear ducts dry. His hand caressed my cheek, a move I never would have expected. I looked back at his face and was met, not with a look of fear, anger or pain, but with a look of regret and compassion.

"I know...I'm dying..."

I hated hearing him speak the inevitable. His speech was softer, causing me to lean in further to him to hear his every word. He moved his hand from my face to my hair, brushing wayward strands away from my eye.

"You...don't...you don't...have to. I'll take you back to headquarters. The doctors...they'll fix you. You'll be fine."

"There's no fixing the damage that has been done to me. I'm not scared, Celaine. I'm free...finally, I'm free again. My only worry is for you."

"Me? Why are you worried about me?"

"You're too good. The most genuine person I've known. Just do me a...a favor."

"Anything."

"Don't let them take your soul. Don't let them blind you. Don't allow them to take your life like I did. Always keep your eyes open to the truth."

"I will," I promised, confused as to what his words meant.

"One more thing."

"Yeah?"

"Lean in closer to me."

I leaned in toward Blake. He had the familiar smirk on his face that I'd grown to find endearing. Expecting him to say something, I was caught off guard when I felt his lips touch mine as he pulled my head in for a passionate embrace. The look on my face after his lips left mine had to have been nothing short of priceless.

"Now I can honestly say that I lived my life without any regrets."

A new round of tears streamed down my face. I laid down next to Blake, holding him for the last few moments of his life, sobbing when I heard him take his final breath.

There are moments that occur in your life that forever alter your existence. Before today, I had two of those moments: the death of my family and the day I met Chase. After today, I had three. Blake's death altered me in an irreparable way, ensuring that I would never walk the Earth the same person again.

# 30

## THE INFINITE SORROW

'ALWAYS KEEP YOUR eyes open to the truth.' Blake's words haunted me. What did they mean? What was the answer to this enigma he presented me with in his last breath?

We stood gathered together around the casket, the late summer sun beating down through the gaps in the leaves of the maples scattered throughout the private cemetery. This would be the eternal resting place of Blake Cohen, and I was the reason for him being here. Victor feels the same way too, or so I believe. Since Blake's death, his steely stare had turned even more ominous towards me. And despite Kara's reassurance that his death had been due in part to his aversion to regular suit maintenance, I knew differently.

I brushed my hand over the pleats of the black dress I'd worn the day I arrived at headquarters; the last day of my former life, and the beginning of my new one with Blake Cohen. Even though I was with everyone I'd gotten to know over the past several weeks, I still felt alone, my mind replaying the events of my encounter with The Man in Black and Blake's final words to me. In the intermittent lapses that followed the grisly scenario looping through my mind, Chase's face appeared, causing guilt to overtake me. Never had I suspected Blake as having held the feelings he revealed to me before he surrendered to eternity. It made me think, if he had survived, whether I would have developed the same feelings for him. Presently, the thought seemed inconceivable, as my heart was still firmly in Chase's possession, but what about a year from now when I'd grown despondent over Chase moving on? This thought made my guilt intensify, worsening the internal conflict that was waging war with my soul.

My tears had dried up. Ignoring my past convictions, I gave in to the raw emotion that had abducted me and succumbed to taking the pills Dr. Lin had given to me. I was hollow, a robot awaiting a command.

I heard none of the sermon the chaplain gave that day, nor the sound of the creaks the wooden casket made when it was lowered into the dark, damp earth. Instead, I became lost in my thoughts, staring off into the oblivion of the cemetery, over every headstone and blade of grass. It wasn't until Kara touched my shoulder that I was brought back down into the sickening reality, ceasing the never-ending loop playing in my head. The funeral was over, as was the life of Blake Cohen. I followed Kara through the iron gate leading out of the cemetery, stealing one last glance back at Blake's grave. A backhoe was in the distance, already on its way to fill it in.

Although I was alone, I still felt a presence around me so intense that it seemed as though it was burning a hole in the back of my head. When I shifted my eyes further away from the grave, I spotted the thrower of this invisible flame.

Victor leaned against a maple tree, cigarette in hand, a look of sheer hatred in his eyes.

# 31
## THE NEW RECRUIT

"YOU'RE LEAVING FOR Norfolk tonight," Cameron announced while we gathered around the table the next morning for breakfast. Kara shook her head as if to be subconsciously telling Cameron, *Not now*.

"Norfolk? Why am I going to Norfolk?"

"Because that's where Ian Grant lives."

I set my fork down. "Okay, Cameron, I'll play along. Who's Ian Grant?"

"Your new partner."

"What?" I stole a glance at the empty seat next to me. "You can't possibly be serious? It's only been a day since Blake's funeral."

"It'd only been a day since Liam's funeral when you were scouted," Victor spoke up from his permanent seat at the head of the table. "Perhaps, you'll be able to keep this partner alive."

Victor's comment struck a nerve. I felt my face flush, my head dizzy with anger. "Excuse me." I stood up from the table, angrily stepping out of the dining hall.

"Celaine, wait." Kara jogged after me into the hallway. "He's an ass."

"Excuse me?"

"Victor. He's a genius, and the reason why this place even exists, but he's also an arrogant, self-righteous ass."

"I usually have a fond appreciation for bluntness, but with him, not so much."

Kara and I walked to one of the couches in the sitting room. On the news, an aerial view of the devastation that was Hope Memorial appeared with a recap of the story surrounding the explosions. Kara looked up at the screen to see what had caught my attention.

"You miss him, don't you?"

"More than you could ever imagine."

"Do you still think it was worth it? Coming here and leaving him?"

"You know...that's the funny thing about this place. The second I think that maybe, just maybe, I've made a horrible mistake by coming here, something happens to completely vanquish that thought. In the warehouse, after I shot The Man in Black...when I saw the look of astonishment in his eyes as that bullet hit him, the look of almost sheer defeat when he took off like the coward he is, I knew that I was doing the right thing. I am doing the right thing. My fate took control of my destiny ten years ago, leaving me to do its bidding, which is why I'm going to Norfolk tonight."

Kara smiled. "You know, it's not like you don't have anyone who cares about you here. It's not as if we view you...your kind, for lack of a better description, as some sort of oddity. We just have to go on with business as usual even through the immense pain it causes. I mean, given your personal experiences with that monster, I think you can appreciate the need for a partner. Besides that, if the public finds out that another one of you has been killed, there will be sheer chaos. They would begin to lose faith in you and us. What good we and our cause have done for societal morale will dissipate and then evil will have won. Besides that, Victor thinks the President is about a stone's throw away from declaring martial law."

"That wouldn't go over well."

"That's what they said about the curfew, but yet his approval ratings went up after the installation of that joke."

"May I ask you something?"

"Shoot."

"Why Ian Grant, Celaine Stevens and Blake Cohen?"

"What do you mean?"

"Why were we chosen? How were we chosen?"

She looked at me for a moment, contemplating her answer as though choosing which one to give. "I honestly don't know," she replied in a whisper, forcing me to believe that she'd chosen the lie over the truth. "Victor is more or less responsible for that, and I believe he relies on his own sources. From what I've been told, it seems to be related to your social security numbers and totally at random. Victor has Inez or Caine check out a bunch of random people and he makes the final selection himself."

"What if one of these random people he chooses declines? They would know a little too much information, wouldn't they?"

"That's what your gun is for." Cameron appeared in the sitting room.

I felt my blood begin to boil as it rose to my face. "What does he mean by that?" I turned back around towards Kara. Her head was in her hands, her eyes fixed to the floor.

"They haven't told you yet? Blake never told you? Wow, he must really have had it bad for you –classic."

Suddenly, it dawned on me. Of course, it all made sense. It wasn't that no one had ever declined their offer – it was more like they *couldn't* decline it. Too furious to speak, I glared at Kara. So much for having choices in life.

Without taking her eyes off the floor, she spoke in an apologetic whisper. "We didn't know you then, Celaine...we...we have to look out for our program here. We can't jeopardize the good work we've done. We can't jeopardize the progress we've made."

"I'm not killing Ian Grant. I won't do it. I'm not a murderer."

"No, you aren't a murderer." Victor joined us in the sitting room, his presence angering me further. "You're merely sacrificing one innocent life for the benefit of millions of innocent lives."

"You can package your bullshit up any way you want, but at the end of the day, it's still just shit, Victor."

Cameron's eyes widened, his head bobbing from me to Victor and back again in disbelief, as though challenging Victor was a cardinal sin.

"That's quite a colorful analogy, but, Ms. Stevens, at the end of the day, you still work for me, and you will follow my instructions to the letter."

The urge to punch him surged through me, and it took all I had to suppress it. In an attempt to avoid further irritation, I turned my back to walk down the hallway, only to be halted by Victor's voice, launching his own brand of kryptonite in my direction. "You wouldn't want your family's death *or* Blake's to have been in vain, would you?"

Later that evening, I was on the road heading toward Norfolk, a gun situated in the holster at my hip. I had never been to Norfolk, but from the photographs I once saw of the Virginia Beach area from Lucy's family vacations, it seemed like a beautiful area, an added bonus. Besides, it was on the ocean and away from the confines of The Epicenter.

Ian Grant. I'd never met him, yet I already knew so much about him. He was tall, standing at 6'2", brown hair, green eyes, a handsome, photogenic man just a couple of years younger than me. Never married and an only child, he had no immediate family, and had been estranged from his mother for the last several years. His father had been killed in the blast at the Flamingo Casino and Resort in Atlantic City just days prior to my family's murder.

An exceedingly intelligent, yet underachieving individual–which was noted as possibly having been the catalyst for the animosity between him and his mother–instead of going to college, he took a job bartending at a local novelty bar about a mile from the naval pier. Where he's been for the last four years, and where he'd be tonight until curfew when, after work, he'd return to his studio apartment, just mere blocks from the bar.

After four hours on the road, I was in Norfolk. When I passed from Maryland into Virginia, my vehicle captured the inquisitive stares of the border patrol, who'd waived me through after scanning the government-issued license plate that granted me adequate clearance for interstate travel. I didn't have a game plan. I didn't know what I was going to say to Ian or how I would broach the subject and doubted that I would be half as convincing as Blake had been with me. Then again, at that time, I hadn't been jaded like I was now.

It was getting late, but there was still a couple of hours left until curfew. Back home, the streets would have already emptied by now.

Norfolk was an entirely different story. Upon approaching the city limits, I was taken back in time ten years to a place where the institution of a curfew was unheard of; where excitement and mischievous fun abounded on the streets without fear of reprimand. But, despite catching a glimmer of life in the eyes of those who were making the most of an enforced situation, I could still tell that in the back of their minds, they knew that any kind of fun they were going to have tonight would be regulated.

It was dusk, the sun's rays having lost their daily battle with the Earth's rotation. The sky was painted with all manners of blues, oranges, and dusty pinks, and over the ocean, the deep purple of nightfall was making its way onto the shore. Lights from local businesses flickered on, creating faux daylight in the short interval between twilight and curfew.

I came upon the street where supposedly, based upon the information Caine was able to dig up, Ian's bar was located. This particular strip was home to what appeared to be numerous hot spots in the Norfolk area, including multiple bars, restaurants and night clubs. A cursory scan of both sides of the street revealed the Concord Bar and Grill nestled between an unidentified storefront and a night club with gaudy neon signs. It was one of those cutesy beach-themed bars that was usually seen in popular tourist towns, and I suspected that its ambiance served only to strip Ian, or any other male employee for that matter, of his masculinity as he walked through its doors day after day. As an added touch, outside of the establishment, a Beach Boys song blared through a speaker connected to the building. *For the love of God, please, don't let that be playing on the inside, too.*

After locating an alleyway a few streets down from the bar, I stowed the car out of sight and headed back down the sidewalk. Most likely feeling sorry for me, Kara had gone out and purchased "street clothes" for me to use. It was a nice gesture; however, she'd misjudged my height and torso length. And as I walked down the street, I found myself rolling my pant leg up with one hand so as not to stumble on the absurd length of the jeans, while pulling my baby blue t-shirt down with the other hand. Yeah, I looked really credible as a government agent. The good news was that I completely fit in with the crowd setting at the Concord, where many of the female patrons were also donning shirts that were a tad too short, but, not surprisingly, they were nowhere near as modest as

I was.

Much to my chagrin, the same music that assaulted the eardrums of those outside the bar was also merrily battering those inside as well. After finding an empty stool, I awkwardly sat down at the bar, where I noticed that the theme of the place had also infected its employees. All of them donned fake tans coupled with unfortunate attire consisting of red and blue Hawaiian shirts and multi-colored leis.

"What can I get for ya, hun?" a bubbly bleached blonde asked from behind the bar.

"May I just have a glass of lemon water, please?"

She gave me a 'You've got to be kidding me' look as she forced a smile and a 'sure thing' response to my request.

*There goes your tip, toots*, I thought, as I returned to scouring the bar for my target. I may not have had a plan or much of anything figured out, but I did know that, if I was to get a "no" response from him, I wasn't going to put a bullet in his head. Let one of them come back down and take care of that, because it wouldn't be me.

The not-so-perky-anymore blonde returned with a glass of water that I was almost certain had been spat in or subjected to other gross scenarios. "Thank you," I greeted her. I wouldn't be drinking the water. She gave me a nod, and I swore I could see her roll her eyes as she turned back towards the other end of the bar.

"Excuse me, Ma'am," I called after her. Being called ma'am always had a way of irritating us younger women. And I took great pleasure in irritating this particular one.

"Yes?" she replied, faking another smile. "Is everything all right with your water?"

*Because messing up water is possible?* I shook my head in disbelief, continuing my inquiry, "No, no, the water is great, but would you mind telling me whether Ian Grant is working tonight, by chance?"

She studied me, the look of annoyance giving way to a look of curiosity, hurt and anger rolled into one. It appeared she was no fan of Mr. Grant's. "That rat bastard?" she replied, confirming my speculations. "Yeah. He's over at the other end of the bar." She pointed at the end of the bar to the same handsome man I'd seen in the photograph back at headquarters. He was doing bar tricks with shot glasses, entertaining a crowd of young women who all seemed smitten by him.

"How much have they had to drink?"

"Surprisingly, not that much. He's just that good." She looked me up and down again. "If I were you, I'd be careful."

"I'll take that into consideration. Would you mind sending him over here when he's done entertaining the children?"

"Sure, but don't be surprised if he ignores you and forgets your name later. He has a habit of doing that."

"Duly noted."

Blonde ambition sulked her way down to the end of the bar, tapping Ian on the shoulder. It took her three taps, the last being just two degrees shy of a punch, before he acknowledged her. He turned around, uttering something that, from reading his lips, appeared to resemble a 'What' response with an irritated look on his face. The blonde bartender pointed down to me, mouthing a few words into his ear. Ian stared at me with a look that resembled intrigue mixed with an expression that screamed, 'Oh, crap, where do I know her from?' After a couple of seconds of contemplation, he waved at me and then spoke into the blonde bartender's ear, turning back to the eager women he'd enraptured at the bar. The blonde walked back over to my stool.

"He said to tell you he'll be over in a minute."

"Thank you."

She continued to stare at me until she finally spoke again. "You know he doesn't remember you." She seemed satisfied with herself for having made that last statement to me. "That's what he does. You're all wonderful and amazing until he gets you in bed and then – you're irrelevant," she said, sighing.

"Well, I will never know that as I have no intention of sleeping with him."

She looked at me surprised, instantly perking up. "Oh..." she replied, and then the embarrassment kicked in. "Oh..." I smiled at her, causing her to walk away with a face as red as the Grenadine she served behind the bar.

I observed Ian, realizing that I'd have my work cut out for me tonight. He left little doubt that he loved showing off and no doubt that he loved the attention from the ladies. They were *oohing* and *ahhing* as he threw random bottles of liquor into the air, spinning them around from hand to hand in a mini juggling act, pouring shots with reckless abandon.

They egged him on for more, of which he was happy to oblige. And when his impromptu performance drew to a close, he took a bow and gave a flirtatious wink to his adoring fans, who awarded him with applause and cat calls the likes of which were only heard at construction sites. The blonde bartender rolled her eyes while the other male bartenders stopped what they were doing to take it all in, envious expressions overcoming their faces.

Ian placed the liquor bottles back on the shelf, looking over at me to make sure I was still there. He smiled at me with a smile that could make even the sourest person's mood brighten. I was sure it only added to his popularity with the ladies, providing him with ridiculous tips. His eyes observed me, piercing right through me, as he stuck his index finger in the air, giving me the universal symbol for *just a second*. His fingers gripped the tap on the sink and turned it as he washed away the sticky film from the cocktail of alcohol that'd spilled on his hands. Once clean enough to meet with his approval, he turned the water off and, drying his hands on his pants, walked over to my place at the bar. On his face was a look of concentration as if he were using every brain cell left in his head to figure out where he'd met me previously.

"Don't worry," I said to him when he was standing before me, "you've never met me before."

The look of concentration left his face, and I could almost see his brain relaxing. "Oh, good," he replied with a sigh of relief. "I was worried this was going to get awkward."

"There's nothing more awkward than basically admitting to a woman you've never met before that you're somewhat of a cad." He wasn't amused with my sarcasm. "Do you mind if we move to a booth or somewhere else to talk?"

"Well, I guess that would all depend on who you are and what you want to talk about."

"I'm a process server, and I want to speak with you about a complaint for child support I was sent here to serve you with."

His eyes widened with nervous agony. With the way he was gazing around the room, I figured he was planning an exit strategy before he passed out.

"Whoa there, Casanova, I'm kidding."

"Oh, thank God. I think I just saw my life flash before my eyes." He pretended to wipe sweat from his brow. "I've had one hell of a good time."

"I bet you have."

I stood up from my bar stool, motioning him to a booth near the back of the restaurant section of the bar. When I turned around to see whether or not he was following me, I was surprised to see that, not only was he following me, but his eyes were stuck to my backside like velcro. Perhaps, I could find it in me to shoot someone after all. I picked a booth completely isolated from the other patrons, with the nearest neighbor being five booths away. French fries and shredded napkins littered the table. With the hem of my shirt, I wiped them away to clear a spot for us.

"Isn't this your job?"

"I'm not a waiter, I'm a bartender."

"Of course. How silly of me." I shook my head as I took a seat in the booth.

"Okay, you've got my undivided attention."

"And how many women have you said that to?"

"How about you come back to my place and I'll tell you." He winked at me in an attempt at flustering me. Although, I was sure his tricks had worked on many other women, they did absolutely nothing for me.

I rolled my eyes. "I don't think so."

His demeanor changed, as he wasn't used to being declined by a woman. "Who are you?" he asked. "What's your name...why are you here? I can't sit here very long. My manager has already given me the evil eye."

"Well, Ian Grant, my name is Celaine, and I'm here to make you an offer."

"How do you know my name?"

"I know a lot about you. For instance, I know you live only a couple of blocks from here in a small studio apartment. I know that you and your mother no longer speak to each other, which may explain your obvious womanizing issue." He stared at me, eyes full of suspicion, an air of discomfort projecting from him. Before he had a chance to speak, I hammered the final nail into the coffin. "Finally, and most importantly, I know that your father was killed by The Man in Black." I'd struck an obvious chord with him. Agitated, he began to get up from the table before he took a deep breath, calmed himself, and sat back down again.

"Is this some kind of sick joke?" He glanced back over at the bar area. "Just a minute," he called, while making the gesture meaning the same to the frazzled manager, a gawky red-headed man who wasn't much older than himself.

I shook my head. "No. This isn't a joke. That's one subject I wouldn't joke about. My entire family was wiped out by that bastard." I looked back up at him, noticing that I'd regained his undivided attention. "What would you do if you had the power to catch him; to make him pay for what he did and to ensure he wouldn't do to another family what he did to yours? Would you sacrifice your life, your hopes, and your dreams just to make him pay for the destruction he's caused? Would you be brave enough to face him?"

"I would do anything to get my father back. After his death, I promised him that I would make my existence worth something." His voice cracked, betraying a sensitive side he'd prefer to keep locked away. It struck me then that this may have been one of the first times he'd ever really opened up about the impact of his father's death and the effect it had on him.

"If I were to tell you that I could give you the tools to live up to the promise you made to your father, would you take them?"

He nodded. "Yeah – definitely."

"You'd have to leave here, your home, your job, your life. You could have no contact with the outside world. It would be as though you'd disappeared off the face of the planet." Ian stared at me, deep in thought. "I'll give you seventy-two hours to think about it, and then I'll be back. Tell no one of our encounter here tonight or there will be consequences." Just as I was about to get up, leaving him behind, the manager came over.

"Ian, break time is over." He was the type of person who talked with his hands, and I found myself having to duck after narrowly avoiding being clocked in the head. "This is the fifth break you've taken on your shift tonight. I've got half a mind to…"

"Shut your yap, Harold." I turned my head toward Ian in shock.

"What did you say to me?" Harold's face was deep red. With the way his body was shaking, I was worried he was going to have a stroke.

"You heard me, Harold. I quit."

"But…but…your shift…this won't look good on a resume."

Ian held his middle finger up in the air for all to see throughout the bar, and kept it up there as he grabbed his wallet and keys from behind the bar, finally allowing his hand to come back down as he walked through the door, exiting the establishment for the last time. We walked down the sidewalk together to his apartment.

"Okay, I've thought about it and I'm in."

"That was quick."

"I've heard that before."

"I'm not taking you anywhere tonight. Not until you've put some thought into everything I told you. You're expected to give up your life, you know."

He laughed. "That's just it. I have no life to give up, so in essence I'm giving up nothing to gain everything I've ever wanted. My family wants nothing to do with me. I can't seem to maintain any kind of lasting, meaningful relationship with a girl. I'm stuck in a dead end job with no benefits because I can't do any better, living off free food from the bar, sneaking booze when Harold isn't looking, only to stumble back to my pit of an apartment at night and waking up to face my horrible decisions the next day."

"You're right. You're life really does suck." I laughed.

"I wouldn't be talking if I were you. Yours must not have been too great either if you're here with me right now."

*Actually, it wasn't great, it was perfect*, I thought, but kept to myself to avoid the barrage of questions that would surely follow if I were to make my thoughts audible.

We came to the glass doorway of Ian's apartment building. He took his keys out of his pocket and unlocked the door, holding it open for me as we entered. To my right was a flight of stairs, which Ian started to ascend. Once upstairs, I followed him down the hall until he stopped at the second door on the left, unlocked it, and motioned for me to enter.

It was the definition of bachelor pad. Dishes piled high in the sink, clothes strewn about the floor in various piles. But it wasn't so much the appearance of the apartment that was as off-putting as the smell that wafted through the air: stale food and body odor. How he was as popular with the ladies as he appeared to be was befuddling to me. I surmised that he either went back to their places or it was purely the work of liquor.

"Sorry about the mess. I usually try to pick up a bit when I know I'm going to have company."

"Well, I can see why you want to get out of here so badly. I'd rather pick up and leave than even attempt to try and clean this cesspool."

I walked through the foyer into the small kitchen, where I had to tiptoe around beer cans like a giant trying to navigate a mini maze. The floor plan of the apartment opened up from the kitchen into the living room, where there were even more clothes in random piles on the floor and health and fitness magazines intermingled between socks, sweatshirts and damp towels. Aside from his obvious disdain for cleaning, there were signs he did, at some point in time, attempt to make his tiny space a home with the photographs that adorned the wall. Photographs featuring friends, family, scenery and random objects in colors, blacks and whites and sepias hung in every square inch of free space in his living room. It was quite evident photography was an enjoyable hobby for him; one of which he was rather talented at. My feet paved a path through the clutter as I walked around the apartment to admire his work, coming upon a space in the wall showcasing an obvious theme. Displayed there were still more photographs, however, unlike the others, these photographs were amateurish and dated. Featured in them was the same young boy throughout various stages of his life along with an older man. There were images of them fishing, camping, and bonding on various family excursions.

"You were close to your father, weren't you?"

"He was more like a brother to me than a father." Ian emerged from his room carrying a small duffel bag, a stoic look etched upon his face. "I was with him the day he died. My mother and I were sleeping in our hotel room while we were on vacation in Atlantic City. Dad wasn't much of the gambler, but mom wanted to be at the casino, so to the casino we went. He was a horrible insomniac, my dad. That's why he was still awake and roaming the casino floors at three in the morning when the blast hit. He didn't die immediately – but he should have. When my mom and I saw him at the hospital a couple of hours after the blast, he was unrecognizable." He took a deep breath in an attempt to counteract the emotional toll recounting the event of his father's death was taking on him. "The...the burns. They were horrible. They were so bad that they haunt my dreams to this day. He was burned over seventy percent of his body. Skin was literally dripping off him as though he were melting away. His agony was horrendous. When we arrived, he was barely clinging to life. The doctors prepared us for the worse, knowing that it could come at any second. My mom sat on one side of his bed and I on the other, but never once did he look at my mother or acknowledge her presence. He only looked at me and, with his last breath, he told me he loved me. Then he was gone. I think that's the real reason why my mother hates me. She'll deny it, but after that night, she never looked at me the same way again."

"I'm sorry." I attempted to console him while gazing upon his memories. "My parents and my brother died in a horrific way, too. Although I would give my own life to get them back, I'm relieved with the thought that it was quick and I didn't have to see them die."

He nodded. "Now you know why I have nothing to think about."

"So, does that mean you want to get on the road tonight?"

"You bet your ass I do."

"How do you know that I'm not some psychotic whack job who's just making this whole thing up just so I can take you out to some wooded area, rob you blind and then off you?"

"Well, first of all, everything you see in here is everything I own. Whatever you want, you can have. Secondly, if I die tonight, I honestly wouldn't care." He walked over to me, standing within inches from my face. "But, most importantly, when I look into your eyes, I don't see someone who is capable of any misdeeds. I see a soul who's kind – caring."

"Okay, Rico Suave, let's go."

# 32
## THE COMMENDATION

CHASE MATTHEWS WAS a hero, and today he would be honored by his colleagues because of it. He stood in front of the mirror in the City Hall bathroom adjusting his tie. Already, the auditorium had filled to capacity with people wanting to hear good news for a change. Normally, he wasn't a nervous person, but the prospect of thousands of eyes on him made him feel like heading for the hills. The fact that he was getting rewarded for saving a few lives was ironic to him. After all, wasn't that what he did every day? He wondered why it was such a big deal now.

Paul recovered after spending a few days in the intensive care unit at Grace University, receiving treatment for severe smoke inhalation, or so Chase had been informed by the staff there. He'd been told that Paul was expected to attend today's ceremony, which made the formality worth it, for the burly man had made an indelible impression on him. Hope Memorial was under heavy construction with its most critical patients having been transported to Grace University, and the less critical to various hospitals further away. It would take a couple of months, but Hope Memorial would be back up and running as if the explosion had never happened.

His parents and sister were here, beaming with pride at their son and brother. They would be joining him on the stage, which was a big deal for them. Still, he didn't like the fuss. If the city felt the need, they could have just called him.   Yes, a phone call would have sufficed instead of an over-the-top ceremony, newspaper articles, and interviews with the local media outlets. He splashed water on his face, knowing he couldn't stall any longer. "Okay," he muttered, taking a deep breath, "let's get this over with." Adjusting his tie one last time, he walked out of the restroom and into the hallway.

"There you are," MaKayla said. "We were beginning to think you ran away."

"I came pretty close."

"You're such a dork." She rolled her eyes. "Seriously, what's so horrible about being called a hero and being worshipped by a bazillion people for a day?"

"The bazillion part."

"It will all be over before you know it."

"So are executions."

He followed MaKayla down the hallway toward the backstage of the auditorium, where he was spotted by the Mayor's over-stressed assistant, who would be introducing him tonight.

"Oh, thank goodness," she gasped in relief. "The natives are getting restless. Not to mention, Mayor Wilson has to be out of here in twenty-five minutes." She took him by the hand and led him toward the stage.

*At least I know this will all be over in twenty-five minutes*, Chase thought.

The Matthews family walked onto the stage, taking their seats in their respective chairs.  From the audience, he could hear a few claps when he appeared on stage, but he didn't look into the crowd until he was seated in the chair next to his father.  For some reason, being seated in a chair as opposed to standing up seemed to calm his nerves, soothing his stage fright somewhat.

He looked through the audience, where he spotted Trey in the front row.  Trey gave him a wink, and he wasn't quite certain whether it was directed toward him or in response to the attractive mini-skirt-sporting woman seated next to him. He smiled at Trey as he continued to scope out the audience.  In the row behind Trey, he saw a couple of individuals whom he aided in escaping Hope Memorial.  One of them, a young woman, mouthed "thank you" to him from her seat.  Perhaps this wouldn't be so bad after all.

Toward the back of the auditorium, near the middle, he found the very person he hoped he would see. Paul, donning a white, button-down dress shirt with a blue and red Hawaiian print tie, sat talking to an older man seated in front of him, his thunderous laughter reaching the far corners of the auditorium. It amused Chase to see that Paul appeared just as uncomfortable with this gathering as he was, and he wondered whether that was why he chose to sit in the back row near the exits. *Smart man*, Chase mused.

As he attempted to return his focus back to the stage, a sight he wasn't expecting caught his eye. Seated next to Paul was a woman who was noticeably staring at him. She was beautiful, probably one of the most beautiful women he'd ever seen. Her long blonde hair fell in ringlets halfway down her arm in a golden cascade, complimenting her peaches-and-cream complexion. Upon noticing that he was now noticing her, the woman smiled at him, a perfect pearly white smile; the kind of smile that wiped a man's mind of his thoughts, causing time to stand still. He shook his head to regain his bearings.

"Are you all right?" his father asked him.

"I think so."

"You look like you've seen a ghost."

"No, not a ghost. An angel maybe, but definitely not a ghost."

Jim looked at him with a confused glance, but before he could ask any more questions, Mayor Wilson took the stage, eliciting a round of applause from the audience. The Matthews family stood up from their seats and joined in the applause with the audience. Moments later, the mayor motioned for everyone to sit down, silencing the room.

"Good evening, ladies and gentlemen," he began. "We are here today to honor a very special member of our community. A man who not only saves lives as a part of his vocation, but who also saves them as a part of his love for his fellow man and respect for his civic duty."

The mayor went into detail about the events of the day, including Chase's plan that had ended up saving several lives, as well as the emergency tracheostomy that had saved Paul's. Chase sat listening, ultimately hearing none of what was said, but remained fixated on the woman who was still eyeing him intently from the audience. Dating hadn't crossed his mind since Celaine left. The thought of it repulsed him, actually. Still, it was unthinkable for him not to at least attempt to be happy again.

He smoothed out a wrinkle in his khaki pants, trying his best to divert his attention away from the blonde beauty. Almost as though sensing a change in her son, Carrie put her arm around the back of Chase's chair, rubbing his shoulder.

"And now allow me to introduce the hero himself, Dr. Chase Matthews."

Applause erupted throughout the auditorium, adding to the tension that encased him. How he made it to the podium, he didn't know, for he didn't remember his feet touching the ground. It was as if some invisible force had picked him up and carried him. While he stood at the podium, he wished for the applause to go on forever, as its death would signal him to begin talking. He'd prepared no speech, preferring to wing it. Still, after the applause had died down, it took him a few speechless seconds, coupled with a blank stare at the back of the auditorium and MaKayla clearing her throat to jump start him into action.

"I want to thank you all for coming out tonight. I see many familiar faces here, which means a lot to me as well as to my family. I'd like to first start out by saying that, although I'm honored and humbled by this recognition, I'm no hero. I did what any selfless human being would and should do." He looked around the audience as a thought occurred to him. "Would all the doctors in the room oblige me by please standing up?"

Confused, the doctors in the audience collectively began to look around at each other, not wanting to be the first to their feet.

"Come on. I'm standing up here for all of you to see. I know you don't want to make me feel stupid up here." One by one, they began to stand up, until close to a third of the auditorium was on its feet. "I want everyone still seated to take a look around at all those people who are now standing. Take a good look because these are the real heroes in the room. Collectively, these individuals have saved hundreds, if not thousands, of lives through their careers. Yet, they aren't the ones being honored tonight. What I did was nothing more admirable than what these individuals before you do on a daily basis. If I'm to be honored with a commendation tonight, then so should they. Please, everyone, give a round of applause to show them the honor they deserve."

Those still seated clapped in response; a round of applause that lasted several minutes, dissipating after it was announced that dinner was being served in the ballroom.

"I'm so proud of you." Carrie hugged Chase backstage, a tear rolling down her cheek.

"If I hadn't already known it, I would swear that we raised one heck of an amazing son," Jim said, shaking his hand.

"Good show, Bro. Good show." MaKayla put her arm around her brother as they walked toward the ballroom.

As they approached the entrance, Chase felt a pair of arms surround him, lifting him up in a bear hug. He whirled around once he was back on his feet again, recognizing Paul's wide-toothed grin.

"Paul," he said. "I hoped I would see you here."

"Are you kidding me, Doc? How could I not show up to thank the man who saved my life?"

"Just doing my job."

"No. What you did was special. I saw a bunch of those other doctors high-tailing it out of there once the bomb threat was announced. You are one of a kind. I don't know what a pediatrician was doing up at the intensive care unit, but my guess is that God put you there for a reason."

Chase's face reddened with the knowledge of the real reason for him having been in the intensive care unit, knowing that it had nothing to do with divine intervention and more to do with his own selfish desires.

"I'm not a hero. I wanted to get out of that hospital the same as everyone else. Don't forget, my life depended on it, too."

"You are far too modest, Doc. You'll always be a hero in my book, no matter what you say."

Carrie tapped Chase on the shoulder to motion their entrance into the ballroom. He nodded, turning back to Paul.

"It was good seeing you again."

"Oh, before you go, Doc. There's somebody I'd like you to meet." Paul turned to reveal the stunning blonde who had caught his eye in the audience. Inexplicably, he felt as though the wind had been knocked out of him at the sight of her. "This is my daughter, Paige."

Chase looked from Paige to Paul and then back again. It was inconceivable to him that the petite vision before him had been created by such a burley, yeti-like man such as Paul. She either took solely after her mother or she was biologically the product of someone else's genes.

"I want to thank you for what you did for my father." Her voice was melodic, complementing her appearance. "I don't know what I would have done had he not made it." Her sing-song voice cracked as she spoke.

And before he knew what had hit him, she flung her arms around him in an embrace that was much stronger than he ever would have anticipated from a girl of her stature. Not sure of what to do, he put his arms around her torso, reciprocating the embrace.

"I'm sorry," she said as she let go. "I just get so emotional when it comes to the big guy here."

"That's understandable."

"Can I take you out for coffee sometime? You know, as a proper 'thank you'?"

"Uh – sure. I'd like that."

*It's just coffee*, he told himself. *It's not as if it's a date.*

"Great. It's a date," Paul announced, causing a shade of crimson to overcome Paige's horrified face.

"Dad..." she warned through gritted teeth.

"Oh, sorry. I'll leave you two alone."

"I'm sorry about him. He's a little overbearing at times, but he means well."

"I couldn't tell."

She laughed, opening her purse to take out a pen and envelope, carefully ripping off a chunk of the envelope to write on.

"Here's my number." She handed the torn piece of envelope to him. "Please use it."

"I will." He tucked the number in his pocket. "It was nice meeting you, Paige."

"It was a pleasure meeting you, Dr. Matthews."

With that, she disappeared into the ballroom to join her father. Even though he knew it was impossible to do, he still felt as though, through this exchange, he'd somehow cheated on Celaine. *No, it's worse than that,* he thought, *I just cheated on my heart.* He walked into the ballroom, spotting his parents at a table in the far corner of the room.

"So," MaKayla began, "who was Ms. America?"

"Her name is Paige, and she seems like a nice girl."

"I don't like her."

"MaKayla," Carrie admonished.

"You don't even know her. How can you possibly say you don't like her?"

"Because she's not Celaine."

# 33
## The Vendetta

IT HAD BEEN a close call, one that would never happen again. While he rested, recuperating from his injuries, The Man in Black couldn't help but wonder whether she could stand a chance against him. Had she listened to her partner, had she not exhibited the foolish behavior that she had, she could have outdone the others who'd come before her. He shuddered at the thought of someone being able to stop him, someone being able to take him down before he could accomplish his ultimate goal.

He forced himself up out of the bed centered in his immaculate master bedroom in the three-bedroom apartment of which he lived alone. Pain shot up his side. He grunted in response, gripping it in a shallow attempt at comfort. The wound where the bullet had pierced his flesh remained very tender, but he still continued to refuse the pain killers being pushed on him regardless. Something about physical pain invigorated him, making him feel more alive. His caretakers had done such a wonderful job with ensuring his survival. Of course, they benefited from it, too. It was a true symbiotic relationship. His armor would be repaired, his wound would heal, and he would return, better than ever.

She was one of the select few who'd been able to draw blood from him, and she would also be the last. Just as her predecessors, she would pay the price for having wounded him. Sooner or later, it always happened. Her partner's death, however satisfied it had made him, wasn't anything he could gloat over, for his fate had been handed to him on a silver platter the second he decided to save her pathetic life. The affections of men ultimately lead to their downfalls.

She would get a new partner, for that was how it seemed to work with them. Recruit. Train. Fight. Die. It was a variable revolving door of would-be superheroes being thrown his way. Still, the woman was good, and she definitely had some sort of ax to grind with him, some sort of vendetta the source of which he must uncover if he was to gain the upper hand.

Pain tore through his body at levels that would bring a normal person to their knees in repentance. Unfazed, he made his way down the hallway, limping the entire way to the kitchen. In the kitchen, he rummaged through the cupboards until he found a coffee mug. From the same cupboard, he grabbed a pitcher, filled it with water from the sink and poured it into the coffee maker. The night before, he'd poured the remaining coffee grounds into the filter in anticipation of a new day, a day closer to the first day of the rest of his life.

While the coffee percolated, he walked over to his window, staring through the glass at the world outside in disgust. Soon, very soon, it would all change. Soon, he would enjoy the view outside his window. It would reflect a world of order in which he would rule, a world where everyone would be too afraid and too defenseless to stop him.

Hanging on the wall behind him was a lone painting, an abstract whose black and red lines curved with purposeful chaos on the canvas. The painting reminded him of himself in the way its strokes manipulated their way around their fabricated world. He was the black streak on the canvas, perfectly blending in with the dance of humanity until finally overtaking it just as the black consumed the red in the portrait. Like the black, he would leave nothing more than a smattering of red in his wake.

The smell of coffee wafted through the air, perking up his senses. His thirst for violence had been quenched for now, but he could already feel the urge emerging from deep within him again. Every once in a while was not going to be enough to satisfy him for too much longer. The attacks would soon have to be spaced closer together, ensuring more and more casualties each time.

ENIGMA BLACK

He stretched his robotic arms, feeling his joints crack. A heavy price
was paid when his attacks didn't go according to plan. Many pieces of
his body had not come from their original biologic assembly line. But the
faux skin-like covering made those areas that lacked organic flesh
virtually unnoticeable, and he could walk out in public without drawing
any attention to himself.

The coffeemaker beeped, alerting him that his caffeine fix was done
brewing. He poured the first cup, returning to his spot at the window.
Washington, D.C. in the early morning. Ironic that he chose to live in
the very place that stood as a symbol for freedom. Freedom. The thought
of it made him laugh. No one was ever truly free. Like it or not,
everyone was under someone else's thumb. Whether it be bosses,
spouses, or the law, there's always someone or something present to rob
people of what they thought they still had. For that's what society
needed, a ruler. Without someone telling them what to do and when to
do it, humanity would crumble. Yes, very soon they would look at
Washington, D.C. in a very different light. Very soon, it would be
known as a symbol of their oppression and the death of life and liberty as
they knew it. When that time came, the black would overcome the red.

As hard as he tried, he couldn't get her out of his mind. The woman
superhero who'd looked at him with such determination, with such
fearlessness. Never before had he felt as though someone could equal
him. Sure, she was just as awkward as a baby bird leaving the nest the
first time, but soon, very soon, she would take flight. And he would have
to clip her wings before that happened. She was a bad habit that needed
to be nipped in the bud, and he knew just the way to do it.

A demonic smile spread across his face as he regaled in the carnage
he would create. There would be blood spilled. He would celebrate in
her exsanguination after she witnessed the torture and death of all those
she cared about, for he now had his own vendetta to fulfill with her.

# 34
## THE CHANGING OF THE GUARDS

TO SAY THAT Ian was excited to begin his transformation was an understatement. Even with the risk of death present, it still couldn't happen fast enough for him. He'd acclimatized to his new home, having known what to expect from my answers to the seemingly million questions he'd posed to me on the ride back to The Epicenter. I was happy to answer them, thankful that the focus of the conversation stayed away from any talk of our personal lives. The only person who didn't seem to be taken with him was Cameron, who I assumed saw him as more competition for attention than anything else. I likened it to a male dominance issue and figured that they'd either duke it out or mark their territory like the grown men they were.

Any awkwardness had been avoided until we were all seated at dinner the night before Ian's procedure.

"So," Cameron began, inciting Kara to roll her eyes. Whenever Cameron began a sentence with the phrases 'so' or 'did you know', whatever followed could be counted on to tread the fine line between insightful and inappropriate. "So, did Celaine tell you about Blake?"

Ian looked puzzled. We'd briefly skimmed over the prospect of there having been others like me, but I hadn't offered up any detailed information on the subject. I gave Cameron the evil eye coupled with what I hoped was an *I'm-going-to-get-you-for-this* look on my face.

Ian focused his gaze in my direction. "Who's Blake?" His tone of voice seemed more concerned now than curious.

"He was my partner."

"Oh," he paused. "Where is he now? Did he quit or something?"

"Not exactly." I stuck a fork full of mashed potatoes into my mouth with the hope that it would delay the conversation enough so the current subject would be dropped in favor of another topic. Desperate, I looked to Kara to intercede, but Cameron beat her to the punch.

"Blake was killed saving Celaine. It seems as though he had a little bit of a crush on her." I looked straight ahead, continuing to eat my dinner even as I felt Ian's eyes boring through the side of my face. "His feelings got the best of him." I really wished Cameron would shut up.

"Well," Ian said, "you don't have to worry about that with me. I'm never going to look at my partner in anything more than a professional way."

Cameron snickered.

"Ditto," I replied, surprising Ian. Surely, no woman had ever turned him down before.

When we returned to what I hoped would be normal conversation, I glanced around at our dysfunctional family dinner table, noticing an obvious absence. "Where's Victor?" I asked.

"I'm not really sure," Kara replied. "I think he's out doing a couple of personal errands or whatnot. He's not here all the time like the rest of us."

"But he will be here tomorrow, right?" Ian asked, worried.

"He'd better," Marcus added from the other end of the table. "He had me working all night last night on putting together a suit for you so that your training could begin as soon as possible."

Ian nodded, a look of obvious relief overcoming his face.

As I lay in bed that night with the soothing visage of Niagara Falls hovering over me, it became apparent that sleep wasn't going to take pity on me. My adrenaline levels remained elevated from the events of the past few days. Eventually, those levels would begin their descent downwards, but until they did, I would remain the definition of restless. On top of everything else, I hadn't seen Chase since before the explosion, which made me nervous. Even though I knew he hadn't been among the dead, I still needed the peace of mind that only seeing him alive would bring, and I knew I wouldn't be able to sleep without it.

I threw my legs over the side of the bed and stood up as I made my way towards the hall, barely making it two steps from my door when I heard a voice behind me.

"Where are you going?"

I turned around to see Ian standing in the hall next to his room. He'd been assigned to Blake's old room, something that didn't set well with me.

"Out," I replied as I turned to keep walking.

Behind me I heard Ian's footsteps following my path, prompting me to swing back around to face him. "Ian, you really should try to get some sleep. You have a long day tomorrow and, as I'm sure they've explained to you, tonight could be the last time you will ever have a measurable amount of sleep as long as you're here."

"Seriously, Celaine, do you think I'm going to sleep tonight?"

"Probably not, but you should try."

"Come on. Why so secretive? I mean, we are going to be partners, right?"

"Right. We are going to be partners. At this very moment, we aren't partners, and even when you officially hold that title, you only embody it when we're on assignment. Not during the off time."

"Working with you is going to be fun."

"It's work; it's not supposed to be fun."

Ian eyed me up and down. "So, is that the fabled suit you're wearing?"

"That it is."

"Is mine going to be that tight? It seems like it would constrict the junk a little."

"I'm sure you have nothing to worry about." I winked at Ian and headed back down the hall toward the garage.

◇◇◇◇

The small beam of light from the motorcycle's headlight was all I had to rely on to navigate me through the pitch black roadways that lead to Chase's apartment. Upon reaching the city, I parked in the same alleyway as I had before, again scaling the fire escape, jumping from rooftop to rooftop until I came upon the one I was looking for. The light was on in Chase's room. With Hope Memorial in shambles and it being past curfew, I figured the likelihood of him being home was probably pretty high. Not to mention, I knew him like the back of my hand. His predictability was unfaltering. I looked up to the night sky in the off chance that the clouds had broken up enough to again reveal the stars as it had done the last time I was here. No such luck. The cloud cover was unrelenting tonight.

My fingers grasped the necklace that hung around my neck as though the heart attached to it were my very own, the latter skipping a beat as a shadow in Chase's bedroom announced his presence. Something seemed different about him, something that hadn't been there the last time I saw him. It was as if a new sense of purpose had overcome him. He was…happy. Yes, that was it. He seemed far happier than he had the last time I'd seen him. A smile spread across my tear streaked face. It was everything I'd wanted for him since I left. If he could be happy without me, maybe there was a chance that I could be happy without him, too.

"Not likely," I sighed, clutching the heart charm.

He leaned over to pick up something from his bedside table I recognized as being his cell phone. Whatever it was that was on that cell phone only made his mood that much sunnier. He hit a button on the phone to make a call, beaming when the person on the other end picked up. Whoever he was speaking with, it made him happy, and even though that was what I wanted, the selfish side of me just hoped that whoever it was he was talking to wasn't trying to fill the imprint I had made on his heart.

He called her. It was awkward and uncomfortable, but he called her. And he was relieved when his call went straight to voice mail. Over the last two years, he'd been bathed in the comfort of Celaine. Dating her had been so easy, so effortless. Even in the beginning, there had been something about her that'd made him feel at ease. That was how he'd known she was the one for him, and that was why he'd spent the last three hours searching for her on every search engine imaginable. Not surprisingly, he'd come up empty-handed with each click of the mouse taking him from one dead end to another. He thought he knew Celaine; he thought he knew what she wanted out of life.

Her sudden departure made him rethink relationships to the point where he gave up trying to understand them. What feelings were normal? What feelings weren't normal? Who was the one? Who wasn't the one? All of that was thrown out the window. For now, he would just go where the wind took him and attempt to regain the happiness he'd lost.

He was tired, his eyes strained from having been glued to the screen of his laptop. Tomorrow, he was going to Grace University Hospital to assist with the overflow of patients from Hope Memorial. One thing he loved about pediatrics was the way his patients tended to bond with him. There'd been a near riot at Grace University when a few of them were first moved there and told that he would no longer be their physician. Their protests were so intense that he'd received a phone call a couple of days after the explosion asking him if he would be willing to donate some of his time to assure his patients that he wasn't going anywhere. For the first time since Celaine, he had something in his life that made him smile from ear to ear.

Before going to bed, he checked his phone again. A missed call indicated that Paige had returned his call. He looked at the clock and, seeing that it wasn't too late, he decided to call her back.

"Hey," she squealed, answering his call on the first ring. "I was so excited when you called the first time that when I called you back and you didn't answer, I thought it was some kind of fluke."

A smile overspread his face. "I'm sorry I didn't catch your call. I was –working."

"Oh, that's okay. I completely understand. I imagine you must be pretty busy, you know, being a doctor and all."

"Yeah, it has its days." Guilt began to overcome him.

"I'll bet it does. So…what's your schedule like this week? Are you still up for that coffee?"

"Definitely. In fact, I was going to ask you what you were doing on Saturday afternoon at about one."

"Having coffee with a very handsome doctor."

He blushed. "Well, okay then. There's this café that I frequent about a half mile down from Hope Memorial on Azalea St."

"Yeah. I think I know which one you're talking about. Meet you there at one o'clock on Saturday then?"

"I'll be there."

"Great," she squealed again, forcing him to pull the phone away from his ear to protect his eardrums. "It's a date, then?"

He wasn't sure if that last sentence was a question or a statement. "It's a date. I'll see you on Saturday."

He set the phone back down on the nightstand and sat on the corner of his bed, rubbing his temples with his index fingers, a sick feeling overtaking his stomach.

*I'm sorry, Celaine*, he thought.

"Are you sure you're ready for this?" I asked Ian, holding his hand as he laid on the operating table. *As if you really have a choice.*

"I'm just a little nervous. I've never had surgery of any kind before."

"It will be all right. I promise, you're in good hands."

"Were you even the slightest bit nervous? You know, after they told you that you could die?"

"Of course I was, but you just have to remember why and who you're here for and the fear drains away."

"I've thought of nothing else but him since I've been here."

I smiled. "Well, there you go. Just imagine him here, sitting next to you as you drift off, giving you a huge thumbs up for your bravery."

"He used to do that all the time. When I would bring home an 'A' on a science project or score a home run. He'd be there to greet me with his big grin and both thumbs reaching for the sky."

"I kind of figured. I saw the pictures in your apartment, remember?"

"I brought a couple of those with me."

"Good. You needed to bring them. Those pictures will be just about the only thing that will enable you to maintain your sanity from now on."

"Celaine," Dr. Harris spoke softly, "we're ready."

"Good luck," I said, letting go of Ian's hand.

"Are you going to stay in the viewing room?"

"Yes, I'll be there."

"Okay." He seemed somewhat relieved. "To think, when I wake up, I'll be a superhero."

"Yeah," I said, smiling, turning around as its fakeness began to wear on me. What was happening to him was anything but super, and the guilt I felt for allowing him to believe otherwise weighed heavily on my soul. I'd led the lamb to the slaughter and, in a sense, was no better than a murderer. This was, in essence, the changing of the guards. I'd taken over Blake's shift and Ian, mine. A seasoned veteran, I was the cynical one while he was the hopeful one who still believed anything was possible.

I opened the door to the viewing room and took a seat facing Ian. Inside the operating room, Dr. Harris turned a valve and placed the anesthesia-filled mask over his face. Before drifting off, he took one last look at me, sleepily putting his thumb up into the air.

# 35

# THE ASSASSINATION

LUCY PIERCE RETURNED home, promptly throwing her keys at–and missing–the kitchen counter as she slumped down in her dining room chair. "Oy," she muttered under her breath, rubbing her temples. Since the day Celaine disappeared, she'd been pulling double duty, thriving as the harried psychiatrist by day, and the tireless private investigator at night. This night her best efforts at maintaining two full-time pursuits were losing to utter exhaustion, exhaustion that wore thin on her gaunt face; exhaustion that caused her to fall asleep while in consult with patients; exhaustion that persistently told her to give up on finding her wayward friend.

Giving up was not an option she was willing to accept. In her heart, she knew there had to be something more to Celaine's sudden departure. With a sigh, she reached across the table and made contact with the stack of flyers she'd made for Celaine, using her fingertips to pull them over to where she sat. She'd read countless materials online about others who'd gone missing under similar circumstances. None of them had ever been found.

On the street, gossip circulated around a group of rebels comprised of everyday citizens of society who moonlighted as members of a secret rebellion committed to overthrowing President Brooks. Evidence of their participation in this rebellion had been found in the homes of several of those members who'd wound up missing over the years, leading Lucy to wonder whether Celaine had been leading a double life too. Lucy sighed as she set the flyers back down on the table. It had been a long several weeks, the longest of her life, and it felt as though she'd aged by years instead of by only a matter of days.

She stood up and shuffled to the bathroom to wash the day away. When she turned on the light in the bathroom, she caught a glimpse of herself in the mirror. Dark circles had invaded the crevices beneath her eyes; once pristine skin had grown pale, appearing sickly. Her hair, normally meticulous without a stray strand in sight, hung haphazardly from her disheveled bun. Lucy turned on the water, finding herself transfixed by her unrecognizable profile until her hands splashed her face with cold water, bringing her back down to reality.

Her stomach rumbled, reminding her that she hadn't yet eaten. She usually ignored her hunger pains, but she knew the discomfort would keep her from falling asleep, making matters worse. Resigned to the inevitable, Lucy turned the bathroom light off and headed back to the kitchen. After rummaging through her cabinets, she settled on a bowl of cereal and took it into the living room, turning on the television. The nightly news was on. No longer live because of the curfew, it was taped at nine o'clock in the evening and timed to air a couple of hours later.

Lucy scraped a spoonful of Cheerios into her mouth, balancing the bowl on her knees. With her eyelids growing increasingly heavy, she leaned her head back on the couch, unaware of the danger lurking behind her.

Concealed by darkness, the young sniper waited for her target. She'd received her orders for this assignment – her first ever – a couple of weeks ago, and it was all she could do to contain her enthusiasm until the big day arrived. Hours were spent in target practice in preparation, in tracking down the ordered target. Hours that turned into days and days that turned into weeks until the arrival of this very second. With her target in sight, the assassin raised herself up to her feet, grabbing the gun from its holster. Excited, she placed her finger on the trigger.

"Stay still, damn you," she scowled as the target bounced around from one room to another. The gun weighed heavy in her hand, sweat beaded on her forehead. Her arm trembled, and she found herself having to steady it as she took a deep breath. "She's dangerous," she repeated, assuring herself. "She needs to be dealt with before it's too late. The rebellion must be stopped."

The target reappeared from the kitchen, bowl in hand, and sat down on the couch.

"Finally," she sighed.

Her victim had become still enough for her to take aim. She looked into her sight and lined up the perfect shot. A shot straight through the back of the head, the perfect kill shot. They would be pleased with her back at the bureau.

"One…," she counted softly, "two…three."

She applied pressure on the trigger, setting the gun off, waking the deadly assault from its slumber. With the silencer on the gun quieting the chaos to those within earshot, the only evidence of her sinister attack was the sound of a window shattering and a bowl breaking to pieces as it fell to the floor.

A wicked smile appeared across the freshly-minted sniper's face as she set down her gun and pulled a phone from her jacket pocket. A voice picked up on the first ring.

"Tell Victor it's been taken care of," she announced to the voice on the other end, hanging up as she'd been instructed to do.

Then, as mysteriously as she appeared, she was gone; lost to the shadows of the night, to the devastation she'd caused.

# 36
## THE NEW THREAT

CARVER BROOKS PACED around the perimeter of his office in an underground bunker on the outskirts of Washington, D.C. Due to the overwhelming tenacity of the rebellion, he'd seen his approval ratings plummet, putting him in danger of losing everything.

This rebellion, this new threat, was gaining supporters at an admirable pace. Its members held demonstrations in the streets, broadcast their messages across the Internet and, most frustrating of all, gained recruits by the day. The people were starting to turn on him, making the prospect of his returning for a fourth term less and less likely. Something had to be done and it had to be done before all of his hard work was brought to an end.

He tapped his fingers on the mahogany desk. The sound of each fingertip hitting the wood sent him into deep, rhythmic thoughts. This underground bunker was his haven. Often times, he came here to think, to plan. Surrounded by photographs of his earlier life, of family and friends long gone, long forgotten, every item he cherished was kept here, as he didn't much care for the professional atmosphere of the White House. From the floor to the ceiling, this office was more...him. The walls were a dark purplish hue; for purple was the color of royalty, of power. Being surrounded by it invigorated him as though the fibers of its very meaning were absorbed through his skin.

Indeed, he'd felt quite powerful the day the public voted him into office, invincible even. How they adored him back then. He'd been on top of the world thanks to the pedestal they'd placed him on. And in return, he'd done all he could to protect them from the dangers within it. For all people were like sheep who, if left unattended for too long, would wander into trouble, getting caught up in the chaos, death and corruption of the world. Like sheep, they needed a leader to herd them back in line, to keep the wolves at bay.

How ungrateful they were. Couldn't they see everything he had done to keep them safe?

Still, more needed to be done in the near future. With crops of new recruits adding to this rebellious threat by the day, drastic measures were going to have to be taken, and they were going to have to be taken soon if peace was going to be restored amongst the herd. He continued his purposeful pace around the office as though every footstep held the key to unraveling his new dilemma, until a sudden and unexpected knock on the door broke his concentration.

"Yes," he answered.

"Mr. President, he's here." His body guard opened the door halfway, sticking his head into the office.

"Send him in and leave us."

"Yes, Mr. President."

Carver sat down at his desk just as the door opened again.

"Ah, Victor, old friend," he greeted his guest, "I trust everything is well with you. Have a seat."

"Why, yes, Carver. Things are going rather well. Thank you." Victor took a seat in a purple velvet-lined chair.

"Could I interest you in a brandy?

"No, thanks. You wanted to see me?"

"We'll get to that. I hear you recently lost your longest running fighter – Blake, was it?"

"Yes, Blake was killed by The Man in Black a few days ago."

"Hmm…that's too bad. I honestly thought he would be the one to defeat that thorn in my side." Carver smirked, removing the bottle of brandy from his desk drawer. He poured a small amount in a glass to take a quick shot.

"Don't be so coy, Carver, we both know there's no one who'll ever be able to defeat The Man in Black."

"I know. I'm counting on that." He took another shot of brandy, relishing it to the last particle. "The new one. The woman."

"Ah, yes, Celaine Stevens," Victor said.

"Yes. She's been receiving a lot of buzz around the country. The first woman fighter has quite the fan base. People are in awe of her."

"She's rather good – perhaps a little too good for a beginner. I must say, she's impressed us all with her abilities thus far. But she lets her feelings get the best of her, and that will most likely be her downfall." Victor rolled his eyes, shifting in his chair.

"Just so long as you keep her death as secretive as possible from the public when she's killed. Blake's death was hidden rather well by their sheer captivation with her, but I fear there may be a genuine revolt if they know she's gone, too."

"Don't worry, when she's gone, no one will know the difference. If it's one thing I've learned, fighters are a dime a dozen."

"Good. How complicit has she been with the program?"

"She gripes a lot and she's a little resistant at times, but when she's reminded what she's there for, ultimately she becomes complicit whether she wants to be or not. She'll be broken just like Blake was."

Carver nodded. "The rebellion is getting stronger, and their message seems to be reaching the ears of the public. As you can figure out, that is going to be detrimental to my presidency. Those vigilante freaks are undoing everything I've worked for." He stuck the cork back into the brandy bottle, throwing it haphazardly back into the drawer. A loud thud erupted as it slid across its wooden interior.

"How do you propose we handle them?" Victor asked.

"Well, that's the reason why I called you in here. The public seems to like these makeshift superheroes you've created. In fact, they seem to like them so much that if they, too, were to oppose the rebellion then perhaps the public would follow suit." A small smile spread across his face as though the realization of his next words had struck him once again. "Yes, if the public hates the rebellion, and if I show a mutual disdain, and then your superheroes follow suit, perhaps all this mutual hatred will unite the country, making people forget why the rebels amassed in the first place."

"That sounds like more of a temporary fix, the likes of which is almost impossible for two people to contain. Celaine and, potentially, Ian can handle a lot, but they can't be in twenty different places at once."

"They won't need to be. A couple of public displays of their disdain towards the rebellion will be all it will take to win the people back over in our favor and back on board with my administration." He arose from his chair, resuming his slow pace around the office before turning to a bookshelf where he nervously fingered the knickknacks its shelves contained. When he turned around again, he faced Victor with a sneer spreading across his face. "Once I'm back in their good graces, then I'll make my move. They thought they were oppressed before…well…they haven't seen oppressed yet. My generosity is about to expire. With an organized, nationwide rebellion looming over the horizon I do believe I can get Congress to approve my decision to enact shore to shore martial law under the guise of it being for the safety and security of those non-troublemakers of society."

"Martial law?" Victor asked, perplexed. "It sounds a little dramatic, don't you think? You'll be raising a lot of eyebrows, and you may find even more problems on your hands than you have now."

"My last ten years in office has raised nothing but eyebrows, has it not? Victor, you should know by now that I always get what I want, and I take care of those who help me obtain it. That's why Congress will do as I ask them. Without me, they're nothing."

"How are you going to justify it? Isn't martial law supposed to be temporary?"

"Wasn't the curfew?"

Victor smiled. "Carver, you're always full of big aspirations, but I believe you're not giving the people much credit. They will question your motives this time."

"Of course they will, but it won't matter. There will always be danger. Clearing out the rebellion will take quite a while, but there will always be The Man in Black to fall back on when the argument is made that the rebellion is no longer a threat, right?"

"I suppose," Victor said in a near whisper.

"You'll see. Martial law will rule the country…and so will I."

# 37

## THE VISIT

I LEARNED OF Lucy's death by accident two months after the fact. In the sitting room, during one of my sleepless nights, I happened to glance at an article on the front page of the newspaper Brian was reading. A headline, a small blurb running down the side of the front page, captured my attention:

### Assassination of Local Doctor Remains Unsolved

Normally, articles about random murders wouldn't have warranted a second glance from me, but this article's colorful use of the word 'assassination' grabbed my attention. I tilted my head and tried to read the article at the angle that Brian was holding the paper. When I was finally able to catch the first few words on the second line, my heart leapt from my chest:

> *"Twenty-eight-year-old psychiatrist Lucy Pierce was murdered..."*

No. It couldn't be. It had to be another Dr. Lucy Pierce. Both 'Lucy' and 'Pierce' were common names. Besides, no one would ever want to hurt Lucy. She wouldn't hurt a fly, let alone make any enemies. Her patients loved her, and she'd never mentioned a disgruntled client or a fear that her life was in jeopardy.

I struggled to see the rest of the article, noticing a photograph that Brian's index finger was blocking. The image was small, allowing his finger to conceal it, but I could still make out a wisp of blonde hair at its tip. I tried to wait patiently, but after only a matter of seconds, I couldn't take it anymore, and I ripped the page from Brian's hands, nearly tearing it in half in the process.

"Was that necessary?" he demanded.

I didn't answer him, and couldn't have if I had wanted to. "No," I said, gasping. My body shook with agony upon recognizing the face in the photograph. Distraught, I stood up, knowing that there was nothing I could do, but nonetheless feeling the need to do something, I took off running down the hall.

"Celaine, are you all right?" Brian's voice echoed behind me.

Nothing was going to stop me. My speed picked up, the world going by me in a blur. I was crying, sobbing, and I didn't care who saw me as I kept on running toward my motorcycle; my only means of escape from the walls that were closing in around me. When I reached the motorcycle, I swung my leg over the seat, threw my helmet on and took off, gripping the throttle tighter when I became unsatisfied with the maximum speed of the cycle. I needed to get back home and I needed to get there now. The motorcycle tore through the pine trees, its tires striking the wet pavement of the roadway as it skidded on its side across both lanes. Unfazed, I squeezed the throttle tighter and shot down the road.

Back home, it was just as dreary and overcast as it had been at The Epicenter. When I pulled up to the entrance of the cemetery, I killed the engine of the motorcycle and typed in one of the many codes I'd learned to disable it, rendering the machine useless to anyone who may be tempted to take it for a spin. What I was doing was not encouraged, but at the moment that didn't matter to me. I was in plain clothing and, even though my body had changed significantly in the last few months, nothing about me screamed superhero.

The damp lawn soaked through my tennis shoes. A breeze blew through me, the fall air sending a chill down my spine. She was buried in the same cemetery as my family. In the newly expanded portion constructed to accommodate the rapidly growing body count the last ten years had amassed. Though I felt guilty, I couldn't see them. Visiting my family and best friend's graves in the same day would be too much for my delicate state. However, as I passed their general vicinity, I turned my head to search for the tree they were buried under, and, after spotting it, I continued my walk mouthing "I love you" in its direction.

The new addition to the cemetery was situated at the bottom of a hill forming a valley of newly minted graves. They were close together, the graves, closer than most cemeteries would've normally allowed, but it was necessary as well as cost effective.

I didn't know where Lucy was buried, and it took me a few moments of aimless wandering before I found her. It was a simple stone, not too presumptuous, just like she had been. Her picture, the picture that was in the paper, adorned her stone along with the lines *Beloved Daughter, Sister, and Friend*. It was generic, but nonetheless true. Beside the stone in a small flower pot were lilies, her favorite flower. After searching for words but coming up empty handed, I recited the first memories that came to mind:

"I remember when we were at sleepovers in high school, you would fall asleep before any of us, and we would draw all over your face with markers. We'd draw the most ridiculous things. Hearts, clouds, sayings, and still you'd never wake up. The next morning, you'd be awake hours before any of us and, instead of retaliating like you should have, you'd just keep the marks on your face the whole day as if you were making some kind of fashion statement. I remember, when I moved to Iowa, you were the only one who would write to me or call me to see how I was doing. You were the only one who didn't see me as damaged goods. Oh, God, Luce...I'm so sorry. I wish I...I wish I could have seen you again. I wish that I could have said goodbye to you properly, face-to-face instead of by letter. I don't know who did this to you, but I swear that I'll find out."

I looked up to the sky, wiping the tears from my eyes, wishing I could have had just one more moment with her to tell her how much her friendship had meant to me, that I'd taken none of it for granted.

"Celaine?" The familiar voice caused me to turn around in surprise, wiping my face once more.

"Ian," I sniffed.

The grief consuming me, I walked toward him, falling into his arms amongst the field of graves. Human contact was something I sorely needed at the moment. Stunned, Ian's body went rigid in my arms, relaxing after a moment as he wrapped his arms around me tightly as if he, too, was happy to receive the nourishment only the touch of another person gave to the soul.

"I'm sorry," he whispered into my ear, rubbing my back.

I pulled away from him, but he kept his arms firmly around me as if letting go would snap him back into a form of dismal reality.

"How did you find me?" I asked.

"It wasn't hard. I just followed the trail of tears and skid marks from the suicide mission you went on to get here."

"She was my best friend and I never got the chance to say goodbye to her. She's gone. It's as if someone was stalking her and found just the right moment, when she was the most vulnerable, to strike. I'm supposed to be saving people, but I can't even save my best friend."

I felt my eyes watering again, a single tear falling down my cheek.

Ian leaned in, wiping the tear from my face. "We'll find the people responsible for this, I promise you."

His smooth, velvety lips caressed my forehead as his arms unleashed me from their grasp. I looked up into his emerald eyes seeing, at last, what scores of other women had already discovered.

"Let's go. They're waiting for us back there."

I nodded and followed him as he led the way back to the entrance of the cemetery, resting his hand on my back for comfort. But as we walked back up the hill, I felt the sudden urge to turn back around as though there was something behind me I was supposed to see, something that was pulling me toward it. When I turned my head, I saw a male figure with his back turned walking in the opposite direction. He wore jeans and a grey hooded sweatshirt with the hood pulled over his head. I stood at the top of the hill, inexplicably mesmerized by the figure that was growing less and less discernible by the second.

"What is it?" Ian asked.

"Nothing. I'm sure it's nothing."

I turned back around to follow Ian out of the cemetery.

◇◇◇◇

Chase hadn't been able to visit Lucy since attending the funeral, where he stood on the sidelines with Luke and Trey who, like him, were uncharacteristically quiet.

"Have you heard anything from Celaine?" Lucy's mother had asked him between tears.

"No, I haven't."

"We've done everything we could think of to find her." She looked solemnly at an unseen entity in the distance, at something only she could see. "Her aunt hasn't even heard a word, or so she says. It's just tragic. She was Lucy's best friend, for heaven sakes. The police found flyers in Lucy's kitchen and multiple searches for Celaine on her computer. She never gave up on Celaine. It's a pity Celaine gave up on her."

"Do they have any leads yet?" Chase was quick to change the subject.

"None – absolutely none. They've questioned poor Luke like crazy because, as you know, after a woman is killed, the ex-boyfriend is the prime suspect. I know he didn't do it. He loved Lucy more than life itself, even though they weren't together anymore." She turned to face him, her eyes heavy and glazed. "I'd like to think that maybe it was just a freak accident, that whoever pulled the trigger didn't mean to shoot her. I'd like to think that somebody didn't hate her that much. But I know that she was the target. Someone wanted her dead, and that someone is still walking the streets with us today."

Chase locked his car door as he walked through the path of stone monuments with flowers in hand. Lucy's death had been like losing Celaine all over again. She'd been the last link he had left. After a couple of dates with Paige, Trey was able to convince him to throw away the box of mementos he'd kept tucked away in his closet, and even that wasn't good enough. If Trey had his way, his mind would have been wiped of all memories of Celaine, but try as he may, Trey couldn't stop his heart from thinking about her and wishing that she would find her way back to him.

His love for Celaine had kept him from allowing Paige to enter his heart or his bed. Meaningless, empty sex didn't appeal to him, and it would be unfair to Paige to allow her to think that it would hold any meaning for him right now.

He walked up the hill overlooking the newer section of the cemetery, stealing a glance at the intricate carvings on each of the stones, finding himself taken off guard when his eyes drifted to Lucy's grave site. Taken aback, his body was rendered breathless as though someone had punched him square in the gut. There she was, just as beautiful as ever. She was slimmer, that he noticed right off the bat. And she had a look of intensity that surrounded her as though she'd been through twenty years of pure hell. Still, in his eyes, she remained breathtaking.

His heart pounded and his feet, no longer at a standstill, were moving towards her. He moved along the stones, cutting through a cluster of trees at the bottom of the hill, keeping just out of her sight. He was unsure of what he was going to say to her, if he even was going to say anything to her at all. He'd just walk up to her and let the words come on their own. But, just as he was about to emerge in full view of her, he saw another sight he hadn't expected.

He was tall, muscular and headed straight for her, concerned. Chase took refuge behind a tree and watched her as she turned around to face the man, wrapping her arms around him in a warm, almost loving embrace; the kind of embrace he'd only been able to long for during his many sleepless nights. She let go of him, but he kept her in his arms, prompting his heart to sink from his chest to the pits of his stomach. He knew he should avert his eyes, for whatever was transpiring between the two of them was private and not something he was going to want to see. Besides that, she looked comfortable with him, almost as if she'd known him for quite some time.

*Is this why she left?* he thought. *Was he why she left?*

A sick, saddened rage overcame him that intensified with every second the man's arms were around her. Part of him wanted to confront her, to see how long this had been going on and why she hadn't had it in her to tell him instead of stringing him along for two years. And the only thing preventing him from acting on his thoughts was the thought that occurred to him next: *Was she happy?*

That was all he'd ever wanted for her and, now that she may finally be, he didn't want to get in the way of it. So, he stood watching them, hidden behind the tree, watching as his replacement leaned in and kissed her tenderly, watching as he guided her away from Lucy's grave back toward the front entrance of the cemetery. Dizzy and still sick, he decided he couldn't go through with visiting Lucy, he couldn't stand where she had just been. He turned back the way he came, pulling his hood up over his head in the offhand chance she would turn around and recognize him.

Upon reaching the top of the hill, he looked back at her, watching her for what he realized may be the last time as she left the cemetery with the other man. The cool air struck him, and he shuddered as he turned back around and disposed of the flowers he'd brought with him in the nearest trash can along with the note he'd attached to them:

*Lucy,*

*I just want you to know that I never blamed you. I believe you and I promise that I will find her and bring her back home.*

Before today, it hadn't been absolutely certain to him that there was no hope of him ever seeing Celaine again. It hadn't been clear to him that they couldn't be together and that their breakup wasn't forever. Now he knew that hope was useless and he'd truly lost her.

The door to Paige's apartment flung open as she greeted his arrival later that evening.

"Chase! Hi…"

Before she could finish her sentence, his lips were on hers in a passionate embrace. Trying to forget, trying to move on, trying to feel life within his soul again, he tossed all of his convictions aside that night and gave into his most primal of needs, with Celaine not far from his thoughts.

# EPILOGUE

*Ever has it been that love knows not its own depth until the hour of separation.*

*~Kahlil Gibran*

I WAS HERE again, at my permanent place on the ledge five months after I left. In the past five months, I'd experienced more raw emotion than I had in the last ten years, and I knew that there would be more to come. Overhead, lights from a jet flew across the sky. If ever I was jealous of an inanimate object it was now. In exchange for being put in the position to be able to carry out my lust for vengeance, I'd given up my freedom. Was it a fair trade? It was a question I was still asking myself five months later.

In the cold, moonless night, I saw him walking down the street. The pediatrics department of Hope Memorial was back up and running. Instead of driving, he'd opted to walk the nearly half mile to work. Chase had always been the health nut, even in the coldest of temperatures. He opened the door to his building, disappearing into its depths. Near where I sat, I heard the sound of footsteps, causing me to spring to my feet, poised for attack.

"Whoa, whoa, whoa. It's just me," Ian's voice appeared within the depths of the darkness.

"What's with your strange preoccupation with stalking me?"

"It's not stalking, it's curiosity. I've learned to walk that tightrope well through the years. Besides, why can't I know where my partner disappears to night after night?"

"It's complicated."

"Oh, a boy, huh? Is that him right there?"

I swung my head around to see Chase's window aglow from his lamp on the nightstand in his bedroom. He was getting ready for the next day, rummaging through his closet for his clothes while making sure his clock was set.

"Yep, that's him. I'd recognize that look from anywhere," Ian commented, sitting down next to me. "You've got it bad."

"Would you please not talk."

"Someone woke up on the wrong side of adrenaline hell this morning."

"And yet, you still continue to run your mouth."

"Seriously, what did you ever see in him anyway? I wouldn't have pegged him as being your type. He's too gangly and pale."

"Oh, really? So who would you peg as being my type? You?"

"No," he said. "You couldn't handle a guy like me."

"I think it's more like I *wouldn't* handle a guy like you."

"Hey…" he sprung to his feet to get a better view of the street, "who's the hot blonde?"

I glanced down at the street just as she entered the apartment building. "I'm not sure."

"Well, perhaps I'll just have to join you up here more often. Maybe I'll even become a peeping tom like you."

"You're funny." Chase left the room, creating what I was sure to be a look of disappointment on my face.

"You regret leaving, don't you?" Ian's voice became consoling.

"I have my days."

"Why did you leave, then? If you had something worth living for, why would you choose to cease existing?"

"It was something I had to do. I can't explain it, but I feel as though I would have been letting them down had I chosen differently." I stared blankly at Chase's empty bedroom, hiding the tear forming in my eye from Ian. "This is the one thing I can do to get justice for them. Once The Man in Black is gone, then I can go on living again, but until then, I feel as though I don't deserve to exist."

Ian sat down on the edge of the rooftop in the hopes of catching another glance of the mystery woman. "There wasn't anything you could have done to help them. Celaine, you deserve to be happy. Don't you think that's what they would have wanted? You…oh…shit."

"What?"

He stared in the direction of Chase's window, eyes wide with surprise. That alone should have told me all I needed to know. But, my gaze, nonetheless, shifted from Ian's shocked expression to the glow of Chase's bedroom. A gasp escaped my lips, cutting through the still night air. At that moment, I felt the pain of my heart being ripped from my chest.

Chase reentered his room, but this time he wasn't alone. The mystery blonde from the street was with him, and it was obvious that their relationship wasn't platonic. My whole body stiffened, stuck to the ledge as though it were adhered to its very surface, as though roots had sprouted from my boots and attached themselves to the cement. Like happening upon a horrible car accident, I knew I should look away, but I couldn't, and my body didn't release itself from its mysterious hold on the ledge until after the light disappeared from Chase's bedroom.

The cool, damp air cut through me. My body shook. Ian put his hand on my shoulder, not knowing what to say. The only thought crossing my mind was that I needed to get away as fast as possible. With a running start, I flung myself from the roof of the dance studio, my body arching into a dive. And as the roadway below appeared closer and closer, I debated whether or not I would deploy the grappling hook or allow myself to slam into the pavement to my death. Even if the fall didn't kill me, I was sure that the pain from my body slamming against the pavement wouldn't even come close to the pain I had just experienced on the rooftop.

In the midst of my freefall, their faces flashed before me, projected onto the pavement as though from an ethereal projector. They stared at me accusingly. There were the usual faces of my family – my father, mother, and Jake – that flashed through my head at every pivotal point in my life. But interspersed amongst the usual images were those images of Blake and Lucy both with "get a grip" looks on their faces, ensuring that I would keep my heart beating until every promise I'd made was fulfilled and every question I had was answered.

I flicked my wrist, releasing the hook from my arm. The rope flew through the air, locating a light pole to cling to, and I glided down into an alleyway, feeling my feet scuff against the pavement. After releasing the hook, I slumped over as I began to dry heave, which caused me to fall to the ground. Lightheaded, I took off my helmet to allow the cool night air to hit my face. No matter how hard I tried, I couldn't get the image of Chase and the mystery blonde out of my head.

"Ugh," I yelled, punching a hole in the bricks of the building that ran along the alleyway.

"I've never seen you like this before." Ian appeared in the alley. "I must say, it's kind of hot."

I shook my head without looking at him. "I wasn't expecting that...I mean...I was...but not this soon."

Ian entered the alley, taking a seat on a discarded plastic bag next to me. "He was your first love, wasn't he?"

"How could you tell that?"

"Let's just say the suicidal roof jump kind of tipped me off a little. That, and the fact that, had anything like that happened before, you would have reacted more indifferently than you just did."

"Indifferently? What difference would it make? First love, second love, tenth love, it's still love. If there was an ounce of indifference in your heart during the relationship, then it really wasn't love at all."

"Interesting point. All I know is that after my heart was shattered the first time, no other woman was able to fully fit the pieces of it back together again. Maybe that's the reason I am who I am. I'm just searching for that loving feeling again, trying to replicate the unique. Going from woman to woman, to woman, to woman, to woman, to woman, to..."

"Okay, I get the point."

"Well, that's a good thing because we'd be sitting here for at least another couple of hours had you not gotten it."

"You're quite the scoundrel." I managed a smile at him through watering eyes.

"I'm not good with this emotional stuff." The plastic bag rustled as he adjusted his body to put his arms around my shoulders. "I'm used to dumping girls via text message, third parties, strategically placed post-it notes on pillows. You know, the usual."

"And to think you're still single. Shocker."

"Hey, so are…" he paused, correcting himself.

"So am I? You can say it."

"I'm sorry, Celaine."

"It's fine. I know it. I know that once The Man in Black is gone, I'll have nothing to come back home to, but there's still this crazy little voice in my head that tells me there's always hope."

"Really? I usually just tell that voice to shut up because it's somewhat of a buzz kill."

I felt around my neck until I located Chase's necklace, rubbing it between my thumb and index finger.

"Are you going to get rid of that?"

"No. The day I get rid of it is the day I know that hope has truly died. I'm not ready to know that yet."

A police car cruised along the street, its headlights illuminating part of the alleyway as it passed.

"I'm thinking that's our cue to leave," Ian said, standing back up.

"Perhaps…" My pager went off, its alarm intensified by the silence. I removed it from my holster and looked at the screen, my body becoming numb.

"What? What is it?" Ian asked, concerned.

"It's Kara. They know who killed Lucy."

They gathered together in a ramshackle cabin deep in the Maryland woods on land owned by their unit's designated leader, Marshall Leitner. The head unit, they were the command post. With meetings held every Monday, Wednesday and Friday, they were comprised of those who'd left the larger cities in search of a life away from the oppression President Brooks had created. Scattered throughout the country were several units like them—diverse groups of people who gathered, each with the goal of restoring democracy.

They communicated between units via encrypted e-mail messages that opened with codes, changing monthly to stay a step ahead of whoever may be spying on their activities. For now, they'd been able to stay under the radar, but they knew that wouldn't be the case for much longer.

The Maryland unit was the largest with just over eighty members, but its proximity to Washington, D.C. is what made it unanimously dubbed the command post, and why members from other units were migrating their way there. Most walked to the cabin, leaving their vehicles at home. None ever spoke of the meetings, as they knew what fate could and would befall them if their actions were made known. Jury trials no longer existed for that kind of infraction anymore. For high treason, they would all be executed.

Marshall Leitner entered the cabin after first extinguishing his cigarette on a stone used to prop the door open. With everyone's eyes on him, he made his way to the podium in the back of the room, mentally preparing himself for the night's meeting as he took in his ever-expanding group. Some were seated in lawn chairs while others stood on their feet, patiently waiting for him. His speech would be broadcast to the units by a camera situated atop a laptop tuned in to a heavily secured site that only unit leaders could access. All eyes were on him as he cleared his throat and began to speak.

"As you all know, there have been a series of heinous acts perpetrated in our name." He looked around the room, surveying the nods that echoed across it. "Our name has been tarnished, dragged through the mud in order to instill a sense of hatred toward our group by those who stay with the herd. They will listen to Dictator Brooks; they will not question his motives because doing so will bring harm to them and their families. But, we stand here strong with our resolve to make our country the great nation it once was. Even if it means the end of us, there will be more to carry on in our name. Our revolution will succeed, and our plan will be put into action. The fall of Brook's tyrannical reign is imminent. We will take our country back."

Applause exploded throughout the cabin. In response, he raised his hand in the air, silencing the room.

"What about these superheroes?" a middle-aged raven haired gentleman asked. "We'll be on their hit list just like The Man in Black."

Marshall chuckled. "No, we'll be hated more than The Man in Black. The Man in Black kills for the sake of killing. Our attacks will have a clear purpose, and our purpose will enact change. This change will go against Brooks. Going against Brooks will inherently wage war against his engineered puppets. Yes, they will come for us. They'll come for us and take many of us in the process, but we will stand strong with our mission to uncover the truth. We will level with Brooks' superheroes, and after all of our attempts have failed, we will do what we must. Like Brooks, they too will fall."

The cabin erupted with deafening applause which, this time, he did nothing to quell.

## TO BE CONTINUED...

# ABOUT THE AUTHOR

Sara "Furlong" Burr was born and raised in Michigan and currently still lives there with her husband, two daughters, a high-strung Lab, and three judgmental cats. When she's not writing, Sara enjoys reading, camping, spending time with her family, and attempting to paint while consuming more amaretto sours than she cares to admit.

You can learn more about Sara at http://sarafurlongburr.blogspot.com, follow her on Twitter via @Sarafurlong, and read more of her ramblings via Facebook at https://www.facebook.com/EnigmaBlackKindle.

Other Books by Sara Furlong Burr include *Vendetta Nation* and *Redemption* (*Enigma Black* Trilogy, Books 2 & 3) *A Second Chance* (a short story), and *One Crazy Night* (an anthology), all available on Amazon.

SARA FURLONG-BURR

# VENDETTA NATION (ENIGMA BLACK #2)

## PROLOGUE

DEATH. BEFORE THE age of seventeen, it had been nothing but a word to me; before The Man in Black, its meaning hadn't ingrained itself into my being. But since that bitter December day, over a decade ago, it has been in the forefront of my mind. I'd experienced its devastating touch with the deaths of my father, mother and brother; and since, with the deaths of my former partner and best friend. Now, I was experiencing it for myself, firsthand.

I lay on the sidewalk where Ian had left me, bleeding. A few feet away, I could hear the sound of glass breaking. What was he doing? As much as I wanted to find out, I had no strength to move, only to lie there and hope that I still had enough blood left in my body to keep my heart beating. Perhaps it was a good thing I couldn't move. With soldiers patrolling the streets in full force, the last thing we needed was to draw attention to ourselves, but I suppose that was the least of my concerns right now.

Seconds later, I felt my body being lifted gently off the ground as pressure was placed on the gunshot wound that had torn a hole in my chest. With what little strength I could muster, I opened my eyes in slits—the furthest they would open. Ian was holding me in his arms while he packed gauze and other bandaging over the wound, taping it securely in place with materials he'd stolen from the drug store that now appeared in my field of vision. Glass littered the ground outside the store's empty window frame.

I shivered uncontrollably, unsure of whether it was due to the cold April rain, falling in endless sheets from the night sky, or whether it was from the sheer loss of blood from the gunshot wound. Either way, I was slipping away, and fast. It was my fault I was dying, really. If only I'd been more careful.

"Stay with me," Ian pleaded as he stood up and ran down the street with my limp body teetering on the brink of life and death in his arms. "Don't close your eyes. Stay awake. We're almost there. Just a little further and we'll be at the car, and then we'll be back at The Epicenter where the doctors...they'll...they'll treat you, and you'll be fine. You'll see. You'll be fine."

I wasn't going to be fine. I began to lose consciousness, my head falling from Ian's shoulder. If this was death, it seemed surprisingly peaceful.

When the bullet had first pierced my flesh, it was as if someone had punched me, and I hadn't immediately grasped the gravity of the situation. Curiously, the throbbing pain hadn't presented itself until after I looked down and realized just what had happened. It had been brief, the pain, and had soon been replaced by a strange, soothing numbness. But now, as death slowly drew nearer, I felt as though my body were floating in air. I had no cares, no worries left in the world other than the pressing thought that this must be what it had been like for my family those many years ago.

In my passage from my earthly life into pseudo consciousness, a field appeared around me. A field filled with grass as tall as my waist, adorned with the occasional yellow, orange or purple flower. In the middle of this field stood a solitary tree with leaves of white that glittered in the sun shining down from the ethereal sky. Something drew me to that tree; someone wanted me to join them there. And as I ran through the field to heed its call, my feet seemingly left the ground, giving me the sensation of flying through the air. The wind carried me like a wayward leaf, lightly caressing my skin and making the pale yellow dress I wore billow in the breeze like rays of sunlight. Halfway through the field, I drifted back to the ground again. As soon as my feet hit the soil, I ran toward the beckoning tree. But even as I was running, stretching my legs as far as they would allow with each bound, it still felt as though I were gliding through the air.

The closer I came to the tree, the more of its trunk was revealed through the depths of the tall grass, and I saw the reason for my summoning. Walking around its massive circumference was a sight I'd only been able to see in my dreams.

"Jake!" I exclaimed. My legs moved as fast as humanly possible to reach my little brother. He watched me approaching him, and a familiar smile creased his face; a face that hadn't aged beyond adolescence. I would finally be going home.

Ian jerked the car door open, setting me down gently in the front seat. Without removing his hand from the bandages that were effectively slowing the blood flow from my chest, he lowered the seat, raising my legs up onto the dashboard. We weren't allowed to seek medical treatment, nor could we now that soldiers were blocking all of the hospital entrances in response to the coup attempted by the rebels, so he had to treat me himself. If he hadn't, I would have been dead already. Instead, my death had been prolonged, leaving me to my subconscious field of dreams from which I was periodically jostled back to partial consciousness. Fastening my seatbelt, Ian hurriedly removed his hand from my wound, shut the door, and hopped into his side of the car, where he removed his helmet, immediately resting his hand back on my chest as though his mere touch was capable of a miracle. Perhaps he was just doing it to assure himself that my heart was still beating, or that my body was still taking in air. Whatever his reasons, it felt reassuring that I wouldn't die alone.

Back in my state of limbo, I remained running to my brother, whose touch I hadn't felt in a lifetime. I was so close to him now; close enough to see strands of his hair blowing ever so slightly in the breeze. He was wearing the same clothes he had on the day he died. His usual blue jeans, filthy from his shenanigans, were no cleaner even in death.

It was a strange thing, being in a pseudo conscious state, stranded halfway between life and death. Not only did I know exactly what was going on before me, but I also knew exactly what was going on around my near lifeless body. It was as though my mind were taking a vacation without putting my body on notice. I heard the squeal of the tires as Ian peeled out onto the roadway, attempting to save my delicate life. I heard Kara's frantic voice over the intercom in the car, urging Ian to go faster, promising him that Dr. Harris and Dr. Martin would be there to greet him in the garage. But, most of all, I heard Chase.

When I came within feet of embracing my little brother, Chase appeared before me, causing me to skid to a stop in shock. I never imagined that it would be possible to improve upon perfection, but this state of limbo proved to be full of the impossible. I stood, looking at him, my dying heart all but speeding up as I stared into his deep blue eyes. Reaching out to him, I stole a glance over his shoulder, seeing Jake still standing behind him.

"Oh, Jake," I called, walking towards him again. He said nothing, only replying with a shake of his head and a parting wave just before he disappeared behind the tree.

"Celaine," Chase called my name.

I turned away from the tree to see Chase's outstretched hand, instantly grabbing me. He pulled me into his waiting arms, holding me like he used to when we were together.

"Chase," I cried.

"Shh." He ran his hand through my hair, holding my body tightly to his. "It's going to be okay. I won't ever let it not be okay." He'd frequently uttered this phrase to me on my particularly difficult days. He was my protector, my personal superhero. "I love you, Celaine."

"I love you, too," I said before I drifted further away into oblivion for what may be the last time.

Ian drove down the highway at speeds that made even him cringe. Back at The Epicenter, they were assembling, waiting to take her from him, and even at the speed he was going, he couldn't get there fast enough. He felt his arm begin to go numb from its steadfast position on her chest, where her heart was barely beating. At the moment, his heart was working enough for the both of them.

"We're almost there," he told her. "Just about another mile and then you'll be okay. We'll be back out there taking care of The Man in Black and Brooks in no time. Just hang in there, Celaine. Please, hang in there for me." His voice shook as he attempted to locate her wayward pulse. "I need you to be there for me," he pleaded. "I need you to be with me." He hesitated, wondering if he should utter the words that had been on his mind; the words he always told himself he'd never be able to say. "Celaine, I think I might... I love you."

"I love you, too."

It was barely above a whisper, but she had said it nonetheless. Skidding the car on the roadway to turn, Ian pulled into the pine tree-laden pathway that lead to The Epicenter, speeding down its dirt surface, through the gates and into the tunnel to the sanctity of the garage, where only Kara stood to await their arrival.

Made in the USA
San Bernardino, CA
27 April 2017